"What's going on, toad?" said Tiffany.

The toad looked a bit shifty. "Miss Tick doesn't really want you to handle this," it said. "She'll be back soon with help—"

"Is she going to be in time?" Tiffany demanded.

"I don't know. Probably. But you shouldn't—"

"You'd better tell me what you know, toad," said Tiffany. "Miss Tick isn't here. I am."

"Another world is colliding with this one," said the toad. "There. Happy now? That's what Miss Tick thinks. But it's happening faster than she expected. All the monsters are coming back."

"Why?"

"There's no one to stop them."

There was silence for a moment.

"There's me," said Tiffany.

ALSO BY TERRY PRATCHETT

TERRY PRATCHETT

❧

The Wee Free Men:
The Beginning

HARPER

An Imprint of HarperCollinsPublishers

Library of Congress catalog card number: 2010927739
ISBN 978-0-06-201217-3

Typography by Hilary Zarycky
10 11 12 13 14 LP/RRDH   10 9 8 7 6 5 4 3 2
❖
First Edition

CONTENTS

THE WEE FREE MEN

CONTENTS

CHAPTER 1

A Clang Well Done

୬୦

Some things start before other things.

It was a summer shower but didn't appear to know it, and it was pouring rain as fast as a winter storm.

Miss Perspicacia Tick sat in what little shelter a raggedy hedge could give her and explored the universe. She didn't notice the rain. Witches dried out quickly.

The exploring of the universe was being done with a couple of twigs tied together with string, a stone with a hole in it, an egg, one of Miss Tick's stockings (which also had a hole in it), a pin, a piece of paper, and a tiny stub of pencil. Unlike wizards, witches learn to make do with a little.

The items had been tied and twisted together to make a . . . device. It moved oddly when she prodded it. One of the sticks seemed to pass right through the egg, for example, and came out the other side without leaving a mark.

"Yes," she said quietly, as rain poured off the rim of her hat. "There it *is*. A definite ripple in the walls of the world. Very worrying. There's probably another world making contact. That's never good. I ought to go there. But . . . according to my left elbow, there's a witch there already."

"She'll sort it out, then," said a small and, for now, mysterious voice from somewhere near her feet.

"No, it can't be right. That's chalk country over that way," said Miss Tick. "You can't grow a good witch on chalk. The stuff's barely harder than clay. You need good hard rock to grow a witch, believe me." Miss Tick shook her head, sending raindrops flying. "But my elbows are generally very reliable."*

"Why talk about it? Let's go and see," said the voice. "We're not doing very well around here, are we?"

That was true. The lowlands weren't good to witches. Miss Tick was making pennies by doing bits of medicine and misfortune-telling,** and slept in barns most nights. She'd twice been thrown into ponds.

"I can't barge in," she said. "Not on another witch's territory. That never, ever works. But . . ." She paused. "Witches don't just turn up out of nowhere. Let's have a look. . . ."

She pulled a cracked saucer out of her pocket and tipped into it the rainwater that had collected on her hat. Then she took a bottle of ink out of another pocket and poured in just enough to turn the water black.

She cupped it in her hands to keep the raindrops out and listened to her eyes.

◆　◆　◆

Tiffany Aching was lying on her stomach by the river, tickling trout. She liked to hear them laugh. It came up in bubbles.

A little way away, where the riverbank became a sort of pebble

---

*People say things like "listen to your heart," but witches learn to listen to other things too. It's amazing what your kidneys can tell you.

**Ordinary fortune-tellers tell you what you *want* to happen; witches tell you what's going to happen whether you want it to or not. Strangely enough, witches tend to be more accurate but less popular.

beach, her brother, Wentworth, was messing around with a stick, and almost certainly making himself sticky.

Anything could make Wentworth sticky. Washed and dried and left in the middle of a clean floor for five minutes, Wentworth would be sticky. It didn't seem to come from anywhere. He just got sticky. But he was an easy child to mind, provided you stopped him from eating frogs.

There was a small part of Tiffany's brain that wasn't too certain about the name Tiffany. She was nine years old and felt that Tiffany was going to be a hard name to live up to. Besides, she'd decided only last week that she wanted to be a witch when she grew up, and she was certain Tiffany just wouldn't work. People would laugh.

Another and larger part of Tiffany's brain was thinking of the word *susurrus*. It was a word that not many people have thought about, ever. As her fingers rubbed the trout under its chin, she rolled the word round and round in her head.

Susurrus . . . according to her grandmother's dictionary, it meant "a low soft sound, as of whispering or muttering." Tiffany liked the *taste* of the word. It made her think of mysterious people in long cloaks whispering important secrets behind a door: *susurruss-susurrusss* . . .

She'd read the dictionary all the way through. No one told her you weren't supposed to.

As she thought this, she realized that the happy trout had swum away. But something else was in the water, only a few inches from her face.

It was a round basket, no bigger than half a coconut shell, coated with something to block up the holes and make it float. A little man, only six inches high, was standing up in it. He had a mass of untidy red hair into which a few feathers, beads, and bits of cloth had been woven. He had a red beard, which was pretty much as bad as the hair. The rest of him that wasn't covered with blue tattoos was covered with a tiny kilt. And he was waving a fist at her and shouting:

"Crivens! Gang awa' oot o' here, ye daft wee hinny! 'Ware the green *heid*!"

With that he pulled at a piece of string that was hanging over the side of his boat, and a second red-headed man surfaced, gulping air.

"Nae time for fishin'!" said the first man, hauling him aboard. "The green heid's coming!"

"Crivens!" said the swimmer, water pouring off him. "Let's offski!"

And with that he grabbed one very small oar and, with rapid back and forth movements, made the basket speed away.

"Excuse me!" Tiffany shouted. "Are you fairies?"

But there was no answer. The little round boat had disappeared in the reeds.

Probably not, Tiffany decided.

Then, to her dark delight, there was a susurrus. There was no wind, but the leaves on the alder bushes by the riverbank began to shake and rustle. So did the reeds. They didn't bend, they just blurred. *Everything* blurred, as if something had picked up the world and was shaking it. The air fizzed. People whispered behind closed doors. . . .

The water began to bubble, just under the bank. It wasn't very deep here—it would only have reached Tiffany's knees if she'd waded—but it was suddenly darker and greener and, somehow, much deeper. . . .

She stood and took a couple of steps backward just before long skinny arms fountained out of the water and clawed madly at the bank where she had been. For a moment she saw a thin face with long sharp teeth, *huge* round eyes, and dripping green hair like waterweed, and then the thing plunged back into the depths.

By the time the water closed over it, Tiffany was already running along the bank to the little beach where Wentworth was making frog pies. She snatched up the child just as a stream of bubbles came around the curve in the bank. Once again the water boiled, the green-haired creature shot up, and the long arms clawed at the mud. Then it screamed and dropped back into the water.

"I wanna go-a *toy-lut*!" screamed Wentworth.

Tiffany ignored him. She was watching the river with a thoughtful expression.

I'm not scared at all, she thought. How strange. I ought to be scared, but I'm just angry. I mean, I can *feel* the scared, like a red-hot ball, but the angry isn't letting it out. . . .

"Wenny wanna wanna *wanna* go-a *toy-lut*!" Wentworth shrieked.

"Go on, then," said Tiffany absentmindedly. The ripples were still sloshing against the bank.

There was no point in telling anyone about this. Everyone would just say, "What an imagination the child has," if they were feeling in a good mood, or, "Don't tell stories!" if they weren't.

She was still very angry. How dare a monster turn up in the river? Especially one so . . . so . . . ridiculous! Who did it think she was?

This is Tiffany, walking back home. Start with the boots. They are big and heavy boots, much repaired by her father, and they

9

belonged to various sisters before her; she wears several pairs of socks to keep them on. They are *big*. Tiffany sometimes feels she is nothing more than a way of moving boots around.

Then there is the dress. It has been owned by many sisters as well and has been taken up, taken out, taken down, and taken in by her mother so many times that it really ought to have been taken away. But Tiffany rather likes it. It comes down to her ankles and, whatever color it had been to start with, is now a milky blue that is, incidentally, exactly the same color as the butterflies skittering beside the path.

Then there is Tiffany's face. Light pink, with brown eyes, and brown hair. Nothing special. Her head might strike anyone watching—in a saucer of black water, for example—as being just slightly too big for the rest of her, but perhaps she'll grow into it.

And then go farther up, and farther, until the track becomes a ribbon and Tiffany and her brother two little dots, and there is her country.

They call it the Chalk. Green downlands roll under the hot midsummer sun. From up here the flocks of sheep, moving slowly, drift over the short turf like clouds on a green sky. Here and there sheepdogs speed over the grass like shooting stars.

And then, as the eyes pull back, it is a long green mound, lying like a great whale on the world . . .

. . . surrounded by the inky rainwater in the saucer.

◆　◆　◆

Miss Tick looked up.

"That little creature in the boat was a Nac Mac Feegle!" she said. "The most feared of all the fairy races! Even trolls run away from the Wee Free Men! And one of them *warned* her!"

"She's the witch, then, is she?" said the voice.

"At that age? Impossible!" said Miss Tick. "There's been no one to teach her! There're no witches on the Chalk! It's too *soft*. And yet . . . she wasn't scared. . . ."

The rain had stopped. Miss Tick looked up at the Chalk, rising above the low, wrung-out clouds. It was about five miles away.

"This child needs watching," she said. "But chalk's too soft to grow a witch on. . . ."

◆　◆　◆

Only the mountains were higher than the Chalk. They stood sharp and purple and gray, streaming long trails of snow from their tops even in summer. "Brides o' the sky," Granny Aching had called them once, and it was so rare that she ever said anything at all, let alone anything that didn't have to do with sheep, that Tiffany had remembered it. Besides, it was exactly right. That's what the mountains looked like in the winter, when they were all in white and the snow streams blew like veils.

Granny used old words and came out with odd, old sayings. She didn't call the downland the Chalk, she called it "the wold." Up on the wold the wind blows cold, Tiffany had thought, and the word had stuck that way.

She arrived at the farm.

People tended to leave Tiffany alone. There was nothing particularly cruel or unpleasant about this, but the farm was big and everyone had their jobs to do, and she did hers very well and so she became, in a way, invisible. She was the dairymaid, and good at it. She made better butter than her mother did, and people commented about how good she was with cheese. It was a talent. Sometimes, when the wandering teachers came to the village, she went and got a bit of education. But mostly she worked in the dairy, which was dark and cool. She enjoyed it. It meant she was doing something for the farm.

It was actually *called* the Home Farm. Her father rented it from the Baron, who owned the land, but there had been Achings farming it for hundreds of years and so, her father said (quietly, sometimes, after he'd had a beer in the evenings), as far as the *land* knew, it was owned by the Achings. Tiffany's mother used to tell him not to speak like that, although the Baron was always very respectful to Mr. Aching since Granny had died two years ago, calling him the finest shepherd in these hills, and was generally held by the people in the village to be not too bad these days. It paid to be respectful, said Tiffany's mother, and the poor man had sorrows of his own.

But sometimes her father insisted that there had been Achings (or Akins, or Archens, or Akens, or Akenns—spelling had been optional) mentioned in old documents about the area for hundreds and hundreds of years. They had these hills in their bones, he said, and they'd always been shepherds.

Tiffany felt quite proud of this, in an odd way, because it might also be nice to be proud of the fact that your ancestors moved around a bit, too, or occasionally tried new things. But you've got to be proud of *something*. And for as long as she could remember, she'd heard her father, an otherwise quiet, slow man, make the Joke, the one that must have been handed down from Aching to Aching for hundreds of years.

He'd say, "Another day of work and I'm still Aching," or "I get up Aching and I go to bed Aching," or even "I'm Aching all over." They weren't particularly funny after about the third time, but she'd miss it if he didn't say at least one of them every week. They didn't have to be funny—they were *father* jokes. Anyway, however they were spelled, all her ancestors had been Aching to stay, not Aching to leave.

There was no one around in the kitchen. Her mother had probably gone up to the shearing pens with a bite of lunch for the men, who were shearing this week. Her sisters Hannah and Fastidia were up there too, rolling fleeces and paying attention to some of the younger men. They were always quite eager to work during shearing.

Near the big black stove was the shelf that was still called Granny Aching's Library by her mother, who liked the idea of having a library. Everyone else called it Granny's Shelf.

It was a small shelf, since the books were wedged between a jar of crystallized ginger and the china shepherdess that Tiffany had won at a fair when she was six.

There were only five books if you didn't include the big farm diary, which in Tiffany's view didn't count as a real book because you had to write it yourself. There was the dictionary. There was the Almanack, which got changed every year. And next to that was *Diseases of the Sheep*, which was fat with the bookmarks that her grandmother had put there.

Granny Aching had been an expert on sheep, even though she called them "just bags of bones, eyeballs, and teeth, lookin' for new ways to die." Other shepherds would walk miles to get her to come and cure their beasts of ailments. *They* said she had the Touch, although she just said that the best medicine for sheep or man was a dose of turpentine, a good cussin', and a kick. Bits of paper with Granny's own recipes for sheep cures stuck out all over the book. Mostly they involved turpentine, but some included cussin'.

Next to the book on sheep was a thin little volume called *Flowers of the Chalk*. The turf of the downs was full of tiny, intricate flowers, like cowslips and harebells, and even smaller ones that somehow survived the grazing. On the Chalk flowers had to be tough and cunning to survive the sheep and the winter blizzards.

Someone had colored in the flowers a long time ago. On the flyleaf of the book was written in neat handwriting *Sarah Grizzel*, which had been Granny's name before she was married. She had probably thought that Aching was at least better than Grizzel.

And finally there was *The Goode Childe's Booke of Faerie Tales*, so old that it belonged to an age when there were far more *e*'s around.

Tiffany stood on a chair and took it down. She turned the pages until she found the one she was looking for and stared at it for a while. Then she put the book back, replaced the chair, and opened the crockery cupboard.

She found a soup plate, went over to a drawer, took out the tape measure her mother used for dressmaking, and measured the plate.

"Hmm," she said. "Eight inches. Why didn't they just *say*?"

She unhooked the largest frying pan, the one that could cook breakfast for half a dozen people all at once, and took some candies from the jar on the dresser and put them in an old paper bag. Then, to Wentworth's sullen bewilderment, she took him by a sticky hand and headed back down toward the stream.

Things still looked very normal down there, but she was not going to let *that* fool her. All the trout had fled, and the birds weren't singing.

She found a place on the riverbank with the right-sized bush. Then she found a stone and hammered a piece of wood into the ground as hard as she could, close to the edge of the water, and tied the bag of sweets to it. Tiffany was the kind of child who always carried a piece of string.

"Candy, Wentworth," she shouted.

She gripped the frying pan and stepped smartly behind the bush.

Wentworth trotted over to the sweets and tried to pick up the bag. It wouldn't move.

"I wanna go-a *toy-lut!*" he yelled, because it was a threat that usually worked. His fat fingers scrabbled at the knots.

Tiffany watched the water carefully. Was it getting darker? Was it getting greener? Was that just waterweed down there? Were those bubbles just a trout, laughing?

No.

She ran out of her hiding place with the frying pan swinging like a bat. The screaming monster, leaping out of the water, met the frying pan coming the other way with a clang.

It was a good clang, with the *oiyoiyoioioioioioinnnnnggggggg* that is the mark of a clang well done.

The creature hung there for a moment, a few teeth and bits of green weed splashing into the water, then slid down slowly and sank with some massive bubbles.

The water cleared and was once again the same old river, shallow and icy cold and floored with pebbles.

"Wanna wanna *sweeties!*" screamed Wentworth, who never noticed anything else in the presence of sweets.

Tiffany undid the string and gave them to him. He ate them far too quickly, as he always did with sweets. She waited until he was sick, then went back home in a thoughtful state of mind.

In the reeds, quite low down, small voices whispered:

"Crivens, Wee Bobby, did yer no' see that?"

"Aye. We'd better offski an' tell the Big Man we've found the hag."

◆ ◆ ◆

Miss Tick was running up the dusty road. Witches don't like to be seen running. It looks unprofessional. It's also not done to be seen carrying things, and she had her tent on her back.

She was also trailing clouds of steam. Witches dry out from the inside.

"It had all those teeth!" said the mystery voice, this time from her hat.

"I know!" snapped Miss Tick.

"And she just hauled off and hit it!"

"Yes. I *know*."

"Just like that!"

"Yes. Very impressive," said Miss Tick. She was getting out of breath. Besides, they were already on early slopes of the downs now, and she wasn't good on chalk. A wandering witch likes firm ground under her, not a rock so soft you could cut it with a knife.

"Impressive?" said the voice. "She used her *brother* as *bait*!"

"Amazing, wasn't it?" said Miss Tick. "Such quick thinking . . . oh, no . . ." She stopped running and leaned against a field wall as a wave of dizziness hit her.

"What's happening? What's happening?" said the voice from the hat. "I nearly fell off!"

"It's this wretched chalk! I can feel it already! I can do magic on honest soil, and rock is always fine, and I'm not too bad on clay, even . . . but chalk's neither one thing nor the other! I'm very *sensitive* to geology, you know."

"What are you trying to tell me?" said the voice.

"Chalk . . . is a hungry soil. I don't really have much power on chalk."

The owner of the voice, who was hidden, said: "Are you going to fall over?"

"No, no! It's just the magic that doesn't work."

Miss Tick did not look like a witch. Most witches don't, at least the ones who wander from place to place. Looking like a witch can be dangerous when you walk among the uneducated. And for that reason she didn't wear any occult jewelry, or have a glowing magical knife or a silver goblet with a pattern of skulls all around it, or carry a broomstick with sparks coming out of it, all of which are tiny hints that there may be a witch around. Her pockets never carried anything more magical than a few twigs, maybe a piece of string, a coin or two, and, of course, a lucky charm.

Everyone in the country carried lucky charms, and Miss Tick had worked out that if you didn't have one, people would suspect that you *were* a witch. You had to be a bit cunning to be a witch.

Miss Tick did have a pointy hat, but it was a stealth hat and pointed only when she wanted it to.

The one thing in her bag that might have made anyone suspicious was a very small, grubby booklet entitled *An Introduction to Escapology, by the Great Williamson*. If one of the risks of your job is being thrown into a pond with your hands tied together, then the ability to swim thirty yards underwater, fully clothed, plus the ability to lurk under the weeds breathing air through a hollow reed, count as nothing if you aren't also *amazingly* good with knots.

"You can't do magic here?" said the voice in the hat.

"No, I can't," said Miss Tick.

She looked up at the sounds of jingling. A strange procession was coming up the white road. It was mostly made up of donkeys pulling small carts with brightly painted covers on them. People walked alongside the carts, dusty to the waist. They were all men, they wore bright robes—or robes, at least, that had been bright before being trailed through mud and dust for years—and every one of them wore a strange black square hat.

Miss Tick smiled.

They looked like tinkers, but there wasn't one among them, she knew, who could mend a kettle. What they did was sell invisible things. And after they'd sold what they had, they still had it. They sold what everyone needed but often didn't want. They sold the key to the universe to people who didn't even know it was locked.

"I can't *do*," said Miss Tick, straightening up. "But I *can* teach!"

◆　◆　◆

Tiffany worked for the rest of the morning in the dairy. There was cheese that needed doing.

There was bread and jam for lunch. Her mother said, "The teachers are coming to town today. You can go, if you've done your chores."

Tiffany agreed that, yes, there were one or two things she'd quite like to know more about.

"Then you can have half a dozen carrots and an egg. I daresay they could do with an egg, poor things," said her mother.

Tiffany took them with her after lunch and went to get an egg's worth of education.

Most boys in the village grew up to do the same jobs as their fathers or, at least, some other job somewhere in the village where someone's father would teach them as they went along. The girls were expected to grow up to be somebody's wife. They were also expected to be able to read and write, those being considered soft indoor jobs that were too fiddly for the boys.

However, everyone also felt that there were a few other things that even the boys ought to know, to stop them wasting time wondering about details like "What's on the other side of the mountains?" and "How come rain falls out of the sky?"

Every family in the village bought a copy of the Almanack every year, and a sort of education came from that. It was big and thick and printed somewhere far off, and it had lots of details about things like phases of the moon and the right time to plant beans. It also contained a few prophesies about the coming year, and mentioned faraway places with names like Klatch and Hersheba. Tiffany had seen a picture of Klatch in the Almanack. It showed a camel standing in a desert. She'd only found out what both those names were because her mother had told her. And that was Klatch, a camel in a desert. She'd wondered if there wasn't a bit more to it, but it seemed that "Klatch = camel, desert" was all anyone knew.

And that was the trouble. If you didn't find some way of stopping it, people would go *on* asking questions.

The teachers were useful there. Bands of them wandered through the mountains, along with the tinkers, portable blacksmiths, miracle medicine men, cloth peddlers, fortune-tellers, and all the other travelers who sold things the people didn't need every day but occasionally found useful.

They went from village to village delivering short lessons on many subjects. They kept apart from the other travelers and were quite mysterious in their ragged robes and strange square hats. They used long words, like *corrugated iron*. They lived rough lives, surviving on what food they could earn from giving lessons to anyone who would listen. When no one would listen, they lived on baked hedgehog. They went to sleep under the stars, which the math teachers would count, the astronomy teachers would measure, and the literature teachers would name. The geography teachers got lost in the woods and fell into bear traps.

People were usually quite pleased to see them. They taught children enough to shut them up, which was the main thing, after all. But they always had to be driven out of the villages by nightfall in case they stole chickens.

Today the brightly colored little booths and tents were pitched in a field just outside the village. Behind them small square areas had been fenced off with high canvas walls and were patrolled by apprentice teachers looking for anyone trying to overhear Education without paying.

The first tent Tiffany saw had a sign that read:

JOGRAFFY! JOGRAFFY! JOGRAFFY!
FOR TODAY ONLY: ALL MAJOR LAND MASSES AND OCEANS
PLUS EVERYTHING YOU NEED TO KNO ABOUT GLASSIERS!
ONE PENNY, OR ALL MAJOR VEJTABLES ACSEPTED!

Tiffany had read enough to know that, while he might be a whiz at major land masses, this particular teacher could have done with some help from the man running the stall next door:

THE WONDERS OF PUNCTUATION AND SPELLING
1 ABSOLUTE CERTAINTY ABOUT THE COMMA!
2 I BEFORE E COMPLETELY SORTED OUT!
3 THE MYSTERY OF THE SEMICOLON REVEALED!!!
4 SEE THE AMPERSAND! (SMALL EXTRA CHARGE)
5 FUN WITH BRACKETS!
** WILL ACCEPT VEGETABLES, EGGS, AND CLEAN USED CLOTHING **

The next stall along was decorated with scenes out of history, generally of kings cutting one another's heads off and similar interesting highlights. The teacher in front was dressed in ragged red robes with rabbit-skin trimmings and wore an old top hat with flags stuck in it. He had a small megaphone that he aimed at Tiffany.

"The Death of Kings Through the Ages?" he said. "Very educational, lots of blood!"

"Not really," said Tiffany.

"Oh, you've *got* to know where you've come from, miss," said the teacher. "Otherwise how will you know where you're going?"

"I come from a long line of Aching people," said Tiffany. "And I think I'm moving on."

She found what she was looking for at a booth hung with pictures of animals including, she was pleased to see, a camel. The sign said:

USEFUL CREATURES—TODAY: OUR FRIEND THE HEDGEHOG!

She wondered how useful the thing in the river had been, but this looked like the only place to find out. A few children were waiting on the benches inside the booth for the lesson to begin, but the teacher was still standing out in front, in the hope of filling up the empty spaces.

"Hello, little girl," he said, which was only his first big mistake. "I'm sure *you* want to know all about hedgehogs, eh?"

"I did this one last summer," said Tiffany.

The man looked closer, and his grin faded. "Oh, yes," he said. "I remember. You asked all those . . . little questions."

"I would like a question answered today," said Tiffany.

"Provided it's not the one about how you get baby hedgehogs," said the man.

"No," said Tiffany patiently. "It's about zoology."

"Zoology, eh? That's a big word, isn't it."

"No, actually it isn't," said Tiffany. "*Patronizing* is a big word. Zoology is really quite short."

The teacher's eyes narrowed further. Children like Tiffany were bad news. "I can see you're a clever one," he said. "But I don't know any teachers of zoology in these parts. Vetin'ry, yes, but not zoology. Any particular animal?"

"Jenny Green-Teeth. A water-dwelling monster with big teeth and claws and eyes like soup plates," said Tiffany.

"What size of soup plates? Do you mean big soup plates, a whole full-portion bowl with maybe some biscuits, possibly even a bread roll, or do you mean the little cup you might get if, for example, you just ordered soup and a salad?"

"The size of soup plates that are eight inches across," said Tiffany, who'd never ordered soup and a salad anywhere in her life. "I checked."

"Hmm, that is a puzzler," said the teacher. "Don't think I know that one. It's certainly not useful, I know that. It sounds made-up to me."

"Yes, that's what *I* thought," said Tiffany. "But I'd still like to know more about it."

"Well, you could try her. She's new."

The teacher jerked his thumb toward a little tent at the end of the row. It was black and quite shabby. There weren't any posters, and absolutely no exclamation marks.

"What does she teach?" Tiffany asked.

"Couldn't say," said the teacher. "She *says* it's thinking, but I don't know how you teach *that*. That'll be one carrot, thank you."

When she went closer, Tiffany saw a small notice pinned to the outside of the tent. It said, in letters that whispered rather than shouted:

I CAN TEACH YOU A LESSON YOU WON'T FORGET IN A HURRY.

CHAPTER 2

Miss Tick

∽

Tiffany read the sign and smiled.

"Aha," she said. There was nothing to knock on, so she added "Knock, knock" in a louder voice.

A woman's voice from within said: "Who's there?"

"Tiffany," said Tiffany.

"Tiffany who?" said the voice.

"Tiffany who isn't trying to make a joke."

"Ah. That sounds promising. Come in."

She pushed aside the flap. It was dark inside the tent, as well as stuffy and hot. A skinny figure sat behind a small table. She had a very sharp, thin nose and was wearing a large black straw hat with paper flowers on it. It was completely unsuitable for a face like that.

"Are you a witch?" said Tiffany. "I don't mind if you are."

"What a strange question to spring on someone," said the woman, looking slightly shocked. "Your Baron bans witches in this country, you know that, and the first thing you say to me is 'Are you a witch?' Why would I be a witch?"

"Well, you're wearing all black," said Tiffany.

"Anyone can wear black," said the woman. "That doesn't

mean a thing."

"And you're wearing a straw hat with flowers in it," Tiffany went on.

"Aha!" said the woman. "That proves it, then. Witches wear tall pointy hats. Everyone knows that, foolish child."

"Yes, but witches are also very clever," said Tiffany calmly. There was something about the twinkle in the woman's eyes that told her to continue. "They sneak about. Probably they often don't look like witches. And a witch coming here would know about the Baron, and so she'd wear the kind of hat that everyone knows witches don't wear."

The woman stared at her. "That was an incredible feat of reasoning," she said at last. "You'd make a good witch finder. You know they used to set fire to witches? Whatever kind of hat I've got on, you'd say it proves I'm a witch, yes?"

"Well, the frog sitting on your hat is a bit of a clue, too," said Tiffany.

"I'm a toad, actually," said the creature, which had been peering at Tiffany from between the paper flowers.

"You're very yellow for a toad."

"I've been a bit ill," said the toad.

"And you talk," said Tiffany.

"You only have my word for it," said the toad, disappearing into the paper flowers. "You can't prove anything."

"You don't have matches on you, do you?" said the woman to Tiffany.

"No."

"Fine, fine. Just checking."

Again there was a pause while the woman gave Tiffany a long stare, as if making up her mind about something.

"My name," she said at last, "is Miss Tick. And I *am* a witch. It's a good name for a witch, of course."

"You mean blood-sucking parasite?" said Tiffany, wrinkling her forehead.

"I'm sorry?" said Miss Tick, coldly.

"Ticks," said Tiffany. "Sheep get them. But if you use turpentine—"

"I *meant* that it *sounds* like 'mystic,'" said Miss Tick.

"Oh, you mean a pune, or play on words," said Tiffany.* "In that case it would be even better if you were Miss *Teak*, a dense foreign wood, because that would sound like 'mystique,' or you could be Miss Take, which would—"

"I can see we're going to get along like a house on fire," said Miss Tick. "There may be no survivors."

"You really *are* a witch?"

"Oh, puh-lease," said Miss Tick. "Yes, yes, I am a witch. I have a talking animal, a tendency to correct other people's pronunciation—it's *pun*, by the way, not 'pune'—and a fascination for poking my nose into other people's affairs and, yes, *a pointy hat*."

"Can I operate the spring now?" said the toad.

"Yes," said Miss Tick, her eyes still on Tiffany. "You can operate the spring."

"I like operating the spring," said the toad, crawling around to the back of the hat.

There was a click, and a slow *thwap-thwap* noise, and the center of the hat rose slowly and jerkily up out of the paper flowers, which fell away.

"Er . . ." said Tiffany.

*Tiffany had read lots of words in the dictionary that she'd never heard spoken, so she had to guess at how they were pronounced.

"You have a question?" said Miss Tick.

With a last *thwop*, the top of the hat made a perfect point.

"How do you know I won't run away right now and tell the Baron?" said Tiffany.

"Because you haven't the slightest desire to do so," said Miss Tick. "You're absolutely fascinated. You want to *be* a witch, am I right? You probably want to fly on a broomstick, yes?"

"Oh, yes!" She'd often dreamed of flying. Miss Tick's next words brought her down to earth.

"Really? You like having to wear really, really thick pants? Believe me, if I've got to fly, I wear two pairs of woolen ones and a canvas pair on the outside which, I may tell you, are not very feminine no matter how much lace you sew on. It can get *cold* up there. People forget that. And then there's the bristles. Don't ask me about the bristles. I will not talk about the bristles."

"But can't you use a keeping-warm spell?" said Tiffany.

"I could. But a witch doesn't do that sort of thing. Once you use magic to keep yourself warm, then you'll start using it for other things."

"But isn't that what a witch is supposed to—" Tiffany began.

"Once you learn about magic, I mean really *learn* about magic, learn everything you *can* learn about magic, then you've got the most important lesson still to learn," said Miss Tick.

"What's that?"

"Not to use it. Witches don't use magic unless they really have to. It's hard work and difficult to control. We do other things. A witch pays attention to everything that's going on. A witch uses her head. A witch is sure of herself. A witch always has a piece of string—"

"I always *do* have a piece of string!" said Tiffany. "It's always handy!"

"Good. Although there's more to witchcraft than string. A witch delights in small details. A witch sees through things and around things. A witch sees farther than most. A witch sees things from the other side. A witch knows where she is, who she is, and *when* she is. A witch would see Jenny Green-Teeth," she added. "What happened?"

"How did you know I saw Jenny Green-Teeth?"

"I'm a witch. Guess," said Miss Tick.

Tiffany looked around the tent. There wasn't much to see, even now that her eyes were getting accustomed to the gloom. The sounds of the outside world filtered through the heavy material.

"I think—"

"Yes?" said the witch.

"I think you heard me telling the teacher."

"Correct. I just used my ears," said Miss Tick, saying nothing at all about saucers of ink. "Tell me about this monster with eyes the size of the kind of soup plates that are eight inches across. Where do soup plates come into it?"

"The monster is mentioned in a book of stories I've got," explained Tiffany. "It said Jenny Green-Teeth has eyes the size of soup plates. There's a picture, but it's not a good one. So I measured a soup plate, so I could be exact."

Miss Tick put her chin on her hand and gave Tiffany an odd sort of smile.

"That was all right, wasn't it?" said Tiffany.

"What? Oh, yes. Yes. Um . . . yes. Very . . . exact. Go on."

Tiffany told her about the fight with Jenny, although she didn't mention Wentworth in case Miss Tick got funny about it. Miss Tick listened carefully.

"Why the frying pan?" she said. "You could've found a stick."

"A frying pan just seemed a better idea," said Tiffany.

"Hah! It *was*. Jenny would've eaten you up if you'd used a stick. A frying pan is made of iron. Creatures of that kidney can't stand iron."

"But it's a monster out of a storybook!" said Tiffany. "What's it doing turning up in our little river?"

Miss Tick stared at Tiffany for a while and then said: "Why do you want to be a witch, Tiffany?"

It had started with The Goode Childe's Booke of Faerie Tales. *Actually, it had probably started with a lot of things, but the stories most of all.*

Her mother had read them to her when she was little, and then she'd read them to herself. And all the stories had, somewhere, the witch. The *wicked old witch*.

And Tiffany had thought, Where's the *evidence*?

The stories never said *why* she was wicked. It was enough to be an old woman, enough to be all alone, enough to look strange because you had no teeth. It was enough to be *called* a witch.

If it came to that, the book never gave you the *evidence* of *anything*. It talked about "a handsome prince" . . . was he really, or was it just because he was a prince that people called him handsome? As for "a girl who was as beautiful as the day was long" . . . well, which day? In midwinter it hardly ever got light! The stories didn't want you to think, they just wanted you to believe what you were told. . . .

And you were told that the old witch lived all by herself in a strange cottage that was made of gingerbread or ran around on giant hen's feet, and talked to animals, and could do magic.

Tiffany only ever knew one old woman who lived all alone in a strange cottage. . . .

Well, no. That wasn't quite true. But she had only ever known one old woman who lived in a strange house *that moved about*, and that was Granny Aching. And she could do magic, sheep magic, and she talked to animals and there was nothing wicked about her. That *proved* you couldn't believe the stories.

And there had been the *other* old woman, the one who *everyone* said was a witch. And what had happened to her had made Tiffany very . . . thoughtful.

Anyway, she preferred the witches to the smug handsome princes and especially to the stupid smirking princesses, who didn't have the sense of a beetle. They had lovely golden hair, too, and Tiffany didn't. Her hair was brown, plain brown. Her mother called it chestnut, or sometimes auburn, but Tiffany knew it was brown, brown, brown, just like her eyes. Brown as earth. And did the book have any adventures for people who had brown eyes and brown hair? No, no, no . . . it was the blond people with blue eyes and the redheads with green eyes who got the stories. If you had brown hair you were probably just a servant or a woodcutter or something. Or a dairymaid. Well, that was not going to happen, even if she *was* good at cheese. She couldn't be the prince, and she'd never be a princess, and she didn't want to be a woodcutter, so she'd be the witch and *know* things, just like Granny Aching—

"Who was Granny Aching?" said a voice.

Who was Granny Aching? People would start asking that now. And the answer was: What Granny Aching was, was there. She was always there. It seemed that the lives of all the Achings revolved around Granny Aching. Down in the village decisions were made, things were done, life went on in the knowledge that in her old wheeled shepherding hut on the hills Granny Aching was there, watching.

And she was the silence of the hills. Perhaps that's why she liked Tiffany, in her awkward, hesitant way. Her older sisters chattered, and Granny didn't like noise. Tiffany didn't make noise when she was up at the hut. She just loved being there. She'd watch the buzzards and listen to the noise of the silence.

It did have a noise, up there. Sounds, voices, animal noises floating up onto the downs somehow made the silence deep and complex. And Granny Aching wrapped this silence around herself and made room inside it for Tiffany. It was always too busy on the farm. There were a lot of people with a lot to do. There wasn't enough time for silence. There wasn't time for listening. But Granny Aching was silent and listened all the time.

"What?" said Tiffany, blinking.

"You just said, 'Granny Aching listened to me all the time,'" said Miss Tick.

Tiffany swallowed. "I think my grandmother was slightly a witch," she said, with a touch of pride.

"Really? How do you know."

"Well, witches can curse people, right?" said Tiffany.

"So it is said," said Miss Tick diplomatically.

"Well, my father said Granny Aching cussed the sky blue," said Tiffany.

Miss Tick coughed. "Well, cussing, now, cussing isn't like genuine *cursing*. Cussing's more like *dang* and *botheration* and *darned* and *drat*, you know? Cursing is more on the lines of 'I hope your nose explodes and your ears go flying away.'"

"I think Granny's cussing was a bit more than that," said Tiffany, in a very definite voice. "And she talked to her dogs."

"And what kind of things did she say to them?" said Miss Tick.

"Oh, things like 'come by' and 'away to me' and 'that'll do,'" said

Tiffany. "They always did what she told them."

"But those are just sheepdog commands," said Miss Tick dismissively. "That's not exactly witchcraft."

"Well, that still makes them familiars, doesn't it?" Tiffany retorted, feeling annoyed. "Witches have animals they can talk to, called familiars. Like your toad there."

"I'm not familiar," said a voice from among the paper flowers. "I'm just slightly presumptuous."

"And she knew about all kinds of herbs," Tiffany persisted. Granny Aching was going to be a witch even if Tiffany had to argue all day. "She could cure anything. My father said she could make a shepherd's pie stand up and baa." Tiffany lowered her voice. "She could *bring lambs back to life. . . .*"

You hardly ever saw Granny Aching indoors in the spring and summer. She spent most of the year sleeping in the old wheeled hut, which could be dragged across the downs after the flocks. But the first time Tiffany could remember seeing the old woman in the farmhouse, she was kneeling in front of the fire, putting a dead lamb in the big black oven.

Tiffany had screamed and screamed. And Granny had gently picked her up, a little awkwardly, and sat her on her lap and shushed her and called her "my little jiggit," while on the floor her sheepdogs, Thunder and Lightning, watched her in doggish amazement. Granny wasn't particularly at home around children, because they didn't baa.

When Tiffany had stopped crying out of sheer lack of breath, Granny had put her down on the rug and opened the oven, and Tiffany had watched the lamb come alive again.

When Tiffany got a little older, she found out that jiggit meant "twenty" in the Yan Tan Tethera, the ancient counting language of the shepherds. The older people still used it when they were counting things they thought of as special. She was Granny Aching's twentieth grandchild.

And when she was older still, she also understood all about the warming oven, which never got more than, well, warm. Her mother would let the bread dough rise in it, and Ratbag the cat would sleep in it, sometimes on the dough. It was just the place to revive a weak lamb that had been born on a snowy night and was near death from the cold. That was how it worked. No magic at all. But that time it had been magic. And it didn't stop being magic just because you found out how it was done.

"Good, but still not *exactly* witchcraft," said Miss Tick, breaking the spell again. "Anyway, you don't have to have a witch ancestor to be a witch. It helps, of course, because of heredity."

"You mean like having talents?" said Tiffany, wrinkling her brow.

"Partly, I suppose," said Miss Tick. "But I was thinking of pointy hats, for example. If you have a grandmother who can pass on her pointy hat to you, that saves a great deal of expense. They are incredibly hard to come by, especially ones strong enough to withstand falling farmhouses. Did Mrs. Aching have anything like that?"

"I don't think so," said Tiffany. "She hardly ever wore a hat except in the very cold weather. She wore an old grain sack as a sort of hood. Um . . . does that count?"

For the first time, Miss Tick looked a little less flinty. "Possibly, possibly," she said. "Do you have any brothers and sisters, Tiffany?"

"I have six sisters," said Tiffany. "I'm the youngest. Most of them don't live with us now."

"And then you weren't the baby anymore because you had a dear little brother," said Miss Tick. "The only boy, too. That must have been a nice surprise."

Suddenly, Tiffany found Miss Tick's faint smile slightly annoying.

"How do you know about my brother?" she said.

The smile faded. Miss Tick thought: This child is *sharp*. "Just a guess," she said. No one likes admitting to spying.

"Are you using persykology on me?" said Tiffany hotly.

"I think you mean psychology," said Miss Tick.

"Whatever," said Tiffany. "You think I don't like him because my parents make a fuss of him and spoil him, yes?"

"Well, it did cross my mind," said Miss Tick, and gave up worrying about the spying. She was a witch, and that was all there was to it. "I think it was the bit when you used him as bait for a slobbering monster that gave me a hint," she added.

"He's just a nuisance!" said Tiffany. "He takes up my time and I'm always having to look after him and he always wants sweets. Anyway," she added, "I had to think fast."

"Quite so," said Miss Tick.

"Granny Aching would have done something about monsters in our river," said Tiffany, ignoring that. "Even if they are out of books." And she'd have done something about what happened to old Mrs. Snapperly, she added to herself. She'd have spoken up, and people would have listened. . . . They always listened when Granny spoke up. Speak up for those who don't have voices, she always said.

"Good," said Miss Tick. "So she should. Witches deal with things. You said the river was very shallow where Jenny leaped up? And the world looked blurred and shaky? Was there a susurrus?"

Tiffany beamed. "Yes, there certainly was!"

"Ah. Something bad is happening."

Tiffany looked worried.

"Can I stop it?"

"And now I'm slightly impressed," said Miss Tick. "You said, 'Can I stop it?' and not 'Can anyone stop it?' or 'Can we stop it?' That's good. You accept responsibility. That's a good start. And you keep a cool head. But no, you can't stop it."

"I walloped Jenny Green-Teeth!"

"Lucky hit," said Miss Tick. "There are worse than her on the way, believe me. I believe an incursion of major proportions is going to start here, and clever though you are, my girl, you have as much chance as one of your lambs on a snowy night. You keep clear. I'll try to fetch help."

"What, from the Baron?"

"Good gracious, no. He'd be no use at all."

"But he protects us," said Tiffany. "That's what my mother says."

"Does he?" said Miss Tick. "Who from? I mean, from whom?"

"Well, from, you know . . . attack, I suppose. From other barons, my father says."

"Has he got a big army?"

"Well, er, he's got Sergeant Roberts, and Kevin and Neville and Trevor," said Tiffany. "We all know them. They mostly guard the castle."

"Any of them got magical powers?" said Miss Tick.

"I saw Neville do card tricks once," said Tiffany.

"A wow at parties, but probably not much use even against something like Jenny," said Miss Tick. "Are there no oth— Are there no witches here at all?"

Tiffany hesitated.

"There was old Mrs. Snapperly," she said. Oh, yes. She'd lived all alone in a strange cottage, all right. . . .

"Good name," said Miss Tick. "Can't say I've heard it before, though. Where is she?"

"She died in the snow last winter," said Tiffany slowly.

"And now tell me what you're not telling me," said Miss Tick, sharp as a knife.

"Er . . . she was begging, people think, but no one opened their doors to her and, er . . . it was a cold night, and . . . she died."

"And she was a witch, was she?"

"Everyone *said* she was a witch," said Tiffany. She really did not want to talk about this. No one in the villages around here wanted to talk about it. No one went near the ruins of the cottage in the woods, either.

"You don't think so?"

"Um . . ." Tiffany squirmed. "You see . . . the Baron had a son called Roland. He was only twelve, I think. And he went riding in the woods by himself last summer and his dogs came back without him."

"Mrs. Snapperly lived in those woods?" said Miss Tick.

"Yes."

"And people think she killed him?" said Miss Tick. She sighed. "They probably think she cooked him in the oven, or something."

"They never actually *said*," said Tiffany. "But I think it was something like that, yes."

"And did his horse turn up?" said Miss Tick.

"No," said Tiffany. "And that was strange, because if it'd turned up anywhere along the hills, the people would have noticed it. . . ."

Miss Tick folded her hands, sniffed, and smiled a smile with no humor in it at all.

"Easily explained," she said. "Mrs. Snapperly must have had a really *big* oven, eh?"

"No, it was really quite small," said Tiffany. "Only ten inches deep."

"I bet Mrs. Snapperly had no teeth and talked to herself, right?" said Miss Tick.

"Yes. And she had a cat. And a squint," said Tiffany. And it all came out in a rush: "And so after he vanished, they went to her cottage and they looked in the oven and they dug up her garden and they threw stones at her old cat until it died and they turned her out of her cottage and piled up all her old books in the middle of the room and set fire to them and burned the place to the ground and everyone said she was an old witch."

"They burned the books," said Miss Tick in a flat voice.

"Because they said they had old writing in them," said Tiffany. "And pictures of stars."

"And when you went to look, did they?" said Miss Tick.

Tiffany suddenly felt cold. "How did you know?" she said.

"I'm good at listening. Well, did they?"

Tiffany sighed. "Yes, I went to the cottage next day, and some of the pages, you know, had kind of floated up in the heat? And I found a part of one, and it had all old lettering and gold and blue edging. And I buried her cat."

"You buried the cat?"

"Yes! Someone had to!" said Tiffany hotly.

"And you measured the oven," said Miss Tick. "I know you did, because you just told me what size it was." And you measure soup plates, Miss Tick added to herself. What *have* I found here?

"Well, yes. I did. I mean . . . it was tiny! And if she could magic away a boy and a whole horse, why didn't she magic away the men who came for her? It didn't make any sense!"

Miss Tick waved her into silence. "And then what happened?"

"Then the Baron said no one was to have anything to do with her," said Tiffany. "He said *any* witches found in the country would be tied up and thrown in the pond. Er, you could be in danger," she added, uncertainly.

"I can untie knots with my teeth and I have a Gold Swimming Certificate from the Quirm College for Young Ladies," said Miss Tick. "All that practice at jumping into the swimming pool with my clothes on was time well spent." She leaned forward.

"Let me guess what happened to Mrs. Snapperly," she said. "She lived from the summer until the snow, right? She stole food from barns, and probably women gave her food at the back door if the men weren't around? I expect the bigger boys threw things at her if they saw her."

"How do you *know* all this?" said Tiffany.

"It doesn't take a huge leap of imagination, believe me," said Miss Tick. "And she wasn't a witch, was she?"

"I think she was just a sick old lady who was no use to anyone and smelled a bit and looked odd because she had no teeth," said Tiffany. "She just looked like a witch in a story. Anyone with half a mind could see that."

Miss Tick sighed. "Yes. But sometimes it's so hard to find half a mind when you need one."

"Can't you teach me what I need to know to be a witch?" said Tiffany.

"Tell me why you *still* want to be a witch, bearing in mind what happened to Mrs. Snapperly."

"So that sort of thing doesn't happen again," said Tiffany.

She even buried the old witch's cat, thought Miss Tick. What kind of child is this?

"Good answer. You might make a decent witch one day," she said. "But I don't teach people to *be* witches. I teach people *about* witches. Witches learn in a special school. I just show them the way, if they're any good. All witches have special interests, and I like children."

"Why?"

"Because they're much easier to fit in the oven," said Miss Tick. But Tiffany wasn't frightened, just annoyed.

"That was a nasty thing to say," she said.

"Well, witches don't have to be *nice*," said Miss Tick, pulling a large black bag from under the table. "I'm glad to see you pay attention."

"There really is a school for witches?" said Tiffany.

"In a manner of speaking, yes," said Miss Tick.

"Where?"

"Very close."

"It is magical?"

"Very magical."

"A wonderful place?"

"There's nowhere quite like it."

"Can I go there by magic? Does, like, a unicorn turn up to carry me there or something?"

"Why should it? A unicorn is nothing more than a big horse that comes to a point, anyway. Nothing to get so excited about," said Miss Tick. "And that will be one egg, please."

"Exactly where can I find the school?" said Tiffany, handing over the egg.

"Aha. A root vegetable question, I think," said Miss Tick. "Two carrots, please."

Tiffany handed them over.

"Thank you. Ready? To find the school for witches, go to a high place near here, climb to the top, open your eyes . . ." Miss Tick hesitated.

"Yes?"

". . . and then open your eyes again."

"But—" Tiffany began.

"Got any more eggs?"

"No, but—"

"No more education, then. But I have a question to ask you."

"Got any eggs?" said Tiffany, instantly.

"Hah! Did you see anything *else* by the river, Tiffany?"

Silence suddenly filled the tent. The sound of bad spelling and erratic geography filtered through from outside as Tiffany and Miss Tick stared into each other's eyes.

"No," lied Tiffany.

"Are you sure?" said Miss Tick.

"Yes."

They continued the staring match. But Tiffany could outstare a cat.

"I *see*," said Miss Tick, looking away. "Very well. In that case, please tell me . . . when you stopped outside my tent just now, you said 'aha' in what I considered to be a smug tone of voice. Were you thinking, 'This is a strange little black tent with a mysterious little sign on the door, so going inside could be the start of an adventure,' *or* were you thinking, 'This could be the tent of some wicked witch like they thought Mrs. Snapperly was, who'll put some horrible spell on me as soon as I go in'? It's all right, you can stop staring now. Your eyes are watering."

"I thought both those things," said Tiffany, blinking.

"But you came in anyway. Why?"

"To find out."

"Good answer. Witches are naturally nosy," said Miss Tick, standing up. "Well, I must go. I hope we shall meet again. I will give you some free advice, though."

"Will it cost me anything?"

"What? I just said it was free!" said Miss Tick.

"Yes, but my father said that free advice often turns out to be expensive," said Tiffany.

Miss Tick sniffed. "You could say this advice is priceless," she said. "Are you listening?"

"Yes," said Tiffany.

"Good. Now . . . if you trust in yourself . . ."

"Yes?"

". . . and believe in your dreams . . ."

"Yes?"

". . . and follow your star . . ." Miss Tick went on.

"Yes?"

". . . you'll still get beaten by people who spent *their* time working hard and learning things and weren't so lazy. Good-bye."

The tent seemed to grow darker. It was time to leave. Tiffany found herself back in the square where the other teachers were taking down their stalls.

She didn't look around. She knew enough not to look around. Either the tent would still be there, which would be a disappointment, or it would have mysteriously disappeared, and that would be worrying.

She headed home and wondered if she should have mentioned the little red-haired men. She hadn't for a whole lot of reasons. She wasn't sure, now, that she'd really seen them, she had a feeling that they wouldn't have wanted her to, and it was nice to have something Miss Tick didn't know. Yes. That was the best part. Miss Tick was a bit too clever, in Tiffany's opinion.

On the way home she climbed to the top of Arken Hill, which

was just outside the village. It wasn't very big, not even as high as the downs above the farm and certainly nothing like as high as the mountains.

The hill was more . . . modest. There was a flat place at the top where nothing ever grew, and Tiffany knew there was a story that a hero had once fought a dragon up there and its blood had burned the ground where it fell. There was another story that said there was a heap of treasure under the hill, *defended* by the dragon, and *another* story that said a king was buried there in armor of solid gold. There were lots of stories about the hill; it was surprising it hadn't sunk under the weight of them.

Tiffany stood on the bare soil and looked at the view.

She could see the village and the river and Home Farm and the Baron's castle, and beyond the fields she knew, she could see gray woods and heathlands.

She closed her eyes and opened them again. And blinked, and opened them *again*.

There was no magic door, no hidden building revealed, no strange signs.

For a moment, though, the air buzzed and smelled of snow.

When she got home, she looked up *incursion* in the dictionary. It meant "invasion."

An incursion of major proportions, Miss Tick had said.

And now little unseen eyes watched Tiffany from the top of the shelf. . . .

CHAPTER 3

Hunt the Hag

༺ঔ৩༻

Miss Tick removed her hat, reached inside, and pulled a piece of string. With little clicks and flapping noises the hat took up the shape of a rather elderly straw hat. She picked up the paper flowers from the ground and stuck them on, carefully.

Then she said: "Phew!"

"You can't just let the kid go like that," said the toad, who was sitting on the table.

"Like what?"

"She's clearly got First Sight *and* Second Thoughts. That's a powerful combination."

"She's a little know-it-all," said Miss Tick.

"Right. Just like you. She impressed you, right? I know she did because you were quite nasty to her, and you always do that to people who impress you."

"Do you want to be turned into a frog?"

"Well, now, let me see . . ." said the toad sarcastically. "Better skin, better legs, likelihood of being kissed by a princess one hundred percent improved . . . why, yes. Whenever you're ready, madam."

"There're worse things than being a toad," said Miss Tick darkly.

"Try it sometime," said the toad. "Anyway, I rather liked her."

"So did I," said Miss Tick briskly. "She hears about an old lady dying because these idiots thought she was a witch, and *she* decides to become a witch so that they don't try that again. A monster roars up out of her river, and she bashes it with a frying pan! Have you ever heard the saying 'The land finds its witch'? It's happened here, I'll bet. But a *chalk* witch? Witches like granite and basalt, hard rock all the way down! Do you know what chalk *is*?"

"You're going to tell me," said the toad.

"It's the shells of billions and billions of tiny, helpless little sea creatures that died millions of years ago," said Miss Tick. "It's . . . tiny, tiny bones. Soft. Soggy. Damp. Even limestone is better than that. But . . . she's grown up on chalk and *she* is hard, and sharp, too. She's a born witch. On *chalk*! Which is *impossible*!"

"She bashed Jenny!" said the toad. "The girl has got talent!"

"Maybe, but she needs more than that. Jenny isn't clever," said Miss Tick. "She's only a Grade 1 Prohibitory Monster. And she was probably bewildered to find herself in a stream, when her natural home is in stagnant water. There'll be much, much worse than her."

"What do you mean, 'a Grade 1 Prohibitory Monster'?" asked the toad. "I've never heard her called that."

"I *am* a teacher as well as a witch," said Miss Tick, adjusting her hat carefully. "Therefore I make lists. I make assessments. I write things down in a neat, firm hand with pens of two colors. Jenny is one of a number of creatures invented by adults to scare children away from dangerous places." She sighed. "If only people would *think* before they make up monsters."

"You ought to stay and help her," said the toad.

"I've got practically no power here," said Miss Tick. "I told you. It's the chalk. And remember the redheaded men. A Nac Mac

Feegle *spoke* to her! *Warned* her! I've never seen one in my life! If she's got *them* on her side, who knows what she can do?"

She picked up the toad. "D'you know what'll be turning up?" she continued. "All the things they locked away in those old stories. All those reasons why you shouldn't stray off the path, or open the forbidden door, or say the wrong word, or spill the salt. All the stories that gave children nightmares. All the monsters from under the biggest bed in the world. Somewhere, all stories are real and all dreams come true. And they'll come true here if they're not stopped. If it wasn't for the Nac Mac Feegle, I'd be really worried. As it is, I'm going to try and get some help. That's going to take me at least two days without a broomstick!"

"It's unfair to leave her alone with them," said the toad.

"She won't be alone," said Miss Tick. "She'll have you."

"Oh," said the toad.

◆   ◆   ◆

Tiffany shared a bedroom with Fastidia and Hannah. She woke up when she heard them come to bed, and she lay in the dark until she heard their breathing settle down and they started to dream of young sheep shearers with their shirts off.

Outside, summer lightning flashed around the hills, and there was a rumble of thunder. . . .

Thunder and Lightning. She knew them as dogs before she knew them as the light and sound of a storm. Granny always had her sheepdogs with her, indoors and out. One moment they would be black-and-white streaks across the distant turf, and then they were suddenly there, panting, eyes never leaving Granny's face. Half the dogs on the hills were Lightning's puppies, trained by Granny Aching.

Tiffany had gone with the family to the big Sheepdog Trials. Every shepherd on the Chalk went to them, and the very best entered the arena to show how well they could work their dogs. The dogs would round up sheep, separate them, drive them into the pens—or sometimes run off, or snap at one another, because even the best dog can have a bad day. But Granny never entered with Thunder and Lightning. She'd lean on the fence with the dogs lying in front of her, watching the show intently and puffing her foul pipe. And Tiffany's father had said that after each shepherd had worked his dogs, the judges would look nervously across at Granny Aching to see what she thought. In fact all the shepherds watched her. Granny never, ever entered the arena, because she was the Trials. If Granny thought you were a good shepherd—if she nodded at you when you walked out of the arena, if she puffed at her pipe and said, "That'll do"—you walked like a giant for a day, you owned the Chalk. . . .

When she was small and up on the wold with Granny, Thunder and Lightning would baby-sit Tiffany, lying attentively a few feet away as she played. And she'd been so proud when Granny had let her use them to round up a flock. She'd run about excitedly in all directions, shouting "Come by!" and "There!" and "Walk up!" and, glory be, the dogs had worked perfectly.

She knew now that they'd have worked perfectly whatever she'd shouted. Granny was just sitting there, smoking her pipe, and by now the dogs could read her mind. They only ever took orders from Granny Aching. . . .

The storm died down after a while, and there was the gentle sound of rain.

At some point Ratbag the cat pushed open the door and jumped onto the bed. He was big to start with, but Ratbag *flowed.* He was so fat that, on any reasonably flat surface, he gradually spread out in a great puddle of fur. He hated Tiffany but would never let personal feelings get in the way of a warm place to sleep.

She must have slept, because she woke up when she heard the voices.

They seemed very close but, somehow, very small.

"Crivens! It's a' verra well sayin' 'find the hag,' but what should we be lookin' for, can ye tell me that? All these bigjobs look just the same tae me!"

"Not-totally-wee Geordie doon at the fishin' said she was a big, big girl!"

"A great help that is, I dinna think! They're all big, big girls!"

"Ye paira dafties! Everyone knows a hag wears a pointy bonnet!"

"So they canna be a hag if they're sleepin', then?"

"Hello?" whispered Tiffany.

There was silence, embroidered with the breathing of her sisters. But in a way Tiffany couldn't quite describe, it was the silence of people trying hard not to make any noise.

She leaned down and looked under the bed. There was nothing there but the guzunder.

The little man in the river had talked just like that.

She lay back in the moonlight, listening until her ears ached.

Then she wondered what the school for witches would be like and why she hadn't seen it yet.

She knew every inch of the country for two miles around. She liked the river best, with the backwaters where striped pike sunbathed just above the weeds and the banks where kingfishers nested. There was a heronry a mile or so upriver, and she liked to creep up on the birds when they came down here to fish in the reeds, because there's nothing funnier than a heron trying to get airborne in a hurry.

She drifted off to sleep again, thinking about the land around the farm. She knew all of it. There were no secret places that she didn't know about.

But maybe there were magical doors. That's what she'd make, if she had a magical school. There should be secret doorways everywhere, even hundreds of miles away. Look at a special rock by, say, moonlight, and there would be yet another door.

But the school, now, the school. There would be lessons in broomstick riding and how to sharpen your hat to a point, and magical meals, and lots of new friends.

"Is the bairn asleep?"

"Aye, I canna hear her movin'."

Tiffany opened her eyes in the darkness. The voices under the bed had a slightly echoey edge. Thank goodness the guzunder was nice and clean.

"Right, let's get oot o' this wee pot, then."

The voices moved off across the room. Tiffany's ears tried to swivel to follow them.

"Hey, see here, it's a hoose! See, with wee chairies and things!"

They've found the doll's house, Tiffany thought.

It was quite a large one, made by Mr. Block the farm carpenter when Tiffany's oldest sister, who already had two babies of her own now, was a little girl. It wasn't the most fragile of items. Mr. Block did not go in for delicate work. But over the years the girls had decorated it with bits of material and some rough-and-ready furniture.

By the sound of it the owners of the voices thought it was a palace.

"Hey, hey, hey, we're in the cushy stuff noo! There's a beid in this room. Wi' pillows!"

"Keep it doon—we don't want any o' them to wake up!"

"Crivens, I'm as quiet as a wee moose! Aargh! There's sojers!"

"Whut d'ye mean, sojers?"

"There's redcoats in the room!"

They've found the toy soldiers, thought Tiffany, trying not to breathe loudly.

Strictly speaking, they had no place in the doll's house, but Wentworth wasn't old enough for them, and so they'd got used as innocent bystanders back in those days when Tiffany had made tea parties for her dolls. Well, what passed for dolls. Such toys as there were in the farmhouse had to be tough to survive intact through the generations and didn't always manage it. Last time Tiffany had tried to arrange a party, the guests had been a rag doll with no head, two wooden soldiers, and three quarters of a small teddy bear.

Thuds and bangs came from the direction of the doll's house.

"I got one! Hey, pal, can yer mammie sew? Stitch this! Aargh! He's got a heid on him like a tree!"

"Crivens! There's a body here wi' no heid at a'!"

"Aye, nae wonder, 'cause here's a bear! Feel ma boot, ye washoon!"

It seemed to Tiffany that although the owners of the three voices were fighting things that couldn't possibly fight back, including a teddy bear with only one leg, the fight still wasn't going all one way.

"I got 'im! I got 'im! I got 'im! Yer gonna get a gummer, ye wee hard disease!"

"Someone bit ma leg! Someone bit ma leg!"

"Come here! Ach, yer fightin' yersels, ye eejits! Ah'm fed up wi' the pairy yees!"

Tiffany felt Ratbag stir. He might be fat and lazy, but he was lightning fast when it came to leaping on small creatures. She couldn't let him get the . . . whatever they were, however bad they sounded.

She coughed loudly.

"See?" said a voice from the doll's house. *"Yer woked them up! Ah'm offski!"*

Silence fell again, and this time, Tiffany decided after a while, it was the silence of no one there rather than the silence of people being incredibly quiet. Ratbag went back to sleep, twitching occasionally as he disemboweled something in his fat cat dreams.

Tiffany waited a little while and then got out of bed and crept toward the bedroom door, avoiding the two squeaky floorboards. She went downstairs in the dark, found a chair by moonlight, fished the book of fairy tales off Granny's shelf, then lifted the latch on the back door and stepped out into the warm midsummer night.

There was a lot of mist around, but a few stars were visible overhead and there was a gibbous moon in the sky. Tiffany knew it was gibbous because she'd read in the Almanack that *gibbous* meant what the moon looked like when it was just a bit fatter than half full, and so she made a point of paying attention to it around those times just so that she could say to herself: "Ah, I see the moon's very gibbous tonight. . . ."

It's possible that this tells you more about Tiffany than she would want you to know.

Against the rising moon the downs were a black wall that filled half the sky. For a moment she looked for the light of Granny Aching's lantern. . . .

Granny never lost a lamb. That was one of Tiffany's first memories: of being held by her mother at the window one frosty night in early spring, with a million brilliant stars glinting over the mountains and, on the darkness of the downs, the one yellow star in the constellation of Granny Aching zigzagging through the night. She wouldn't go to bed while a lamb was lost, however bad the weather. . . .

There was only one place where it was possible for someone in a large family to be private, and that was in the privy. It was a three-holer, and it was where everyone went if they wanted to be alone for a while.

There was a candle in there, and last year's Almanack hanging on a string. The printers knew their readership and printed the Almanack on soft, thin paper.

Tiffany lit the candle, made herself comfortable, and looked at the book of fairy tales. The moon gibbous'd at her through the crescent-shaped hole cut in the door.

She'd never really liked the book. It seemed to her that it tried to tell her what to do and what to think. Don't stray from the path, don't open that door, but hate the wicked witch because she is *wicked*. Oh, and believe that shoe size is a good way of choosing a wife.

A lot of the stories were highly suspicious, in her opinion. There was the one that ended when the two good children pushed the wicked witch into her own oven. Tiffany had worried about that after all that trouble with Mrs. Snapperly. Stories like this stopped people thinking properly, she was sure. She'd read that one and thought, Excuse me? *No one* has an oven big enough to get a whole person in, and what made the children think they could just walk around eating people's houses in any case? And why does some boy too stupid to know a cow is worth a lot more than five beans have the *right* to murder a giant and steal all his gold? Not to mention commit an act of ecological vandalism? And some girl who can't tell the difference between a wolf and her grandmother must either have been as dense as teak or come from an extremely ugly family. The stories *weren't real*. But Mrs. Snapperly had died because of stories.

She flicked past page after page, looking for the right picture. Because although the stories made her angry, the pictures, ah, the pictures were the most wonderful things she'd ever seen.

She turned a page and there it was.

Most of the pictures of fairies were not very impressive. Frankly, they looked like a small girls' ballet class that'd just had to run through a bramble patch. But this one . . . was different. The colors were strange, and there were no shadows. Giant grasses and daisies grew everywhere, so the fairies must have been quite small, but they *looked* big. They looked like rather strange humans. They certainly didn't look much like fairies. Hardly any of them had wings. They were odd shapes, in fact. In fact, some of them looked like monsters. The girls in the tutus wouldn't have stood much chance.

And the odd thing was that, alone of all the fairy pictures in the book, *this* one looked as if it had been done by an artist who had painted what was in front of him. The other pictures, the ballet girls and the romper-suit babies, had a made-up, syrupy look. This one didn't. This one said that the artist had been there . . .

. . . at least in his head, Tiffany thought.

She concentrated on the bottom left-hand corner, and there it was. She'd seen it before, but you had to know where to look. It was definitely a little red-haired man, naked except for a kilt and a skinny vest, scowling out of the picture. He looked very angry. And . . . Tiffany moved the candle to see more clearly . . . he was *definitely* making a gesture with his hand.

Even if you didn't know it was a rude one, it was easy to guess.

She heard voices. She pushed the door open with her foot to hear them better, because a witch always listens to other people's conversations.

The sound was coming from the other side of the hedge, where there was a field that should have been full of nothing but sheep waiting to go to market. Sheep are not known for their conversation. She snuck out carefully in the misty dawn and found a small gap that had been made by rabbits, which just gave her a good enough view.

There was a ram grazing near the hedge, and the conversation was coming from it or, rather, somewhere in the long grass underneath it. There seemed to be at least four speakers, who sounded bad-tempered.

"*Crivens! We wanna coo beastie, no' a ship beastie!*"

"*Ach, one's as goo' as t'other! C'mon, lads, a' grab aholt o' a leg!*"

"*Aye, all the coos are inna shed, we tak what we can!*"

"*Keep it doon, keep it doon, will ya!*"

"*Ach, who's listenin'? Okay, lads—yan . . . tan . . . teth'ra!*"

The sheep rose a little in the air, and bleated in alarm as it started to go across the field backward. Tiffany thought she saw a hint of red hair in the grass around its legs, but that vanished as the ram was carried away into the mist.

She pushed her way through the hedge, ignoring the twigs that scratched at her. Granny Aching wouldn't have let anyone get away with stealing a sheep, even if they *were* invisible.

But the mist was thick, and now Tiffany heard noises from the henhouse.

The disappearing-backward sheep could wait. Now the *hens* needed her. A fox had got in twice in the last two weeks, and the hens that hadn't been taken were barely laying.

Tiffany ran through the garden, catching her nightdress on pea sticks and gooseberry bushes, and flung open the henhouse door.

There were no flying feathers, and nothing like the panic a fox would cause. But the chickens were clucking excitedly, and Prunes, the cockerel, was strutting nervously up and down. One of the hens looked a bit embarrassed. Tiffany lifted it up quickly.

There were two tiny blue, red-haired men underneath. They were each holding an egg clasped in their arms. They looked up with very guilty expressions.

"Ach, no!" said one. "It's the bairn! *She's* the hag . . ."

"You're stealing our eggs," said Tiffany. "How dare you! And I'm *not* a hag!"

The little men looked at one another, and then at the eggs.

"Whut eiggs?" said one.

"The eggs you are holding," said Tiffany meaningfully.

"Whut? Oh, these? These are *eiggs*, are they?" said the one who'd spoken first, looking at the eggs as if he'd never seen them before. "There's a thing. And there was us thinking they was, er, stones."

"Stones," said the other one nervously.

"We crawled under yon chookie for a wee bitty warmth," said the first one. "And there was all these things, we though' they was stones, which was why the puir fowl was clucking all the time . . ."

"Clucking," said the second one, nodding vigorously.

". . . so we took pity on the puir thing and—"

"*Put* . . . the . . . eggs . . . *back*," said Tiffany slowly.

The one who hadn't been doing much talking nudged the other one. "Best do as she says," he said. "It's a' gang agley. Ye canna cross an Aching, an' this one's a hag. She dinged Jenny, an' no one ha' ever done *that* afore."

"Aye, I didna think o' that. . . ."

Both of the tiny men put the eggs back very carefully. One of them even breathed on the shell of his and made a show of polishing it with the ragged hem of his kilt.

"No harm done, mistress," he said. He looked at the other man. And then they vanished. But there was a suspicion of a red blur in the air, and some straw by the henhouse door flew up in the air.

"And I'm a miss!" shouted Tiffany. She lowered the hen back onto the eggs and went to the door. "And I'm *not* a hag! Are you fairies of some sort? And what about our ship? I mean, sheep?" she added.

There was no answer but a clanking of buckets near the house, which meant that other people were getting up.

She rescued the fairy tales, blew out the candle, and made her way into the house. Her mother was lighting the fire and asked what she was doing up, and she said that she'd heard a commotion in the henhouse and had gone out to see if it was the fox again. That wasn't a lie. In fact, it was completely true.

Tiffany was on the whole quite a truthful person, but it seemed to her that there were times when things didn't divide easily into "true" and "false," but instead could be things that people needed to know at the moment and things that they didn't need to know at the moment.

Besides, she wasn't sure what *she* knew at the moment.

There was porridge for breakfast. She ate it hurriedly, meaning to get back out into the paddock and see about that sheep. There might be tracks in the grass, or something. . . .

She looked up, not knowing why.

Ratbag had been asleep in front of the oven. Now he was sitting up, alert. Tiffany felt a prickling on the back of her neck and tried to see what the cat was looking at.

On the dresser was a row of blue-and-white jars that weren't very useful for anything. They'd been left to her mother by an elderly aunt, and she was proud of them because they looked nice but were completely useless. There was little room on the farm for useless things that looked nice, so they were treasured.

Ratbag was watching the lid of one of them. It was rising very slowly, and under it was a hint of red hair and two beady, staring eyes.

It lowered again when Tiffany gave it a long stare. A moment later she heard a faint rattle, and when she looked up, the pot was wobbling back and forth and there was a little cloud of dust rising along the top of the dresser. Ratbag was looking around in bewilderment.

They certainly were *very* fast.

She ran out into the paddock and looked around. The mist was off the grass now, and skylarks were rising on the downs.

"If that sheep doesn't come back *this minute*," she shouted at the sky, "there will be a *reckoning*!"

The sound bounced off the hills. And then she heard, very faint but close by, the sound of small voices:

"*Whut did the hag say?*" said the first voice.

"*She said there'd be a reck'ning'!*"

"*Oh, waily, waily, waily! We're in trouble noo!*"

Tiffany looked around, face red with anger.

"We have a *duty*," she said, to the air and the grass.

It was something Granny Aching had said once, when Tiffany had been crying about a lamb. She'd said: "We are as gods to the beasts o' the field, my jiggit. We order the time o' their birth and the time o' their death. Between times, we ha' a duty."

"We have a duty," Tiffany repeated, more softly. She glared around the field. "I know you can hear me, whoever you are. If that sheep doesn't come back, there will be . . . trouble. . . ."

The larks sang over the sheepfolds, making the silence deeper.

Tiffany had to do the chores before she had any more time to herself. That meant feeding the chickens and collecting the eggs, and feeling slightly proud of the fact that there were two more than there might otherwise have been. It meant fetching six buckets of water from the well and filling the log basket by the stove, but she put those jobs off because she didn't like doing them much. She did quite like churning butter, though. It gave her time to think.

When I'm a witch with a pointy hat and a broomstick, she thought as she pumped the handle, I'll wave my hand and the butter will come just like *that*. And any little red-headed devils who even *think* about taking our beasts will be—

There was a slopping sound behind her, where she'd lined up the six buckets to take to the well.

One of them was now full of water, which was still sloshing backward and forward.

She went back to the churning as if nothing had happened but stopped after a while and went over to the flour bin. She took a small handful of flour and dusted it over the doorstep, and then went back to the churning.

A few minutes later there was another watery sound behind her. When she turned around, there was, yes, another full bucket. And in the flour on the stone doorstep were just two lines of footprints, one leading out of the dairy and one coming back.

It was all Tiffany could do to lift one of the heavy wooden

buckets when it was full.

So, she thought, they are immensely strong as well as being incredibly fast. I'm really being very calm about this.

She looked up at the big wooden beams that ran across the room, and a little dust fell down, as if something had quickly moved out of the way.

I think I ought to put a stop to this right now, she thought. On the other hand, there's no harm in waiting until *all* the buckets are filled up.

"And then I'll have to fill the log box in the scullery," she said aloud. Well, it was worth a try.

She went back to the churning and didn't bother to turn her head when she heard four more sloshes behind her. Nor did she look around when she heard little *whooshwhoosh* noises and the clatter of logs in the box. She turned to see only when the noise stopped.

The log box was full up to the ceiling, and all the buckets were full. The patch of flour was a mass of footprints.

She stopped churning. She had a feeling that eyes were watching her, a *lot* of eyes.

"Er . . . thank you," she said. No, that wasn't right. She sounded nervous. She let go of the butter paddle and stood up, trying to look as fierce as possible.

"And what about our sheep?" she said. "I won't believe you're really sorry until I see the sheep come back!"

There was a bleating from the paddock. She ran out to the bottom of the garden and looked through the hedge.

The sheep *was* coming back, backward and at high speed. It jerked to a halt a little way from the hedge and dropped down as the little men let it go. One of the red-headed men appeared for a moment on its head. He huffed on a horn, polished it with his kilt, and vanished in a blur.

Tiffany walked back to the dairy looking thoughtful.

When she got back, the butter had been churned. Not just churned, in fact, but patted into a dozen fat golden oblongs on the marble she used when she did it. There was even a sprig of parsley on each one.

Are they brownies? she wondered. According to the *Faerie Tales*, brownies hung around the house doing chores in exchange for a saucer of milk. But in the picture they'd been cheery little creatures with long pointy hoods. The red-haired men didn't look as if they'd ever drunk milk in their lives, but perhaps it was worth a try.

"Well," she said aloud, still aware of the hidden watchers. "That'll do. Thank you. I'm glad you're sorry for what you did."

She took one of the cat's saucers from the pile by the sink, washed it in the sink, filled it with milk from today's churn, then put it down on the floor and stood back. "Are you brownies?" she said.

The air blurred. Milk splashed across the floor, and the saucer spun around and around.

"I'll take that as a no, then," said Tiffany. "So what are you?"

There were unlimited supplies of no answer at all.

She lay down and looked under the sink, and then peered behind the cheese shelves. She stared up into the dark, spidery shadows of the room. It felt empty.

And she thought: I think I need a whole egg's worth of education, in a hurry.

◆　◆　◆

Tiffany had walked along the steep track from the farm into the village hundreds of times. It was less than half a mile long, and over the centuries the carts had worn it down so that it was more like a gully in the chalk and ran like a milky stream in wet weather.

She was halfway down when the susurrus started. The hedges rustled without a wind. The skylarks stopped singing, and while she hadn't really noticed their song, their silence was a shock. Nothing's louder than the end of a song that's always been there.

When she looked up at the sky, it was like looking through a diamond. It sparkled, and the air went cold so quickly that it was like stepping into an icy bath.

Then there was snow underfoot, snow on the hedges. And the sound of hooves.

They were in the field beside her. A horse was galloping through the snow, behind the hedge that was now, suddenly, just a wall of white.

The hoofbeats stopped. There was a moment of silence and then a horse landed in the lane, skidding on the snow. It pulled itself upright, and the rider turned it to face Tiffany.

The rider himself couldn't face Tiffany. He had no face. He had no head to hang it on.

She ran. Her boots slipped on the snow as she moved, but suddenly her mind was cold as the ice.

She had two legs, slipping on ice. A horse had twice as many legs to slip. She'd seen horses try to tackle this hill in icy weather. She had a chance.

She heard a breathy, whistling noise behind her, and a whinny from the horse. She risked a glance. The horse was coming after her, but slowly, half walking and half sliding. Steam poured off it.

About halfway down the slope the lane passed under an arch of trees, looking like crashed clouds now under their weight of snow. And beyond them, Tiffany knew, the lane flattened out. The headless man would catch her on the flat. She didn't know what would happen after that, but she was sure it would be unpleasantly short.

Flakes of snow dropped on her as she passed under the trees, and she decided to make a run for it. She might reach the village. She was good at running.

But if she got there, then what? She'd never reach a door in time. And people would shout, and run about. The dark horseman didn't look like someone who'd take much notice of that. No, she had to *deal* with it.

If only she'd brought the frying pan.

"Here, wee hag! Stannit ye still, right noo!"

She stared up.

A tiny blue man had poked his head up out of the snow on top of the hedge.

"There's a headless horseman after me!" she shouted.

"He'll no' make it, hinny. Stand ye still! Look him in the eye!"

"He hasn't got any eyes!"

"Crivens! Are ye a hag or no'? Look him in the eyes he hasna got!"

The blue man disappeared into the snow.

Tiffany turned around. The horseman was trotting under the trees now, the horse more certain as the ground leveled. He had a sword in his hand, and he *was* looking at her, with the eyes he didn't have. There was the breathy noise again, not good to hear.

The little men are watching me, she thought. I can't run. Granny Aching wouldn't have run from a thing with no head.

She folded her arms and glared.

The horseman stopped, as if puzzled, and then urged the horse forward.

A blue-and-red shape, larger than the other little men, dropped out of the trees. He landed on the horse's forehead, between its eyes, and grabbed an ear in each hand.

Tiffany heard the man shout: "Here's a face full o' dandruff for ye, yer bogle, courtesy of Big Yan!" and then the man hit the horse between the eyes *with his head*.

To her amazement the horse staggered sideways.

"Aw right?" shouted the tiny fighter. "Big toughie, is ye? Once more wi' *feelin'*!"

This time the horse danced uneasily the other way, and then its back legs slid from under it and it collapsed in the snow.

Little blue men erupted from the hedge. The horseman, trying to get to his feet, disappeared under a blue-and-red storm of screaming creatures—

And vanished. The snow vanished. The horse vanished.

The blue men, for a moment, were in a pile on the hot, dusty road. One of them said, "Aw, crivens! I kicked meself in me own heid!" And then they, too, vanished, but for a moment Tiffany saw blue-and-red blurs disappearing into the hedge.

Then the skylarks were back. The hedges were green and full of flowers. Not a twig was broken, not a flower disturbed. The sky was blue, with no flashes of diamond.

Tiffany looked down. On the toes of her boots, snow was melting. She was, strangely, glad about that. It meant that what had just happened was magical, not madness. Because if she closed her eyes, she could still hear the wheezy breathing of the headless man.

What she needed right now was people, and ordinary things happening. But more than anything else, she wanted answers.

Actually, what she wanted more than anything else was not to hear the wheezy breathing when she shut her eyes. . . .

◆ ◆ ◆

The tents had gone. Except for a few pieces of broken chalk, apple cores, some stamped-down grass, and, alas, a few chicken feathers, there was nothing at all to show that the teachers had ever been there.

A small voice said, "Psst!"

She looked down. A toad crept out from under a dock leaf.

"Miss Tick said you'd be back," it said. "I expect there's some things you need to know, right?"

"*Everything,*" said Tiffany. "We're swamped with tiny men! I can't understand half of what they say! They keep calling me a hag!"

"Ah, yes," said the toad. "You've got Nac Mac Feegles!"

"It snowed, and then it hadn't! I was chased by a horseman with no *head*! And one of the . . . what did you say they were?"

"Nac Mac Feegles," said the toad. "Also known as pictsies. *They* call themselves the Wee Free Men."

"Well, one of them head-butted the horse! It fell over! It was a huge horse, too!"

"Ah, that sounds like a Feegle," said the toad.

"I gave them some milk and they tipped it over!"

"You gave the Nac Mac Feegle *milk?*"

"Well, you said they're pixies!"

"Not pixies, *pictsies.* They certainly don't drink milk!"

"Are they from the same place as Jenny?" Tiffany demanded.

"No. They're rebels," said toad.

"Rebels? Against who?"

"Everyone. Anything," said the toad. "Now pick me up."

"Why?"

"Because there's a woman at the well over there giving you a funny look. Put me in your apron pocket, for goodness' sake."

Tiffany snatched up the toad and smiled at the woman. "I'm making a collection of pressed toads," she said.

"That's nice, dear," said the woman, and hurried away.

"That wasn't very funny," said the toad from her apron.

"People don't listen anyway," said Tiffany.

She sat down under a tree and took the toad out of her pocket.

"The Feegles tried to steal some of our eggs and one of our sheep," she said. "But I got them back."

"You got something back from the Nac Mac Feegle?" said the toad. "Were they ill?"

"No. They were a bit . . . well, sweet, actually. They even did the chores for me."

"The *Feegle* did *chores*?" said the toad. "They *never* do chores! They're not helpful at all!"

"And then there was the headless horseman!" said Tiffany. "He had no *head*!"

"Well, that is the major job qualification," said the toad.

"What's going on, toad?" said Tiffany. "Is it the Feegles who are invading?"

The toad looked a bit shifty. "Miss Tick doesn't really want you to handle this," it said. "She'll be back soon with help—"

"Is she going to be in time?" Tiffany demanded.

"I don't know. Probably. But you shouldn't—"

"I want to know what is happening!"

"She's gone to get some other witches," said the toad. "Uh . . . she doesn't think you should—"

"You'd better tell me what you know, toad," said Tiffany. "Miss Tick isn't here. I am."

"Another world is colliding with this one," said the toad. "There. Happy now? That's what Miss Tick thinks. But it's happening faster than she expected. All the monsters are coming back."

"Why?"

"There's no one to stop them."

There was silence for a moment.

"There's me," said Tiffany.

CHAPTER 4

The Wee Free Men

Nothing happened on the way back to the farm. The sky stayed blue, none of the sheep in the home paddocks appeared to be traveling backward very fast, and an air of hot emptiness lay over everything.

Ratbag was on the path leading up to the back door, and he had something trapped in his paws. As soon as he saw Tiffany, he picked it up and exited around the corner of the house urgently, legs spinning in the high-speed slink of a guilty cat. Tiffany was too good a shot with a clod of earth.

But at least there wasn't something red-and-blue in his mouth.

"Look at him," she said. "Great cowardly blob! I really wish I could stop him catching baby birds—it's so sad!"

"You haven't got a hat you can wear, have you?" said the toad, from her apron pocket. "I hate not being able to see."

They went into the dairy, which Tiffany normally had to herself for most of the day.

In the bushes by the door there was a muffled conversation. It went like this:

"Whut did the wee hag say?"

"She said she wants yon cat to stop scraffin' the puir wee burdies."

"Is that a'? Crivens! Nae problemo!"

◆ ◆ ◆

Tiffany put the toad on the table as carefully as possible.

"What do you eat?" she said. It was polite to offer guests food, she knew.

"I've got used to slugs and worms and stuff," said the toad. "It wasn't easy. Don't worry if you don't have any. I expect you weren't expecting a toad to drop in."

"How about some milk?"

"You're very kind."

Tiffany fetched some and poured it into a saucer. She watched while the toad crawled in.

"Were you a handsome prince?" she asked.

"Yeah, right, maybe," said the toad, dribbling milk.

"So why did Miss Tick put a spell on you?"

"Her? Huh, she couldn't do that," said the toad. "It's serious magic, turning someone into a toad but leaving them thinking they're human. No, it was a fairy godmother. Never cross a woman with a star on a stick, young lady. They've got a mean streak."

"Why did she do it?"

The toad looked embarrassed. "I don't know," it said. "It's all a bit . . . foggy. I just *know* I've been a person. At least, I think I know. It gives me the willies. Sometimes I wake up in the night and I think, was I ever *really* human? Or was I just a toad that got on her nerves and she made me *think* I was human once? That'd be a real torture, right? Supposing there's nothing for me to turn back into?" The toad turned worried yellow eyes on her. "After all, it can't be very hard to mess with a toad's head, yeah? It must be much simpler than turning, oh, a one-hundred-and-sixty-pound human into eight ounces of toad, yes? After all, where's the rest of the mass going to go, I ask myself? Is it just sort of, you know, left over? Very worrying. I mean, I've got one or two memories of being a human, of course, but what's a memory? Just a thought in your brain. You can't be sure it's *real*. Honestly, on nights when I've eaten a bad slug, I wake up screaming, except all that comes out is a croak. Thank you for the milk, it was very nice."

Tiffany stared in silence at the toad.

"You know," she said, "magic is a lot more complicated than I thought."

"*Flappitty-flappitty flap! Cheep, cheep! Ach, poor wee me, cheepitty-cheep!*"

Tiffany ran over to the window.

There was a Feegle on the path. It had made itself some crude wings out of a piece of rag, and a kind of beaky cap out of straw, and was wobbling around in a circle like a wounded bird.

"Ach, cheepitty-cheep! Fluttery-flutter! I certainly hope dere's no' a pussycat aroound! Ach, dearie me!" it yelled.

And down the path Ratbag, archenemy of all baby birds, slunk closer, drooling. As Tiffany opened her mouth to yell, he leaped and landed with all four feet on the little man.

Or at least where the little man had been, because he had somersaulted in midair and was now right in front of Ratbag's face and had grabbed a cat ear with each hand.

"Ach, see you, pussycat, scunner that y'are!" he yelled. "Here's a giftie from the t' wee burdies, yah schemie!"

He butted the cat hard on the nose. Ratbag spun in the air and landed on his back with his eyes crossed. He squinted in cold terror as the little man leaned down at him and shouted, "*CHEEP!*"

Then he levitated in the way that cats do and became a ginger streak, rocketing down the path through the open door, and shooting past Tiffany to hide under the sink.

The Feegle looked up, grinning, and saw Tiffany.

"Please don't go—" she began quickly, but he went, in a blur.

Tiffany's mother was hurrying down the path. Tiffany picked up the toad and put it back in her apron pocket just in time. The door was flung open.

"Where's Wentworth? Is he here?" her mother asked urgently. "Did he come back? Answer me!"

"Didn't he go up to the shearing with you, Mum?" said Tiffany, suddenly nervous. She could feel the panic pouring off her mother like steam.

"We can't find him!" There was a wild look in her mother's eyes. "I turned my back for only a minute! Are you *sure* you haven't seen him?"

"But he couldn't come all the way back here—"

"Go and look in the house! Go on!"

Mrs. Aching hurried away. Hastily, Tiffany put the toad on the floor and urged him under the sink. She heard him croak, and Ratbag, mad with fear and bewilderment, came out from under the sink in a whirl of legs and rocketed out of the door.

She stood up. Her first, shameful thought was: He *wanted* to go up to watch the shearing. How could he get lost? He went with Mum and Hannah and Fastidia!

And how closely would Fastidia and Hannah watch him with all those young men up there?

She tried to pretend she hadn't thought that, but she was treacherously good at spotting when she was lying. That's the trouble with a brain—it thinks more than you sometimes want it to.

But he's never interested in moving far away from people! It's half a mile up to the shearing pens! And he doesn't move that fast. After a few feet he flops down and demands sweets!

But it would be a bit more peaceful around here if he did *get lost. . . .*

There it went again, a nasty, shameful thought, which she tried to drown out by getting busy. But first she took some candy out of the jar, as bait, and rustled the bag as she ran from room to room.

She heard boots in the yard as some of the men came down from the shearing sheds, but she got on with looking under beds and in cupboards, even ones so high that a toddler couldn't possibly reach them, and then looked *again* under beds that she'd already looked under, because it was that kind of search. It was the kind of search where you go and look in the attic, even though the door is always locked.

After a few minutes there were two or three voices outside, calling for Wentworth, and she heard her father say, "Try down by the river!"

. . . and that meant he was frantic too, because Wentworth would never walk that far without a bribe. He was not a child who was happy away from people with sweets.

It's your fault.

The thought felt like a piece of ice in her mind.

It's *your* fault because you didn't love him very much. He turned up and you weren't the youngest anymore, and you had to have him trailing around after you, and you kept wishing, didn't you, that he'd go away.

"That's not true!" Tiffany whispered to herself. "I . . . quite liked him. . . ."

Not very much, admittedly. Not all the time. He didn't know how to play properly, and he never did what he was told. *You* thought it would be better if he *did* get lost.

Anyway, she added in her head, you can't love people all the time when they have a permanently runny nose. Any *anyway* . . . I wonder . . .

"I wish I could find my brother," she said aloud.

This seemed to have no effect. But the house was full of people, opening and shutting doors and calling out and getting in one another's way, and the . . . Feegles were shy, despite many of them having faces like a hatful of knuckles.

Don't *wish*, Miss Tick had said. *Do* things.

She went downstairs. Even some of the women who'd been packing fleeces up at the shearing had come down. They were clustered around her mother, who was sitting at the table crying. No one noticed Tiffany. That often happened.

She slipped into the dairy, closed the door carefully behind her, and leaned down to peer under the sink.

The door burst open again and her father ran in. He stopped. Tiffany looked up guiltily.

"He can't be under there, girl!" her father said.

"Well, er . . ." said Tiffany.

"Did you look upstairs?"

"Even the attic, Dad—"

"Well." Her father looked panicky and impatient at the same time. "Go and . . . do something!"

"Yes, Dad."

When the door had shut, Tiffany peered under the sink again.

"Are you there, toad?"

"Very poor pickings under here," the toad answered, crawling out. "You keep it very clean. Not even a spider."

"This is *urgent*!" snapped Tiffany. "My little brother has gone missing. In broad daylight! Up on the downs, where you can see for miles!"

"Oh, *croap*," said the toad.

"Pardon?" said Tiffany.

"Er, that was, er, swearing in Toad," said the toad. "Sorry, but—"

"Has what's going on got something to do with magic?" said Tiffany. "It has, hasn't it . . . ?"

"I hope it hasn't," said the toad, "but I think it has."

"Have those little men stolen Wentworth?"

"Who, the Feegles? *They* don't steal children!"

There was something in the way the toad said it. *They* don't steal . . .

"Do you know who *has* taken my brother, then?" Tiffany demanded.

"No. But . . . they might," said the toad. "Look, Miss Tick told me that you were not to—"

"My brother has been *stolen*," said Tiffany sharply. "Are you going to tell me not to do anything about it?"

"No, but—"

"Good! Where are the Feegles now?"

"Lying low, I expect. The place is full of people searching, after all, but—"

"How can I bring them back? I *need* them!"

"Um, Miss Tick said—"

"How can I bring them back?"

"Er . . . you want to bring them back, then?" said the toad, looking mournful.

"Yes!"

"It's just that's something not many people have ever wanted to do," said the toad. "They're not like brownies. If you get Nac Mac

Feegle in the house, it's usually best to move away." He sighed. "Tell me, is your father a drinking man?"

"He has a beer sometimes," said Tiffany. "What's that got to do with anything?"

"Only beer?"

"Well, I'm not supposed to know about what my father calls the Special Sheep Liniment," said Tiffany. "Granny Aching used to make it in the old cowshed."

"Strong stuff, is it?"

"It dissolves spoons," said Tiffany. "It's for special occasions. Father says it's not for women because it puts hairs on your chest."

"Then if you want to be *sure* of finding the Nac Mac Feegle, go and fetch some," said the toad. "It will work, believe me."

Five minutes later Tiffany was ready. Few things are hidden from a quiet child with good eyesight, and she knew where the bottles were stored and she had one now. The cork was hammered in over a piece of rag, but it was old and she was able to lever it out with the tip of a knife. The fumes made her eyes water.

She went to pour some of the golden-brown liquid into a saucer—

"No! We'll be trampled to death if you do that," said the toad. "Just leave the cork off."

Fumes rose from the top of the bottle, wavering like the air over rocks on a hot day.

She felt it—a sensation, in the dim, cool room, of riveted attention.

She sat down on a milking stool and said, "All right, you can come out now."

There were *hundreds*. They rose up from behind buckets. They lowered themselves on string from the ceiling beams. They sidled sheepishly from behind the cheese racks. They crept out from under the sink. They came out of places where you'd think a man with hair like an orange gone nova couldn't possibly hide.

They were all about six inches tall and mostly colored blue, although it was hard to know if that was the actual color of their skins or just the dye from their tattoos, which covered every inch that wasn't covered with red hair. They wore short kilts, and some wore other bits of clothing too, like skinny vests. A few of them wore rabbit or rat skulls on their heads, as a sort of helmet. And every single one of them carried, slung across his back, a sword nearly as big as he was.

However, what Tiffany noticed more than anything else was that they were scared of her. Mostly they were looking at their own feet, which was no errand for the faint-hearted because their feet were large, dirty, and half tied up with animal skins to make very bad shoes. None of them wanted to look her in the eye.

"You were the people who filled the water buckets?" she said.

There was a lot of foot shuffling and coughing and a chorus of ayes.

"And the wood box?"

There were more ayes.

Tiffany glared at them.

"And what about the sheep?"

This time they all looked down.

"Why did you steal the sheep?"

There was a lot of muttering and nudging, and then one of the tiny men removed his rabbit-skull helmet and twiddled it nervously in his hands.

"We wuz hungerin', mistress," he muttered. "But when we kenned it was thine, we did put the beastie back in the fold."

They looked so crestfallen that Tiffany took pity on them.

"I expect you wouldn't have stolen it if you weren't so hungry, then," she said.

There were several hundred astonished looks.

"Oh, we would, mistress," said the helmet twiddler.

"You would?"

Tiffany sounded so surprised that the twiddler looked around at his colleagues for support. They all nodded.

"Yes, mistress. We have tae. We are a famously stealin' folk. Aren't we, lads? Whut's it we're famous for?"

"Stealin'!" shouted the blue men.

"And what else, lads?"

"Fightin'!"

"And what else?"

"Drinkin'!"

"And what else?"

There was a certain amount of thought about this, but they all reached the same conclusion.

"Drinkin' *and* fightin'!"

"And there was summat else," muttered the twiddler. "Ach, yes. Tell the hag, lads!"

"Stealin' an' drinkin' an' fightin'!" shouted the blue men cheerfully.

"Tell the wee hag who we are, lads," said the helmet twiddler.

There was the scrape of many small swords being drawn and thrust into the air.

"Nac Mac Feegle! The Wee Free Men! Nae king! Nae quin! Nae laird! Nae master! *We willna be fooled again!*"

Tiffany stared at them. They were all watching her to see what she was going to do next, and the longer she said nothing, the more worried they become. They lowered their swords, looking embarrassed.

"But we wouldna dare deny a powerful hag, except mebbe for strong drink," said the twiddler, his helmet spinning desperately in his hands and his eyes on the bottle of Special Sheep Liniment. "Will ye no' help us?"

"Help you?" said Tiffany. "I want you to help me! Someone has taken my brother in broad daylight."

"Oh waily, waily waily!" said the helmet twiddler. "She's come, then. She's come a-fetchin'. We're too late! It's the Quin!"

"What, there were four of them?" said Tiffany.

"They mean the Queen," said the toad. "The Queen of the—"

"Hush yer gob!" shouted the helmet twiddler, but his voice was lost in the wails and groans of the Nac Mac Feegle. They were pulling at their hair and stamping on the ground and shouting, "Alackaday!" and "Waily waily waily!" and the toad was arguing with the helmet twiddler and everyone was getting louder to make themselves heard—

Tiffany stood up. "Everybody shut up right now!" she said.

Silence fell, except for a few sniffs and faint wailys from the back.

"We wuz only dreeing our weird, mistress," said the helmet twiddler, almost crouching in fear.

"But not in here!" snapped Tiffany, shaking with anger. "This is a *dairy*! I have to keep it clean!"

"Er . . . *dreeing your weird* means 'facing your fate,'" said the toad.

"'Cause if the Quin is here, then it means our kelda is weakenin' fast," said the helmet twiddler. "An' we'll ha' naeone tae look after us."

No one to look after us, thought Tiffany. Hundreds of tough

little men who could each win the Worst Broken Nose Contest need someone to look after them?

She took a deep breath.

"My mother's in the house crying," she said, "and . . ." I don't know how to comfort her, she added to herself. I'm no *good* at this sort of thing, I never know what I should be saying. Out loud she said: "And she wants him back. Er. A lot." She added, hating to say it, "He's her favorite."

She pointed to the helmet twiddler, who backed away.

"First of all," she said, "I can't keep thinking of you as the helmet twiddler, so what is your name?"

A gasp went up from the Nac Mac Feegle, and Tiffany heard one of them murmur, "Aye, she's the hag, sure enough. That's a hag's question!"

The helmet twiddler looked around at them as if seeking help.

"We dinna give oour names," he muttered. But another Feegle, somewhere safe at the back said, "Wheest! You canna refuse a hag!"

The little man looked up, very worried.

"I'm the Big Man o' the clan, mistress," he said. "An' my name it is . . ." He swallowed. "Rob Anybody Feegle, mistress. But I beg ye not to use it agin me!"

The toad was ready for this.

"They think names have magic in them," he murmured. "They don't tell them to people in case they are written down."

"Aye, an' put upon comp-li-cated documents," said a Feegle.

"An' summonses and such things," said another.

"Or 'Wanted' posters!" said another.

"Aye, an' bills an' affidavits," said another.

"Writs of distrainment, even!" The Feegles looked around in panic at the very thought of written-down things.

"They think written words are even more powerful," whispered the toad. "They think all writing is magic. Words worry them. See their swords? They glow blue in the presence of lawyers."

"All *right*," said Tiffany. "We're getting somewhere. I promise not to write his name down. Now tell me about this Queen who's taken Wentworth. Queen of what?"

"Canna say it aloud, mistress," said Rob Anybody. "She hears her name wherever it's said, and she comes callin'."

"Actually, that's true," said the toad. "You do not want to meet her, ever."

"She's bad?"

"Worse. Just call her the Queen."

"Aye, the Quin," said Rob Anybody. He looked at Tiffany with bright, worried eyes. "Ye dinna ken o' the Quin? An' you the wean o' Granny Aching, who had these hills in her bones? Ye dinna ken the ways? She did not show ye the ways? Ye're no' a hag? How can this be? Ye slammered Jenny Green-Teeth and stared the Heidless Horseman in the eyes he hasna got, and you dinna ken?"

Tiffany gave him a brittle smile and then whispered to the toad, "Who's Ken? And what about his dinner? And what's a wean of Granny Aching?"

"As far as I can make out," said the toad, "they're amazed that you don't know about the Queen and . . . er, the magical ways, what with you being a child of Granny Aching and standing up to the monsters. *Ken* means 'know.'"

"And his dinner?"

"Forget about his dinner for now," said the toad. "They thought Granny Aching told you her magic. Hold me up to your ear, will you?" Tiffany did so, and the toad whispered, "Best not to disappoint them, eh?"

She swallowed. "But she never told me about any magic—" she began. And stopped. It was true. Granny Aching hadn't told her about any magic. But she showed people magic every day.

There was the time when the Baron's champion hound was caught killing sheep. It was a hunting dog, after all, but it had got out onto the downs and, because sheep run, it had chased. . . .

The Baron knew the penalty for sheep worrying. There were laws on the Chalk, so old that no one remembered who made them, and everyone knew this one: Sheep-killing dogs were killed.

But this dog was worth five hundred gold dollars, and so—the story went—the Baron sent his servant up onto the downs to Granny's hut on wheels. She was sitting on the step, smoking her pipe and watching the flocks.

The man rode up on his horse and didn't bother to dismount. That was not a good thing to do if you wanted Granny Aching to be your friend. Iron-shod hooves cut the turf. She didn't like that.

He said: "The Baron commands that you find a way to save his dog, Mistress Aching. In return, he will give you a hundred silver dollars."

Granny had smiled at the horizon, puffed at her pipe for a while, and replied: "A man who takes arms against his lord, that man is hanged. A starving man who steals his lord's sheep, that man is hanged. A dog that kills sheep, that dog is put to death. Those laws are on these hills and these hills are in my bones. What is a baron, that the law be brake for him?"

She went back to staring at the sheep.

"The Baron owns this country," said the servant. "It is his law."

The look Granny Aching gave him turned the man's hair white. That was the story, anyway. But all stories about Granny Aching had a bit of fairy tale about them.

"If it is, as ye say, his law, then let him break it and see how things may then be," she said.

A few hours later the Baron sent his bailiff, who was far more important but had known Granny Aching for longer. He said: "Mrs. Aching, the Baron requests that you use your influence to save his dog. He will happily give you fifty gold dollars to help ease this difficult situation. I am sure you can see how this will benefit everyone concerned."

Granny smoked her pipe and stared at the new lambs and said: "Ye speak for your master, your master speaks for his dog. Who speaks for the hills? Where is the Baron, that the law be brake for him?"

They said that when the Baron was told this, he went very quiet. But although he was pompous, and often unreasonable, and far too haughty, he was not stupid. In the evening he walked up to the hut and sat down on the turf nearby. After a while Granny Aching said: "Can I help you, my lord?"

"Granny Aching, I plead for the life of my dog," said the Baron.

"Bring ye siller? Bring ye gilt?" said Granny Aching.

"No silver. No gold," said the Baron.

"Good. A law that is brake by siller or gilt is no worthwhile law. And so, my lord?"

"I plead, Granny Aching."

"Ye try to break the law with a word?"

"That's right, Granny Aching."

Granny Aching, the story went, stared at the sunset for a while and then said: "Then be down at the little old stone barn at dawn tomorrow, and we'll see if an old dog can learn new tricks. There will be a reckoning. Good night to ye."

Most of the village was hanging around the old stone barn the next morning. Granny arrived with one of the smaller farm wagons. It held a ewe with her newborn lamb. She put them in the barn.

Some of the men turned up with the dog. It was nervous and snappy, having spent the night chained up in a shed, and kept trying to bite the men who were holding it by two leather straps. It was hairy. It had fangs.

The Baron rode up with the bailiff. Granny Aching nodded at them and opened the barn door.

"You're putting the dog into the barn with a sheep, Mrs. Aching?" said the bailiff. "Do you want it to choke to death on lamb?"

This didn't get much of a laugh. No one liked the bailiff much.

"We shall see," said Granny. The men dragged the dog to the doorway, threw it inside the barn, and slammed the door quickly. People rushed to the little windows.

There was the bleating of the lamb, a growl from the dog, and then a baa from the lamb's mother. But this wasn't the normal baa of a sheep. It had an edge to it.

Something hit the door and it bounced on its hinges. Inside, the dog yelped.

Granny Aching picked up Tiffany and held her to a window.

The shaken dog was trying to get to its feet, but it didn't manage it before the ewe charged again, seventy pounds of enraged sheep slamming into it like a battering ram.

Granny lowered Tiffany again and lit her pipe. She puffed it peacefully as the building behind her shook and the dog yelped and whimpered.

After a couple of minutes she nodded at the men. They opened the door.

The dog came out limping on three legs, but it hadn't managed to get more than a few feet before the ewe shot out behind it and butted it so hard that it rolled over.

It lay still. Perhaps it had learned what would happen if it tried to get up again.

Granny Aching had nodded to the men, who picked the sheep up and dragged it back into the barn.

The Baron had been watching with his mouth open.

"He killed a wild boar last year!" he said. "What did you do to him?"

"He'll mend," said Granny Aching, carefully ignoring the question. "'Tis mostly his pride that's hurt. But he won't look at a sheep again, you have my thumb on that." And she licked her right thumb and held it out.

After a moment's hesitation, the Baron licked his thumb, reached down, and pressed it against hers. Everyone knew what it meant. On the Chalk, a thumb bargain was unbreakable.

"For you, at a word, the law was brake," said Granny Aching. "Will ye mind that, ye who sit in judgment? Will ye remember this day? Ye'll have cause to."

The Baron nodded to her.

"That'll do," said Granny Aching, and their thumbs parted.

Next day the Baron technically did give Granny Aching gold, but it was only the gold-colored foil on an ounce of Jolly Sailor, the cheap and horrible pipe tobacco that was the only one Granny Aching would ever smoke. She was always in a bad mood if the peddlers were late and she'd run out. You'd couldn't bribe Granny Aching for all the gold in the world, but you could definitely attract her attention with an ounce of Jolly Sailor.

Things were a lot easier after that. The bailiff was a little less unpleasant when rents were late, the Baron was a little more polite to people, and Tiffany's father said one night after two beers that the Baron had been shown what happens when sheep rise up, and things might be different one day, and her mother hissed at him not to talk like that because you never knew who was listening.

And one day Tiffany heard him telling her mother, quietly: "'Twas an old shepherds' trick, that's all. An old ewe will fight like a lion for her lamb, we all know that."

That was how it worked. No magic at all. But that time it had been magic. And it didn't stop being magic just because you found out how it was done. . . .

The Nac Mac Feegle were watching Tiffany carefully, with occasional longing glances at the bottle of Special Sheep Liniment.

I haven't even found the witches' school, she thought. I don't know a single spell. I don't even have a pointy hat. My talents are an instinct for making cheese and not running around panicking when things go wrong. Oh, and I've got a toad.

And I don't understand half of what these little men are saying. But they know who's taken my brother.

Somehow I don't think the Baron would have a clue how to deal with this. I don't, either, but I think I can be clueless in more sensible ways.

"I . . . remember a lot of things about Granny Aching," she said. "What do you want me to do?"

"The kelda sent us," said Rob Anybody. "She sensed the Quin comin'. She kenned there wuz going to be trouble. She tole us, it's gonna be bad, find the new hag who's kin to Granny Aching, she'll ken what to do."

Tiffany looked at the hundreds of expectant faces. Some of the Feegle had feathers in their hair and necklaces of mole teeth. You couldn't tell someone with half his face dyed dark blue and a sword as big as he was that you weren't really a witch. You couldn't disappoint someone like that.

"And will you help me get my brother back?" she said. The Feegles' expressions didn't change. She tried again. "Can you help me steal my brother back from the Quin?"

Hundred of small yet ugly faces brightened up considerably.

"Ach, *noo* yer talkin' *oour* language," said Rob Anybody.

"Not . . . quite," said Tiffany. "Can you all just wait a moment? I'll just pack some things," she said, trying to sound as if she knew what she was doing. She put the cork back on the bottle of Special

Sheep Liniment. The Nac Mac Feegle sighed.

She darted back into the kitchen, took some bandages and ointments out of the medicine box, put the bottle of Special Sheep Liniment into her apron pocket, because her father said it always did *him* good, and, as an afterthought, added the book *Diseases of the Sheep* and picked up the frying pan. Both might come in useful.

The little men were nowhere to be seen when she went back into the dairy.

She knew she ought to tell her parents what was happening. But it wouldn't work. It would be "telling stories." Anyway, with any luck she could get Wentworth back before she was even missed. But, just in case . . .

She kept a diary in the dairy. Cheese needed to be kept track of, and she always wrote down details of the amount of butter she'd made and how much milk she'd been using.

She turned to a fresh page, picked up her pencil, and, with her tongue sticking out of the corner of her mouth, began to write.

The Nac Mac Feegle gradually reappeared. They didn't obviously step out from behind things, and they certainly didn't pop magically into existence. They appeared in the same way that faces appear in clouds and fires; they seemed to turn up if you just looked hard enough and wanted to see them.

They watched the moving pencil in awe, and she could hear them murmuring.

"Look at that writin' stick noo, will ye, bobbin' along. That's hag business."

"Ach, she has the kenning o' the writin', sure enough."

"But you'll no' write doon oour names, eh, mistress?"

"Aye, a body can be put in the pris'n if they have written evidence."

Tiffany stopped writing and read the note:

Dear Mum and Dad, I have gone to look for Wentworth. I am ~~perfectly probably~~ quite safe, because I am with some ~~friends acquaintances~~ people who knew Granny. PS The cheeses on rack three will need turning tomorrow if I'm not back.

Love, Tiffany

Tiffany looked up at Rob Anybody, who had shinned up the table leg and was watching the pencil intently, in case it wrote something dangerous.

"You could have just come and asked me right at the start," she said.

"We didna ken it was thee we were lookin' for, mistress. Lots of bigjob women walkin' around this farm. We didna ken it was thee until you caught Daft Wullie."

It might not be, thought Tiffany.

"Yes, but stealing the sheep and the eggs, there was no need for that," she said sternly.

"But they wasna nailed doon, mistress," said Rob Anybody, as if that was an excuse.

"You can't nail down an egg!" snapped Tiffany.

"Ach, well, you'd have the kennin' o' wise stuff like that, mistress," said Rob Anybody. "I see you's done wi' the writin', so we'd best be goin'. Ye hae a besom?"

"Broomstick," murmured the toad.

"Er, no," said Tiffany. "The important thing about magic," she added haughtily, "is to know when not to use it."

"Fair enough," said Rob Anybody, sliding back down the table leg. "Come here, Daft Wullie." One of the Feegles who looked very much like that morning's egg thief came and stood by Rob

Anybody, and they both bent over slightly. "If you'd care to step on us, mistress," said Rob Anybody.

Before Tiffany could open her mouth, the toad said out of the corner of its mouth, and being a toad that means quite a lot of corner, "One Feegle can lift a grown man. You couldn't squash one if you tried."

"I don't *want* to try!"

Tiffany very cautiously raised a big boot. Daft Wullie ran underneath it, and she felt the boot being pushed upward. She might as well have trodden on a brick.

"Now t'other wee bootie," said Rob Anybody.

"I'll fall over!"

"Nae, we're *good* at this. . . ."

And then Tiffany was standing up on two pictsies. She felt them moving backward and forward underneath her, keeping her balanced. She felt quite secure, though. It was just like wearing really *thick* soles.

"Let's gae," said Rob Anybody, down below. "An' don't worry about yon pussycat scraffin' the wee burdies. Some of the lads is stayin' behind to mind things!"

◆　◆　◆

Ratbag crept along a branch. He wasn't a cat who was good at changing the ways he thought. But he was good at finding nests. He'd heard the cheeping from the other end of the garden, and even from the bottom of the tree he'd been able to see three little yellow beaks in the nest. Now he advanced, drooling. Nearly there . . .

Three Nac Mac Feegle pulled off their straw beaks and grinned happily at him.

"Hello, Mister Pussycat," said one of them. "Ye dinna learn, do ye? *Cheep!*"

CHAPTER 5

The Green Sea

໑ৡৡ

Tiffany flew a few inches above the ground, standing still. Wind rushed around her as the Feegles sped out of the farmyard's top gate and onto the turf of the downs. . . .

This is the girl, flying. At the moment there's a toad on her head, holding on to her hair.

Pull back, and here is the long green whaleback of the downs. Now she's a pale-blue dot against the endless grass, mowed by the sheep to the height of a carpet. But the green sea isn't unbroken. Here and there humans have been.

Last year Tiffany had spent three carrots and an apple on half an hour of geology, although she'd been refunded a carrot after explaining to the teacher that 'Geology' shouldn't be spelled on his sign as "G olly G." He said that the chalk had been formed underwater millions of years before from tiny seashells.

That made sense to Tiffany. Sometimes you found little fossils in the chalk. But the teacher didn't know much about the flint. You found flints, harder than steel, in chalk, the softest of rocks. Sometimes the shepherds chipped the flints, one flint against another, into knives. Not even the best steel knives could take an edge as sharp as flint.

And men in what was called on the Chalk "the olden days" had dug pits for it. They were still there, deep holes in the rolling green, filled with thickets of thorn and brambles.

Huge, knobbly flints still turned up in the village gardens. Sometimes they were larger than a man's head. They often looked like heads, too. They were so melted and twisted and curved that you could look at a flint and see almost anything—a face, a strange animal, a sea monster. Sometimes the more interesting ones would be put on garden walls, for show.

The old people called those *calkins*, which meant "chalk children." They'd always seemed ... odd to Tiffany, as if the stone was striving to become alive. Some flints looked like bits of meat, or bones, or something off a butcher's slab. In the dark, under the sea, it looked as though the chalk had been trying to make the shapes of living creatures.

There weren't just the chalk pits. Men had been everywhere on the Chalk. There were stone circles, half fallen down, and burial mounds like green pimples where, it was said, chieftains of the olden days had been buried with their treasure. No one fancied digging into them to find out.

There were odd carvings in the chalk, too, which the shepherds sometimes weeded when they were out on the downs with the flocks and there was not a lot to do. The chalk was only a few inches under the turf. Hoofprints could last a season, but the carvings had lasted for thousands of years. They were pictures of horses and giants, but the strange thing was that you couldn't see them properly from anywhere on the ground. They looked as if they'd been made for viewers in the sky.

And then there were the weird places, like Old Man's Forge, which was just four big flat rocks placed so they made a kind of half-buried hut in the side of a mound. It was only a few feet deep. It didn't look like anything special, but if you shouted your name into it, it was several seconds before the echo came back.

There were signs of people everywhere. The Chalk had been *important*.

Tiffany left the shearing sheds way behind. No one was watching. Sheared sheep took no notice at all of a girl moving without her feet touching the ground.

The lowlands dropped away behind her, and now she was properly on the downs. Only the occasional baa of a sheep or scream of a buzzard disturbed a busy silence, made up of bee buzzes and breezes and the sound of a ton of grass growing every minute.

On either side of Tiffany the Nac Mac Feegle ran in a spread-out ragged line, staring grimly ahead.

They passed some of the mounds without stopping, and ran up and down the sides of shallow valleys without a pause. And it was then that Tiffany saw a landmark ahead.

It was a small flock of sheep. There were only a few, freshly sheared, but there were always a handful of sheep at this place. Strays would turn up there, and lambs would find their way to it when they'd lost their mothers.

This was a magic place.

There wasn't much to see now, just the iron wheels sinking into the turf and the pot-bellied stove with its short chimney. . . .

On the day Granny Aching died, the men had cut and lifted the turf around the hut and stacked it neatly some way away. Then they'd dug a deep hole in the chalk, six feet deep and six feet long, lifting out the chalk in great damp blocks.

Thunder and Lightning had watched them carefully. They didn't whine or bark. They seemed more interested than upset.

Granny Aching had been wrapped in a woolen blanket, with a tuft of raw wool pinned to it. That was a special shepherd thing. It was there to tell any gods who might get involved that the person being buried there was a shepherd, and spent a lot of time on the hills, and what with lambing and one thing and another couldn't always take much time out for religion, there being no churches or temples up there, and therefore it was generally hoped that the gods would understand and look kindly on them. Granny Aching, it had to be said, had never been seen to pray to anyone or anything in her life, and it was agreed by all that, even now, she wouldn't have any time for a god who didn't understand that lambing came first.

The chalk had been put back over her, and Granny Aching, who always said that the hills were in her bones, now had her bones in the hills.

Then they burned the hut. That wasn't usual, but her father had said that there wasn't a shepherd anywhere on the Chalk who'd use it now.

Thunder and Lightning wouldn't come when he called, and he knew better than to be angry, so they were left sitting quite contentedly by the glowing embers of the hut.

Next day, when the ashes were cold and blowing across the raw chalk, everyone went up onto the downs and with very great care put the turf back, so all that was left to see were the iron wheels on their axles, and the pot-bellied stove.

At which point—so everyone said—the two sheepdogs had looked up, their ears pricking, and had trotted away over the turf and were never seen again.

The pictsies carrying her slowed down gently, and Tiffany flailed her arms as they dropped her onto the grass. The sheep lumbered away slowly, then stopped and turned to watch her.

"Why're we stopping? Why're we stopping *here*? We've got to catch her!"

"Got to wait for Hamish, mistress," said Rob Anybody.

"Why? Who's Hamish?"

"He might have the knowin' of where the Quin went with your wee laddie," said Rob Anybody soothingly. "We canna just rush in, ye ken."

A big, bearded Feegle raised his hand. "Point 'o order, Big Man. Ye *can* just rush in. We *always* just rush in."

"Aye, Big Yan, point well made. But ye gotta know *where* ye're just gonna rush in. Ye canna just rush in *anywhere*. It looks bad, havin' to rush oot again straight awa'."

Tiffany saw that all the Feegles were staring intently upward and paying her no attention at all.

Angry and puzzled, she sat down on one of the rusty wheels and looked at the sky. It was better than looking around. There was Granny Aching's grave somewhere around here, although you couldn't find it now, not precisely. The turf had healed.

There were a few little clouds above her and nothing else at all, except the distant circling dots of the buzzards. There were always buzzards over the Chalk.

The shepherds had taken to calling them Granny Aching's chickens, and some of them called clouds like those up there today "Granny's little lambs." And Tiffany *knew* that even her father called the thunder "Granny Aching cussin'."

And it was said that some of the shepherds, if wolves were troublesome in the winter, or a prize ewe had got lost, would go to the site of the old hut in the hills and leave an ounce of Jolly Sailor tobacco, just in case. . . .

Tiffany hesitated. Then she shut her eyes. I want that to be true, she whispered to herself. I want to know that other people think she hasn't really gone too.

She looked under the wide rusted rim of the wheels and shivered. There was a brightly colored little packet there.

She picked it up. It looked quite fresh, so it had probably been there for only a few days. There was the Jolly Sailor on the front, with his big grin and big yellow rain hat and big beard, with big blue waves crashing behind him.

Tiffany had learned about the sea from Granny Aching and the Jolly Sailor wrappings. She'd heard it was big, and roared. There was a tower in the sea, which was a lighthouse that carried a big light on it at night to stop boats from crashing into the rocks. In the pictures the beam of the lighthouse was a brilliant white. She knew about it so well, she'd dreamed about it, and had woken up with the roar of the sea in her ears.

She'd heard one of her uncles say that if you looked at the tobacco label upside down, then part of the hat and the sailor's ear and a bit of his collar made up a picture of a woman with no clothes on, but Tiffany had never been able to make it out and couldn't see what the point would be in any case.

She carefully pulled the label off the packet and sniffed at it. It smelled of Granny. She felt her eyes begin to fill with tears. She'd never cried for Granny Aching before, never. She'd cried for dead lambs and cut fingers and for not getting her own way, but never for Granny. It hadn't seemed right.

And I'm not crying now, she thought, carefully putting the label in her apron pocket. Not for Granny being dead. . . .

It was the smell. Granny Aching smelled of sheep, turpentine, and Jolly Sailor tobacco. The three smells mixed together and become one smell, which was, to Tiffany, the smell of the Chalk. It followed Granny Aching like a cloud, and it meant warmth, and silence, and a space around which the whole world revolved. . . .

A shadow passed overhead. A buzzard was diving down from the sky toward the Nac Mac Feegle.

She leaped up and waved her arms. "Run away! Duck! It'll kill you!"

They turned and looked at her for a moment as though she'd gone mad.

"Dinna fash yersel', mistress," said Rob Anybody.

The bird curved up at the bottom of its dive, and as it climbed again a dot dropped from it. As it fell, it seemed to grow two wings and started to spin like a sycamore leaf, which slowed down the fall somewhat.

It was a pictsie, still spinning madly when he hit the turf a few feet away, where he fell over. He got up, swearing loudly, and fell over again. The swearing continued.

"A good landin', Hamish," said Rob Anybody. "The spinnin' certainly slows ye doon. Ye didna drill right into the ground this time hardly at a'."

Hamish got up more slowly this time and managed to stay upright. He had a pair of goggles over his eyes.

"I dinna think I can tak' much more o' this," he said, trying to untie a couple of thin bits of wood from his arms. "I feel like a fairy wi' the wings on."

"How can you survive that?" Tiffany asked.

The very small pilot tried to look her up and down, but only managed to look her up and farther up.

"Who's the wee bigjob who knows sich a lot aboot aviation?" he said.

Rob Anybody coughed. "She's the hag, Hamish. Spawn o' Granny Aching."

Hamish's expression changed to a look of terror. "I didna mean to speak out o' turn, mistress," he said, backing away. "O' course, a hag'd have the knowing of anythin'. But 'tis nae as bad as it looks, mistress. I allus make sure I lands on my heid."

"Aye, we're very resilient in the heid department," said Rob Anybody.

"Have you seen a woman with a small boy?" Tiffany demanded. She hadn't much liked being called "spawn."

Hamish gave Rob Anybody a panicky look, and Rob nodded.

"Aye, I did," said Hamish. "Onna black horse. Riding up from the lowlan's goin' hell for—"

"We dinna use bad language in front o' a hag!" Rob Anybody thundered.

"Begging your pardon, mistress. She was ridin' heck for leather," said Hamish, looking more sheepish than the sheep. "But she kenned I was spyin' her and called up a mist. She's gone to the other side, but I dinna ken where."

"'Tis a perilous place, the other side," said Rob Anybody slowly. "Evil things there. A cold place. Not a place to tak' a wee babbie."

It was hot on the downs, but Tiffany felt a chill. However bad it is, she thought, I'm going to have to go there. I know it. I don't have a choice.

"The *other* side?" she said.

"Aye. The magic world," said Rob Anybody. "There's . . . bad things there."

"Monsters?" said Tiffany.

"As bad as ye can think of," said Rob Anybody. "*Exactly* as bad as ye can think of."

Tiffany swallowed hard and closed her eyes. "Worse than Jenny? Worse than the headless horseman?" she said.

"Oh, aye. They were wee pussycats compared to the scunners over there. 'Tis an ill-fared country that's come callin', mistress. 'Tis a land where dreams come true. That's the Quin's world."

"Well, that doesn't sound too—" Tiffany began. Then she remembered some of the dreams she'd had, the ones where you were so glad to wake up. . . . "We're not talking about nice dreams, are we?" she said.

Rob Anybody shook his head. "Nay, mistress. The other kind."

And me with my frying pan and *Diseases of the Sheep*, thought Tiffany. And she had a mental picture of Wentworth among horrible monsters. They probably wouldn't have any sweeties at all.

She sighed. "All right," she said. "How do I get there?"

"Ye dinna ken the way?" said Rob Anybody.

It wasn't what she'd been expecting. What she *had* been expecting was more like "Ach, ye canna do that, a wee lass like you, oh deary us no!" She wasn't so much expecting that as hoping it, in fact. But, instead, they were acting as if it was a perfectly reasonable idea. . . .

"No!" she said. "I don't dinna any ken at all! I haven't done this before! Please help me!"

"That's true, Rob," said a Feegle. "She's new to the haggin'. Tak' her to the kelda."

"Not e'en Granny Aching ever went to see the kelda in her ain cave!" snapped Rob Anybody. "It's no a—"

"Quiet!" hissed Tiffany. "Can't you hear that?"

The Feegles looked around.

"Hear what?" said Hamish.

"It's a susurration!"

The turf was trembling. The sky looked as though Tiffany was inside a diamond. And there was the smell of snow.

Hamish pulled a pipe out of his waistcoat and blew it. Tiffany couldn't hear anything, but there was a scream from high above.

"I'll let ye know what's happenin'!" cried the pictsie, and started to run across the turf. As he ran, he raised his arms over his head.

He was moving fast by then, but the buzzard sped down and across the turf even faster and plucked him neatly into the air. As it beat at the air to rise again, Tiffany saw Hamish climbing up through the feathers.

The other Feegles had formed a circle around Tiffany, and this time they'd drawn their swords.

"Whut's the plan, Rob?" said one of them.

"Okay, lads, this is what we'll do. As soon as we see somethin', we'll attack it. Right?"

This caused a cheer.

"Ach, 'tis a good plan," said Daft Wullie.

Snow formed on the ground. It didn't fall, it . . . did the opposite of melting, rising up fast until the Nac Mac Feegle were waist deep, and then buried up to their necks. Some of the smaller ones began to disappear, and there was muffled cursing from under the snow.

And then the dogs appeared, lumbering toward Tiffany with a nasty purpose. They were big, black, and heavily built, with orange eyebrows, and she could hear the growling from where she stood.

She plunged her hand into her apron pocket and pulled out the toad. It blinked in the sharp light.

"Wazzup?"

Tiffany turned him around to face the things. "What are *these*?" she said.

"Oh, doak! Grimhounds! Bad! Eyes of fire and teeth of razor blades!"

"What should I do about them?"

"Not be here?"

"Thank you! You've been very helpful!" Tiffany dropped him back in her pocket and gripped the frying pan.

It wasn't going to be good enough, she knew that. The black dogs were big, and their eyes *were* flames, and when they opened their mouths to snarl, she could see the light glint on steel. She'd never been afraid of dogs, but these dogs weren't from anywhere outside of a nightmare.

There were three of them, but they circled so that no matter how she turned, she could only see two at once. She knew it would be the one behind her that attacked first.

"Tell me something more about them!" she said, turning the other way to the circle so that she could watch all three.

"Said to haunt graveyards!" said a voice from her apron.

"Why is there snow on the ground?"

"This has become the Queen's land. It's always winter there! When she puts out her power, it comes here too!"

But Tiffany could see green some way off, beyond the circle of snow.

Think, think . . .

The Queen's land. A magical place where there really were monsters. Anything you could dream of in nightmares. Dogs with eyes of flame and teeth of razors, yes. You didn't get them in the real world, they wouldn't work. . . .

They were drooling now, red tongues hanging out, enjoying her fear. And part of Tiffany thought: It's amazing their teeth don't rust. . . .

. . . and took charge of her legs. She dived between two of the dogs and ran toward the distant green.

There was a growl of triumph behind her, and she heard the crunch of paws on snow.

The green didn't seem to be getting nearer.

She heard yells from the pictsies and a snarl that turned into a wail, but there was something behind her as she jumped over the last of the snow and rolled on the warm turf.

A grimhound leaped after her. She jerked herself away as it snapped, but it was already in trouble.

No eyes of fire, no teeth of razors. Not here, not in the *real* world, on the home turf. It was blind here and blood was already dripping from its mouth. You shouldn't jump with a mouthful of razors. . . .

Tiffany almost felt sorry for it as it whined in pain, but the snow was creeping toward her and she hit the dog with the frying pan. It went down heavily and lay still.

There was a fight going on back in the snow, which was flying up like a mist, but she could see two dark shapes in the middle, spinning around and snapping.

She banged on the pan and shouted, and a grimhound sprang from the whirling snow and landed in front of her, a Feegle hanging from each ear.

The snow flowed toward Tiffany. She backed away, watching the advancing, snarling dog. She held the pan like a bat.

"Come on," she whispered. "Jump!"

The eyes flamed at her, and then the dog looked down at the snow.

And vanished. The snow sank into the ground. The light changed.

Tiffany and the Wee Free Men were alone on the downs. Feegles were picking themselves up around her.

"Are you fine, mistress?" said Rob Anybody.

"Yes!" said Tiffany. "It's easy! If you get them off the snow, they're just dogs!"

"We'd best move on. We lost some of the lads."

The excitement drained away.

"You mean they're dead?" Tiffany whispered. The sun was shining brightly again, the skylarks were back . . . and people were dead.

"Ach, no," said Rob. "*We're* the one's who's deid. Did ye not know that?"

CHAPTER 6

The Shepherdess

❧

"**Y**ou're *dead*?" said Tiffany. She looked around. Feegles were picking themselves up and grumbling, but no one was going "Waily waily waily." And Rob Anybody wasn't making any sense at all.

"Well, if you think you're dead, then what are they?" she went on, pointing to a couple of small bodies.

"Oh, they've gone back to the land o' the livin'," said Rob Anybody cheerfully. "It's nae as good as this one, but they'll bide fine and come back before too long. No sense in grievin'."

The Achings were not very religious, but Tiffany thought she knew how things ought to go, and they started out with the idea that you were alive and not dead yet.

"But you *are* alive!" she said.

"Ach, no, mistress," said Rob, helping another pictsie to his feet. "We *wuz* alive. And we wuz good boys back in the land o' the livin', and so when we died there, we wuz borned into this place."

"You mean . . . you think . . . that you sort of died somewhere else and then came here?" said Tiffany. "You mean this is like . . . *heaven*?"

"Aye! Just as advertised!" said Rob Anybody. "Lovely sunshine, good huntin', nice pretty flowers, and wee burdies goin' cheep."

"Aye, and then there's the fightin'," said another Feegle. And then they all joined in.

"An' the stealin'!"

"An' the drinkin' and fightin'!"

"An' the kebabs!" said Daft Wullie.

"But there's bad things here!" said Tiffany. "There's monsters!"

"Aye," said Rob, beaming happily. "Grand, isn't it? Everythin' you could ever ask for, even things to fight!"

"But *we* live here!" said Tiffany.

"Ach, well, mebbe all you humans wuz good in the Last World, too," said Rob Anybody generously. "I'll just round up the lads, mistress."

Tiffany reached into her apron and pulled out the toad as Rob walked away.

"Oh. We survived," it said. "Amazing. There are very definite grounds for an action against the owner of those dogs, by the way."

"What?" said Tiffany, frowning. "What are you *talking* about?"

"I . . . I . . . don't know," said the toad. "The thought just popped into my head. Perhaps I knew something about dogs when I was human?"

"Listen, the Feegle think they're in heaven! They think they died and came here!"

"And?" said the toad.

"Well, that can't be right! You're supposed to be alive here and then die and end up in some heaven somewhere else!"

"Well, that's just saying the same thing in a different way, isn't it? Anyway, lots of warrior tribes think that when they die, they go to a heavenly land somewhere," said the toad. "You know, where they can drink and fight and feast forever? So maybe this is theirs."

"But this is a real place!"

"So? It's what they believe. Besides, they're only small. Maybe the universe is a bit crowded and they have to put heavens anywhere there's room? I'm a toad, so you'll appreciate that I'm having to guess a lot here. Maybe they're just wrong. Maybe you're just wrong. Maybe *I'm* just wrong."

A small foot kicked Tiffany on the boot.

"We'd best be moving on, mistress," said Rob Anybody. He had a dead Feegle over his shoulder. Quite a few of the others were carrying bodies, too.

"Er . . . are you going to bury them?" said Tiffany.

"Aye, they dinna need these ol' bodies noo, an' it's no' tidy to leave 'em lyin' aboot," said Rob Anybody. "Besides, if the bigjobs find little wee skulls and bones aroound, they'll start to wonder, and we don't want anyone pokin' aboot. Savin' your presence, mistress," he added.

"No, that's very, er . . . practical thinking," said Tiffany, giving up.

The Feegle pointed to a distant mound with a thicket of thorn trees growing on it. A lot of the mounds had thickets on them. The trees took advantage of the deeper soil. It was said to be unlucky to cut them down.

"It's nae very far noo," he said.

"You live in one of the mounds?" Tiffany asked. "I thought they were, you know, the graves of ancient chieftains?"

"Ach, aye, there's some ol' dead kingie in the chamber next door, but he's nae trouble," said Rob. "Dinna fret, there's nae skelingtons or any such in oour bit. It's quite roomy, we've done it up a treat."

Tiffany looked up at the endless blue sky over the endlessly green downland. It was all so peaceful again, a world away from headless men and big savage dogs.

What if I hadn't taken Wentworth down to the river? she thought. What would I be doing now? Getting on with the cheese, I suppose. . . .

I never knew about all this. I never knew I lived in heaven, even if it's only heaven to a clan of little blue men. I didn't know about people who flew on buzzards.

I never killed monsters before.

"Where do they come from?" she said. "What's the name of the place the monsters *come* from?"

"Ach, ye prob'ly ken the place well," said Rob Anybody. As they grew nearer to the mound, Tiffany thought she could smell smoke in the air.

"Do I?" she said.

"Aye. But it's no' a name I'll say in open air. It's a name to be whispered in a safe place. I'll no' say it under this sky."

◆　◆　◆

It was too big to be a rabbit hole and badgers didn't live up here, but the entrance to the mound was tucked among the thorn roots, and no one would have thought it was anything but the home of some kind of animal.

Tiffany was slim, but even so she had to take off her apron and crawl on her stomach under the thorns to reach it, dragging the apron behind her. And it still needed several Feegles to push her through.

At least it didn't smell bad and, once you were through the hole, it opened up a lot. Really, the entrance was just a disguise. Underneath, the space was the size of quite a large room, open in the center but with Feegle-sized galleries around the walls from floor to ceiling. They were crowded with pictsies of all sizes, washing clothes, arguing, sewing and, here and there, fighting, and doing everything as loudly as possible. Some had hair and beards tinged with white. Much younger ones, only a few inches tall, were running around with no clothes on, and yelling at one another at the tops of their little voices. After a couple of years of helping to bring up Wentworth, Tiffany knew what *that* was all about.

There were no girls, though. No Wee Free Women.

No . . . there was one.

The squabbling, bustling crowds parted to let her through. She came up to Tiffany's ankle. She was prettier than the male Feegles, although the world was full of things prettier than, say, Daft Wullie. But, like them, she had red hair and an expression of determination.

She curtsied, then said, "Are ye the bigjob hag, mistress?"

Tiffany looked around. She was the only person in the cavern who was over seven inches tall.

"Er, yes," she said. "Er . . . more or less. Yes."

"I am Fion. The kelda says to tell you the wee boy will come to nae harm yet."

"She's found him?" said Tiffany quickly. "Where is he?"

"Nae, nae, but the kelda knows the way of the Quin. She didna want you to fash yersel' on that score."

"But she stole him!"

"Aye. 'Tis comp-li-cate-ed. Rest a wee while. The kelda will see you presently. She is . . . not strong now."

Fion turned around with a swirl of skirts, strode back across the chalk floor as if she was a queen herself, and disappeared behind a large round stone that leaned against the far wall.

Tiffany, without looking down, carefully lifted the toad out of her pocket and held it close to her lips. "Am I fashing myself?" she whispered.

"No, not really," said the toad.

"You would tell me if I was, wouldn't you?" said Tiffany urgently. "It'd be terrible if everyone could see I was fashing and I didn't know."

"You haven't a clue what it means, have you . . . ?" said the toad.

"Not exactly, no."

"She just doesn't want you to get upset, that's all."

"Yes, I thought it was probably something like that," lied Tiffany. "Can you sit on my shoulder? I think I might need some help here."

The ranks of the Nac Mac Feegle were watching her with interest, but at the moment it appeared that she had nothing to do but hurry up and wait. She sat down carefully, drumming her fingers on her knees.

"Whut d'ye think of the wee place, eh?" said a voice from below. "It's great, yeah?"

She looked down. Rob Anybody Feegle and a few of the pictsies she'd already met were lurking there, watching her nervously.

"Very . . . cozy," said Tiffany, because that was better than saying "how sooty" or "how delightfully noisy." She added: "Do you cook for all of you on that little fire?"

The big space in the center held a small fire, under a hole in the roof that let the smoke get lost in the bushes above and in return brought in a little extra light.

"Aye, mistress," said Rob Anybody.

"The small stuff, bunnies an' that," added Daft Wullie. "The big stuff we roasts in the chalk pi— mmph mmph . . ."

"Sorry, what was that?" said Tiffany.

"What?" said Rob Anybody innocently, his hand firmly over the mouth of the struggling Wullie.

"What was Wullie saying about roasting 'big stuff'?" Tiffany demanded. "You roast 'big stuff' in the chalk pit? Is this the kind of big stuff that goes 'baa'? Because that's the only big stuff you'll find in these hills!"

She knelt down on the grimy floor and brought her face to within an inch of Rob Anybody's face, which was grinning madly and sweating.

"*Is it?*"

"Ach . . . ah . . . weel . . . in a manner o' speakin' . . ."

"*It is?*"

" 'Tis not thine, mistress!" shrieked Rob Anybody. "We ne'er took an Aching ship wi'out the leave o' Granny!"

"Granny Aching let you have sheep?"

"Aye, she did, did, did that! As p-payment!"

"Payment? For what?"

"No Aching ship ever got caught by wolves!" Rob Anybody gabbled. "No foxes took an Aching lamb, right? Nor no lamb e'er had its een pecked out by corbies, not wi' Hamish up in the sky!"

Tiffany looked sideways at the toad.

"Crows," said the toad. "They sometimes peck out the eyes of—"

"Yes, yes, I know what they do," said Tiffany. She calmed down a little. "Oh. I see. You kept away the crows and wolves and foxes for Granny, yes?"

"Aye, mistress! No' just kept 'em awa', neither!" said Rob Anybody triumphantly. "There's good eatin' on a wolf."

"Aye, they kebabs up a treat, but they're no' as good as a ship, tho . . . mmph mmph . . ." Wullie managed, before a hand was clamped over his mouth again.

"From a hag ye only tak' what ye's given," said Rob Anybody, holding his struggling brother firmly. "Since she's gone, though, weel . . . we tak' the odd old ewe that would've deid anywa', but ne'er one wi' the Aching mark, on my honor."

"On your honor as a drunken rowdy thief?" said Tiffany.

Rob Anybody beamed. "Aye!" he said. "An' I got a lot of good big reputation to protect there! That's the truth o' it, mistress. We keeps an eye on the ships of the hills, in mem'ry o' Granny Aching, an' in return we tak' what is hardly worth a thing."

"And the baccy too, o' course . . . mmph mmph . . ." and then, once again, Daft Wullie was struggling to breathe.

Tiffany took a deep breath, not a wise move in a Feegle colony. Rob Anybody grinned nervously.

"You take the tobacco? The tobacco the shepherds leave for . . . my grandmother?"

"Ach, I forgot about that," squeaked Rob Anybody. "But we allus wait a few days in case she comes to collect it hersel'. Ye can ne'er tell wi a hag, after all. And we do mind the ships, mistress. And she wouldna grudge us, mistress! Many's a night she'd share a pipe wi' the kelda outside o' her house on the wheelies! She'd not be one to let good baccy get all rainy! Please, mistress!"

Tiffany felt intensely angry, and what made it worse was that she was angry with herself.

"When we find lost lambs and suchlike, we drives 'em here for when the shepherds come lookin'," Rob Anybody added anxiously.

What did I think happened? Tiffany thought. Did I think she'd come back for a packet of Jolly Sailor? Did I think she was still somehow walking the hills, looking after the sheep? Did I think she . . . was still here, watching for lost lambs?

Yes! I want that to be true. I don't want to think she's just . . . gone. Someone like Granny Aching can't just . . . not be there anymore. And I want her back so much, because she didn't know how to talk to me and I was too scared to talk to her, and so we never talked and we turned silence into something to share.

I know *nothing* about her. Just some books, and some stories she tried to tell me, and things I didn't understand, and I remember big red soft hands and that smell. I never knew who she really was. I mean, she must have been nine too, once. She was Sarah Grizzel. She got married and had children, two of them in the shepherding hut. She must've done all sorts of things I don't know about.

And into Tiffany's mind, as it always did sooner or later, came the figure of the blue-and-white china shepherdess, swirling in red mists of shame. . . .

Tiffany's father took her to the fair at the town of Yelp one day not long before her seventh birthday, when the farm had some rams to sell. That was a ten-mile journey, the farthest she'd ever been. It was off the Chalk. Everything looked different. There were far more fenced fields and lots of cows and the buildings had tiled roofs instead of thatch. She considered that this was foreign travel.

Granny Aching had never been there, said her father on the way. She hated leaving the Chalk, he said. She said it made her dizzy.

It was a great day. Tiffany was sick on cotton candy, had her fortune told by a little old lady who said that many, many men would want to marry her, and won the shepherdess, which was made of china painted white and blue.

She was the star prize on the hoop-la stall, but Tiffany's father had said that it was all cheating, because the base was so wide that not one throw in a million could ever drop the hoop right over it.

She'd thrown the ring any old how, and it had been the one in a million. The stall holder hadn't been very happy about it landing over the shepherdess rather than the gimcrack rubbish in the rest of the stall. He handed it over when her father spoke sharply to him, though, and she'd hugged it all the way home on the cart, while the stars came out.

Next morning she'd proudly presented it to Granny Aching. The old woman had taken it very carefully in her wrinkled hands and stared at it for some time.

Tiffany was sure, now, that it had been a cruel thing to do.

Granny Aching had probably never heard of shepherdesses. People who cared for sheep on the Chalk were all called shepherds, and that was all there was to it. And this beautiful creature was as much unlike Granny Aching as anything could be.

The china shepherdess had an old-fashioned long dress, with the bulgy bits at the side that made it look as though she had saddlebags in her knickers. There were blue ribbons all over the dress, and all over the rather showy straw bonnet, and on the shepherd's crook, which was a lot more curly than any crook Tiffany had ever seen.

There were even blue bows on the dainty foot poking out from the frilly hem of her dress.

This wasn't a shepherdess who'd ever worn big old boots stuffed with wool and tramped the hills in the howling wind with the sleet being driven along like nails. She'd never tried in that dress to pull out a ram who'd got his horns tangled in a thorn patch. This wasn't a shepherdess who'd kept up with the champion shearer for seven hours, sheep for sheep, until the air was hazy with grease and wool and blue with cussing, and the champion gave up because he couldn't cuss sheep as well as Granny Aching. No self-respecting sheepdog would ever "come by" or "walk up" for a simpering girl with saddlebags in her pants. It was a lovely thing but it was a joke of a shepherdess, made by someone who'd probably never seen a sheep up close.

What had Granny Aching thought about it? Tiffany couldn't guess. She'd seemed happy, because it's the job of grandmothers to be happy when grandchildren give them things. She'd put it up on her shelf and then taken

Tiffany on her knee and called her "my little jiggit" in a nervous sort of way, which she did when she was trying to be grandmotherly.

Sometimes, in the rare times Granny was down at the farm, Tiffany would see her take down the statue and stare at it. But if she saw Tiffany watching, she'd put it back quickly and pretend she'd meant to pick up the sheep book.

Perhaps, Tiffany thought wretchedly, the old lady had seen it as a sort of insult. Perhaps she thought she was being told that this was what a shepherdess should look like. She shouldn't be an old lady in a muddy dress and big boots, with an old sack around her shoulders to keep the rain off. A shepherdess should sparkle like a starry night. Tiffany hadn't meant to, she'd never meant to, but perhaps she had been telling Granny that she wasn't . . . right.

And then a few months after that Granny had died, and in the years since then everything had gone wrong. Wentworth had been born, and then the Baron's son had vanished, and then there had been that bad winter when Mrs. Snapperly died in the snow.

Tiffany kept worrying about the statue. She couldn't talk about it. Everyone else was busy, or not interested. Everyone was edgy. They'd have said that worrying about a silly statue was . . . silly.

Several times she nearly smashed the shepherdess, but she didn't because people would notice.

She wouldn't have given something as wrong as that to Granny Aching now, of course. She'd grown up.

She remembered that the old lady would smile oddly, sometimes, when she looked at the statue. If only she'd said something. But Granny liked silence.

And now it turned out that she made friends with a lot of little blue men, who walked the hills looking after the sheep, because they liked her, too. Tiffany blinked.

It made a kind of sense. In memory of Granny Aching, the men left the tobacco. And in memory of Granny Aching, the Nac Mac Feegle minded the sheep. It all worked, even if it wasn't magic. But it took Granny away.

"Daft Wullie?" she said, staring hard at the struggling pictsie and trying not to cry.

"Mmph?"

"Is it true what Rob Anybody told me?"

"Mmph!" Daft Wullie's eyebrows went up and down furiously.

"Mr. Feegle, you can please take your hand away from his mouth," said Tiffany. Daft Wullie was released. Rob Anybody had looked worried, but Daft Wullie was terrified. He dragged his hat off and stood holding it in his hands, as if it was some kind of shield.

"Is all that true, Daft Wullie?" said Tiffany.

"Oh waily waily—"

"Just a simple yes or—a simple aye or nay, please."

"Aye! It is!" blurted out Daft Wullie. "Oh waily waily—"

"Yes, thank you," said Tiffany, sniffing and trying to blink the tears away. "All right. I understand."

The Feegles eyed her cautiously.

"Ye're nae gonna get nasty aboot it?" said Rob Anybody.

"No. It all . . . works."

She heard it echo around the cavern, the sound of hundreds of little men sighing with relief.

"She didna turn me intae a pismire!" said Daft Wullie, grinning happily at the rest of the pictsies. "Hey, lads, I talked wi' the hag and she didna e'en look at me crosswise! She *smiled* at me!" He beamed at Tiffany and went on: "An' d'ye ken, mistress, that if'n you hold the baccy label upside-doon, then part o' the sailor's bonnet and his ear became a lady wi' nae mmph mmph . . ."

"Ach, there I goes again, accidentally nearly throttlin' ye," said Rob Anybody, his hand clamping over Wullie's mouth.

Tiffany opened her mouth, but stopped when her ears tickled strangely.

In the roof of the cave, several bats woke up and hastily flew out of the smoke hole.

Some of the Feegles were busy on the far side of the chamber. What Tiffany had thought was a strange round stone was being rolled aside, revealing a large hole.

Now her ears squelched and felt as though all the wax was running out. The Feegles were forming up in two rows, leading to the hole.

Tiffany prodded the toad. "Do I want to know what a pismire is?" she whispered.

"It's an ant," said the toad.

"Oh? I'm . . . slightly surprised. And this sort of high-pitched noise?"

"I'm a toad. We're not good at ears. But it's probably him over there."

There was a Feegle walking out of the hole from which came, now that Tiffany's eyes had become accustomed to the gloom, a faint golden light.

The newcomer's hair was white instead of red, and while he was tall for a pictsie, he was as skinny as a twig. He was holding some sort of fat skin bag, bristling with pipes.

"Now there's a sight I don't reckon many humans have seen and lived," said the toad. "He's playing the mousepipes!"

"They make my ears tingle!" Tiffany tried to ignore the two

little ears still on the bag of pipes.

"High-pitched, see?" said the toad. "Of course, the pictsies hear sounds differently than humans do. He's probably their battle poet, too."

"You mean he makes up heroic songs about famous battles?"

"No, no. He recites poems that frighten the enemy. Remember how important words are to the Nac Mac Feegle? Well, when a well-trained gonnagle starts to recite, the enemy's ears explode. Ah, it looks as though they're ready for you."

In fact Rob Anybody was tapping politely on Tiffany's toecap. "The kelda will see you now, mistress," he said.

The piper had stopped playing and was standing respectfully beside the hole. Tiffany felt hundreds of bright little eyes watching her.

"Special Sheep Liniment," whispered the toad.

"Pardon?"

"Take it in with us," the toad said insistently. "It'd be a good gift!"

The pictsies watched her carefully as she lay down again and crawled through the hole behind the stone, the toad hanging on tightly. As she got closer, she realized that what she'd thought was a stone was an old round shield, green-blue and corroded with age. The hole it had covered was indeed wide enough for her to go through, but she had to leave her legs outside because it was impossible to get all of her into the room beyond. One reason was the bed, small though it was, which held the kelda. The other reason was that what the room was mostly full of, piled up around the walls and spilling across the floor, was gold.

CHAPTER 7

First Sight and Second Thoughts

‹∿›

Glint, glisten, glitter, gleam . . .

Tiffany thought a lot about words, in the long hours of churning butter. "Onomatopoeic," she'd discovered in the dictionary, meant words that sounded like the noise of the thing they were describing, like *cuckoo*. But *she* thought there should be a word meaning a word that sounds like the noise a thing would make if that thing made a noise even though, actually, it doesn't, but would if it did.

Glint, for example. If light made a noise as it reflected off a distant window, it'd go *glint!* And the light of tinsel, all those little glints chiming together, would make a noise like *glitterglitter*. *Gleam* was a clean, smooth noise from a surface that intended to shine all day. And *glisten* was the soft, almost greasy sound of something rich and oily.

The little cave contained all of these at once. There was only one candle, which smelled of sheep fat, but gold plates and cups gleamed, glistened, glinted, and glittered the light back and forth until the one little flame filled the air with a light that even *smelled* expensive.

The gold surrounded the bed of the kelda, who was sitting up against a pile of pillows. She was much, much fatter than the male pictsies; she looked as if she'd been made of round balls of slightly squashy dough, and was the color of chestnuts.

Her eyes were closed as Tiffany slid in, but they flicked open the moment she'd stopped pulling herself forward. They were the sharpest eyes she'd ever seen, much sharper even than Miss Tick's.

"Soo . . . you'll be Sarah Aching's wee girl?" said the kelda.

"Yes. I mean, aye," said Tiffany. It wasn't very comfortable lying on her stomach. "And you're the kelda?"

"Aye. I mean, yes," said the kelda, and the round face became a mass of lines as the kelda smiled. "What was your name, now?"

"Tiffany, er, kelda." Fion had turned up from some other part of the cave and was sitting down on a stool by the bed, watching Tiffany intently with a disapproving expression.

"A good name. In our tongue you'd be Tir-far-thóinn, Land Under Wave," said the kelda. It sounded like "Tiffan."

"I don't think anyone *meant* to name—"

"Ach, what people mean to do and what is done are two different things," said the kelda. Her little eyes shone. "Your wee brother is . . . safe, child. Ye could say he's safer where he is noo than he has ever been. No mortal ills can touch him. The Quin wouldna harm a hair o' his heid. And there's the evil o' it. Help me up here, girl."

Fion leaped up immediately and helped the kelda struggle up higher among her cushions.

"Where wuz I?" the kelda continued. "Ah, the wee laddie. Aye, ye could say he bides well where he is, in the Quin's own country. But I daresay there's a mother grievin'?"

"And our father, too," said Tiffany.

"An' his wee sister?" said the kelda.

Tiffany felt the words *yes, of course* trot automatically onto her tongue. She also knew that it would be very stupid to let them go any further. The little old woman's dark eyes were seeing right into her head.

"Aye, you're a born hag, right enough," said the kelda, holding her gaze. "Ye got that little bitty bit inside o' you that holds on, right? The bitty bit that watches the rest o' ye. 'Tis the First Sight and Second Thoughts ye have, and 'tis a wee gift an' a big curse to ye. You see and hear what others canna, the world opens up its secrets to ye, but ye're always like the person at the party with the wee drink in the corner who canna join in. There's a little bitty bit inside ye that willna melt and flow. Ye're Sarah Aching's line, right enough. The lads fetched the right one."

Tiffany didn't know what to say to that, so she didn't say anything. The kelda watched her, eyes twinkling, until Tiffany felt awkward.

"Why would the Queen take my brother?" she asked eventually. "And why is she after me?"

"Ye think she is?"

"Well, yes, actually! I mean, Jenny might have been a coincidence, but the horseman? And the grimhounds? And taking Wentworth?"

"She's bending her mind to ye," said the kelda. "When she does, something of her world passes into this one. Mebbe she just wants to test you."

"*Test* me?"

"To see how good you are. Ye're the hag noo, the witch who guards the edges and the gateways. So wuz yer granny, although she wouldna ever call hersel' one. And so wuz I until noo, and I'll pass the duty to ye. She'll ha' to get past ye, if she wants this land.

Ye have the First Sight and the Second Thoughts, just like yer granny. That's rare in a bigjob."

"Don't you mean second sight?" Tiffany asked. "Like people who can see ghosts and stuff?"

"Ach, no. That's typical bigjob thinking. *First Sight* is when you can see what's really there, not what your heid tells you *ought* to be there. Ye saw Jenny, ye saw the horseman, ye saw them as real thingies. Second sight is dull sight, it's seeing only what you expect to see. Most bigjobs ha' that. Listen to me, because I'm fadin' noo and there's a lot you dinna ken. Ye think this is the whole world? That is a good thought for sheep and mortals who dinna open their eyes. Because in truth there are more worlds than stars in the sky. Understand? They are everywhere, big and small, close as your skin. They are *everywhere*. Some ye can see an' some ye canna, but there are doors, Tiffan. They might be a hill or a tree or a stone or a turn in the road, or they might e'en be a thought in yer heid, but they are there, all aroound ye. You'll have to learn to see 'em, because you walk among them and dinna know it. And some of them . . . is poisonous."

The kelda stared at Tiffany for a moment and then continued: "Ye asked why the Quin should take your boy. The Quin likes children. She has none o' her own. She dotes on them. She'll give the wee boy everything he wants, too. *Only* what he wants."

"He only wants sweets!" said Tiffany.

"Is that so? An' did ye gi' them to him?" asked the kelda, as if she was looking into Tiffany's mind. "But what he *needs* is love an' care an' teachin' an' people sayin' no to him sometimes an' things o' that nature. He needs to be growed up strong. He willna get that fra' the Quin. He willna grow up. He'll get sweeties. Forever."

Tiffany wished the kelda would stop looking at her like that.

"But I see he has a sister willin' to take any pains to bring him back," said the little old woman, taking her eyes away from Tiffany. "What a lucky wee boy he is, to be so fortunate. Ye ken how to be strong, do ye?"

"Yes, I think so."

"Good. D'ye ken how to be weak? Can ye bow to the gale, can ye bend to the storm?" The kelda smiled again. "Nay, ye needna answer that. The wee burdie always has tae leap from the nest to see if it can fly. Anyway, ye have the feel o' Sarah Aching about ye, and no word e'en o' mine could turn her once she had set her mind to something. Ye're no' a woman yet, and that's no' bad thing, because where ye'll be goin' is easy for children, hard for adults."

"The world of the Queen?" ventured Tiffany, trying to keep up.

"Aye. I can feel it noo, lyin' over this one like a fog, as far awa' as the other side o' a mirror. I'm weakenin', Tiffan. I canna defend this place. So here is my bargain, child. I'll point ye toward the Quin an', in return, ye'll tak' over as kelda."

That surprised Fion as much as Tiffany. Her head shot up sharply and her mouth opened, but the kelda had raised a wrinkled hand.

"When *ye* are a kelda somewhere, my girl, ye'll expect people to do your biddin'. So dinna give me the argument. That's my offer, Tiffan. Ye won't get a better."

"But she *canna*—" Fion began.

"Can she not?" said the kelda.

"She's nae a *pictsie*, mother!"

"She's a bit on the large side, aye," said the kelda. "Dinna fret, Tiffan. It willna be for long. I just need ye to mind things for a wee while. Mind the land like yer granny did, and mind my boys. Then when yer wee boy is back home, Hamish'll fly up to the mountains and let it be known that the Chalk Hill clan has want o' a kelda. We've got a good place here, and the girls'll come flockin'. What d'ye say?"

"She disna know our ways!" Fion protested. "Ye're overtired, mother!"

"Aye, I am," said the kelda. "But a daughter canna run her mother's clan, ye know that. Ye're a dutiful girl, Fion, but it's time ye were pickin' your bodyguard and going awa' seeking a clan of your own. Ye canna stay here." The kelda looked up at Tiffany again. "Will ye, Tiffan?" She held up a thumb the size of a match head and waited.

"What will I have to do?" said Tiffany.

"The thinkin'," said the kelda, still holding up her thumb. "My lads are good lads, there's none braver. But they think their heids is most useful as weapons. That's lads for ye. We pictsies aren't like you big folk, ye ken. Ye have many sisters? Fion here has none. She's my only daughter. A kelda might be blessed wi' only one daughter in her whole life, but she'll have hundreds and hundreds o' sons."

"They are *all* your sons?" said Tiffany, aghast.

"Oh aye," said the kelda, smiling. "Oh, dinna look so astonished. The bairns are really wee when they're borned, like little peas in a pod. And they grow up fast." She sighed. "But sometimes I think all the brains is saved for the daughters. They're good boys, but they're no' great thinkers. You'll have to help them help ye."

"Mother, she canna carry oot the *duties* o' a kelda!" Fion protested.

"I don't see why not, if they're explained to me," said Tiffany.

"Oh, do you not?" said Fion sharply. "Weel, that's gonna be most *interesting*!"

"I recall Sarah Aching talkin' aboot ye," said the kelda. "She said ye were a strange wee one, always watchin' and listenin'. She said ye had a heid full o' words that ye ne'er spoke aloud. She wondered what'd become o' ye. Time for ye to find oot, aye?"

Aware of Fion glaring at her, and maybe *because* of Fion glaring at her, Tiffany licked her thumb and touched it gently against the kelda's tiny thumb.

"It is done, then," said the kelda. She lay back suddenly, and just as suddenly seemed to shrink. There were more lines in her face now. "Never let it be said I left my sons wi'oot a kelda to mind them," she muttered. "Now I can go back to the Last World. Tiffan is the kelda for now, Fion. In her hoose, ye'll do what she says."

Fion looked down at her feet. Tiffany could see that she was angry.

The kelda lay back. She beckoned Tiffany closer, and in a weaker voice said: "There. 'Tis done. And now for my part o' the bargain. Listen. Find . . . the place where the time disna fit. There's the way in. It'll shine out to ye. Bring him back to ease yer puir mother's heart and mebbe also your ain head—"

Her voice faltered, and Fion leaned quickly toward the bed.

The kelda sniffed.

She opened one eye.

"Not quite yet," she murmured to Fion. "Do I smell a wee drop of Special Sheep Liniment on ye, kelda?"

Tiffany looked puzzled for a moment and then said: "Oh, me. Oh. Yes. Er . . . here. . . ."

The kelda struggled to sit up again. "The best thing humans ever made," she said. "I'll just have a large wee drop, Fion."

"It puts hairs on your chest," Tiffany warned.

"Ach, weel, for a drop of Sarah Aching's Special Sheep Liniment

wo," said the old kelda. She took from Fion a

he size of a thimble and held it up.

would be good for ye, mother," said Fion.

o' that at this time," said the kelda. "One drop

afore I go, please, Kelda Tiffan."

Tiffany tipped the bottle slightly. The kelda shook the cup irritably.

"It was a larger drop I had in mind, kelda," she said. "A kelda has a generous heart."

She took something too small to be a gulp but too large to be a sip.

"Aye, it's a lang time since I tasted this brose," she said. "Your granny and I used to ha' a sip or two in front o' the fire on cold nights. . . ."

Tiffany saw it clearly in her head, Granny Aching and this little fat woman, sitting around the pot-bellied stove in the hut on wheels, while the sheep grazed under the stars.

"Ah, ye can see it," said the kelda. "I can feel yer eyes on me. That's the First Sight workin'." She lowered the cup. "Fion, go and fetch Rob Anybody and William the gonnagle."

"The bigjob is blockin' the hole," said Fion sulkily.

"I daresay there's room to wriggle past," said the old kelda in the kind of calm voice that said a stormy voice could follow if people didn't do what they were told.

With a smoldering glance at Tiffany, Fion squeezed past.

"Ye ken anyone who keeps bees?" said the kelda. When Tiffany nodded, the little old woman went on, "Then you'll know why we dinna have many daughters. You canna ha' two quins in one hive wi'oot a big fight. Fion must take her pick o' them that will follow her and seek a clan that needs a kelda. That is our way. She thinks there's another way, as gels sometimes do. Be careful o' her."

Tiffany felt something move past her, and Rob Anybody and the bard came into the room. There was more rustling and whispering, too. An unofficial audience was gathering outside.

When things had settled down a little, the old kelda said: "It is a bad thing for a clan to left wi'oot a kelda to watch o'er it e'en for an hour. So Tiffan will be your kelda until a new one can be fetched."

There was a murmur beside and behind Tiffany. The old kelda looked at William the gonnagle.

"Am I right that this has been done before?" she said.

"Aye. The songs say twice before," said William. He frowned, and added: "Or you could say it was three times if you include the time when the Quin was—"

He was drowned out by the cry that went up behind Tiffany:

"Nae quin! Nae king! Nae laird! Nae master! We willna be fooled again!"

The old kelda raised a hand. "Tiffan is the spawn of Granny Aching," she said. "Ye all ken of her."

"Aye, and ye saw the wee hag stare the heidless horseman in the eyes he hasna got," said Rob Anybody. "Not many people can do that!"

"And I have been your kelda for seventy years and my words canna be gainsaid," said the old kelda. "So the choice is made. I tell ye, too, that ye'll help her steal back her wee baby brother. That is the fate I lay on you all in memory of me and Sarah Aching."

She lay back in her bed and in a quieter voice added, "An' now I would have the gonnagle play 'The Bonny Flowers,' and hope to see yez all again in the Last World. To Tiffan I say be wary." The kelda took a deep breath. "Somewhere, a' stories are

:rue. . . ."

fell silent. William the gonnagle inflated the bag
and blew into one of the tubes. Tiffany felt the
rs of music too high-pitched to hear.

After a few moments Fion leaned over the bed to look at her
mother, then started to cry.

Rob Anybody turned and looked up at Tiffany, his eyes running
with tears. "Could I just ask ye to go out intae the big chamber,
kelda?" he said, quietly. "We ha' things to do, ye ken how it is. . . ."

Tiffany nodded and, with great care, feeling pictsies scuttle out
of her way, backed out of the room. She found a corner where she
didn't seem to be in anyone's way and sat there with her back to
the wall.

She'd expected a lot of "waily waily waily," but it seemed the
death of the kelda was too serious for that. Some Feegles were
crying, and some were staring at nothing, and as the news spread,
the tiered hall filled up with a wretched, sobbing silence. . . .

. . . The hills had been silent on the day Granny Aching died.

Someone went up every day with fresh bread and milk and scraps for
the dogs. It didn't need to be quite so often, but Tiffany had heard her parents talking and her father had said, "We ought to keep an eye on Mam
now."

Today had been Tiffany's turn, but she'd never thought of it as a chore.
She liked the journey.

But she'd noticed the silence. It was no longer the silence of many little
noises, but a dome of quiet all around the hut.

She knew then, even before she went in at the open door and found
Granny lying on the narrow bed.

She'd felt coldness spread though her. It even had a sound—it was like a thin, sharp musical note. It had a voice, too. Her own voice. It was saying: It's too late, tears are no good, no time to say anything, there are things to be done.

And . . . then she fed the dogs, who were waiting patiently for their breakfast. It would have helped if they'd done something soppy, like whine or lick Granny's face, but they hadn't. And still Tiffany heard the voice in her mind: No tears, don't cry. Don't cry for Granny Aching.

Now, in her head, she watched the slightly smaller Tiffany move around the hut like a little puppet.

She'd tidied up the hut. Besides the bed and the stove there really wasn't much there. There was the clothes sack and the big water barrel and the food box, and that was it. Oh, stuff to do with sheep was all over the place—pots and bottles and sacks and knives and shears—but there was nothing there that said a person lived here, unless you counted the hundreds of blue-and-yellow Jolly Sailor wrappers pinned on one wall.

She'd taken one of them down—it was still underneath her mattress at home—and remembered the Story.

It was very unusual for Granny Aching to say more than a sentence. She used words as if they cost money. But there'd been one day when she'd taken food up to the hut, and Granny had told her a story. A sort of a story. She'd unwrapped the tobacco, and looked at the wrapper, and then looked at Tiffany with that slightly puzzled look she used, and said: "I must've looked at a thousand o' these things, and I never once saw his bo-ut." That was how she pronounced boat.

Of course Tiffany had rushed to have a look at this label, but she couldn't see any boat, any more than she could see the naked lady.

"That's 'cause the bo-ut is just where you can't see it," Granny had said. "He's got a bo-ut for chasin' the great white whale fish on the salt sea. He's always chasing it, all round the world. It's called Mopey. It's a beast like a big cliff of chalk, I heard tell. In a book."

"Why's he chasing it?" Tiffany had asked.

"To catch it," Granny had said. "But he never will, the reason being, the world is round like a big plate and so is the sea, and so they're chasing one another, so it is almost like he is chasing hisself. Ye never want to go to sea, jiggit. That's where worse things happen. Everyone says that. You stop along here, where's the hills is in yer bones."

And that was it. It was one of the very few times Granny Aching had ever said anything to Tiffany that wasn't, in some way, about sheep. It was the only time she ever acknowledged that there was a world beyond the Chalk. Tiffany used to dream about the Jolly Sailor chasing the whale fish in his boat. And sometimes the whale fish would chase her, but the Jolly Sailor always arrived in his mighty ship just in time and their chase would start again.

Sometimes she'd run to the lighthouse, and wake up just as the door swung open. She'd never seen the sea, but one of the neighbors had an old picture on the wall that showed a lot of men clinging to a raft in what looked like a huge lake full of waves. She hadn't been able to see the lighthouse at all.

And Tiffany had sat by the narrow bed and thought about Granny Aching, and about the little girl Sarah Grizzel very carefully painting the flowers in the book, and about the world losing its center.

She missed the silence. What there was now wasn't the same kind of silence there had been before. Granny's silence was warm, and brought you inside. Granny Aching might sometimes have had trouble remembering the difference between children and lambs, but in her silence you were welcome and belonged. All you had to bring was a silence of your own.

Tiffany wished that she'd had a chance to say sorry about the shepherdess.

Then she'd gone home and told everyone that Granny was dead. She was seven, and the world had ended.

Someone was tapping politely on her boot. She opened her eyes and saw the toad. It was holding a small rock in its mouth. It spat it out.

"Sorry about that," it said. "I'd have used my arms, but we're a very soggy species."

"What am I supposed to *do*?" said Tiffany.

"Well, if you hit your head on this low ceiling, you would have a definite claim for damages," said the toad. "Er . . . did I just say that?"

"Yes, and I hope you wish you hadn't," said Tiffany. "Why did you say it?"

"I don't know, I don't know," moaned the toad. "Sorry, what were we talking about?"

"I *meant* what do the pictsies want me to *do* now?"

"Oh, I don't think it works like that," said the toad. "You're the kelda. *You* say what's to be done."

"Why can't Fion be kelda? She's a pictsie!"

"Can't help you there," said the toad.

"Can I be of serrrvice?" said a voice by Tiffany's ear.

She turned her head and saw, on one of the galleries that ran around the cave, William the gonnagle.

Up close, he was noticeably different from the other Feegles. His hair was neater, and braided into one pigtail. He didn't have as many tattoos. He spoke differently too, more clearly and slowly than the others, sounding his Rs like a drumroll.

"Er, yes," said Tiffany. "Why can't Fion be kelda here?"

William nodded. "A good question," he said politely. "But, ye ken, a kelda cannot wed her brrrrotherrrr. She must go to a new clan and wed a warrrrior there."

"Well, why couldn't that warrior come here?"

"Because the Feegles here would not know him. They'd have no rrrrespect for him." William made 'respect' sound like an avalanche.

"Oh. Well . . . what was that about the Queen? You were going to say something and they stopped you."

William looked embarrassed. "I don't think I can tell you aboot—"

"I *am* the temporary kelda," said Tiffany stiffly.

"Aye. Well . . . there was a time when we lived in the Queen's world and served her, before she grew so cold. But she tricked us, and we rrrrebelled. It was a dark time. She does not like us. And that is all I will say," William added.

Tiffany watched Feegles going in and out of the kelda's chamber. Something was going on in there.

"They're burying her in the other part of the mound," said William without being asked. "Wi' the other keldas o' this clan."

"I thought they would be more . . . noisy," said Tiffany.

"She was their motherrr," said William. "They do not want to shout. Their hearts are too full for worrrrds. In time we will hold a wake to help her back to the land o' the living, and that'll be a loud one, I can promise ye. We'll dance the FiveHundredAndTwelvesome Reel to the tune o' 'The Devil Among The Lawyers' and eat and drink, and I daresay my nephews will ha' headaches the size o' a sheep." The old Feegle smiled briefly. "But for now, each Feegle remembers her in silence. We dinna mourn like ye do, ye ken. We mourn for them that has tae stay behind."

"Was she your mother too?" said Tiffany quietly.

"Nay. She was my sister. Did she no' tell ye that when a kelda goes to a new clan, she takes a few o' her brothers with her? To be alone among strangers would be too much for a heart to bear."

The gonnagle sighed. "Of course, in time, after the kelda weds, the clan is full of her sons and is no' so lonely for her."

"It must be for you, though," said Tiffany.

"You're a quick one, I'll grant ye that," said William. "I am the last o' those who came. When this is o'er, I'll seek the leave of the next kelda to return to my ain folk in the mountains. This is a fiiine fat country and this is a fiiine bonny clan my nephews have, but I would like to die in the heather where I was borrrned. If you will excuse me, kelda . . ."

He walked away and was lost in the shadows of the mound.

Tiffany suddenly wanted to go home. Perhaps it was just William's sadness, but now she felt shut up in the mound.

"I've got to get out of here," she muttered.

"Good idea," said the toad. "You've got to find the place where the time is different, for one thing."

"But how can I do that?" wailed Tiffany. "You can't *see* time!"

She stuck her arms through the entrance hole and pulled herself up into the fresh air.

There was a big old clock in the farmhouse, and the time on it got set once a week. That is, when her father went to the market in Creel Springs, he made a note of the position of the hands on the big clock there, and when he got home, he moved the hands on their clock to the same position. It was really just for show, anyway. Everyone took their time from the sun, and the sun couldn't go wrong.

Now Tiffany lay among the trunks of the old thorn bushes, whose leaves rustled continuously in the breeze. The mound was like a little island in the endless turf; late primroses and even a few ragged foxgloves grew up here in the shelter of the thorn roots.

"She could have just told me where to look," she said.

"But she didn't know where it would be," said the toad. "She just knew the signs to look for."

Tiffany rolled over carefully and stared up at the sky between the low branches. It'll shine out, the kelda had said. . . .

"I think I ought to talk to Hamish," she said.

"Right ye are, mistress," said a voice by her ear. She turned her head.

"How long have you been there?" she said.

"A' the time, mistress," said the pictsie. Others poked their heads around the trees and out from under leaves. There were at least twenty on the mound.

"You've been watching me all the time?"

"Aye, mistress. 'Tis oour task to watch o'er our kelda. I'm up here most o' the time anyway, because I'm studying to become a gonnagle." The young Feegle flourished a set of mousepipes. "An' they willna let me play doon there on account o' them sayin' my playin' sounds like a spider tryin' to fart through its ears, mistress."

"But what happens if I want to spend a— have a— go to the— what happens if I say I don't want you to guard me?"

"If it's a wee call o' nature ye're talkin' aboout, mistress, the cludgie is o'er there in the chalk pit. Ye'll just sing oot to us where ye're goin' and no one'll go peeking, ye'll have oour word on it," said the attendant Feegle.

Tiffany glared at him as he stood in the primroses, beaming with pride and anxious duty. He was younger than most of them, without as many scars and lumps. Even his nose wasn't broken.

"What's your name, pictsie?" she said.

"No'-as-big-as-Medium-Sized-Jock-but-bigger-than-Wee-Jock-Jock, mistress. There's no' that many Feegle names, ye ken, so we ha' to share."

"Well, Not-as-big-as-Little-Jock—" Tiffany began.

"That'd be Medium-Sized Jock, mistress," said Not-as-big-as-Medium-Sized-Jock-but-bigger-than-Wee-Jock-Jock.

"Well, Not-as-big-as-Medium-Sized-Jock-but-bigger-than-Wee-Jock, I can—"

"That's No'-as-big-as-Medium-Sized-Jock-but-bigger-than-Wee-Jock-*Jock*, mistress," said Not-as-big-as-Medium-Sized-Jock-but-bigger-than-Wee-Jock-Jock. "Ye were one jock short," he added helpfully.

"You wouldn't be happier with, say, Henry?" said Tiffany, helplessly.

"Ach, nay, mistress." Not-as-big-as-Medium-Sized-Jock-but-bigger-than-Wee-Jock-Jock wrinkled his face. "There's nay history tae the name, ye ken. But there have been a number o' brave warriors called No'-as-big-as-Medium-Sized-Jock-but-bigger-than-Wee-Jock-Jock. Why, 'tis nearly as famous a name as Wee Jock itself! An', o' course, should Wee Jock hisself be taken back to the Last World, then I'll get the name o' Wee Jock, which isna to say that I mislike the name o' No'-as-big-as-Medium-Sized-Jock-but-bigger-than-Wee-Jock-Jock, ye ken. There's been many a fine story o' the exploits o' No'-as-big-as-Medium-Sized-Jock-but-bigger-than-Wee-Jock-Jock," the pictsie added, looking so earnest that Tiffany didn't have the heart to say that they must have been very long stories.

Instead she said: "Well, er, please, I want to talk to Hamish the aviator."

"Nae problem," said Not-as-big-as-Medium-Sized-Jock-but-bigger-than-Wee-Jock-Jock. "He's up there right noo."

He vanished. A moment later Tiffany heard—or, rather, felt with her ears—the bubbling sensation of a Feegle whistle.

Tiffany pulled *Diseases of the Sheep*, which was now looking very battered, out of her apron. There was a blank page at the back. She tore it out, feeling like a criminal for doing so, and took out her pencil.

"Dear Mum and Dad," she wrote carefully. "How are you, I am well. Wentworth is also well but I have to go and fetch him from ~~the Qu~~ where he is staying. Hope to be back soon, Tiffany. PS I hope the cheese is all right."

She was just considering this when she heard a rush of wings overhead. There was a whirring noise, a moment of silence, and then a small, weary, and rather muffled voice said: "Ach, crivens . . ."

She looked out onto the turf. The body of Hamish was upside down a few feet away. His arms with their twirlers were still outstretched.*

It took some time to get him out. If he landed headfirst and spinning, Tiffany was told, he had to be unscrewed in the opposite direction so that his ears wouldn't come off.

When he was upright and swaying unsteadily, Tiffany said: "Can you wrap this letter in a stone and drop it in front of the farmhouse where people will see it?"

"Aye, mistress."

"And . . . er . . . does it hurt when you land headfirst like that?"

"Nay, mistress, but it is awfu' embarrassing."

"Then there's a sort of toy we used to make that might help you," said Tiffany. "You make a kind of . . . bag of air—"

"Bag o' air?" said the aviator, looking puzzled.

---

*No words could describe what a Feegle in a kilt looks like upside down, so they won't try.

"Well, you know how things like shirts billow out on a clothes-line when it's windy? Well, you just make a cloth bag and tie some strings to it and a stone to the strings, and when you throw it up, the bag fills with air and the stone floats down."

Hamish stared at her.

"Do you understand me?" said Tiffany.

"Oh, aye. I wuz just waitin' to see if you wuz goin' to tell me anything else," said Hamish politely.

"Do you think you could, er, *borrow* some fine cloth?"

"Nay, mistress, but I ken well where I can steal some," said Hamish.

Tiffany decided not to comment on this. She said: "Where was the Queen when the mist came down?"

Hamish pointed. "Aboot a half mile yonder, mistress."

In the distance Tiffany could see some more mounds, and a few stones from the old days.

Trilithons, they were called, which just meant "three stones." The only stones found naturally on the downs were flints. But the giant stones of the trilithons had been dragged from at least ten miles away, and were stacked like a child stacks toy bricks. Here and there the big stones had been stood in circles; sometimes one stone had been placed all alone. It must have taken a lot of people a long time to do all that. Some people said there'd been human sacrifices up there. Some said they were part of some old religion. Some said they marked ancient graves.

Some said they were a warning: Avoid this place.

Tiffany hadn't. She'd been there with her sisters a few times, as a dare, just in case there were any skulls. But the mounds around the stones were thousands of years old. All that you found there now were rabbit holes.

"Anything else, mistress?" said Hamish politely. "Nay? Then I'll just be goin'...."

He raised his arms over his head and started to run across the turf. Tiffany jumped as the buzzard skimmed down a few feet away from her and snatched him back up into the sky.

"How can a man six inches high train a bird like that?" she asked as the buzzard circled again for height.

"Ach, all it takes is a wee drop o' kindness, mistress," said Not-as-big-as-Medium-Sized-Jock-but-bigger-than-Wee-Jock-Jock.

"Really?"

"Aye, an' a big dollop o' cruelty," Not-as-big-as-Medium-Sized-Jock-but-bigger-than-Wee-Jock-Jock said. "Hamish trains 'em by runnin' aroound in a rabbit skin until a bird pounces on him."

"That sounds awful!" said Tiffany.

"Ach, he's not too nasty aboot it. He just knocks them out wi' his heid, and then he's got a special oil he makes which he blows up their beak," Not-as-big-as-Medium-Sized-Jock-but-bigger-than-Wee-Jock-Jock went on. "When they wakes up, they thinks he's their mammy and'll do his biddin'."

The buzzard was already a distant speck.

"He hardly seems to spend any time on the ground!" said Tiffany.

"Oh, aye. He sleeps in the buzzard's nest at night, mistress. He says it's wunnerfully warm. An' he spends all his time in the air," Not-as-big-as-Medium-Sized-Jock-but-bigger-than-Wee-Jock-Jock added. "He's ne'er happy unless he's got the wind under his kilt."

"And the birds don't mind?"

"Ach, no, mistress. All the birds and beasts up here know it's good luck to be friends wi' the Nac Mac Feegle, mistress."

"They do?"

"Well, to tell ye the truth, mistress, it's more that they know it's unlucky *not* to be friends wi' the Nac Mac Feegle."

Tiffany looked at the sun. It was only a few hours away from setting.

"I must find the way in," she said. "Look, Not-as-small-as—"

"No'-as-big-as-Medium-Sized-Jock-but-bigger-than-Wee-Jock-Jock, mistress," said the pictsie, patiently.

"Yes, yes, thank you. Where is Rob Anybody? Where is *every-body*, in fact?"

The young pictsie looked a bit embarrassed.

"There's a bit o' a debate goin' on down below, mistress," he said.

"Well, we have got to find my brother, okay? I *am* the kelda in this vicinity, yes?"

"It's a wee bit more comp-li-cat-ed than that, mistress. They're, er, discussin' ye . . ."

"Discussing *what* about me?"

Not-as-big-as-Medium-Sized-Jock-but-bigger-than-Wee-Jock-Jock looked as if he really didn't want to be standing there.

"Um, they're discussing . . . er . . . they . . ."

Tiffany gave up. The pictsie was blushing. Since he was blue to begin with, this turned him an unpleasant violet color. "I'll go back down the hole. Give my boots a push, will you, please?"

She slid down the dry dirt, and Feegles scattered in the cave below as she landed.

When her eyes got accustomed to the gloom once more, she saw that the galleries were crowded with pictsies again. Some of them were in the middle of washing, and many of them had, for some reason, smoothed down their red hair with grease. They all stared at her as if caught in the act of something dreadful.

"We ought to be going if we're to follow the Queen," she said, looking down at Rob Anybody, who'd been washing his face in a basin made of half a walnut shell. Water dripped off his beard, which he'd braided up. There were three braids in his long hair now too. If he turned suddenly, he could probably whip somebody to death.

"Ach, weel," he said, "there's a wee matter we got tae sort oout, kelda." He twiddled the tiny washcloth in his hands. When Rob Anybody twiddled, he was worried.

"Yes?" said Tiffany.

"Er . . . will ye no ha' a cup o' tea?" said Rob Anybody, and a pictsie staggered forward with a big gold cup that must have been made for a king.

Tiffany took it. She *was* thirsty, after all. There was a sigh from the crowd when she sipped the tea. It was actually quite good.

"We stole a bag o' it fra' a peddler who was asleep down by the high road," said Rob Anybody. "Good stuff, eh?" He patted down his hair with his wet hands.

Tiffany's cup stopped halfway to her lips. Perhaps the pictsies didn't realize how loudly they whispered, because her ear was on a level with a conversation.

"Ach, she's a bit on the big side, no offense to her."

"Aye, but a kelda has to be big, ye ken, to have lots of wee babbies."

"Aye, fair enough, big wimmin is a' very well, but if a laddie was tae try tae cuddle this one, he'd have tae leave a chalk mark to show where he left off yesterday."

"An' she's a bit young."

"She needna have any babbies yet, then. Or mebbe not too many at a

time, say. Nae more than ten, mebbe."

"Crivens, lads, what're ye talkin' aboout? 'Tis Rob Anybody she'll choose anyway. Ye can see the big man's poor wee knees knocking fra' here!"

Tiffany lived on a farm. Any little beliefs that babies are delivered by storks or found under bushes tend to get sorted out early on if you live on a farm, especially when a cow is having a difficult calving in the middle of the night. And she'd helped with the lambing, when small hands could be very useful in difficult cases. She knew all about the bags of red chalk the rams had strapped to their chests, and why you knew later on that the ewes with the red smudges on their backs were going to be mothers in the spring. It's amazing what a child who is quiet and observant can learn, and this includes things people don't think she is old enough to know.

Her eye spotted Fion, on the other side of the hall. She was smiling, in a worrying way.

"What's happening, Rob Anybody?" she said, laying the words down carefully.

"Ah, weel . . . it's the clan rules, ye ken," said the Feegle awkwardly. "Ye being the new kelda an', an', weel, we're bound to ask ye, see, nae matter what we feel, we gotta ask ye mutter mutter mutter . . ." He stepped back quickly.

"I didn't quite catch that," said Tiffany.

"We've scrubbed up nice, ye ken," Rob Anybody said. "Some o' the lads actually had a bath in the dewpond, e'en though 'tis only May, and Big Yan washed under his arms for the first time ever, and Daft Wullie has picked ye a bonny bunch of flowers . . ."

Daft Wullie stepped forward, swollen with nervous pride, and thrust the aforesaid bouquet into the air. They probably *had* been nice flowers, but he didn't have much idea of what a bunch was or how you picked one. Stems and leaves and dropping petals stuck out of his fist in all directions.

"Very nice," said Tiffany, taking another sip of the tea.

"Guid, guid," said Rob Anybody, wiping his forehead. "So mebbe you'd like tae tell us mutter mutter mutter . . ."

"They want to know which one of them you're going to marry," said Fion loudly. "It's the rules. Ye have to choose, or quit as kelda. Ye have to choose yer man an' name the day."

"Aye," said Rob Anybody, not meeting Tiffany's eye.

Tiffany held the cup perfectly steady, but only because suddenly she couldn't move a muscle. She was thinking: *Aaargh! This is not happening to me! I can't—he couldn't—we wouldn't—they're not even— this is ridiculous! Run away!*

But she was aware of hundreds of nervous faces in the shadows. How you deal with this is going to be important, said her Second Thoughts. They're all watching you. And Fion wants to see what you'll do. You really oughtn't to dislike a girl four feet shorter than you, but you do.

"Well, this is very unexpected," she said, forcing herself to smile. "A big honor, of course."

"Aye, aye," said Rob Anybody, looking at the floor.

"And there's so many of you, it'd be so hard to choose," Tiffany went on, still smiling. And her Second Thoughts said: He's not happy about it either!

"Aye, it will that," said Rob Anybody.

"I'd just like to have a little fresh air while I think about it," said Tiffany, and didn't let the smile fade until she was out on the mound again.

She crouched down and peered among the primrose

leaves. "Toad!" she yelled.

The toad crawled out, chewing something. "Hm?" it said.

"They want to *marry* me!"

"Mm phmm ffm mm?"

"What are you eating?"

The toad swallowed. "A very undernourished slug," it said.

"I said they want to marry me!"

"And?"

"And? Well, just—just *think*!"

"Oh, right, yeah, the height thing," said the toad. "It might not seem much now, but when you're five feet seven he'll still be six inches high—"

"Don't laugh at me! I'm the kelda!"

"Well, of course, that's the point, isn't it," said the toad. "As far as they're concerned, there's rules. The new kelda marries the warrior of her choice and settles down and has lots and lots of Feegles. It'd be a terrible insult to refuse—"

"I am not going to marry a Feegle! I can't have hundreds of babies! Tell me what to do!"

"Me? Tell the kelda what to do? I wouldn't dare," said the toad. "And I don't like being shouted at. Even toads have their pride, you know." He crawled back into the leaves.

Tiffany took a deep breath, ready to shout, and then closed her mouth.

The old kelda must've known about this, she thought. So . . . she must have thought I'd be able to deal with it. It's just the rules, and they didn't know what to do about them. None of them wanted to marry a big girl like her, even if none of them would admit it. It was just the rules.

There must be a way round it. There had to be. But she had to accept a husband and she had to name the day. They'd told her that.

She stared at the thorn trees for a moment. Hmm, she thought.

She slid back down the hole.

The pictsies were waiting nervously, every scarred and bearded face watching hers.

"I accept *you*, Rob Anybody," she said.

Rob Anybody's face became a mask of terror. She heard him mutter, "Aw crivens!" in a tiny voice.

"But of course, it's the bride who names the day, isn't it?" said Tiffany cheerfully. "Everyone knows that."

"Aye," Rob Anybody quavered. "That's the tradition, right enough."

"Then I shall." Tiffany took a deep breath. "At the end of the world is a great big mountain of granite rock a mile high," she said. "And every year, a tiny bird flies all the way to the rock and wipes its beak on it. Well, when the little bird has worn the mountain down to the size of a grain of sand . . . that's the day I'll marry you, Rob Anybody Feegle!"

Rob Anybody's terror turned to outright panic, but then he hesitated and, very slowly, started to grin.

"Aye, guid idea," he said slowly. "It doesna do tae rush these things."

"Absolutely," said Tiffany.

"And that'd gi' us time tae sort oout the guest list an a' that," the pictsie went on.

"That's right."

"Plus there's a' that business wi' the wedding dress and buckets o' flowers and a' that kind of stuff," said Rob Anybody, looking more cheerful by the second. "That sort thing can tak' forever, ye ken."

"Oh yes," said Tiffany.

"But she's really just said no!" Fion burst out. "It'd take millions of years for the bird to—"

"She said aye!" Rob Anybody shouted. "Ye a' heard her, lads! An' she's named the day! That's the rules!"

"Nae problem aboot the mountain, neither," said Daft Wullie, still holding out the flowers. "Just ye tell us where it is and I reckon we could ha' it doon a lot faster than any wee burdie—"

"It's got to be the bird!" yelled Rob Anybody desperately. "Okay? The wee burdie! Nae more arguin'! Anyone feelin' like arguin' will feel ma boot! Some o' us ha' got a wee laddie to steal back fra' the Quin!" He drew his sword and waved it in the air. "Who's coming wi' me?"

That seemed to work. The Nac Mac Feegle liked clear goals. Hundreds of swords and battleaxes, and one bunch of battered flowers in the case of Daft Wullie, were thrust into the air, and the war cry of the Nac Mac Feegle echoed around the chamber. The period of time it takes a pictsie to go from normal to mad fighting mood is so tiny, it can't be measured on the smallest clock.

Unfortunately, since the pictsies were very individualistic, each one had his own cry and Tiffany could only make out a few over the din:

"They can tak' oour lives but they canna tak' oour troousers!"

"Ye'll tak' the high road an' I'll tak' yer wallet!"

"There can only be one t'ousand!"

"Ach, stick it up yer trakkans!"

But the voices gradually came together in one roar that shook the walls:

"Nae King! Nae Quin! Nae laird! Nae master! We willna be fooled again!"

This died away, a cloud of dust dropped from the roof, and there was silence.

"Let's gae!" cried Rob Anybody.

As one Feegle, the pictsies swarmed down the galleries and across the floor and up the slope to the hole. In a few seconds the chamber was empty, except for the gonnagle and Fion.

"Where have they gone?" said Tiffany.

"Ach, they just go," said Fion, shrugging. "I'm going tae stay here and look after the fire. *Someone* ought to act like a proper kelda." She glared at Tiffany.

"I do hope you find a clan for yourself soon, Fion," said Tiffany sweetly. The pictsie scowled at her.

"They'll run arroond for a while, mebbe stun a few bunnies and fall over a few times," said William. "They'll slow down when they find oout they don't ken what they're supposed to do yet."

"Do they always just run off like this?" said Tiffany.

"Ach, well, Rob Anybody disna want too much talk about marryin'," said William, grinning.

"Yes, we have a lot in common in that respect," said Tiffany.

She pulled herself out of the hole and found the toad waiting for her.

"I listened in," he said. "Well done. Very clever. Very diplomatic."

Tiffany looked around. There were a few hours to sunset, but the shadows were already lengthening.

"We'd better be going," she said, tying on her apron. "And you're coming, toad."

"Well, I don't know much about how to get into—" the toad began, trying to back away. But toads can't back up easily, and Tiffany grabbed him and put him in her apron pocket.

She headed for the mounds and stones. My brother will never

grow up, she thought, as she ran across the turf. That's what the old lady said. How does that work? What kind of a place is it where you never grow up?

The mounds got nearer. She saw William and Not-as-big-as-Medium-Sized-Jock-but-bigger-than-Wee-Jock-Jock running along beside her, but there was no sign of the rest of the Nac Mac Feegle.

And then she was among the mounds. Her sisters had told her that there were more dead kings buried under there, but it had never frightened her. Nothing on the downs had ever frightened her.

But it was cold here. She'd never noticed that before.

Find a place where the time doesn't fit. Well, the mounds were history. So were the old stones. Did they fit here? Well, yes, they belonged to the past, but they'd ridden on the hills for thousands of years. They'd grown old here. They were part of the landscape.

The low sun made the shadows lengthen. That was when the Chalk revealed its secrets. At some places, when the light was right, you could see the edges of old fields and tracks. The shadows showed up what brilliant noonlight couldn't see.

Tiffany had made up *noonlight*.

She couldn't even see hoof prints. She wandered around the trilithons, which looked a bit like huge stone doorways, but even when she tried walking through them both ways, nothing happened.

This wasn't according to plan. There should have been a magic door. She was sure of that.

A bubbling feeling in her ear suggested that someone was playing the mousepipes. She looked around and saw William the gonnagle standing on a fallen stone. His cheeks were bulging, and so was the bag of the mousepipes.

She waved at him. "Can you see anything?" she called.

William took the pipe out of his mouth, and the bubbling stopped. "Oh, aye," he said.

"The way to the Queen's land?"

"Oh, aye."

"Well, would you care to *tell* me?"

"I dinna need to tell a kelda," said William. "A kelda would see the clear way hersel'."

"But you *could* tell me!"

"Aye, and you coulda said please," said William. "I'm ninety-six years old. I'm nae a dolly in yer dolly hoose. Yer granny was a fiiine wuman, but I'll no' be ordered about by a wee chit of a girl."

Tiffany stared for a moment and then lifted the toad out of her apron pocket.

"Chit?" she said.

"It means something very small," said the toad. "Trust me."

"*He's* calling *me* small!"

"I'm biggerrr on the inside!" said William. "And I daresay your da' wouldna be happy if a big giant of a wee girl came stampin' aroound ordering *him* aboout!"

"The old kelda ordered people about!"

"Aye! Because she'd earned rrrespect!" The gonnagle's voice seemed to echo around the stones.

"Please, I don't know what to *do*!" wailed Tiffany.

William stared at her. "Ach, weel, yer no' doin' too badly so far," he said, in a nicer tone of voice. "Ye got Rob Anybody out of marryin' ye wi'oout breakin' the rules, and ye're a game lass, I'll gi' ye that. Ye'll find the way if ye tak' yer time. Just don't stamp yer foot and expect the world to do yer biddin'. A' ye're doing is shoutin' for sweeties, ye ken. Use yer eyes. Use yer heid."

He put the pipe back in his mouth, puffed his cheeks until the skin bag was full, and made Tiffany's ears bubble again.

"What about you, toad?" said Tiffany.

"You're on your own, I'm afraid," said the toad. "Whoever I used to be, I didn't know much about finding invisible doors. And I resent being press-ganged, too, I may say."

"But . . . I don't know what to do! Is there a magic word I should say?"

"I don't know, *is* there a magic word you should say?" said the toad, and turned over.

Tiffany was aware that the Nac Mac Feegle were turning up. They had a nasty habit of being really quiet when they wanted to.

Oh, no, she thought. They think I know what to do! This isn't *fair*! I haven't got any training for this. I haven't been to the witch school! I can't even find *that*! The opening must be somewhere around here, and there must be clues, but I don't know what they are!

They're watching me to see if I'm any good. And I'm good at cheese, and that's all. *But a witch deals with things. . . .*

She put the toad back in her pocket and felt the weight of the book *Diseases of the Sheep*.

When she pulled it out, she heard a sigh go up from the assembled pictsies.

They think words are magical. . . .

She opened the book at random, and frowned.

"Cloggets," she said aloud. Around her, the pictsies nodded their heads and nudged one another.

"Cloggets are a trembling of the greebs in hoggets," she read, "which can lead to inflammation of the lower pasks. If untreated, it may lead to the more serious condition of Sloke. Recommended treatment is the daily dosing with turpentine until there is no longer either any trembling, or turpentine, or sheep."

She risked looking up. Feegles were watching her from every stone and mound. They looked impressed.

However, the words in *Diseases of the Sheep* cut no ice with magic doorways.

"Scrabbity," said Tiffany. There was a ripple of anticipation.

"Scrabbity is a flaky skin condition, particularly around the lollets. Turpentine is a useful remedy—"

And then she saw, out of the corner of her eye, the teddy bear.

It was very small, and the kind of red you don't quite get in nature. Tiffany knew what it was. Wentworth loved the teddy-bear candies. They tasted like glue mixed with sugar and were made of 100% Artificial Additives.

"Ah," she said aloud. "My brother was certainly brought here . . ."

This caused a stir.

She walked forward, reading aloud about Garget of the Nostrils and the Staggers but keeping an eye on the ground. And there was another teddy bear, green this time and quite hard to see against the turf.

O-kay, Tiffany thought.

There was one of the three-stone arches a little way away; two big stones with another one laid across the top of them. She'd walked through it before and nothing had happened.

But nothing *should* happen, she thought. You can't leave a doorway into your world that *anyone* can walk through, otherwise people would wander in and out by accident. You'd have to know it was there.

Perhaps that's the only way it would work.

Fine. Then I'll believe that this is the entrance.

She stepped through and saw an astonishing sight: green grass, blue sky becoming pink around the setting sun, a few little white clouds late for bed, and a general warm, honey-colored look to everything. It was amazing that there could be a sight like this. The fact that Tiffany had seen it nearly every day of her life didn't make it any less fantastic. As a bonus, you didn't even have to look through any kind of stone arch to see it. You could see it by standing practically *anywhere*.

Except . . .

. . . something was wrong. Tiffany walked through the arch several times and still wasn't quite sure. She held up a hand at arm's length, trying to measure the sun's height against the horizon.

And then she saw the bird. It was a swallow, hunting flies, and a swoop took it behind the stones.

The effect was . . . odd, and almost upsetting. It passed behind the stone and she felt her eyes move to follow the swoop . . . but it was late. There was a moment when the swallow should have appeared, and it didn't.

Then it passed across the gap *and for a moment was on both sides of the other stone at the same time.*

Seeing it made Tiffany feel that her eyeballs had been pulled out and turned around.

Look for a place where the time doesn't fit. . . .

"The world seen through that gap is at least one second behind the time here," she said, trying to sound as certain as possible. "I thi— I *know* this is the entrance."

There was some whooping and clapping from the Nac Mac Feegle, and they surged across the turf toward her.

"That was *great*, a' that readin' ye did!" said Rob Anybody. "I didna understand a single word o' it!"

"Aye, it must be powerful language if you canna make oout what the heel it's goin' on aboot!" said another pictsie.

"Ye definitely ha' got the makin's of a kelda, mistress," said Not-as-big-as-Medium-Sized-Jock-but-bigger-than-Wee-Jock-Jock.

"Aye!" said Daft Wullie. "It was smashin' the way you spotted them candies and didna let on! We didna think you'd see the wee green one, too!"

The rest of the pictsies stopped cheering and glared at him.

"What did I say? What did I say?" he said.

Tiffany sagged. "You all knew that was the way through, didn't you," she said.

"Oh, aye," said Rob Anybody. "We ken that kind of stuff. We used tae live in the Quin's country, ye ken, but we rebelled against her evil rule—"

"And we did that, an' then she threw us oout on account o' bein' drunk an' stealin' and fightin' a' the time," said Daft Wullie.

"It wasna like that at a'!" roared Rob Anybody.

"And you were waiting to see if I *could* find the way, right?" said Tiffany, before a fight could start.

"Aye. Ye did well, lassie."

Tiffany shook her head. "No, I didn't," she said. "I didn't do any real magic. I don't know how. I just looked at things and worked them out. It was cheating, really."

The pictsies looked at one another.

"Ah, weel," said Rob Anybody. "What's magic, eh? Just wavin' a stick an' sayin' a few wee magical words. An' what's so clever aboot that, eh? But lookin' at things, really *lookin'* at 'em, and then workin' 'em oout, now, that's a *real* skill."

"Aye, it is," said William the gonnagle, to Tiffany's surprise. "Ye used yer eyes and used yer heid. That's what a real hag does. The magicking is just there for advertisin'."

"Oh," said Tiffany, cheering up. "Really? Well, then . . . there's our door, everyone!"

"Right," said Rob Anybody. "Now show us the way through."

Tiffany hesitated and then thought: I can feel myself thinking. I'm *watching* the way I'm thinking. And what am I thinking? I'm thinking: I walked through this arch before, and nothing happened.

But I wasn't looking then. I wasn't thinking, either. Not properly.

The world I can see through the arch isn't actually real. It just looks as though it is. It's a sort of . . . magical picture, put there to disguise the entrance. And if you don't pay attention, well, you just walk in and out of it and you don't realize it.

Aha . . .

She walked through the arch. Nothing happened. The Nac Mac Feegle watched her solemnly.

Okay, she thought. I'm still being fooled, aren't I? . . .

She stood in front of the stones and stretched out her hands on either side of her, and shut her eyes. Very slowly she stepped forward . . .

Something crunched under her boots, but she didn't open her eyes until she couldn't feel the stones anymore. When she did open them . . .

. . . it was a black-and-white landscape.

CHAPTER 8

Land of Winter

∽

"Aye, she's got First Sight, sure enough," said William's voice behind Tiffany as she stared into the world of the Queen. "She's seein' what's *really* there. . . ."

Snow stretched away under a sky so dirty white that Tiffany might have been standing inside a Ping-Pong ball. Only black trunks and scribbly branches of the trees, here and there, told her where the land stopped and the sky began.

Those, and, of course, the hoofprints. They stretched away toward a forest of black trees, boughed with snow.

The cold was like little needles all over her skin.

She looked down and saw the Nac Mac Feegle pouring through the gate, waist deep in the snow. They spread out without speaking. Some of them had drawn their swords.

They weren't laughing and joking now. They were watchful.

"Right, then," said Rob Anybody. "Well done. You wait here for us and we'll get your wee brother back, nae problemo—"

"I'm coming too!" snapped Tiffany.

"Nay, the kelda disna—"

"This one dis!" said Tiffany, shivering. "I mean *does*! He's my brother. And *where* are we?"

Rob Anybody glanced up at the pale sky. There was no sun anywhere. "Ye're here noo," he said, "so mebbe there's nae harm in tellin' ye. This is what ye call Fairyland."

"*Fairyland?* No, it's not! I've seen pictures! Fairyland is . . . is all trees and flowers and sunshine and, and tinklyness! Dumpy little babies in romper suits with horns! People with wings! Er . . . and weird people! I've seen pictures!"

"It isna always like this," said Rob Anybody shortly. "An' ye canna come wi' us because ye ha' nae weapon, mistress."

"What happened to my frying pan?" said Tiffany.

Something bumped against her heels. She looked around and saw Not-as-big-as-Medium-Sized-Jock-but-bigger-than-Wee-Jock-Jock hold up the pan triumphantly.

"Okay, ye have the pan," said Rob Anybody, "but what ye need here is a sword of thunderbolt iron. That's like the, you know, official weapon for invadin' Fairyland. . . ."

"I know how to use the pan," said Tiffany. "And I'm—"

"Incomin'!" yelled Daft Wullie.

Tiffany saw a line of black dots in the distance and felt someone climb up her back and stand on her head.

"It's the black dogs," Not-as-big-as-Medium-Sized-Jock-but-bigger-than-Wee-Jock-Jock announced. "Dozens o' 'em, Big Man."

"We'll never outrun the dogs!" Tiffany cried, grabbing her pan.

"Dinna need to," said Rob Anybody. "We got the gonnagle wi' us this time. Ye might like to stick yer fingers in yer ears, though."

William, with his eyes fixed on the approaching pack, was unscrewing some of the pipes from the mousepipes and putting them in a bag he carried hanging from his shoulder.

The dogs were much closer now. Tiffany could see the razor teeth and the burning eyes.

Slowly William took out some much shorter, smaller pipes that had a silvery look to them and screwed them into place. He had the look of someone who wasn't going to rush.

Tiffany gripped the handle of her pan. The dogs weren't barking. It would have been slightly less scary if they were.

William swung the mousepipes under his arm and blew into one until the bag bulged.

"I shall play," he announced, as the dogs got close enough for Tiffany to see the drool, "that firrrrm favorite, 'The King Underrrr Waterrrr.'"

As one pictsie, the Nac Mac Feegle dropped their swords and put their hands over their ears.

William put the mouthpiece to his lips, tapped his foot once or twice, and, as a dog gathered itself to leap at Tiffany, began to play.

A lot of things happened at more or less the same time. All Tiffany's teeth started to buzz. The pan vibrated in her hands and dropped onto the snow. The dog in front of her went cross-eyed and, instead of leaping, tumbled forward.

The grimhounds paid no attention to the pictsies. They howled. They spun around. They tried to bite their own tails. They stumbled and ran into one another. The line of panting death broke into dozens of desperate animals, twisting and writhing and trying to escape from their own skins.

The snow was melting in a circle around William, whose cheeks were red with effort. Steam was rising.

He took the pipe from his mouth. The grimhounds, struggling in the slush, raised their heads. And then, as one dog, they put their tails between their legs and ran like greyhounds back across the snow.

"Weel, they ken we're here noo," said Rob Anybody, wiping tears from his eyes.

"Ot aggened?" said Tiffany, touching her teeth to check that they were all still there.

"He played the notes o' pain," Rob Anybody explained. "Ye canna hear 'em 'cause they're pitched so high, but the doggies can. Hurts 'em in their heids. Now we'd better get movin' before she sends somethin' else."

"The Queen sent them? But they're like something out of nightmares!" said Tiffany.

"Oh aye," said Rob Anybody. "That's where she got them."

Tiffany looked at William the gonnagle. He was calmly replacing the pipes. He saw her staring at him, looked up, and winked.

"The Nac Mac Feegle tak' music verrrrrra seriously," he said. And then he nodded at the snow near Tiffany's foot.

There was a sugary yellow teddy bear in the snow, made of 100% Artificial Additives.

And the snow, all around Tiffany, was melting away.

◆　◆　◆

Two pictsies carried Tiffany easily. She skimmed across the snow, the clan running beside her.

No sun in the sky. Even on the dullest days you could generally see where the sun was, but not here. And there was something else that was strange, something she couldn't quite give a name to. This didn't feel like a real place. She didn't know why she felt that, but something was wrong with the horizon. It looked close enough to touch, which was silly.

And things were not . . . finished. Like the trees in the forest they were heading toward, for example. A tree is a tree, she thought. Close up or far away, it's a tree. It has bark and branches and roots.

And you know they're *there*, even if the tree is so far away that it's a blob.

The trees here, though, were different. She had a strong feeling that they *were* blobs, and were growing the roots and twigs and other details as she got closer, as if they were thinking, "Quick, someone's coming! Look real!"

It was like being in a painting where the artist hadn't bothered much with the things in the distance, but quickly rushed a bit of realness anywhere you were looking.

The air was cold and dead, like the air in old cellars.

The light grew dimmer as they reached the forest. In between the trees it became blue and eerie.

No birds, she thought.

"Stop," she said.

The pictsies lowered her to the ground, but Rob Anybody said: "We shouldna hang aroound here too long. Heids up, lads."

Tiffany lifted out the toad. It blinked at the snow.

"Oh, shoap," it muttered. "This is not good. I should be hibernating."

"Why is everything so . . . strange?"

"Can't help you there," said the toad. "I just see snow, I just see ice, I just see freezing to death. I'm listening to my inner toad here."

"It's not that cold!"

"Feels cold . . . to . . . me. . . ." The toad shut his eyes. Tiffany sighed and lowered him into her pocket.

"I'll tell ye where ye are," said Rob Anybody, his eyes still scanning the blue shadows. "Ye ken them wee bitty bugs that cling on to the sheeps and suck theirsel' full o' blood and then drop off again? This whole world is like one o' them."

"You mean like a, a tick? A parasite? A *vampire*?"

"Oh, aye. It floats aroound until it finds a place that's weak on a world where no one's payin' attention, and opens a door. Then the Quin sends in her folk. For the stealin', ye ken. Raidin' o' barns, rustlin' of cattle—"

"We used to like stealin' the coo beasties," said Daft Wullie.

"Wullie," said Rob Anybody, pointing his sword, "you ken I said there wuz times you should *think* before opening yer big fat gob?"

"Aye, Rob."

"Weel, that wuz one o' them times." Rob turned and looked up at Tiffany rather bashfully. "Aye, we wuz wild champion robbers for the Quin," he said. "People wouldna e'en go a-huntin' for fear o' little men. But 'twas ne'er enough for her. She always wanted more. But we said it's no' *right* to steal an ol' lady's only pig, or the food from them as dinna ha' enough to eat. A Feegle has nae worries about stealin' a golden cup from a rich bigjob, ye ken, but takin' awa' the—"

—cup an old man kept his false teeth in made them feel ashamed, they said. The Nac Mac Feegle would fight and steal, certainly, but who wanted to fight the weak and steal from the poor?

Tiffany listened, at the end of the shadowy wood, to the story of a little world where nothing grew, where no sun shone, and where everything had to come from somewhere else. It was a world that took, and gave nothing back except fear. It raided—and people learned to stay in bed when they heard strange noises at night, because if anyone gave her trouble, the Queen could control their dreams.

Tiffany couldn't quite pick up how she did this, but that's where things like the grimhounds and the headless horseman came from. These dreams were . . . more real. The Queen could take dreams and make them more . . . solid. You could step inside them and vanish. And you didn't wake up just as the monsters caught up with you.

The Queen's people wouldn't just take food. They'd take people, too—

"—like pipers," said William the gonnagle. "Fairies can't make music, ye ken. She'll steal a man awa' for the music he makes."

"And she takes children," said Tiffany.

"Aye. Your wee brother's not the first," said Rob Anybody. "There's no' a lot of fun and laughter here, ye ken. She thinks she's good wi' children."

"The old kelda said she wouldn't harm him," said Tiffany. "That's true, isn't it?"

You could read the Nac Mac Feegle like a book. And it would be a big, simple book with pictures of Spot the Dog and a Big Red Ball and one or two short sentences on each page. What they were thinking turned up right there on their faces, and now they were all wearing a look that said: Crivens, I hope she disna ask us the question we dinna want tae answer. . . .

"That *is* true, isn't it?" she said.

"Oh, aye," said Rob Anybody, slowly. "She didna lie to ye there. The Quin'll try to be kind to him, but she disna know how. She's an elf. They're no' very good at thinking of other people."

"What will happen to him if we don't get him back?"

Again there was that "we dinna like the way this is going" look.

"I *said*—" Tiffany repeated.

"I darrresay she'll send him back, in due time," said William. "An' he willna be any olderr. Nothing grows old here. Nothing grows. Nothing at all."

"So he'll be all right?"

Rob Anybody made a noise in his throat. It sounded like a voice that was trying to say aye but was being argued with by a brain that knew the answer was no.

"Tell me what you're not telling me," said Tiffany.

Daft Wullie was the first to speak. "That's a lot o' stuff," he said. "For example, the meltin' point o' lead is—"

"Time passes slower the deeper you go intae this place," said Rob Anybody quickly. "Years pass like days. The Quin'll get tired o' the wee lad after a coupla months, mebbe. A coupla months *here*, ye ken, where the time is slow an' heavy. But when he comes back into the mortal world, you'll be an old lady, or mebbe you'll be deid. So if youse has bairns o' yer own, you'd better tell them to watch out for a wee sticky kid wanderin' the hills shoutin' for sweeties, 'cause that'll be their Uncle Wentworth. That wouldna be the worst o' it, neither. Live in dreams for too long and ye go mad—ye can never wake up prop'ly, ye can never get the hang o' reality again."

Tiffany stared at him.

"It's happened before," said William.

"I *will* get him back," said Tiffany quietly.

"We doon't doubt it," said Rob Anybody. "An' where'er ye go, we'll come with ye. The Nac Mac Feegle are afeared o' nothing!"

A cheer went up, but it seemed to Tiffany that the blue shadows sucked all the sound away.

"Aye, nothin' exceptin' lawyers mmph mmph," Daft Wullie tried to say, before Rob managed to shut him up.

Tiffany turned back to the line of hoofprints and began to walk.

The snow squeaked unpleasantly underfoot.

She went a little way, watching the trees get realer as she approached them, and then looked around.

All the Nac Mac Feegle were creeping along behind her. Rob Anybody gave her a cheery nod. And all her footprints had become holes in the snow, with grass showing through.

The trees began to annoy her. The way things changed was more frightening than any monster. You could hit a monster, but you couldn't hit a forest. And she wanted to hit *something*.

She stopped and scraped some snow away from the base of a tree, and just for a moment there was nothing but grayness where it had been. As she watched, the bark grew down to where the snow was. Then it just stayed there, pretending it had been there all the time.

It was a lot more worrying than the grimhounds. They were just monsters. They could be beaten. This was ... frightening.

She was second thinking again. She felt the fear grow, she felt her stomach become a red hot lump, she felt her elbows begin to sweat. But it was ... not connected. She *watched* herself being frightened, and that meant that there was still this part of herself, the watching part, that wasn't.

The trouble was, it was being carried on legs that were. It had to be very careful.

And that was where it went wrong. Fear gripped her, all at once. She was in a strange world, with monsters, being followed by hundreds of little blue thieves. And ... black dogs. Headless horsemen. Monsters in the river. Sheep whizzing backward across fields. Voices under the bed ...

The terror took her. But because she was Tiffany, she ran toward it, raising the pan. She had to get through the forest, find the Queen, get her brother, leave this place!

Somewhere behind her, voices started to shout—

She woke up.

There was no snow, but there *was* the whiteness of the bedsheet and the plaster ceiling of her bedroom. She stared at it for a while, then leaned down and peered under the bed.

There was nothing there but the guzunder. When she flung open the door of the doll's house, there was no one inside but the two toy soldiers and the teddy bear and the headless dolly.

The walls were solid. The floor creaked as it always did. Her slippers were the same as they always were: old, comfortable, and with all the pink fluff worn off.

She stood in the middle of the floor and said, very quietly, "Is there anybody there?"

Sheep baa'd on the distant hillside, but they probably hadn't heard her.

The door squeaked open and the cat, Ratbag, came in. He rubbed up against her legs, purring like a distant thunderstorm, and then went and curled up on her bed.

Tiffany got dressed thoughtfully, daring the room to do something strange.

When she got downstairs, breakfast was cooking. Her mother was busy at the sink.

Tiffany darted out through the scullery and into the dairy. She scrambled on hands and knees around the floor, peering under the sink and behind cupboards.

"You can come out now, honestly," she said.

No one came. She was alone in the room. She'd often been alone in the room, and had enjoyed it. It was almost her private territory. But now, somehow, it was too empty, too clean.

When she wandered back into the kitchen, her mother was still standing by the sink, washing dishes, but a plate of steaming porridge had been put down in the one set place on the table.

"I'll make some more butter today," said Tiffany carefully, sitting down. "I might as well, while we're getting all this milk."

Her mother nodded and put a plate on the drainboard beside the sink.

"I haven't done anything wrong, have I?" said Tiffany.

Her mother shook her head.

Tiffany sighed. "And then she woke up and it was all a dream." It was just about the worst ending you could have to any story. But it had all seemed so *real*. She could remember the smoky smell in the pictsies' cave, and the way . . . who was it . . . oh, yes, he'd been called Rob Anybody . . . the way Rob Anybody had always been so nervous about talking to her.

It was strange, she thought, that Ratbag had rubbed up against her. He'd sleep on her bed if he could get away with it, but during the day he kept well out of Tiffany's way. How odd.

There was a rattling noise near the mantelpiece. The china shepherdess on Granny's shelf was moving sideways of its own accord, and as Tiffany watched with her porridge spoon halfway to her mouth, it slid off and smashed on the floor.

The rattling went on. Now it was coming from the big oven. She could see the door actually shaking on its hinges.

She turned to her mother and saw her put another plate down by the sink. But it wasn't being held in a hand.

The oven door burst off the hinges and slid across the floor.

"Dinna eat the porridge!"

Nac Mac Feegles spilled out into the room, hundreds of them, pouring across the tiles.

The walls were shifting. The floor moved. And now the thing turning around at the sink was not even human but just . . . stuff, no more human than a gingerbread man, gray as old dough, changing shape as it lumbered toward Tiffany.

The pictsies surged past her in a flurry of snow.

She looked up at the thing's tiny black eyes.

The scream came from somewhere deep inside. There was no Second Thought, no First Thought, just a scream. It seemed to spread out as it left Tiffany's mouth until it became a black tunnel in front of her, and as she fell into it, she heard, in the commotion behind her:

"Who d'yer think ye're lookin' at, pal? Crivens, but ye're gonna get sich a kickin'!"

◆   ◆   ◆

Tiffany opened her eyes.

She was lying on damp ground in the snowy, gloomy wood. Pictsies were watching her carefully but, she saw, there were others behind them staring outward, into the gloom among the tree trunks.

There was . . . stuff in the trees. Lumps of stuff. It was gray, and it hung there like old cloth.

She turned her head and saw William standing beside her, looking at her with concern.

"That was a dream, wasn't it?" she said.

"Weel, noo," said William. "It was, ye ken, and therrre again, it wasna. . . ."

Tiffany sat up suddenly, causing the pictsies to leap back.

"But that . . . thing was in it, and then you all came out of the oven!" she said. "You were *in* my dream! What is—*was* that creature?"

William the gonnagle stared at her as if trying to make up his mind.

"That was what we call a drome," he said. "Nothing here really

159

belongs here, remember? Everything is a reflection from outside, or something kidnaped from another worrrld, or mebbe something the Quin has made outa magic. It was hidin' in the trees, and ye was goin' so fast, ye didna see it. Ye ken spiders?"

"Of course!"

"Well, spiders spin webs. Dromes spin dreams. It's easy in this place. The world you come from is nearly real. This place is nearly unreal, so it's almost a dream anywa'. And the drome makes a dream for ye, wi' a trap in it. If ye eats anything in the dream, ye'll never want tae' leave it."

He looked as though Tiffany should have been impressed.

"What's in it for the drome?" she asked.

"It likes watchin' dreams. It has fun watching *ye* ha' fun. An' it'll watch ye eatin' dream food, until ye starve to death. Then the drome'll eat ye. Not right away, o' course. It'll wait until ye've gone a wee bit runny, because it hasna teeth."

"So how can anyone get out?"

"The best way is to find the drome," said Rob Anybody. "It'll be in the dream with you, in disguise. Then ye just gives it a good kickin'."

"By kicking you mean—?"

"Choppin' its heid off generally works."

Now, Tiffany thought, I am impressed. I wish I wasn't. "And this is Fairyland?" she said.

"Aye. Ye could say it's the bit the tourists dinna see," said William. "An' ye did well. Ye were fightin' it. Ye knew it wasna right."

Tiffany remembered the friendly cat, and the falling shepherdess. She'd been trying to send messages to herself. She should have listened.

"Thank you for coming after me," she said, meekly. "How did you do it?"

"Ach, we can generally find a way intae *anywhere*, even a dream," said William, smiling. "We're a stealin' folk, after all." A piece of the drome fell out of the tree and flopped onto the snow.

"One of them won't get me again!" said Tiffany.

"Aye. I believe you. Ye have murrrder in yer eyes," said William, with a touch of admiration. "If I was a drome, I'd be pretty fearful noo, if I had a brain. There'll be more of them, mark you, and some of 'em are cunning. The Quin uses 'em as guards."

"I won't be fooled!" Tiffany remembered the horror of the moment when the thing had lumbered around changing shape. It was worse because it was in her house, her *place*. She'd felt real terror as the big shapeless thing crashed across the kitchen, but the anger had been there too. It was invading *her place*.

The thing wasn't just trying to kill her, it was *insulting* her.

William was watching her.

"Aye, ye're lookin' mighty fierce," he said. "Ye must love your wee brother to face a' these monsters for him."

And Tiffany couldn't stop her thoughts. I don't love him. I know I don't. He's just so . . . sticky, and can't keep up, and I have to spend too much time looking after him, and he's always screaming for things. I can't talk to him. He just *wants* all the time.

But her Second Thinking said: He's *mine*. My place, my home, my brother! How dare anything touch what's *mine*!

She'd been brought up not to be selfish. She knew she wasn't, not in the way people meant. She tried to think of other people. She never took the last slice of bread. This was a different feeling.

She wasn't being brave or noble or kind. She was doing this

because it had to be done, because there was no way that she could not do it. She thought of:

. . . Granny Aching's light, weaving slowly across the downs, on freezing, sparkly nights or in storms like a raging war, saving lambs from the creeping frost or rams from the precipice. She froze and struggled and tramped through the night for idiot sheep that never said thank you and would be just as stupid tomorrow, and get into the same trouble again. And she did it because not doing it was unthinkable.

There had been the time when they met the peddler and the donkey in the lane. It was a small donkey and could hardly be seen under the pack piled on it. And the peddler was thrashing it because it had fallen over.

Tiffany had cried to see that, and Granny had looked at her and then said something to Thunder and Lightning.

The peddler had stopped when he heard the growling. The sheepdogs had taken up positions on either side of the man, so that he couldn't quite see them both at once. He raised his stick as if to hit Lightning, and Thunder's growl grew louder.

"I'd advise ye not to do that," said Granny.

He wasn't a stupid man. The eyes of the dogs were like steel balls. He lowered his arm.

"Now throw down the stick," said Granny. The man did so, dropping it into the dust as though it had suddenly grown red-hot.

Granny Aching walked forward and picked it up. Tiffany remembered that it was a willow twig, long and whippy.

Suddenly, so fast that her hand was a blur, Granny sliced it across the man's face twice, leaving two long red marks. He began to move, and some desperate thought must have saved him, because now the dogs were almost frantic for the command to leap.

"Hurts, don't it?" said Granny, pleasantly. "Now, I knows who you are,

and I reckon you knows who I am. You sell pots and pans and they ain't bad, as I recall. But if I put out the word, you'll have no business in my hills. Be told. Better to feed your beast than whip it. You hear me?"

With his eyes shut and his hands shaking, the man nodded.

"That'll do," said Granny Aching, and instantly the dogs became, once more, two ordinary sheepdogs, who came and sat on either side of her with their tongues hanging out.

Tiffany watched the man unpack some of the load and strap it to his own back and then, with great care, urge the donkey on along the road. Granny watched him go while filling her pipe with Jolly Sailor. Then, as she lit it, she said, as if the thought had just occurred to her:

"Them as can do has to do for them as can't. And someone has to speak up for them as has no voices."

Tiffany thought: Is this what being a witch is? It wasn't what I expected! When do the *good* bits happen?

She stood up. "Let's keep going," she said.

"Aren't ye tired?" said Rob.

"We're going to keep going!"

"Aye? Weel, she's probably headed for her place beyond the wood. If we dinna carry ye, it'll tak' aboout a coupla hours—"

"I'll walk!" The memory of the huge dead face of the drome was trying to come back into her mind, but fury gave it no space. "Where's the frying pan? Thank you! Let's go!"

She set off through the strange trees. The hoofprints almost glowed in the gloom. Here and there other tracks crossed them, tracks that could have been bird feet, rough round footprints that could have been made by anything, squiggly lines that a snake might make, if there were such things as snow snakes.

The pictsies were running in line with her on either side.

Even with the edge of the fury dying away, it was hard looking at things here without her head aching. Things that seemed far off got closer too quickly, trees changed shape as she passed them.

Almost unreal, William had said. Nearly a dream. This world didn't have enough reality in it for distances and shapes to work properly. Once again the magic artist was painting madly. If she looked hard at a tree, it changed and became more treelike and less like something drawn by Wentworth with his eyes shut.

This is a made-up world, Tiffany thought. Almost like a story. The trees don't have to be very detailed because who looks at trees in a story?

She stopped in a small clearing and stared hard at a tree. It seemed to know it was being watched. It became more real. The bark roughened, and proper twigs grew on the ends of the branches.

The snow was melting around her feet, too. Although *melting* was the wrong word. It was just disappearing, leaving leaves and grass.

If I was a world that didn't have enough reality to go around, Tiffany thought, then snow would be quite handy. It doesn't take a lot of effort. It's just white stuff. Everything looks white and simple. But *I* can make it complicated. I'm more real than this place.

She heard a buzzing overhead and looked up.

And suddenly the air was filling with small people, smaller than the Feegle, with wings like dragonflies'. There was a golden glow around them. Tiffany, entranced, reached out a hand—

At the same moment what felt like the entire clan of Nac Mac Feegle landed on her back and sent her sliding into a snowdrift.

When she struggled out, the clearing was a battlefield. The

pictsies were jumping and slashing at the flying creatures, which buzzed around them like wasps. As she stared, two of them dived onto Rob Anybody and lifted him off his feet by his hair.

He rose in the air, yelling and struggling. Tiffany leaped up and grabbed him around the waist, flailing at the creatures with her other hand. They let go of the pictsie and dodged easily, zipping through the air as fast as hummingbirds. One of them bit her on the finger before buzzing away.

Somewhere a voice went: "Oooooooooooooooeeerrrrrr . . ."

Rob struggled in Tiffany's grip. "Quick, put me doon!" he yelled. "There's gonna be poetry!"

CHAPTER 9

Lost Boys

⌘

The moan rolled around the clearing, as mournful as a month of Mondays.

"... rrrrrraaaaaaaaaaaaooooooooo ..."

It sounded like some animal in terrible pain. But it was, in fact, Not-as-big-as-Medium-Sized-Jock-but-bigger-than-Wee-Jock-Jock, who was standing on a snowdrift with one hand pressed to his heart and the other outstretched, very theatrically.

He was rolling his eyes, too.

"... ooooooooooooooooooooooo ..."

"Ach, the muse is a terrible thing to have happen to ye," said Rob Anybody, putting his hands over his ears.

"... ooooooiiiiiit *is* with grreat lamentation and much worrying dismay," the pictsie groaned, "That we rrregard the doleful prospect of Fairyland in considerrrable decay ..."

In the air the flying creatures stopped attacking and began to panic. Some of them flew into one another.

"... With quite a large number of drrrrrrreadful incidents happening everrry day," Not-as-big-as-Medium-Sized-Jock-but-bigger-than-Wee-Jock-Jock recited, "Including, I am sorrrry to say, an aerial attack by the otherwise quite attractive fey ..."

The fliers screeched. Some crashed into the snow, but the ones still capable of flight swarmed off among the trees.

". . . Witnessed by all of us at this time, and celebrated in this hasty rhyme!" Not-as-big-as-Medium-Sized-Jock-but-bigger-than-Wee-Jock-Jock shouted after them.

And they were gone.

Feegles were picking themselves up off the ground. Some were bleeding where the fairies had bitten them. Several were lying curled up and groaning.

Tiffany looked at her own finger. The bite of the fairy had left two tiny holes.

"It isna too bad," Rob Anybody shouted up from below. "No one taken by them, just a few cases where the lads didna put their hands o'er their ears in time."

"Are they all right?"

"Oh, they'll be fine wi' counsellin'."

On the mound of snow William clapped Not-as-big-as-Medium-Sized-Jock-but-bigger-than-Wee-Jock-Jock on the shoulder in a friendly way.

"That, lad," he said proudly, "was some of the worst poetry I have heard for a long time. It was offensive to the ear and a torrr-ture to the soul. The last couple of lines need some work, but ye has the groanin' off fiiine. All in all, a verrry commendable effort! We'll make a gonnagle out of ye yet!"

Not-as-big-as-Medium-Sized-Jock-but-bigger-than-Wee-Jock-Jock blushed happily.

In Fairyland words *really* have power, Tiffany thought. And I am more real. I'll remember that.

The pictsies assembled into battle order again, although it was pretty disorderly, and set off. Tiffany didn't rush too far ahead this time.

"That's yer little people wi' wings," said Rob, as Tiffany sucked at her finger. "Are ye happier now?"

"Why were they trying to carry you away?"

"Ach, they carries their victims off to their nest, where their young ones—"

"Stop!" said Tiffany. "This is going to be horrible, right?"

"Oh, aye. Gruesome," said Rob, grinning.

"And you used to *live* here?"

"Ah, but it wasna so bad then. It wasna perfect, mark you, but the Quin wasna as cold in them days. The King was still aroound. She was always happy then."

"What happened? Did the King die?"

"No. They had words, if ye tak' my meanin'," said Rob.

"Oh, you mean like an argument—"

"A bit, mebbe," said Rob. "But they was *magical* words. Forests destroyed, mountains explodin', a few hundred deaths, that kind of thing. And he went off to his own world. Fairyland was never a picnic, ye ken, even in the old days. But it was fine if you kept alert, an' there was flowers and burdies and summertime. Now there's the dromes and the hounds and the stinging fey and such stuff creepin' in from their own worlds, and the whole place has gone doon the tubes."

Things taken from their own worlds, thought Tiffany, as she tramped through the snow. Worlds all squashed together like peas in a sack, or hidden inside one another like bubbles inside other bubbles.

She had a picture in her head of things creeping out of their own world and into another, in the same way that mice invaded the larder. Only there were worse things than mice.

What would a drome do if it got into our world? You'd never

know it was there. It'd sit in the corner and you'd never see it, because it wouldn't let you. And it'd change the way you saw the world, give you nightmares, make you want to die.

Her Second Thoughts added: I wonder how many have got in already and we don't know?

And I'm in Fairyland, where dreams can hurt. Somewhere all stories are real, all songs are true. I thought that was a strange thing for the kelda to say. . . .

Tiffany's Second Thoughts said: Hang on, was that a First Thought?

And Tiffany thought: No, that was a Third Thought. I'm thinking about how I think about what I'm thinking. At least, I think so.

Her Second Thoughts said: Let's all calm down, please, because this is quite a small head.

The forest went on. Or perhaps it was a small forest and, somehow, moved around them as they walked. This was Fairyland, after all. You couldn't trust it.

And the snow still vanished where Tiffany walked, and she had only to look at a tree for it to smarten up and make an effort to look like a real tree.

The Queen is . . . well, a queen, Tiffany thought. She's got a world of her own. She could do *anything* with it. And all she does is steal things, mess up people's lives . . .

There was the thud of hoofbeats in the distance.

It's her! What shall I do? What shall I say?

The Nac Mac Feegles leaped behind the trees.

"Come away oot o' the path!" whispered Rob Anybody.

"She might still have him!" said Tiffany, gripping the pan handle nervously and staring at the blue shadows between the trees.

"So? We'll find a wa' to steal him! She's the *Quin*! Ye canna beat the Quin face-to-face!"

The hoofbeats were louder, and now it sounded as though there was more than one animal.

A stag appeared through the trees, steam pouring off it. It stared at Tiffany with wild red eyes and then, bunching up, leaped over her. She smelled the stink of it as she ducked, she felt its sweat on her neck.

It was a real animal. You couldn't imagine a reek like that.

And here came the dogs.

The first one she caught with the edge of the pan, bowling it over. The other turned to snap at her, then looked down in amazement as pictsies erupted from the snow under each paw. It was hard to bite anyone when all four of your feet were moving away in different directions, and then other pictsies landed on its head and biting anything ever again soon became . . . impossible. The Nac Mac Feegle hated grimhounds.

Tiffany looked up at a white horse. That was real, too, as far as she could tell. And there was a boy on it.

"Who are *you*?" he said. He made it sound like "What sort of thing are you?"

"Who are you?" said Tiffany, pushing her hair out of her eyes. It was the best she could do right now.

"This is *my* forest," said the boy. "I command you to do what I say!"

Tiffany peered at him. The dull, secondhand light of Fairyland was not very good, but the more she looked, the more certain she was. "Your name is Roland, isn't it?" she said.

"You will not speak to me like that!"

"Yes, it is. You're the Baron's son!"

"I demand that you stop talking!" The boy's expression was

strange now, creased up and pink, as if he was trying not to cry. He raised his hand with a riding whip in it—

There was a very faint *thwap*. Tiffany glanced down. The Nac Mac Feegle had formed a pile under the horse's belly, and one of them, climbing up on their shoulders, had just cut through the saddle girth.

She held up a hand quickly. "Stand still!" she shouted, trying to sound commanding. "If you move, you'll fall off your horse!"

"Is that a spell? Are you a witch?" The boy dropped the whip and pulled a long dagger from his belt. "Death to witches!"

He urged the horse forward with a jerk, and then there was one of those long moments, a moment when the whole universe said, "Uh-oh" and, still holding the dagger, the boy swiveled around the horse and landed in the snow.

Tiffany knew what would happen next. Rob Anybody's voice echoed among the trees:

"You're in trouble noo, pal! *Get him!*"

"No!" Tiffany yelled. "Get away from him!"

The boy scrambled backward, staring at Tiffany in horror.

"I do know you," she said. "Your name *is* Roland. You're the Baron's son. They said you'd died in the forest—"

"You mustn't talk about that!"

"Why not?"

"Bad things happen!"

"They're already happening," said Tiffany. "Look, I'm here to rescue my—"

But the boy had got to his feet and was running back through the forest. He turned and shouted, "Stay away from me!"

Tiffany ran after him, jumping over snow-covered logs, and saw him ahead, dodging from tree to tree. Then he paused and looked back.

She ran up to him, saying, "I know how to get you out—"

—and danced.

She was holding the hand of a parrot or, at least someone with the head of a parrot.

Her feet moved under her, perfectly. They twirled her around, and this time her hand was caught by a peacock, or at least someone with the head of a peacock. She glanced over his shoulder and saw that she was now in a room, no, a *ballroom* full of masked people, dancing.

Ah, she thought. Another dream. I should have looked where I was going.

The music was strange. There was a kind of rhythm to it, but it sounded muffled and odd, as if it was being played backward, underwater, by musicians who'd never seen their instruments before.

And she *hoped* the dancers were wearing masks. She realized she was looking out through the eyeholes of one and wondered what she was. She was also wearing a long dress, which glittered.

O-kay, she thought carefully. There was a drome there, and I didn't stop to look. And now I'm in a dream. But it's not mine. It must make use of what it finds in your head, and I've never been to anything like this.

"Fwa waa fwah waa wha?" said the peacock. The voice was like the music. It sounded almost like a voice, but it wasn't.

"Oh, yes," said Tiffany. "Fine."

"Fwaa?"

"Oh. Er . . . wuff fawf fwaff?"

This seemed to work. The peacock-headed dancer bobbed a little bow, said "Mwa waf waf" sadly, and wandered off.

Somewhere in here is the drome, said Tiffany to herself. And it must be a pretty good one. This is a *big* dream.

Little things were wrong, though. There were hundreds of people in the room, but the ones in the distance, although they were moving about in quite a natural way, seemed the same as the trees—blobs and swirls of color. You had to look hard to notice this, though.

First Sight, Tiffany thought.

People in brilliant costumes and still more masks walked arm in arm past her, as if she was just another guest. Those who weren't joining the new dance were heading for the long tables at one side of the hall, which were piled with food.

Tiffany had seen such food only in pictures. People didn't starve on the farm, but even when food was plentiful, at Hogswatch or after harvest, it never looked like this. The farm food was mostly shades of white or brown. It was never pink and blue, and never wobbled.

There were things on sticks, and things that gleamed and glistened in bowls. Nothing was simple. Everything had cream on it, or chocolate whirls, or thousands of little colored balls. Everything was spun or glazed or added to or mixed up. This wasn't food—it was what food became if it had been good and had gone to food heaven.

It wasn't just for eating, it was for show. It was piled up against mounds of greenery and enormous arrangements of flowers. Here and there huge transparent carvings were landmarks in this landscape of food. Tiffany reached up and touched a glittering cockerel. It was ice, damp under her fingertips. There were others, too—a jolly fat man, a bowl of fruits all carved in ice, a swan.

Tiffany was, for a moment, tempted. It seemed a very long time since she had eaten anything. But the food was too obviously not food at all. It was bait. It was supposed to say: Hello, little kiddie. Eat me.

I'm getting the hang of this, thought Tiffany. Good thing it didn't think of cheese—

—and there was cheese. Suddenly, *cheese had always been there.*

She'd seen pictures of lots of different cheeses in the Almanack. She was good at cheese and had always wondered what the others tasted like. They were faraway cheeses with strange-sounding names, cheeses like Treble Wibbley, Waney Tasty, Old Argg, Red Runny, and the legendary Lancre Blue, which had to be nailed to the table to stop it attacking other cheeses.

Just a taste wouldn't hurt, surely. It wasn't the same as eating, was it? After all, she was in control, wasn't she? She'd seen right through the dream straight away, hadn't she? So it couldn't have any effect, could it?

And . . . well, *cheese* was hardly temptation for anyone.

Okay, the drome must've put the cheese in as soon as she'd thought of it, but . . .

She was already holding the cheese knife. She didn't quite remember picking it up.

A drop of cold water landed on her hand. It made her glance up at the nearest glittering ice carving.

It showed a shepherdess, with a saddlebag dress and a big bonnet. Tiffany was sure it had been a swan when she'd looked at it before.

The anger came back. She'd nearly been fooled! She looked at the cheese knife. "Be a sword," she said. After all, the drome was making her dream, but she was doing the dreaming. She was real. Part of her wasn't asleep.

There was a clang.

"Correction," said Tiffany. "Be a sword that isn't so heavy." And this time she got something she could actually hold.

There was a rustling in the greenery and a red-haired face poked out.

"Psst," it whispered. "Dinna eat the canapés!"

"You're a bit late!"

"Ach, weel, it's a cunnin' ol' drome ye're dealin' with here," said Rob Anybody. "The dream wouldna let us in unless we wuz properly dressed."

He stepped out, looking very sheepish in a black suit with a bow tie. There was more rustling and other pictsies pushed their way out of the greenery. They looked a bit like redheaded penguins.

"Properly dressed?" said Tiffany.

"Aye," said Daft Wullie, who had a piece of lettuce on his head. "An' these troosers are a wee bit chafin' around the nethers, I don't mind tellin' ye."

"Have ye spotted the creature yet?" said Rob Anybody.

"No! It's so crowded!"

"We'll help ye look," said Rob Anybody. "The thing canna hide if ye're right up close. Be careful, mind you! If it thinks ye're gonna whap it one, there's nae tellin' what it'll try! Spread oot, lads, and pretend ye're enjoying the cailey."

"Whut? D'ye mean get drunk and fight an' that?" said Daft Wullie.

"Crivens, ye wouldna believe it," said Rob Anybody, rolling his eyes. "Nae, ye pudden! This is a *posh* party, ye ken? That means ye mak' small talk an' mingle!"

"Ach, I'm a famous mingler! They won't even know we're here!" said Daft Wullie. "C'mon!"

Even in a dream, even at a posh ball, the Nac Mac Feegle knew how to behave. You charged in madly, and you screamed . . . politely.

"Lovely weather for the time o' year, is it not, ye wee scunner!"

"Hey, jimmy, ha' ye no got a pommes frites *for an ol' pal?"*

"The band is playin' divinely, I dinna think!"

"Make my caviar deep fried, wilya?"

There *was* something wrong with the crowd. No one was panicking or trying to run away, which was *certainly* the right response to an invasion of Feegles.

Tiffany set off again through the crowd. The masked people at the party paid her no attention either. And that's because they're background people, she thought, just like the background trees. She walked along the room to a pair of double doors and pulled them open.

There was nothing but blackness beyond it.

So . . . the only way out was to find the drome. She hadn't really expected anything else. It could be anywhere. It could be behind a mask, it could be a table. It could be anything.

Tiffany stared at the crowd. And it was then she saw Roland.

He was sitting at a table by himself. It was spread with food, and he had a spoon in his hand.

She ran over and knocked it onto the floor. "Haven't you got any sense at all?" she said, pulling him upright. "Do you want to stay here forever?"

And then she felt the movement behind her. Later on, she was sure she hadn't heard anything. She'd just known. It was a dream, after all.

She glanced around, and there was the drome. It was almost hidden behind a pillar.

Roland just stared at her.

"Are you all right?" said Tiffany desperately, trying to shake him. "Have you eaten anything?"

"Fwa fwa faff," murmured the boy.

Tiffany turned back to the drome. It was moving toward her, but very slowly, trying to stay in the shadows. It looked like a little snowman made of dirty snow.

The music was getting louder. The candles were getting brighter. Out on the huge dance floor the animal-headed couples whirled faster and faster. And the floor shook. The dream was in trouble.

The Nac Mac Feegles were running to her from every part of the floor, trying to be heard above the din.

The drome was lurching toward her, pudgy white fingers grasping the air.

"First Sight," breathed Tiffany.

She cut Roland's head off.

◆　◆　◆

The snow had melted all across the clearing, and the trees looked real and properly treelike.

In front of Tiffany the drome fell backward. She was holding the old frying pan in her hand, but it had cut beautifully. Odd things, dreams.

She turned and faced Roland, who was staring at her with a face so pale, he might as well have been a drome.

"It was frightened," she said. "It wanted me to attack you instead. It tried to look like you and made *you* look like a drome. But it didn't know how to speak. You do."

177

"You might have killed me!" he said hoarsely.

"No," said Tiffany. "I just explained. Please don't run away. Have you seen a baby boy here?"

Roland's face wrinkled. "What?" he said.

"The Queen took him," said Tiffany. "I'm going to fetch him home. I'll take you too, if you like."

"You'll never get away," whispered Roland.

"I got in, didn't I?"

"Getting in is easy. No one gets out!"

"I mean to find a way," said Tiffany, trying to sound a lot more confident than she felt.

"She won't let you!" Roland started to back away again.

"Please don't be so . . . so *stupid*," said Tiffany. "I'm going to find the Queen and get my brother back, whatever you say. Understand? I've got this far. And I've got help, you know."

"Where?" said Roland.

Tiffany looked around. There was no sign of the Nac Mac Feegle.

"They always turn up," she said. "Just when I need them."

It struck her that there was suddenly something very . . . empty about the forest. It seemed colder, too.

"They'll be here any minute," she added, hopefully.

"They got trapped in the dream," said Roland flatly.

"They can't have. I killed the drome!"

"It's more complicated than that," said the boy. "You don't know what it's like here. There's dreams inside dreams. There's . . . other things that live inside dreams, horrible things. You never know if you've really woken up. And the Queen controls them all. They're fairy people, anyway. You can't trust them. You can't trust anyone. I don't trust you. You're probably just another dream."

He turned his back and walked away, following the line of hoof-prints.

Tiffany hesitated. The only other real person was going away, leaving her here with nothing but the trees and the shadows.

And, of course, anything horrible that was running toward her through them.

"Er . . ." she said. "Hello? Rob Anybody? William? Daft Wullie?"

There was no reply. There wasn't even an echo. She was alone, except for her heartbeats.

Well, of *course* she'd fought things and won, hadn't she? But the Nac Mac Feegle had been there and, somehow, that'd made it easy. They never gave up, they'd attack absolutely anything, and they didn't know the meaning of the word *fear*.

Tiffany, who had read her way through the dictionary, had a Second Thought there. *Fear* was only one of thousands of words the pictsies probably didn't know the meaning of. Unfortunately, she *did* know what it meant. And the taste and feel of fear, too. She felt it now.

She gripped the pan. It didn't seem quite such a good weapon anymore.

The cold blue shadows between the trees seemed to be spreading out. They were darkest ahead of her, where the hoofprints led. Strangely enough, the wood behind her seemed almost light and inviting.

Someone doesn't want me to go on, she thought. That was . . . quite encouraging. But the twilight was misty and shimmered unpleasantly. Anything could be waiting.

She was waiting, too. She realized that she was waiting for the Nac Mac Feegle, hoping against hope that she'd hear a sudden cry, even of "Crivens!" (She was sure it was a swearword.)

She pulled out the toad, which lay snoring on the palm of her hand, and gave it a prod.

"Whp?" it croaked.

"I'm stuck in a wood of evil dreams and I'm all alone and I think it's getting darker," said Tiffany. "What should I do?"

The toad opened one bleary eye and said: "Leave."

"That is not a lot of help!"

"Best advice there is," said the toad. "Now put me back—the cold makes me lethargic."

Reluctantly, Tiffany put the creature back in her apron pocket, and her hand touched *Diseases of the Sheep*.

She pulled it out and opened it at random. There was a cure for the Steams, but it had been crossed out in pencil. Written in the margin, in Granny Aching's big, round, *careful* handwriting was:

This dunt work. One desert spoonfull of terpentine do.

Tiffany closed the book with care and put it back gently so as not to disturb the sleeping toad. Then, gripping the pan's handle tightly, she stepped into the long blue shadows.

How do you get shadows when there's no sun in the sky? she thought, because it was better to think about things like this than all the other, much worse things that were on her mind.

But these shadows didn't need light to create them. They crawled around on the snow of their own accord, and backed away when she walked toward them. That, at least, was a relief.

They piled up behind her. They were following her. She turned and stamped her foot a few times, and they scurried off behind the trees, but she knew they were flowing back when she wasn't looking.

She saw a drome in the distance ahead of her, standing half hidden behind a tree. She screamed at it and waved the pan threateningly, and it lumbered off quickly.

When she looked around, she saw two more behind her, a long way back.

The track led uphill a little, into what looked like a much thicker mist. It glowed faintly. She headed for it. There was no other way to go.

When she reached the top of the rise, she looked down into a shallow valley.

There were four dromes in it—big ones, bigger than any she'd seen so far. They were sitting down in a square, their dumpy legs stretched out in front of them. Each one had a gold collar around its neck, attached to a chain.

"Tame ones?" Tiffany wondered, aloud. "But—"

Who could put a collar around the neck of a drome? Only someone who could dream as well as they could.

We tamed the sheepdogs to help us herd sheep, she thought. The Queen uses dromes to herd dreams.

In the center of the square formed by the dromes the air was full of mist. The hoof tracks, and the tracks of Roland, led down past the tame dromes and into the cloud.

Tiffany spun around. The shadows darted back.

There was nothing else nearby. No birds sang, nothing moved in the woods. But she could make out three more dromes now, their big round soggy faces peering at her around tree trunks.

She was being herded.

At a time like this it would be nice to have someone around to say something like "No! It's too dangerous! Don't do it!"

Unfortunately, there wasn't. She was going to commit an act of extreme bravery and no one would know if it all went wrong. That was frightening, but also . . . annoying. That was it—*annoying*.

THE WEE FREE MEN

This place annoyed her. It was all stupid and strange.

It was the same feeling she'd had when Jenny had leaped out of the river. Out of *her* river. And the Queen had taken *her* brother. Maybe it was selfish to think like that, but anger was better than fear. Fear was a damp cold mess, but anger had an edge. She could use it.

They were *herding* her! Like a—a sheep!

Well, an angry sheep could send a vicious dog away, whimpering. So . . .

Four big dromes, sitting in a square.

It was going to be a big dream.

Raising the pan to shoulder height, to swipe at anything that came near, and suppressing a dreadful urge to go to the toilet, Tiffany walked slowly down the slope, across the snow, through the mist . . .

. . . and into summer.

CHAPTER 10

Master Stroke

∞

The heat struck like a blowtorch, so sharp and sudden that she gasped.

She'd had sunstroke once, up on the downs, when she'd gone without a bonnet. And this was like that; the world around here was in worrying shades of dull green, yellow, and purple, without shadows. The air was so full of heat that she felt she could squeeze smoke out of it.

She was in . . . reeds, they looked like, much taller than her . . .

. . . with sunflowers growing in them, except . . .

. . . the sunflowers were white . . .

. . . because they *weren't*, in fact, sunflowers at all.

They were daisies. She knew it. She'd stared at them dozens of times, in that strange picture in the *Faerie Tales*. They were daisies, and these weren't giant reeds around her, they were blades of grass and she was very, very small.

She was in the weird picture. The picture was the dream, or the dream was the picture. Which way around didn't matter, because she was right in the middle of it. If you fell off a cliff, it wouldn't matter if the ground was rushing up or you were rushing down. You were in trouble either way.

Somewhere in the distance there was a loud *crack!* and a ragged cheer. Someone clapped and said, in a sleepy sort of voice, "Well done. Good man. Ver' well done."

With some effort Tiffany pushed her way between the blades of grass.

On a flat rock a man was cracking nuts half as big as he was, with a two-handed hammer. He was being watched by a crowd of people. Tiffany used the word *people* because she couldn't think of anything else that was suitable, but it was stretching the word a bit to make it fit all the . . . people.

They were different sizes, for one thing. Some of the men were taller than her, even if you allowed for the fact that *everyone* was shorter than the grass. But others were tiny. Some of them had faces that you wouldn't look at twice. Others had faces that no one would want to look at even *once*.

This is a dream, after all, Tiffany told herself. It doesn't have to make sense, or be nice. It's a dream, not a daydream. People who say things like "May all your dreams come true" should try living in one for five minutes.

She stepped out into the bright, stiflingly hot clearing just as the man raised his hammer again, and said, "Excuse me?"

"Yes?" he said.

"Is there a Queen around here?" said Tiffany.

The man wiped his forehead and nodded toward the other side of the clearing.

"Her Majesty has gone to her bower," he said.

"That being a nook or resting place?" said Tiffany.

The man nodded and said, "Correct again, Miss Tiffany."

Don't ask how he knows your name, Tiffany told herself.

"Thank you," she said, and because she had been brought up to be polite, she added, "Best of luck with the nut cracking."

"This one's the toughest yet," said the man.

Tiffany walked off, trying to look as if this collection of strange nearly-people was just another crowd. Probably the scariest ones were the big women, two of them.

Big women were valued on the Chalk. Farmers liked big wives. Farmwork was hard, and there was no call for a wife who couldn't carry a couple of piglets or a bale of hay. But these two could have carried a horse each. They stared haughtily at her as she walked past.

They had tiny, stupid little wings on their backs.

"Nice day for watching nuts being cracked!" said Tiffany cheerfully as she went past. Their huge pale faces wrinkled, as if they were trying to work out what she was.

Sitting down near them, watching the nut cracker with an expression of concern, was a little man with a large head, a fringe of white beard, and pointy ears. He was wearing very old-fashioned clothes, and his eyes followed Tiffany as she went past.

"Good morning," she said.

"*Sneebs!*" he said, and in her head appeared the words: "Get away from here!"

"Excuse me?" she said.

"*Sneebs!*" said the man, wringing his hands. And the words appeared, floating in her brain: "It's terribly dangerous!"

He waved a pale hand as if to brush her away. Shaking her head, Tiffany walked on.

There were lords and ladies, people in fine clothes and even a few shepherds. But some of them had a pieced-together look. They looked, in fact, like a picture book back in her bedroom.

It was made of thick card, its edges worn raggedy by generations of Aching children. Each page showed a character, and each was cut into four strips that could be turned over independently. The point of the whole thing was that a bored child could turn over parts of the pages and change the way the characters were dressed. You could end up with a soldier's head on a baker's chest wearing a maid's dress and a farmer's big boots.

Tiffany had never been bored enough. She considered that even things that spend their whole lives hanging from the undersides of branches would never be bored enough to spend more than five seconds with that book.

The people around here looked as though they'd either been taken from that book or had dressed for a fancy-dress party in the dark. One or two of them nodded to her as she passed but didn't seem surprised to see her.

She ducked under a round leaf much bigger than she was and took out the toad again.

"Whap? It's sti' cooold," said the toad, hunching down on her hand.

"Cold? The air's baking!"

"There's just snow," said the toad. "Put me back, I'm freezing!"

Just a minute, thought Tiffany. "Do toads dream?" she said.

"No!"

"Oh . . . so it's not really hot?"

"No! You just think it is!"

"Psst," said a voice.

Tiffany put the toad away and wondered if she dared to turn her head.

"It's me!" said the voice.

Tiffany turned toward a clump of daisies twice the height of a man. "That's not a lot of help."

"Are you crazy?" said the daisies.

"I'm looking for my brother," said Tiffany sharply.

"The horrible child who screams for candy all the time?"

The daisy stems parted and the boy Roland darted out and joined her under the leaf.

"Yes," she said, edging away and feeling that only a sister has a right to call even a brother like Wentworth horrible.

"And threatens to go to the toilet if he's left alone?" said Roland.

"Yes! Where is he?"

"*That's* your brother? The one who's permanently sticky?"

"I told you!"

"And you really want him back?"

"Yes!"

"Why?"

He's my brother, Tiffany thought. What's *why* got to do with it?

"Because he's my brother! Now tell me where he is?"

"Are you sure you can get out of here?" said Roland.

"Of course," Tiffany lied.

"And you can take me with you?"

"Yes." Well, she hoped so.

"All right. I'll let you do that," said Roland, relaxing.

"Oh, you'll *let* me, will you?" said Tiffany.

"Look, I didn't know what you were, all right?" said Roland. "There's always weird things in the forest. Lost people, bits of dreams that're still lying around . . . you have to be careful. But if you really know the way, then I ought to get back before my father worries too much."

Tiffany felt the Second Thoughts starting. They said: Don't change your expression. Just . . . check.

"How long have you been here?" she asked carefully. "Exactly?"

"Well, the light doesn't really change much," said the boy. "It feels like I've been here . . . oh, hours. Maybe a day."

Tiffany tried hard not to let her face give anything away, but it didn't work. Roland's eyes narrowed.

"I have, haven't I?" he said.

"Er . . . why do you ask?" said Tiffany, desperately.

"Because in a way it . . . feels like . . . longer. I've only been hungry two or three times, and been to the . . . you know . . . twice, so it can't be *very* long. But I've done all kinds of things . . . it's been a busy day. . . ." His voice trailed off.

"Um. You're right," said Tiffany. "Time goes slowly here. It's been . . . a bit longer."

"A hundred years? Don't tell me it's a hundred years! Something magical has happened and it's a hundred years, yes?"

"What? No! Um . . . nearly a year."

The boy's reaction was surprising. This time he looked *really* frightened. "Oh, no! That's worse than a hundred years!"

"How?" said Tiffany, bewildered.

"If it was a hundred years, I wouldn't get a thrashing when I got home!"

Hmm, thought Tiffany. "I don't think that's going to happen," she said aloud. "Your father has been very miserable. Besides, it's not your fault you were stolen by the Queen—" She hesitated, because this time it was *his* expression that gave it all away. "Was it?"

"Well, there was this fine lady on a horse with bells all over its harness, and she galloped past me when I was out hunting and she was laughing, so of *course* I spurred my horse and chased after her, and . . ." He fell silent.

"That probably wasn't a good decision," said Tiffany.

"It's not . . . *bad* here," said Roland. "It just keeps changing. There's . . . doorways everywhere. I mean, entrances into other places . . ." His voice tailed off.

"You'd better start at the beginning," said Tiffany.

◆ ◆ ◆

"It was great at first," said Roland. "I thought it was, you know, an adventure? She fed me sweetmeats—"

"What are they, exactly?" said Tiffany. Her dictionary hadn't included that one. "Are they like sweetbreads?"

"I don't know. What are sweetbreads?"

"The pancreas or thymus gland of a cow," said Tiffany. "Not a very good name, I think."

Roland's face went red with the effort of thought. "These were more like nougat."

"Right. Go on," said Tiffany.

"And then she told me to sing and dance and skip and play," said Roland. "She said that's what children were supposed to do."

"Did you?"

"Would you? I'd feel like an idiot. I'm twelve, you know." Roland hesitated. "In fact, if what you say is true, I'm thirteen now, right?"

"Why did she want you to skip and play?" said Tiffany, instead of saying, "No, you're still twelve and act like you're eight."

"She just said that's what children do," said Roland.

Tiffany wondered about this. As far as she could see, children mostly argued, shouted, ran around very fast, laughed loudly, picked their noses, got dirty, and sulked. Any seen dancing *and* skipping *and* singing had probably been stung by a wasp.

"Strange," she said.

"And then when I wouldn't, she gave me more sweets."

"More nougat?"

"Sugarplums," said Roland. "They're like plums. You know? With sugar on? She's always trying to feed me sugar! She thinks I like it!"

A small bell rang in Tiffany's memory. "You don't think she's trying to fatten you up before she bakes you in an oven and eats you, do you?"

"Of course not. Only wicked witches do that."

Tiffany's eyes narrowed. "Oh yes," she said carefully. "I forgot. So you've been living on sweeties?"

"No, I know how to hunt! Real animals get in here. I don't know how. Sneebs thinks they find the doorways in by accident. And then they starve to death, because it's always winter here. Sometimes the Queen sends out robbing parties if a door opens into an interesting world, too. This whole place is like . . . a pirate ship."

"Yes, or a sheep tick," said Tiffany, thinking aloud.

"What're they?"

"They're insects that bite sheep and suck blood and don't drop off until they're full," said Tiffany.

"Yuck. I suppose that's the kind of thing peasants have to know about," said Roland. "I'm glad I don't. I've seen through the doorways to one or two worlds. They wouldn't let me out, though. We got potatoes from one, and fish from another. I think they frighten people into giving them stuff. Oh, and there was the world where the dromes come from. They laughed about that and said if I wanted to go in there, I was welcome. I didn't! It's all red, like a sunset. A great huge sun on the horizon, and a red sea that hardly moves, and red rocks, and long shadows. And those horrible creatures sitting on the rocks. They live off crabs and spidery things and little scribbity creatures. It was awful. There was this sort of ring of little claws and shells and bones around every one of them."

"Who are they?" said Tiffany, who had noted the word *peasants*.

"What do you mean?"

"You keep talking about 'they,'" said Tiffany. "Who do you mean? The people out there?"

"Those? Most of them aren't even real," said Roland. "I mean the elves. The fairies. That's who she's queen of. Didn't you know?"

"I thought they were small!"

"I think they can be any size they like," said Roland. "They're not exactly real. They're like . . . dreams of themselves. They can be thin as air or solid as a rock. Sneebs says."

"Sneebs?" said Tiffany. "Oh . . . the little man that just says *sneebs* but real words turn up in your head?"

"Yes, that's him. He's been here for *years*. That's how I knew about the time being wrong. Sneebs got back to his own world once, and it was all different. He was so miserable, he found another doorway and came straight back."

"He *came* back?" said Tiffany, astonished.

"He said it was better to belong where you don't belong than not to belong where you used to belong, remembering when you used to belong there," said Roland. "At least, I think that's what he said. He said it's not too bad here if you keep out of the Queen's way. He says you can learn a lot."

Tiffany looked back at the hunched figure of Sneebs, who was still watching the nut cracking. He didn't look as though he was learning anything. He just looked like someone who'd been frightened for so long, it had become part of his life, like freckles.

"But you mustn't make the Queen angry," said Roland. "I've

seen what happens to people who make her angry. She sets the Bumblebee women on them."

"Are you talking about those huge women with the tiny wings?"

"Yes! They've vicious. And if the Queen gets really angry with someone, she just stares at them, and . . . they change."

"Into what?"

"Other things. I don't want to have to draw you a picture." Roland shuddered. "And if I did, I'd need a lot of red and purple crayon. Then they get dragged off and left for the dromes." He shook his head. "Listen, dreams are real here. *Really* real. When you're inside them you're not . . . exactly here. The nightmares are real, too. You can *die*."

This doesn't *feel* real, Tiffany told herself. This feels like a dream. I could almost wake up from it.

I must always remember what's real.

She looked down at her faded blue dress, with the bad stitching around the hem caused by it being let out and taken in as its various owners had grown. That was real.

And she was real. Cheese was real. Somewhere not far away was a world of green turf under a blue sky, and that was real.

The Nac Mac Feegle were real, and once again she wished they were here. There was something about the way they shouted "Crivens!" and attacked everything in sight that was so very comforting.

Roland was probably real.

Almost everything else was really a dream, in a robber world that lived off the real worlds and where time nearly stood still and horrible things could happen at any moment. I don't want to know anything more about it, she decided. I just want to get my brother and go home, while I'm still angry.

Because when I stop being angry, that'll be the time to get frightened again, and I'll be *really* frightened this time. Too frightened to think. As frightened as Sneebs. And I must think. . . .

"The first dream I fell into was like one of mine," she said. "I've had dreams where I wake up and I'm still asleep. But the ballroom, I've never—"

"Oh, that was one of mine," said Roland. "From when I was young. I woke up one night and went down to the big hall and there were all these people with masks on, dancing. It was just so . . . bright." He looked wistful for a moment. "That was when my mother was still alive."

"This one's a picture from a book I've got," said Tiffany. "She must have got that from me—"

"No, she often uses it," said Roland. "She likes it. She picks up dreams from everywhere. She collects them."

Tiffany stood and picked up the frying pan again. "I'm going to see the Queen," she said.

"Don't," said Roland. "You're the only other real person here except Sneebs, and he's not very good company."

"I'm going to get my brother and go home," said Tiffany flatly.

"I'm not going to come with you, then," said Roland. "I don't want to see what she turns you into."

Tiffany stepped out into the heavy, shadowless light and followed the path up the slope. Giant grasses arched overhead. Here and there more strangely dressed, strangely shaped people turned to watch her but then acted as though she was just a passing wanderer, of no interest whatsoever.

She glanced behind her. In the distance the nut cracker had found a bigger hammer and was getting ready to strike.

"Wanna wanna *wanna* sweetie!"

Tiffany's head shot around like a weathercock in a tornado. She ran along the path, head down, ready to swing the pan at anything that stood in her way, and burst through a clump of grass into a space lined with daisies. It could well have been a bower. She didn't bother to check.

Wentworth was sitting on a large, flat stone, surrounded by sweets. Many of them were bigger than he was. Smaller ones were in piles, large ones lay like logs. And they were in every color sweets can be, such as Not-Really-Raspberry Red, Fake-Lemon Yellow, Curiously-Chemical Orange, Some-Kind-of-Acidy Green, and Who-Knows-What Blue.

Tears were falling off his chin in blobs. Since they were landing among the sweets, serious stickiness was already taking place.

Wentworth howled. His mouth was a big red tunnel with the wobbly thing that no one knows the name of bouncing up and down in the back of his throat. He stopped crying only when it was time to either breathe in or die, and even then it was only for one huge sucking moment before the howl came back again.

Tiffany knew what the problem was immediately. She'd seen it before, at birthday parties. Her brother was suffering from tragic sweet deprivation. Yes, he was surrounded by sweets. But the moment he took any sweet at all, said his sugar-addled brain, that meant he was *not taking all the rest*. And there were so many sweets *he'd never be able to eat them all*. It was too much to cope with. The only solution was to burst into tears.

The only solution at home was to put a bucket over his head until he calmed down, and to take almost all the sweets away. He could deal with a few handfuls at a time.

Tiffany dropped the pan and swept him up in her arms. "It's

Tiffy," she whispered. "And we're going home."

And this is where I meet the Queen, she thought. But there was no scream of rage, no explosion of magic . . . nothing.

There was just the buzz of bees in the distance, and the sound of wind in the grass, and the gulping of Wentworth, who was too shocked to cry.

She could see now that the far side of the bower contained a couch of leaves, surrounded by hanging flowers. But there was no one there.

"That's because I'm behind you," said the voice of the Queen in her ear.

Tiffany turned around quickly.

There was no one there.

"*Still* behind you," said the Queen. "This is *my* world, child. You'll never be as fast as me, or as clever as me. Why are you trying to take my boy away?"

"He isn't yours! He's ours!" said Tiffany.

"You never loved him. You have a heart like a little snowball. I can see it."

Tiffany's forehead wrinkled. "Love?" she said. "What's that got to do with it? He's my *brother*! *My* brother!"

"Yes, that's a very witchy thing, isn't it," said the voice of the Queen. "Selfishness? Mine, mine, mine? All a witch cares about is what's *hers*."

"You stole him!"

"Stole? You mean you thought you *owned* him?"

Tiffany's Second Thoughts said: She's finding your weaknesses. Don't listen to her.

"Ah, you have Second Thoughts," said the Queen. "I expect you think that makes you very witchy, do you?"

"Why won't you let me see you?" said Tiffany. "Are you frightened?"

"Frightened?" said the voice of the Queen. "Of something like *you?*"

And the Queen was there, in front of her. She was much taller than Tiffany, but just as slim; her hair was long and black, her face pale, her lips cherry red, her dress black and white and red. And it was all, very slightly, wrong.

Tiffany's Second Thoughts said: It's because she's perfect. Completely perfect. Like a doll. No one real is as perfect as that.

"That's not you," said Tiffany, with absolute certainty. "That's just your dream of you. That's not you at all."

The Queen's smile disappeared for a moment and came back all edgy and brittle.

"Such rudeness, and you hardly know me," she said, sitting down on the leafy seat. She patted the space beside her.

"Do sit down," she said. "Standing there like that is so confrontational. I will put your bad manners down to simple disorientation." She gave Tiffany a beautiful smile.

Look at the way her eyes move, said Tiffany's Second Thoughts. I don't think she's using them to see you with. They're just beautiful ornaments.

"You have invaded my home, killed some of my creatures, and generally acted in a mean and despicable way," said the Queen. "This offends me. However, I understand that you have been badly led by disruptive elements—"

"You stole my brother," said Tiffany, holding Wentworth tightly. "You steal all sorts of things." But her voice sounded weak and tinny in her ears.

"He was wandering around lost," said the Queen calmly. "I

brought him home and comforted him."

And what there was about the Queen's voice was this: It said, in a friendly, understanding way, that she was right and you were wrong. And this wasn't your fault, exactly. It was probably the fault of your parents', or your food, or something so terrible you've completely forgotten about it. It wasn't *your* fault, the Queen understood, because *you* were a nice person. It was just such a terrible thing that all these bad influences had made you make the wrong choices. If only you'd admit that, Tiffany, then the world would be a much happier place—

—this cold place, guarded by monsters, in a world where nothing grows older, or up, said her Second Thoughts. A world with the Queen in charge of everything. Don't listen.

She managed to take a step backward.

"Am I a monster?" said the Queen. "All I wanted was a little bit of company."

And Tiffany's Second Thoughts, quite swamped by the Queen's wonderful voice, said: Miss Female Infant Robinson . . .

She'd come to work as a maid at one of the farms many years ago. They said that she'd been brought up in a Home for the Destitute in Yelp. They said she'd been born there after her mother had arrived during a terrible storm and the master had written in his big black diary: "To Miss Robinson, female infant," and her young mother hadn't been very bright and was dying in any case and had thought that was the baby's name. After all, it had been written down in an official book.

Miss Robinson was quite old now, never said much, never ate much, but you never saw her not doing something. No one could scrub a floor like Miss Female Infant Robinson. She had a thin, wispy face with a pointed red nose, and thin, pale hands with red knuckles, which were always busy. Miss Robinson worked hard.

Tiffany hadn't understood a lot of what was going on when the crime happened. The women talked about it in twos and threes at garden gates, their arms folded, and they'd stop and look indignant if a man walked past.

She picked up bits of conversation, though sometimes they seemed to be in a kind of code, like: "Never really had anyone of her own, poor old soul. Wasn't her fault she was skinnier'n a rake," and "They say that when they found her, she was cuddling it and said it was hers," and "The house was full of baby clothes she'd knitted!" That last one had puzzled Tiffany at the time, because it was said in the same tone of voice that someone'd use to say, "And the house was full of human skulls!"

But they all agreed on one thing: We can't have this. A crime's a crime. The Baron's got to be told.

Miss Robinson had stolen a baby, Punctuality Riddle, who had been much loved by his young parents even though they'd named him Punctuality (reasoning that if children could be named after virtues like Patience, Faith, and Prudence, what was wrong with a little good time-keeping?).

He'd been left in his crib in the yard and had vanished. And there had been all the usual searchings and weepings, and then someone had mentioned that Miss Robinson had been taking home extra milk.

It was kidnaping. There weren't many fences on the Chalk, and very few doors with locks. Theft of all kinds was taken very seriously. If you couldn't turn your back on what was yours for five minutes, where would it all end? The law's the law. A crime's a crime.

Tiffany had overheard bits of arguments all over the village, but the same phrases cropped up over and over again. Poor thing never meant no harm. She was a hard worker, never complained. She's not right in the head. The law's the law. A crime's a crime.

And so the Baron was told, and he held a court in the Great Hall, and everyone who wasn't wanted up on the hills turned up, including Mr. and Mrs. Riddle, she looking worried, he looking determined, and Miss Robinson, who just stared at the ground with her red-knuckled hands on her knees.

It was hardly a trial. Miss Robinson was confused about what she was accused of, and it seemed to Tiffany that so was everyone else. They weren't certain why they were there, and they'd come to find out.

The Baron had been uneasy, too. The law was clear. Theft was a dreadful crime, and stealing a human being was much worse. There was a prison in Yelp, right beside the Home for the Destitute; some said there was even a connecting door. That was where thieves went.

And the Baron wasn't a big thinker. His family had held the Chalk by not changing their mind about anything for hundreds of years. He sat and listened and drummed his fingers on the table and looked at people's faces and acted like a man sitting on a very hot chair.

Tiffany was in the front row. She was there when the man started to give his verdict, umming and ahhing, trying not to say the words he knew he'd have to say, when the door at the back of the hall opened and the sheepdogs Thunder and Lightning trotted in.

They came down the aisle between the rows of benches and sat down in front of the Baron, looking bright-eyed and alert.

Only Tiffany craned to see back up the aisle. The doors were still slightly ajar. They were far too heavy even for a strong dog to push them open. And she could just make out someone looking through the crack.

The Baron stopped and stared. He, too, looked at the other end of the hall.

And then, after a few moments, he pushed the law book aside and said: "Perhaps we should do this a different way."

And there was a different way, involving people paying a little more attention to Miss Robinson. It wasn't perfect, and not everyone was happy, but it worked.

Tiffany smelled the scent of Jolly Sailor outside the hall when the meeting was over, and thought about the Baron's dog. "Remember this day," Granny Aching had said, and, "Ye'll have cause to."

Barons needed reminding.

"Who will speak up for you?" Tiffany said aloud.

"Speak up for me?" answered the Queen, her fine eyebrows arching.

And Tiffany's Third Thoughts said: Watch her face when she is worried.

"There isn't anyone, is there?" said Tiffany, backing away. "Is there anyone you've been kind to? Anyone who'll say you're not just a thief and a bully? Because that's what you are. You've got a . . . You're like the dromes, you've just got one trick."

And there it was. Now she could see what her Third Thoughts had spotted. The Queen's face *flickered* for a moment.

"And that's not your body," said Tiffany, plunging on. "That's just what you want people to see. It's not real. It's just like everything else here, it's hollow and empty—"

The Queen ran forward and slapped her much harder than a dream should be able to. Tiffany landed in the moss and Wentworth rolled away, yelling, "Wanna go-a toy-lut!"

Good, said Tiffany's Third Thoughts.

"Good?" said Tiffany aloud.

"Good?" said the Queen.

Yes, said her Third Thoughts, because she doesn't know you can have Third Thoughts and your hand is only a few inches from the frying pan and things like her hate iron, don't they? She's angry.

Now make her furious, so that she doesn't think. Hurt her.

"You just live here in a land full of winter and all you do is dream of summers," said Tiffany. "No wonder the king went away."

The Queen stood still for a moment, like the beautiful statue she so much resembled. Again, the walking dream flickered and Tiffany thought she saw . . . something. It was not much bigger than her, and almost human, and a little shabby and, just for a moment, shocked. Then the Queen was back, tall and angry, and she drew a deep breath—

Tiffany grabbed the pan and swung it as she rolled onto her feet. It hit the tall figure only a glancing blow, but the Queen wavered like air over a hot road, and screamed.

Tiffany didn't wait to see what else was going to happen. She grabbed her brother again, and ran away, down through the grass, past the strange figures looking around at the sound of the Queen's anger.

Now shadows moved in the shadowless grasses. Some of the people—the joke people, the ones that looked like a flap-the-pages picture book—changed shape and started to move after Tiffany and her screaming brother.

There was a booming noise on the other side of the clearing. The two huge creatures that Roland had called the Bumblebee women were rising off the ground, their tiny wings blurring with the effort.

Somebody grabbed her and pulled her into the grasses. It was Roland.

"Can you get out now?" he demanded, his face red.

"Er . . ." Tiffany began.

"Then we'd better just run," he said. "Give me your hand. Come *on*!"

"Do *you* know a way out?" Tiffany panted, as they dashed through giant daisies.

"No," Roland panted back. "There isn't one. You saw . . . the dromes outside . . . this is a really *strong* dream."

"Then why are we running?"

"To keep out of her way. If you hide long enough . . . Sneebs says she . . . forgets."

I don't think she's going to forget me very quickly, Tiffany thought.

Roland had stopped, but she pulled her hand away and ran onward, with Wentworth clinging to her in silent amazement.

"Where are you going?" shouted Roland behind her.

"I *really* want to keep out of her way!"

"Come back! You're running right back!"

"No I'm not! I'm running in a straight line!"

"This is a dream!" Roland shouted, but it was louder now because he was catching up to her. "You're running right around—"

Tiffany burst into a clearing . . .

. . . *the* clearing.

The Bumblebee women landed on either side of her, and the Queen stepped forward.

"You know," said the Queen, "I really expected better of you, Tiffany. Now, give me back the boy, and I shall decide what to do next."

"It's not a big dream," mumbled Roland behind her. "If you go too far, you end up coming back—"

"I could make a dream for you that's even smaller than you are," said the Queen pleasantly. "That can be quite painful!"

The colors were brighter. And sounds were louder. Tiffany

could smell something, too, and what was strange about that was that up until now there had been no smells.

It was a sharp, bitter smell that you never forgot. It was the smell of snow. And underneath the insect buzzings in the grass, she heard the faintest of voices.

"Crivens! I canna find the way oot!"

CHAPTER 11

Awakening

cℕɔ

On the other side of the clearing, where the nut-cracking man had been at work, was the last nut, half as high as Tiffany. And it was rocking gently. The cracker took a swipe at it with the hammer, and it rolled out of the way.

See what's really there, said Tiffany to herself, and laughed.

The Queen gave her a puzzled look. "You find this funny?" she demanded. "What's funny about this? What is amusing about this situation?"

"I just had a funny thought," said Tiffany. The Queen glared, as people without a sense of humor do when they're confronted with a smile.

You're not very clever, thought Tiffany. You've never needed to be. You can get what you want just by dreaming it. You believe in your dreams, so you never have to *think*.

She turned and whispered to Roland, "Crack the nut! Don't worry about what I do, crack the nut!" The boy looked at her blankly.

"What did you say to him?" snapped the Queen.

"I said good-bye," said Tiffany, holding on tightly to her brother. "I'm not handing my brother over, no matter what you do!"

"Do you know what color your insides are?" said the Queen. Tiffany shook her head mutely.

"Well, now you'll find out," said the Queen, smiling sweetly.

"You're not powerful enough to do anything like that," said Tiffany.

"You know, you are right," said the Queen. "That kind of physical magic is, indeed, very hard. But I can make you *think* I've done the most . . . terrible things. And that, little girl, is all I need to do. Would you like to beg for mercy now? You may not be able to later."

Tiffany paused. "No-o," she said at last. "I don't think I will."

The Queen leaned down. Her gray eyes filled Tiffany's world. "People here will remember this for a long time," she said.

"I hope so," said Tiffany. "Crack . . . the . . . nut."

For a moment the Queen looked puzzled again. She was not good at dealing with sudden changes. "What?"

"Eh? Oh. Right," muttered Roland.

"What did you say to him?" the Queen demanded, as the boy ran toward the hammer man.

Tiffany kicked her on the leg. It wasn't a witch thing. It was *so* nine years old, and she wished she could have thought of something better. On the other hand, she had hard boots and it was a good kick.

The Queen shook her. "Why did you *do* that?" she said. "Why won't you do what I say? Everyone could be so happy if only they'd do what I say!"

Tiffany stared at the woman's face. The eyes were gray now, but the pupils were like silver mirrors.

I know what you are, said her Third Thoughts. You're something that's never learned anything. You don't know *anything* about people. You're just . . . a child that's got old.

"Want a sweetie?" she whispered.

There was a shout behind her. She twisted in the Queen's grip and saw Roland fighting for the hammer. As she watched, he turned desperately and raised the heavy thing over his head, knocking over the elf behind him.

The Queen pulled her around savagely as the hammer fell. "Sweetie?" she hissed. "I'll show you swe—"

"Crivens! It's the Quin! An' she's got oour kelda, the ol' topher!"

"Nae Quin! Nae Laird! Wee Free Men!"

"I could murrrder a kebab!"

"Get her!"

Tiffany might have been the only person, in all the worlds that there are, to be happy to hear the sound of the Nac Mac Feegle.

They poured out of the smashed nut. Some were still wearing bow ties. Some were back in their kilts. But they were all in a fighting mood and, to save time, were fighting with one another to get up to speed.

The clearing . . . cleared. Real or dreams, the people could see trouble when it rolled toward them in a roaring, cursing, red-and-blue tide.

Tiffany ducked out of the Queen's grasp and hurried into the grasses to watch.

Big Yan ran past, carrying a struggling full-sized elf over his head. Then he stopped suddenly and tossed it high over the clearing.

"An' away he goes, right on his *heid!*" he yelled, then turned and ran back into the battle.

The Nac Mac Feegle couldn't be trodden on or squeezed. They worked in groups, running up one another's backs to get high enough to punch an elf or, preferably, bash it with their heads. And once anyone was down, it was all over bar the kicking.

There was some method in the way the Nac Mac Feegle fought. For example, they always chose the biggest opponent because, as Rob Anybody said later, "It makes them easier to hit, ye ken." And they simply didn't *stop*. It was that which wore people down. It was like being attacked by wasps with fists.

It took them a little while to realize that they'd run out of people to fight. They went on fighting one another for a bit anyway, since they'd come all this way, and then settled down and began to go through the pockets of the fallen in case there was any loose change.

Tiffany stood up.

"Ach, weel, no' a bad job though I says it mysel'," said Rob Anybody, looking around. "A very neat fight, an' we didna e'en ha' to resort to usin' poetry."

"How did you get into the nut?" said Tiffany. "I mean, it was . . . a nut!"

"Only way we could find in," said Rob Anybody. "It's got to be a way that fits. 'Tis difficult work, navigatin' in dreams."

"Especially when ye're a wee bittie sloshed," said Daft Wullie, grinning broadly.

"What? You've been . . . drinking?" said Tiffany. "I've been facing the Queen and you've been in a *pub*?"

"Ach, no!" said Rob Anybody. "Ye ken that dream wi' the big party? When you had the pretty frock an' a'? We got stuck in it."

"But I killed the drome!"

Rob looked a little shifty. "Weeeel," he said, "we didna get oout as easily as you. It took us a wee while."

"Until we finished all the drink," said Daft Wullie helpfully.

Rob glared at him. "Ye didna ha' to put it like that!" he snapped.

"You mean the dream keeps on going?" said Tiffany.

"If ye're thirsty enough," said Daft Wullie. "An' it wasna just the drink—there was can-a-pays as well."

"But I thought if you ate or drank in a dream, you stayed there!" said Tiffany.

"Aye, for most creatures," said Rob Anybody. "Not for us, though. Hooses, banks, dreams, 'tis a' the same to us. There's nothing we canna get in or oot of."

"Except maybe pubs," said Big Yan.

"Oh, aye," said Rob Anybody cheerfully. "Gettin' oot o' pubs sometimes causes us a cerrrtain amount o' difficulty, I'll grant ye that."

"And where did the Queen go?" she said.

"Ach, she did an offski as soon as we arrived," said Rob Anybody. "An' so should we, kelda, afore the dream changes." He nodded at Wentworth. "Is this the wee bairn? Ach, what a noseful o' bogeys!"

"Wanna sweetie!" shouted Wentworth, on automatic candy pilot.

"Weeel, ye canna ha' none!" shouted Rob Anybody. "An' stop snivelin' and come awa' wi' us and stop bein' a burden to your wee sister!"

Tiffany opened her mouth to protest—and shut it again when Wentworth, after a moment of shock, chuckled.

"Funny!" he said. "Wee man! Weewee man!"

"Oh dear," said Tiffany. "You've got him started now."

But she was very surprised, nonetheless. Wentworth never showed this much interest in anyone who wasn't a jelly baby.

"Rob, we've got a real one here," a pictsie called out. To her horror, Tiffany saw that several of the Nac Mac Feegle were holding up Roland's unconscious head. He was full length on the ground.

"Ah, that was the laddie who wuz rude to ye," said Rob. "An' he tried to hit Big Yan wi' a hammer, too. That wasna a clever thing to try. What shall we do with him?"

The grasses trembled. The light was fading from the sky. The air was growing colder, too.

"We can't leave him here!" said Tiffany.

"Okay, we'll drag him along," said Rob Anybody. "Let's move right *noo!*"

"Wee wee man! Wee wee man!" shouted Wentworth gleefully.

"He'll be like this all day, I'm afraid," said Tiffany. "Sorry."

"Run for the door," said Rob Anybody. "Can ye no' see the door?"

Tiffany looked around desperately. The wind was bitter now.

"See the door!" Rob Anybody commanded. She blinked and spun around.

"Er . . . er . . ." she said. The sense of a world beneath that had come to her when she was frightened of the Queen did not turn up so easily now. She tried to concentrate. The smell of snow . . .

It was ridiculous to talk about the smell of snow. It was just pure frozen water. But Tiffany always knew, when she woke up, if it had snowed in the night. Snow had a smell like the taste of tin. Tin *did* have a taste, although admittedly it tasted like the smell of snow.

She thought she heard her brain creak with the effort of thinking. If she was in a dream, she had to wake up. But it was no use running. Dreams were full of running. But there was one direction that looked . . . thin, and white.

She shut her eyes and thought about snow, crisp and white as fresh bed sheets. She concentrated on the feel of it under her feet. All she had to do was wake up. . . .

She *was* standing in snow.

"Right," said Rob Anybody.

"I got out!" said Tiffany.

"Ach, sometimes the door's in yer ain heid," said Rob Anybody. "Noo let's move!"

Tiffany felt herself lifted into the air. Nearby, a snoring Roland rose up on dozens of small blue legs as the Feegles got underneath him.

"Nae stoppin' until we get right oout o' here!" said Rob Anybody. "Feegles wha hae!"

They skimmed over the snow, with parties of Feegles running on ahead. After a minute or two Tiffany looked behind them and saw the blue shadows spreading. They were getting darker, too.

"Rob—" she said.

"Aye, I ken," said Rob. "Run, lads!"

"They're moving *fast*, Rob!"

"I ken that, too!"

Snow stung Tiffany's face. Trees blurred with the speed. The forest sped past. But the shadows were spreading across the path ahead, and every time the party ran through them, they seemed to have a certain solidity, like fog.

Now the shadows behind were night black in the middle.

But the pictsies has passed the last tree, and the snowfields stretched ahead.

They stopped, so quickly that Tiffany almost toppled into the snow.

"What's happened?"

"Where's all oour old footprints gone?" said Daft Wullie. "They wuz there a moment ago! Which way *noo*?"

The trampled track, which had led them on like a line, had vanished.

Rob Anybody spun around and looked back at the forest. Darkness curled above it like smoke, spreading along the horizon.

"She's sendin' nightmares after us," he growled. "This is gonna be a toughie, lads."

Tiffany saw shapes in the spreading night. She hugged Wentworth tightly.

"Nightmares," repeated Rob Anybody, turning to her. "Ye wouldna want to know about *them*. We'll hold 'em off. Ye must mak' a run for it. Get awa' wi' ye, noo!"

"I've got nowhere to run to!" said Tiffany.

She heard a high-pitched noise, a sort of chittering, insect noise, coming from the forest. The pictsies had drawn together. Usually they grinned like anything if they thought a fight was coming up, but this time they looked deadly serious.

"Ach, she's a bad loser, the Quin," said Rob.

Tiffany turned to look at the horizon behind her. The boiling blackness was there, too, a ring that was closing in from all sides.

Doors everywhere, she thought. The old kelda said there's doors everywhere. I must find a door. But there's just snow and a few trees. . . .

The pictsies drew their swords.

"What, er, kind of nightmares are coming?" said Tiffany.

"Ach, long-leggity things with muckle legs and huge teeth, and flappy wings and a hundred eyes, that kinda stuff," said Daft Wullie.

"Aye, and wuss than that," said Rob Anybody, staring at the speeding dark.

"What's worse than that?" said Tiffany.

"Normal stuff gone wrong," said Rob.

Tiffany looked blank for a moment, and then shuddered. Oh *yes*, she knew about those nightmares. They didn't happen often, but they were horrible when they did. She'd woken up once shaking at the thought of Granny Aching's boots, which had been chasing her, and another time it was a box of sugar. Anything could be a nightmare.

She could put up with monsters. But she didn't want to face mad boots.

"Er . . . I have an idea," she said.

"So do I," said Rob Anybody. "Dinna be here—that's my idea!"

"There's a clump of trees over there," said Tiffany.

"So what?" said Rob. He was staring at the line of nighmares. Things were visible in it now—teeth, claws, eyes, ribs. From the way he was glaring, it was obvious that whatever happened later, the first few monsters were going to face a serious problem. If they had faces, anyway.

"Can you *fight* nightmares?" said Tiffany. The chittering noise was getting a lot louder.

"There's no' a thing we canna fight," growled Big Yan. "If it's got a heid, we can gie it a faceful o' dandruff. If it disna have a heid, it's due a good kickin'!"

Tiffany stared at the onrushing . . . things.

"Some of them have got *more* than one head!" she said.

"It's oour lucky day, then," said Daft Wullie.

The pictsies shifted their weight, ready to fight.

"Piper," said Rob Anybody to William the gonnagle, "play us a lament. We'll fight to the sound of the mousepipes—"

"No!" said Tiffany. "I'm not standing for this! The way to fight nightmares is to wake up! I am your kelda! This is an order! We're heading for those trees right now! Do what I say!"

"Weewee man!" yelled Wentworth.

The pictsies glanced at the trees and then at Tiffany.

"Do it!" she yelled, so loudly that some of them flinched. "Right now! Do what I tell you! There's a better way!"

"Ye canna cross a hag, Rob," muttered William.

"I'm going to get you home!" snapped Tiffany. I hope, she added to herself. But she'd seen a small, round, pale face staring at them around a tree trunk. There was a drome in those trees.

"Ach, aye, but—" Rob Anybody glanced past Tiffany and added: "Aw no, look at that . . ."

There was a pale dot in front of the racing line of monstrousness.

Sneebs was making a break for it. His arms pumped like pistons. His little legs seemed to spin. His cheeks were like balloons.

The tide of nightmares rolled over him and kept coming.

Rob sheathed his sword. "Ye heard oour kelda, lads!" he shouted. "Grab her! We'rrre offski!"

Tiffany was lifted up. Feegles raised the unconscious Roland. And everyone ran for the trees.

Tiffany pulled her hand out of her apron pocket and looked at the crumpled wrapper of Jolly Sailor tobacco. It was something to focus on, to remind her of a dream . . .

People *said* you could see the sea from the very top of the downs, but Tiffany had stared hard on a fine winter's day, when the air was clear, and seen nothing but the hazy blue of distance. But the sea on the Jolly Sailor packet was deep blue, with white crests on the waves. It *was* the sea, for Tiffany.

It had looked like a *small* drome in the trees. That meant it wasn't very powerful. She hoped so. She had to hope so. . . .

The trees got closer. So did the ring of nightmares. Some of the sounds were horrible, of cracking bones and crushing rocks and stinging insects and screaming cats, getting nearer and nearer and nearer.

CHAPTER 12

Jolly Sailor

ᕦᕤ

There was sand around her, and white waves crashing, and water draining off the pebble beach and sounding like an old woman sucking a hard mint.

"Crivens! Where are we noo?" said Daft Wullie.

"Aye, and why're we all lookin' like yellow mushrooms?" Rob Anybody added.

Tiffany looked down and giggled. Every pictsie was wearing a Jolly Sailor outfit, with an oilskin coat and a huge yellow oilskin rain hat that covered most of his face. They started to wander about, bumping into one another.

My dream! Tiffany thought. The drome uses what it can find in your head . . . but this is *my* dream. I can *use* it.

Wentworth had gone quiet. He was staring at the waves.

There was a boat pulled up on the beach. As one pictsie, or small yellow mushroom, the Nac Mac Feegle were flocking toward it and clambering up the sides.

"What are you doing?" said Tiffany.

"Best if we wuz leavin'," said Rob Anybody. "It's a good dream ye've found us, but we canna stay here."

"But we should be safe here!"

"Ach, the Quin finds a way in everywhere," said Rob, as a hundred pictsies raised an oar. "Dinna fash yersel', we know all about boats. Did ye no' see Not-totally-wee-Georgie pike fishin' wi' Wee Bobby in the stream the other day? We is no strangers to the piscatorial an' nautical arts, ye ken."

And they did indeed seem to know about boats. The oars were heaved into the oarlocks, and a party of Feegles pushed the boat down the stones and into the waves.

"Now you just hand us the wee bairn," shouted Rob Anybody from the stern. Uncertainly, her feet slipping on the wet stones, Tiffany waded through the cold water and handed Wentworth over.

He seemed to think it was very funny.

"Weewee mens!" he yelled as they lowered him into the boat. It was his only joke, so he wasn't going to stop.

"Aye, that's right," said Rob Anybody, tucking him under the seat. "Noo just you bide there like a good boy and no yellin' for sweeties or Uncle Rob'll gie ye a skelpin' across the earhole, okay?"

Wentworth chuckled.

Tiffany ran back up the beach and hauled Roland to his feet. He opened his eyes and looked blearily at her.

"Wha's happening?" he said. "I had this strange drea—" and then he shut his eyes again and sagged.

"Get in the boat!" Tiffany shouted, dragging him across the shingle.

"Crivens, are we takin' this wee streak o' uselessness?" said Rob, grabbing Roland's trousers and heaving him aboard.

"Of course!" Tiffany hauled herself in afterward and landed in the bottom of the boat as a wave took it. The oars creaked and splashed, and the boat jerked forward. It jolted once or twice, as more waves hit it, and then began to plunge across the sea. The pictsies were strong, after all. Even though each oar was a battleground as pictsies hung from it, or piled up on one another's shoulders or just heaved anything they could grasp, both oars were almost bending as they were dragged through the water.

Tiffany picked herself up and tried to ignore the sudden uncertain feeling in her stomach.

"Head for the lighthouse!" she said.

"Aye, I ken that," said Rob Anybody. "It's the only place there is! And the Quin disna like light." He grinned. "It's a good dream, lady. Have ye no' looked at the sky?"

"It's just a blue sky," said Tiffany.

"It's no' *exactly* a sky," said Rob Anybody. "Look behind ye."

Tiffany turned. It was a blue sky. Very blue. But above the retreating beach, halfway up the sky, was a band of yellow. It looked a long way away, and hundreds of miles across. And in the middle of it, looming over the world as big as a galaxy and gray-blue with distance, was a life preserver.

On it, in letters larger than the moon, were the words:

ЯO⅃IАƧ Y⅃⅃Oꞁ

"We *are* in the label?" said Tiffany.

"Oh, aye," said Rob Anybody.

"But the sea feels . . . real. It's salty and wet and cold. It's not like paint! I didn't dream it salty or so cold!"

"Nae kiddin'? Then it's a picture on the outside, and it's real on the inside." Rob nodded. "Ye ken, we've been robbin' and running aroound on all kinds o' worlds for a lang time, and I'll tell ye this: The universe is a lot more comp-li-cated than it looks from the ooutside."

Tiffany took the grubby label out of her pocket and stared at it again. There was the life preserver, and the lighthouse. But the Jolly Sailor himself wasn't there. What *was* there, so tiny as to be little bigger than a dot on the printed sea, was a tiny rowboat.

She looked up. There were storm clouds in the sky in front of the huge, hazy life preserver. They were long and ragged, curling as they came.

"It didna take her long to find a way in," muttered William.

"No," said Tiffany, "but this is my dream. I know how it goes. Keep rowing!"

Tangling and tumbling, some of the clouds passed overhead and then swooped toward the sea. They vanished beneath the waves like a waterspout in reverse.

It began to rain hard, so hard that a haze of mist rose over the sea.

"Is that it?" Tiffany wondered. "Is that all she can do?"

"I doot it," said Rob Anybody. "Bend them oars, lads!"

The boat shot forward, bouncing through the rain from wave-top to wavetop.

But, against all normal rules, it was now trying to go uphill. The water was mounding up and up, and the boat washed backward in the streaming surf.

Something was rising. Something white was pushing the seas aside. Great waterfalls poured off the shining dome that climbed toward the storm sky.

It rose higher, and still there was more. And eventually there was an eye. It was tiny compared to the mountainous head above it, and it rolled in its socket and focused on the tiny boat.

"Now, *that's* a heid that'd be a day's work e'en for BigYan," said Rob Anybody. "I reckon we'd have to come back tomorrow! Row, boys!"

"It's a dream of mine," said Tiffany, as calmly as she could manage. "It's the whale fish."

I never dreamed the smell, though, she added to herself. But here it is, a huge, solid, world-filling smell of salt and water and fish and ooze—

"Whut does it eat?" Daft Wullie asked.

"Ah, I know that," said Tiffany, as the boat rocked on the swell. "Whales aren't dangerous, because they just eat very small things . . ."

"Row like the blazes, lads!" Rob Anybody yelled.

"How d'ye ken it only eats wee stuff?" said Daft Wullie as the whale fish's mouth began to open.

"I paid a whole cucumber once for a lesson on beasts of the deep," said Tiffany as a wave washed over them. "Whales don't even have proper teeth!"

There was a creaking sound and a gust of fishy halitosis about the size of a typhoon, and the view was full of enormous, pointy teeth.

"Aye?" said Wullie. "Weel, no offense meant, but I dinna think this beastie went to the same school as ye!"

The surge of water was pushing them away. And Tiffany could see the whole of the head now, and in a way she couldn't possibly describe, the whale looked like the Queen. The Queen was *there*, somewhere.

The anger came back.

"This is *my* dream," she shouted at the sky. "I've dreamed it dozens of times! You're not allowed in here! And whales don't eat people! Everyone who isn't very stupid knows that!"

A tail the size of a field rose and slapped down on the sea. The whale shot forward.

Rob Anybody threw off his yellow hat and drew his sword.

"Ach, weel, we tried," he said. "This wee beastie's gonna get the worst belly ache there ever wuz!"

"Aye, we'll cut oour way out!" shouted Daft Wullie.

"No, keep rowing!" said Tiffany.

"It's ne'er be said that the Nac Mac Feegle turned their back on a foe!" Rob yelled.

"But you're rowing *facing* backward!" Tiffany pointed out.

The pictsie looked crestfallen. "Oh, aye, I hadna thought o' it like that," he said, sitting down again.

"Just row!" Tiffany insisted. "We're nearly at the lighthouse!"

Grumbling, because even if they *were* facing the right way, they were still going the wrong way, the pictsies hauled on the oars.

"That's a great big heid he's got there, ye ken," said Rob Anybody. "How big would you say that heid is, gonnagle?"

"Ach, I'd say it's *verrra* big, Rob," said William, who was with the team on the other oar. "Indeed, I might commit myself to sayin' it's enorrrrmous."

"Ye'd go as far as that, would ye?"

"Oh, aye. Enorrrrmous is fully justified."

It's nearly on us, Tiffany thought.

This has got to work. It's my dream. Any moment. Any moment now . . .

"An' how near us would you say it is, then?" asked Rob conversationally, as the boat wallowed and jerked just ahead of the whale.

"That's a verrra good question, Rob," said William. "And I'd answer it by sayin' it's verrra close indeed."

Any moment now, thought Tiffany. I know Miss Tick said you

shouldn't believe in your dreams, but she meant you shouldn't just *hope*.

Er . . . any moment now, I . . . hope. He's never missed. . . .

"In fact I'd go so farrr as to say *exceedingly* close—" William began.

Tiffany swallowed and hoped that the whale wouldn't. There was only about thirty yards of water between the teeth and the boat.

And then it was filled with a wooden wall that blurred as it went past, making a *zipzipzip* noise.

Tiffany looked up, her mouth open. White sails flashed across the storm clouds, pouring rain like waterfalls. She looked up at rigging and ropes and sailors lined up on the spars, and cheered.

And then the stern of the Jolly Sailor's ship was disappearing into the rain and mist, but not before Tiffany saw the big bearded figure at the wheel, dressed in yellow oilskins. He turned and waved just once, before the ship vanished into the murk.

She managed to stand up again, as the boat rocked in the swell, and yelled at the towering whale: "You've got to chase him! That's how it has to work! You chase him, he chases you! *Granny Aching said so!* You can't *not* do it and still be the whale fish! This is *my* dream! My rules! I've had more practice at it than you!"

"Big fishy!" yelled Wentworth.

That was more surprising than the whale. Tiffany stared at her little brother as the boat rocked again.

"Big fishy!" said Wentworth again.

"That's right!" Tiffany said, delighted. "Big fishy! And what makes it *particularly* interesting is that a whale isn't a fish! It is in fact a mammal, just like a cow!"

Did you just say that? said her Second Thoughts, as all the

pictsies stared at her and the boat spun in the surf. The first time he's ever said anything that wasn't about sweeties or weewee and you just *corrected* him?

Tiffany looked at the whale. It was having trouble. But it was *the* whale, the whale she'd dreamed about many times after Granny Aching had told her that story, and not even the Queen could control a story like that.

It turned reluctantly in the water and dived in the wake of the Jolly Sailor's ship.

"Big fishy gone!" said Wentworth.

"No, it's a mammal—" Tiffany's mouth said, before she could stop it.

The pictsies were still staring at her.

"It's just that he ought to get it right," she mumbled, ashamed of herself. "It's a mistake lots of people make. . . ."

You're going to turn into somebody like Miss Tick, said her Second Thoughts. Do you really want that?

"Yes," said a voice, and Tiffany realized that it was hers again. The anger rose up, joyfully. "Yes! I'm *me*! I am careful and logical and I look up things I don't understand! When I hear people use the wrong words, I get edgy! I am good with cheese. I read books fast! I *think*! And I always have a piece of string! That's the kind of person I am!"

She stopped. Even Wentworth was staring at her now. He blinked.

"Big water cow gone," he suggested meekly.

"That's right! Good boy!" said Tiffany. "When we get home, you can have *one* sweet!"

She saw the massed ranks of the Nac Mac Feegle still looking at her with worried expressions.

"Is it okay wi' you if we get on?" asked Rob Anybody, holding up a nervous hand. "Before yon whale fi—before yon whale cow comes back?"

Tiffany looked past them. The lighthouse wasn't far. A little jetty stretched out from its tiny island.

"Yes, please. Er . . . thank you," she said, calming down a bit. The ship and the whale had vanished into the rain, and the sea was merely lapping at the shore.

A drome was sitting on the rocks with its pale, fat legs sticking out in front of it. It was staring out to sea and didn't appear to notice the approaching boat. It thinks it's home, Tiffany thought. I've given it a dream it likes.

Pictsies poured onto the jetty and tied up the boat.

"Okay, we're here," said Rob Anybody. "We'll just chop yon creature's heid off and we'll be right oout o' here . . ."

"Don't!" said Tiffany.

"But it—"

"Leave it alone. Just . . . leave it alone, all right? It's not interested." And it knows about the sea, she added to herself. It's probably homesick for the sea. That's why it's such a *real* dream. I'd have never have got it right by myself.

A crab crawled out of the surf by the drome's feet and settled down to dream crab dreams.

It looks as though a drome can get lost in its own dream, she thought. I wonder if it'll ever wake up?

She turned to the Nac Mac Feegle. "In my dream I always wake up when I reach the lighthouse," she said.

The pictsies looked up at the red-and-white tower and, as one Feegle, drew their swords.

"We dinna trust the Quin," said Rob. "She'll let ye think ye're safe, and just when ye've dropped your guard, she'll leap oout. She'll be waitin' behind the door, ye can bet on it. Ye'll let us go in first."

It was an instruction, not a question. Tiffany nodded and watched the Nac Mac Feegle swarm over the rocks toward the tower.

Alone on the jetty, except for Wentworth and the unconscious Roland, she lifted the toad out of her pocket. It opened its yellow eyes and stared at the sea.

"Either I'm dreaming or I'm on a beach," it said. "And toads don't dream."

"In my dream they can," said Tiffany. "And this is *my* dream."

"Then it is an extremely dangerous one!" said the toad ungratefully.

"No, it's lovely," said Tiffany. "It's wonderful. Look at the way the light dances on the waves."

"Where are the notices warning people they could drown?" complained the toad. "No life preservers or shark nets. Oh, dear. Do I see a qualified lifeguard? I think not. Supposing someone was to—"

"It's a beach," said Tiffany. "Why are you talking like this?"

"I—I don't know," said the toad. "Can you put me down, please? I feel a headache coming on."

Tiffany put it down, and it shuffled into some seaweed. After a while she heard it eating something.

The sea was calm.

It was peaceful.

It was exactly the moment anyone sensible should distrust.

But nothing happened. It was followed by nothing else happening. Wentworth picked up a pebble from the beach and put it in his mouth, on the basis that anything might be a candy.

Then, suddenly, there were noises from the lighthouse. Tiffany heard muffled shouts, and thuds, and once or twice the sound of breaking glass. At one point there was a noise like something heavy falling down a long spiral staircase and hitting every step on the way.

The door opened. The Nac Mac Feegle came out. They looked satisfied.

"Nae problemo," said Rob Anybody. "No one there."

"But there was a lot of noise!"

"Oh, aye. We had to make sure," said Daft Wullie.

"Weewee men!" shouted Wentworth.

"I'll wake up when I go through the door," said Tiffany, pulling Roland out of the boat. "I always do. It must work. This is my dream." She hauled the boy upright. "Can you bring Wentworth?"

"Aye."

"And you won't get lost or—or drunk or anything?"

Rob Anybody looked offended. "We ne'er get lost!" he said. "We always ken where we are! It's just sometimes mebbe we aren't sure where everything else is, but it's no' our fault if *everything else* gets lost! The Nac Mac Feegle are never lost!"

"What about drunk?" said Tiffany, dragging Roland toward the lighthouse.

"We've ne'er been lost in oour lives! Is that no' the case, lads?" said Rob Anybody. There was a murmur of resentful agreement. "The words *lost* and *Nac Mac Feegle* shouldna turn up in the same sentence!"

"And drunk?" said Tiffany again, laying Roland down on the beach.

"Gettin' lost is something that happens to other people!"

declared Rob Anybody. "I want to make that point perfectly clear!"

"Well, at least there shouldn't have been anything to drink in a lighthouse," said Tiffany. She laughed. "Unless you drank the lamp oil, and *no one* would dare do that!"

The pictsies suddenly fell silent.

"What would that be, then?" said Daft Wullie in a slow, careful voice. "Would it be the stuff in a kind o' big bottle kind o' thingie?"

"Wi' a wee skull and crossbones on it?" said Rob Anybody.

"Yes, probably, and it's horrible stuff," said Tiffany. "It'd make you terribly ill if you drank it."

"Really?" said Rob Anybody thoughtfully. "That's verra . . . interesting. What sort o' ill would that be, kind o' thing?"

"I think you'd probably die," said Tiffany.

"We're already dead," said Rob Anybody.

"Well, you'd be very, very, sick, then," said Tiffany. She gave him a strong look. "It's flammable, too. It's a good thing you didn't drink it, isn't it?"

Daft Wullie belched loudly. There was a strong smell of kerosene.

"Aye," he said.

Tiffany went and fetched Wentworth. Behind her, there was some muffled whispering as the pictsies went into a huddle.

"I told yez the wee skull on it meant we shouldna touch it!"

"Big Yan said that showed it wuz strong stuff! An' things ha' come to a pretty pass, ye ken, if people are going to leave stuff like that aroound where innocent people could accidentally smash the door doon and lever the bars aside and take the big chain off 'f the cupboard and pick the lock and drink it!"

"What's flammable mean?"

"It means it catches fire!"

"Okay, okay, dinna panic. No belchin', and none of youse is to tak' a leak anywhere near any naked flames, okay? And act nat'ral."

Tiffany smiled to herself. Pictsies seemed very hard to kill. Perhaps believing you were already dead made you immune.

She turned and looked toward the lighthouse door. She had never actually seen it opened in her dream. She'd always thought that the lighthouse was full of light, on the basis that on the farm the cowshed was full of cows and the woodshed was full of wood.

"All right, all right," she said, looking down at Rob Anybody. "I'm going to carry Roland, and I want you to bring Wentworth."

"Don't you want to carry the wee lad?" said Rob.

"Weewee man!" shouted Wentworth.

"You bring him," said Tiffany shortly. She meant: I'm not sure this is going to work, and he might be safer with you than with me. I hope I'm going to wake up in my bedroom. Waking up in my bedroom would be nice. . . .

Of course, if everyone else wakes up there, too, there might be some difficult questions asked, but anything's better than the Queen—

There was a rushing, rattling noise behind her. She turned and saw the sea disappearing, very quickly. It was pulling back down the shore. As she watched, rocks and clumps of seaweed rose above the surf and then were suddenly high and dry.

"Ah," she said, after a moment. "It's all right. I know what this is. It's the tide. The sea does this. In goes in and out every day."

"Aye?" said Rob Anybody. "Amazin'. It looks like it's pourin' awa' though a hole. . . ."

About fifty yards away the last rivulets of seawater were disappearing over an edge, and some of the pictsies were already heading toward it.

Tiffany suddenly had a moment of something that wasn't exactly panic. It was a lot slower and nastier than panic. It began with just a nagging little doubt that said: Isn't the tide a bit slower?

The teacher (Wonders of the Nattral Wurld, One Apple) hadn't gone into much detail. But there were fish flapping on the exposed seabed, and surely the fish in the sea didn't die every day?

"Er, I think we'd better be careful," she said, trailing after Rob Anybody.

"Why? It's nae as though the water's risin'," he said. "When does the tide come back?"

"Um, not for hours, I think," said Tiffany, feeling the slow, nasty panic getting bigger. "But I'm not sure this—"

"Tons o' time, then," said Rob Anybody.

They'd reached the edge, where the rest of the pictsies were lined up. A little bit of water still trickled over their feet, pouring down into the gulf beyond.

It was like looking down into a valley. At the far side, miles and miles away, the retreating sea was just a gleaming line.

Below them, though, were the shipwrecks. There were a lot of them. Galleons and schooners and clippers, masts broken, rigging hanging, hulls breached, lay strewn across the puddles in what had been the bay.

The Nac Mac Feegle, as one pictsie, sighed happily.

"Sunken treasure!"

"Aye! Gold!"

"Bullion!"

"Jools!"

"What makes you think they've got treasure in them?" said Tiffany.

The Nac Mac Feegle looked amazed, as if she'd suggested that rocks could fly.

"There's *got* to be treasure in 'em," said Daft Wullie. "Otherwise what's the point of lettin' 'em sink?"

"That's right," said Rob Anybody. "There's got t'be gold in sunken ships, otherwise it wouldna be worth fighting all them sharkies and octopussies and stuff. Stealin' treasure fra' the ocean's bed, that's aboout the biggest, best thievin' *ever!*"

And now what Tiffany felt was real, honest panic.

"That's a lighthouse!" she said, pointing. "Can you see it? A lighthouse so ships don't run into the rocks! Right? Understand? This is a trap made just for you! The Queen's still around!"

"Mebbe just can we go down and look inside one wee ship?" said Rob Anybody wistfully.

"No! Because"—Tiffany looked up; a gleam had caught her eye—"because . . . the sea . . . is . . . coming . . . back . . ." she said.

What looked like a cloud on the horizon was getting bigger, and glittering as it came. Tiffany could already hear the roar.

She ran back up the beach and got her hands under Roland's armpits, so that she could drag him to the lighthouse. She looked back, and the pictsies were still watching the huge, surging wave.

And there was Wentworth, watching the wave happily, and bending down slightly so that, if *they* stood on tiptoe, he could hold hands with two Feegles.

The image branded itself on her eyes. The little boy, and the pictsies, all with their backs to her, and all staring with interest at the rushing, glittering, sky-filling wall of water.

"Come on!" Tiffany yelled. "I was wrong, this isn't the tide, this is the Queen—"

Sunken ships were lifted up and spun around in the hissing mountain of surf.

"Come *on*!"

Tiffany managed to haul Roland across her shoulder and, staggering across the rocks, made it to the lighthouse door as the water crashed behind her—

—for a moment the world was full of white light—

—and snow squeaked underfoot.

It was the silent, cold land of the Queen. There was no one around and nothing to see except snow and, in the distance, the forest. Black clouds hovered over it.

Ahead of her, and only just visible, was a picture in the air. It showed some turf, and a few stones, lit with moonlight.

It was the other side of the door back home.

She turned around desperately.

"Please!" she shouted. It wasn't a request to anyone special. She just needed to shout. "Rob? William? Wullie? *Wentworth?*"

Away toward the forest there was the barking of the grimhounds.

"Got to get out," muttered Tiffany. "Got to get away."

She grabbed Roland by the collar and dragged him toward the door. At least he slid better on snow.

No one and nothing tried to stop her. The snow spilled a little way through the doorway between the stones and onto the turf, but the air was warm and alive with nighttime insect noises. Under a real moon, under a real sky, she pulled the boy over to a fallen stone and sat him up against it. She sat down next to him, exhausted to the bone, and tried to get her breath back.

Her dress was soaked and smelled of the sea.

She could hear her own thoughts, a long way off:

They could still be alive. It was a dream, after all. There must be a way back. All I have to do is find it. I've got to go back in there.

The dogs sounded very loud.

She stood up again, although what she really wanted to do was sleep.

The three stones of the door were a black shape against the stars.

And as she watched, they fell down. The one on the left slipped over, slowly, and the other two ended up leaning against it.

She ran over and hauled at the tons of stone. She prodded the air around them in case the doorway was still there. She squinted madly, trying to see it.

Tiffany stood under the stars, alone, and tried not to cry.

"What a shame," said the Queen. "You've let everybody down, haven't you?"

CHAPTER 13

Land Under Wave

❧

The Queen walked over the turf toward Tiffany. Where she'd trodden, frost gleamed for a moment. The little part of Tiffany that was still thinking thought: That grass will be dead in the morning. She's killing *my* turf.

"The whole of life is but a dream, when you come to think of it," said the Queen in the same infuriatingly calm, pleasant voice. She sat down on the fallen stones. "You humans are such dreamers. You dream that you're clever. You dream that you're important. You dream that you're special. You know, you're almost better than dromes. You're certainly more imaginative. I have to thank you."

"What for?" said Tiffany, looking at her boots. Terror clamped her body in red-hot wires. There wasn't anywhere to run to.

"I never realized how wonderful your world *is*," said the Queen. "I mean, the dromes . . . well, they're not much more than a kind of walking sponge, really. Their world is ancient. It's nearly dead. They're not really *creative* anymore. With a little help from me, your people could be a lot better. Because, you see, you dream all the time. *You*, especially, dream all the time. Your picture of the world is a landscape with you in the middle of it, isn't it? Wonderful. Look at you, in that rather horrible dress and those clumpy boots.

You dreamed you could invade my world with a frying pan. You had this dream about Brave Girl Rescuing Little Brother. You thought you were the heroine of a *story*. And then you left him behind. You know, I think being hit by a billion tons of seawater must be like having a mountain of iron drop on your head, don't you?"

Tiffany couldn't think. Her head was full of hot, pink fog. It *hadn't* worked.

Her Third Thoughts were somewhere in the fog, trying to make themselves heard.

"Got Roland out," she muttered, still staring at her boots.

"But he's not yours," said the Queen. "He is, let us face it, a rather stupid boy with a big red face and brains made of pork, just like his father. You left your little brother behind with a bunch of little thieves and you rescued a spoiled little fool."

There was no *time*! shrieked Tiffany's Third Thoughts. You wouldn't have got to him *and* got back to the lighthouse! You nearly didn't get away as it was! You got Roland out! It was the logical thing to do! You don't have to be guilty about it! What's better, to try to save your brother and be brave, courageous, stupid, and dead, or save the boy and be brave, courageous, sensible, and alive?

But something kept saying that stupid and dead would have been more . . . right.

Something kept saying: Would you say to Mum that you could see there wasn't time to rescue your brother so you rescued someone else instead? Would she be *pleased* that you'd worked that out? Being right doesn't always work.

It's the Queen! yelled her Third Thoughts. It's her voice! It's like hypnotism! You've got to stop listening!

"I expect it's not your fault you're so cold and heartless," said the Queen. "It's probably all to do with your parents. They probably never gave you enough time. And having Wentworth was a very cruel thing to do—they really should have been more careful. And they let you read too many books. It can't be good for a young brain, knowing words like *paradigm* and *eschatological*. It leads to behavior such as using your own brother as monster bait." The Queen sighed. "Sadly, that kind of thing happens all the time. I think you should be proud of not being worse than just deeply introverted and socially maladjusted."

She walked around Tiffany.

"It's so sad," she continued. "You dream that you are strong, sensible, logical . . . the kind of person who always has a bit of string. But that's just your excuse for not being really, properly human: You're just a brain, no heart at all. You didn't even cry when Granny Aching died. You *think* too much, and now your precious thinking has let *you* down. Well, *I* think it's best if I just kill you, don't you?"

Find a stone! her Third Thoughts screamed. Hit her!

Tiffany was aware of other figures in the gloom. There were some of the people from the summer pictures, but there were also dromes and the headless horseman and the Bumblebee women.

Around her, frost crept over the ground.

"I think we'll like it here," said the Queen.

Tiffany felt the cold creeping up her legs. Her Third Thoughts, hoarse with effort, shouted: Do *something*!

She should have been better organized, she thought dully. She shouldn't have relied on dreams. Or . . . perhaps I should have been a real human being. More . . . feeling. But I couldn't help not crying! It just wouldn't come! And how can I stop thinking? And thinking about thinking? And even thinking about thinking about thinking?

She saw the smile in the Queen's eyes, and thought: Which one of all those people doing all that thinking is *me*?

Is there really any *me* at all?

Clouds poured across the sky like a stain. They covered the stars. They were the inky clouds from the frozen world, the clouds of nightmare. It began to rain, rain with ice in it. It hit the turf like bullets, turning it into chalky mud. The wind howled like a pack of grimhounds.

Tiffany managed to take a step forward. The mud sucked at her boots.

"A bit of spirit at last?" said the Queen, stepping back.

Tiffany tried another step, but things were not working anymore. She was too cold and too tired. She could feel her *self* disappearing, getting lost.

"So sad, to end like this," said the Queen.

Tiffany fell forward, into the freezing mud.

The rain grew harder, stinging like needles, hammering on her head and running like icy tears down her cheeks. It struck so hard, it left her breathless.

She felt the cold drawing all the heat out of her. And that was the only sensation left, apart from a musical note.

It sounded like the smell of snow, or the sparkle of frost. It was high and thin and drawn out.

She couldn't feel the ground under her and there was nothing to see, not even the stars. The clouds had covered everything.

She was so cold, she couldn't *feel* the cold anymore, or her fingers. A thought managed to trickle through her freezing mind. Is there any me at all? Or do my thoughts just dream of me?

The blackness grew deeper. Night was never as black as this, and winter never as cold. It was colder than the deep winters when the snow came down and Granny Aching would plod from snowdrift to snowdrift, looking for warm bodies. The sheep could survive the snow if the shepherd had some wits, Granny used to say. The snow kept the cold away, the sheep surviving in warm hollows under roofs of snow while bitter wind blew harmlessly over them.

But this was as cold as those days when even the snow couldn't fall, and the wind was pure cold itself, blowing ice crystals across the turf. Those were the killer days in early spring, when the lambing had begun and winter came howling down one more time.

There was darkness everywhere, bitter and starless.

There was a speck of light, a long way off.

One star. Low down. Moving . . .

It got bigger in the stormy night.

It zigzagged as it came.

Silence covered Tiffany and drew her into itself.

The silence smelled of sheep, and turpentine, and tobacco.

And then came movement, as if she was falling through the ground, very fast.

And gentle warmth and, just for a moment, the sound of waves.

And her own voice, inside her head.

This land is in my bones.

Land under wave.

Whiteness.

It tumbled through the warm, heavy darkness around her, something like snow but as fine as dust. It piled up somewhere below her, because she could see a faint whiteness.

A creature like an ice-cream cone with lots of tentacles shot past her and jetted away.

I'm underwater, thought Tiffany.

I remember . . .

This is the million-year rain under the sea, this is the new land being born underneath an ocean. It's not a dream. It's . . . a memory. The land under wave. Millions and millions of tiny shells . . .

This land was *alive*.

All the time there was the warm, comforting smell of the shepherding hut, and the feeling of being held in invisible hands.

The whiteness below her rose up and over her head, but it didn't seem uncomfortable. It was like being in a mist.

Now I'm inside the chalk, like a flint, like a calkin . . .

She wasn't sure how long she spent in the warm deep water, or if indeed any time really had passed, or if the millions of years went past in a second, but she felt movement again, and a sense of rising.

More memories poured into her mind.

There's always been someone watching the borders. They didn't decide to. It was decided for them. Someone has to care. Sometimes they have to fight. Someone has to speak for that which has no voice. . . .

She opened her eyes. She was still lying in the mud, and the Queen was laughing at her, and overhead the storm still raged.

But she felt warm. In fact, she felt hot, red-hot with anger . . . anger at the bruised turf, anger at her own stupidity, anger at this beautiful creature whose only talent was control.

This . . . creature was trying to take her *world*.

All witches are selfish, the Queen had said. But Tiffany's Third Thoughts said: Then turn selfishness into a weapon! Make all things yours! Make other lives and dreams and hopes yours! Protect them! Save them! Bring them into the sheepfold! Walk the gale for them! Keep away the wolf! My dreams! My brother! My family! My land! My world! How dare you try to take these things, because *they are mine!*

I have a duty!

The anger overflowed. She stood up, clenched her fists, and screamed at the storm, putting into the scream all the rage that was inside her.

Lightning struck the ground on either side of her. It did so twice.

And it stayed there, crackling, and two dogs formed.

Steam rose from their coats, and blue light sparked from their ears as they shook themselves. They looked attentively at Tiffany.

The Queen gasped and vanished.

"Come by, Lightning!" shouted Tiffany. "Away to me, Thunder!" And she remembered the time when she'd run across the downs, falling over, shouting all the wrong things, while the two dogs had done exactly what needed to be done.

Two streaks of black and white sped away across the turf and up toward the clouds.

They herded the storm.

Clouds panicked and scattered, but always there was a comet streaking across the sky and they were turned. Monstrous shapes writhed and screamed in the boiling sky, but Thunder and Lightning had worked many flocks; there was an occasional snap of lightning-sparked teeth, and a wail. Tiffany stared upward, rain pouring off her face, and shouted commands that no dog could possibly have heard.

Jostling and rumbling and screaming, the storm rolled off the hills and away toward the mountains, where there were deep canyons that could pen it.

Out of breath, glowing with triumph, Tiffany watched until the dogs came back and settled, once again, on the turf. And then she remembered something else: It *didn't* matter *what* orders she gave those dogs. They were not her dogs. They were working dogs.

Thunder and Lightning didn't take orders from a little girl.

And the dogs weren't looking at her.

They were looking just behind her.

She'd have turned if someone had told her a horrible monster was behind her. She'd have turned if they'd said it had a thousand teeth. She didn't want to turn around now. Forcing herself was the hardest thing she'd ever done.

She was not afraid of what she might see. She was terribly, mortally frightened, afraid to the center of her bones of what she might not see. She shut her eyes while her cowardly boots shuffled her around and then, after a deep breath, she opened them again.

There was a gust of Jolly Sailor tobacco, and sheep, and turpentine.

Sparkling in the dark, light glittering off the white shepherdess dress and every blue ribbon and silver buckle of it, was Granny Aching, smiling hugely, radiant with pride. In one hand she held the huge ornamental crook, hung with blue bows.

She pirouetted slowly, and Tiffany saw that while she was a brilliant, sparkling shepherdess from hat to hem, she still had her huge old boots on.

Granny Aching took her pipe out of her mouth and gave Tiffany the little nod that was, from her, a round of applause. And then—she wasn't.

Real starlit darkness covered the turf, and the nighttime sounds filled the air. Tiffany didn't know if what had just happened was a dream or had happened somewhere that wasn't quite *here* or had happened only in her head. It didn't matter. It had *happened*. And now—

"But I'm still here," said the Queen, stepping in front of her. "Perhaps it *was* all a dream. Perhaps you have gone a little mad, because you are after all a very strange child. Perhaps you had help. How good are *you?* Do you really think that *you* can face me alone? I can make you think whatever I please—"

"Crivens!"

"Oh no, not *them*," said the Queen, throwing up her hands.

It wasn't just the Nac Mac Feegle but also Wentworth, a strong smell of seaweed, a lot of water, and a dead shark. They appeared in midair and landed in a heap between Tiffany and the Queen. But a pictsie was always ready for a fight, and they bounced, rolled, and came up drawing their swords and shaking seawater out of their hair.

"Oh, 'tis you, izzut?" said Rob Anybody, glaring up at the Queen. "Face to face wi' ye at last, ye bloustie ol' callyack that ye are! Ye canna' come here, unnerstan'? Be off wi' ye! Are ye goin' to go quietly?"

The Queen stamped heavily on him. When she took her foot away, only the top of his head was visible above the turf.

"Well, are ye?" he said, pulling himself out as if nothing had happened. "I don't want tae have tae lose my temper wi' ye! An' it's no good sendin' your pets against us, 'cause you ken we can take 'em tae the cleaners!" He turned to Tiffany, who hadn't moved. "You just leave this tae us, kelda. Us an' the Quin, we go way back!"

The Queen snapped her fingers. "Always leaping into things you don't understand," she hissed. "Well, can you face these?"

Every Nac Mac Feegle sword suddenly glowed blue.

Back in the crowd of eerily lit pictsies, a voice that sounded very much like that of Daft Wullie said:

"Ach, we're in *real* trouble noo . . ."

Three figures had appeared in the air, a little way away. The middle one, Tiffany saw, had a long red gown, a strange long wig, and black tights with buckles on his shoes. The others were just ordinary men, it seemed, in ordinary gray suits.

"Oh, ye are a harrrrrd wumman, Quin," said William the gonnagle, "to set the lawyers ontae us."

"See the one on the left there," whimpered a pictsie. "See, he's got a briefcase! It's a *briefcase*! Oh, waily, waily, a briefcase, waily . . ."

Reluctantly, a step at a time, pressing together in terror, the Nac Mac Feegle began to back away.

"Oh, waily waily, he's snappin' the clasps," groaned Daft Wullie. "Oh, waily waily waily, 'tis the sound o' Doom when a lawyer does that!"

"Mister Rob Anybody Feegle and sundry others?" said one of the figures in a dreadful voice.

"There's naebody here o' that name!" shouted Rob Anybody. "We dinna know anythin'!"

"We have here a list of criminal and civil charges totaling nineteen thousand, seven hundred and sixty-three separate offenses—"

"We wasna there!" yelled Rob Anybody desperately. "Isn't that right, lads?"

"—including more than two thousand cases of Making an Affray, Causing a Public Nuisance, Being Found Drunk, Being Found Very Drunk, Using Offensive Language (taking into account ninety-seven counts of Using Language That Was Probably Offensive If Anyone Else Could Understand It), Committing a Breach of the Peace, Malicious Lingering—"

"It's mistaken identity!" shouted Rob Anybody. "It's no' oour fault! We wuz only standing there an' someone else did it and ran awa'!"

"—Grand Theft, Petty Theft, Burglary, Housebreaking, Loitering with Intent to Commit a Felony—"

"We wuz misunderstood when we was wee bairns!" yelled Rob Anybody. "Ye're only pickin' on us 'cause we're blue! We always get blamed for everythin'! The polis hate us! We wasna even in the country!"

But, to groans from the cowering pictsies, one of the lawyers produced a big roll of paper from his briefcase. He cleared his throat and read out: "Angus, Big; Angus, Not-as-big-as-Big-Angus; Angus, Wee; Archie, Big; Archie, One-Eyed; Archie, Wee Mad—"

"They've got oour names!" sobbed Daft Wullie. "They've got oour *names*! It's the pris'n hoose for us!"

"Objection! I move for a writ of *habeas corpus*," said a small voice. "And enter a plea of *vis-ne faciem capite repletam*, without prejudice."

There was absolute silence for a moment. Rob Anybody turned to look at the frightened Nac Mac Feegle and said: "Okay, okay, which of youse said that?"

The toad crawled out of the crowd and sighed. "It suddenly all came back to me," he said. "I remember what I was now. The legal language brought it all back. I'm a toad now, but"—he swallowed—"once I was a lawyer. And this, people, is illegal. These charges are a complete tissue of lies based on hearsay evidence."

He raised yellow eyes toward the Queen's lawyers. "I further move that the case be adjourned *sine die* on the basis of *potest-ne mater tua suere, amice*."

The lawyers had pulled large books out of nowhere and were thumbing through them hastily.

"We're not familiar with counsel's terminology," said one of them.

"Hey, they're sweatin'," said Rob Anybody. "You mean we can have lawyers on *oour* side as well?"

"Yes, of course," said the toad. "You can have defense lawyers."

"Defense?" said Rob Anybody. "Are you tellin' me we could get awa' wi' it 'cause of a tishoo o' lies?"

"Certainly," said the toad. "And with all the treasure you've stolen, you can pay enough to be very innocent indeed. My fee will be—"

He gulped as a dozen glowing swords were swung toward him.

"I've just remembered *why* that fairy godmother turned me into a toad," he said. "So, in the circumstances, I'll take this case *pro bono publico*."

The swords didn't move.

"That means for free," he added.

"Oh, right, we like the sound o' that," said Rob Anybody, to the sound of swords being sheathed. "How come ye're a lawyer *an'* a toad?"

"Oh, well, it was just bit of an argument," said the toad. "A fairy godmother gave my client three wishes—the usual health, wealth, and happiness package—and when my client woke up one wet morning and didn't feel *particularly* happy, she got me to bring an action for breach of contract. It was a definite first in the history of fairy godmothering. Unfortunately, as it turned out, so was turning the client into a small hand mirror and her lawyer, as you see before you, into a toad. I think the worst part was when the judge applauded. That was hurtful, in my opinion."

"But ye can still remember all that legal stuff? *Guid*," said Rob Anybody. He glared at the other lawyers. "Hey, youse scunners, we got a cheap lawyer and we're no' afraid tae use him!"

The other lawyers were pulling more and more paperwork out

of the air now. They looked worried, and a little frightened. Rob Anybody's eyes gleamed as he watched them.

"What does all that viznee-facey-em stuff mean, my learned friend?" he said.

"*Vis-ne faciem capite repletam,*" said the toad. "It was the best I could do in a hurry, but it means, approximately"—he gave a little cough—"'Would you like a face which is full of head?'"

"And tae think we didna know legal talkin' was that simple," said Rob Anybody. "We could all be lawyers, lads, if we knew the fancy words! Let's *get* them!"

The Nac Mac Feegle could change mood in a moment, especially at the sound of a battle cry. They raised their swords in the air.

"*Twelve hundred angry men!*" they shouted.

"*Nae more courtroom drama!*"

"*We ha' the law on oour side!*"

"*The law's made to tak' care o' raskills!*"

"No," said the Queen, and waved her hand.

Lawyers and pictsies faded away. There was just her and Tiffany, facing one another on the turf at dawn, the wind hissing around the stones.

"What have you done with them?" Tiffany shouted.

"Oh, they're around . . . somewhere," said the Queen airily. "It's all dreams, anyway. And dreams within dreams. You can't rely on anything, little girl. Nothing is real. Nothing lasts. Everything goes. All you can do is learn to dream. And it's too late for that. And I . . . I have had longer to learn."

Tiffany wasn't sure which of her thoughts was operating now. She was tired. She felt as though she was watching herself from above and a little behind. She saw herself set her boots firmly on the turf, and then . . .

. . . and then . . .

. . . and then, like someone rising from the clouds of a sleep, she felt the deep, deep Time below her. She sensed the breath of the downs and the distant roar of ancient, ancient seas trapped in millions of tiny shells. She thought of Granny Aching, under the turf, becoming part of the chalk again, part of the land under wave. She felt as if huge wheels, of time and stars, were turning slowly around her.

She opened her eyes and then, somewhere inside, opened her eyes again.

She heard the grass growing, and the sound of worms below the turf. She could feel the thousands of little lives around her, smell all the scents on the breeze, and see all the shades of the night.

The wheels of stars and years, of space and time, locked into place. She knew exactly where she was, and who she was, and what she was.

She swung a hand. The Queen tried to stop her, but she might as well have tried to stop a wheel of years. Tiffany's hand caught her face and knocked her off her feet.

"Now I know why I never cried for Granny," she said. "She has never left me."

She leaned down, and centuries bent with her.

"The secret is not to dream," she whispered. "The secret is to wake up. Waking up is harder. I have woken up and I am real. I know where I come from and I know where I'm going. You cannot fool me anymore. Or touch me. Or anything that is mine."

I'll never be like this again, she thought, as she saw the terror in the Queen's face. I'll never again feel as tall as the sky and as old as the hills and as strong as the sea. I've been given something for a while, and the price of it is that I have to give it back.

And the *reward* is giving it back, too. No human could live like this. You could spend a day looking at a flower to see how wonderful it is, and that wouldn't get the milking done. No wonder we dream our way through our lives. To be awake, and see it all as it really is . . . no one could stand that for long.

She took a deep breath and picked the Queen up. She was aware of things happening, of dreams roaring around her, but they didn't affect her. She was real and she was awake, more aware than she'd ever been. She had to concentrate even to think against the storm of sensations pouring into her mind.

The Queen was as light as a baby and changed shape madly in Tiffany's arms—into monsters and mixed-up beasts, things with claws and tentacles. But at last she was small and gray, like a monkey, with a large head and big eyes and a little downy chest that went up and down as she panted.

She reached the stones. The arch still stood. It was never down, Tiffany thought. The Queen had no strength, no magic, just one trick. The worst one.

"Stay away from here," said Tiffany. "Never come back. Never touch what is mine." And then, because the thing was so weak and babylike, she added: "But I hope there's someone who'll cry for you. I hope the king comes back."

"You *pity* me?" growled the thing that had been the Queen.

"Yes. A bit," said Tiffany. "But don't count on it."

She put the creature down. It scampered across the snow of Fairyland, turned, and became the beautiful Queen again.

"You won't win," the Queen said. "There's always a way in. People dream."

"Sometimes we waken," said Tiffany. "Don't come back . . . or there *will be* a reckoning. . . ."

She concentrated, and now the stones framed nothing more—or less—than the country beyond.

I shall have to find a way of sealing that, said her Third Thoughts. Or her Twentieth Thoughts, perhaps. Her head was *full* of thoughts.

She managed to walk a little way and then sat down, hugging her knees. Imagine getting stuck like this, she thought. You'd have to wear earplugs and noseplugs and a big black hood over your head, and *still* you'd see and hear too much . . .

She closed her eyes, and closed her eyes again.

She felt it all draining away. It *was* like falling asleep, sliding from that strange wide-awakeness into just normal, everyday . . . well, being awake. It felt as if everything was blurred and muffled.

This is how we always feel, she thought. We sleepwalk through our lives, because how could we live if we were always this awake?

Someone tapped her on the boot.

CHAPTER 14

Small, Like Oak Trees

❧

"Hey, where did you get to?" shouted Rob Anybody, glaring up at her. "One minute we was just aboout to give them lawyers a good legal seein'-to, next minute you and the Quin wuz gone!"

Dreams within dreams, Tiffany thought, holding her head. But they were over, and you couldn't look at the Nac Mac Feegle and not know what was real.

"It's over," she said.

"Didja kill her?"

"No."

"She'll be back then," said Rob Anybody. "She's awfu' stupid, that one. Clever with the dreaming, I'll grant ye, but not a brain in her heid."

Tiffany nodded. The blurred feeling was going. The moment of wide-awakeness was fading like a dream. *But I must remember that it wasn't a dream.*

"How did you get away from the huge wave?" she asked.

"Ach, we're fast movers," said Rob Anybody. "An' it was a strong lighthoose. O' course, the water came up pretty high."

"A few sharks were involved, that kind of thing," said Not-as-big-as-Medium-Sized-Jock-but-bigger-than-Wee-Jock-Jock.

"Oh, aye, a few sharkies," said Rob Anybody, shrugging. "And one o' them octopussies—"

"It was a giant squid," said William the gonnagle.

"Aye, well, it was a kebab pretty quickly," said Daft Wullie.

"Ha' a heidful o' heid, you wee weewee!" shouted Wentworth, overcome with wit.

William coughed politely. "And the big wave threw up a lot of sunken vessels full o' trrrreasure," he said. "We stopped off for a wee pillage."

The Nac Mac Feegle held up wonderful jewels and big gold coins.

"But that's just dream treasure, surely?" said Tiffany. "Fairy gold! It'll turn into rubbish in the morning!"

"Aye?" said Rob Anybody. He glanced at the horizon. "Okay, ye heard the kelda, lads! We got mebbe half an hour to sell it to someone! Permission to go offski?" he added to Tiffany.

"Er . . . oh, yes. Fine. Thank you—"

They were gone, in a split-second blur of blue and red.

But William the gonnagle remained for a moment. He bowed to Tiffany.

"Ye didna do at all badly," he said. "We're proud o' ye. So would yer grrranny be. Remember that. Ye are not unloved."

Then he vanished too.

There was a groan from Roland, lying on the turf. He began to move.

"Weewee men all gone," said Wentworth sadly in the silence that followed. "Crivens all gone."

"What *were* they?" muttered Roland, sitting up and holding his head.

"It's all a bit complicated," said Tiffany. "Er . . . do you remember much?"

"It all seems like . . . a dream . . ." said Roland. "I remember . . . the sea, and we were running, and I cracked a nut which was full of those little men, and I was hunting in this huge forest with shadows—"

"Dreams can be very funny things," said Tiffany carefully. She went to stand up and thought: I must wait here awhile. I don't know why I know, I just know. Perhaps I knew and have forgotten. But I must wait for something.

"Can you walk down to the village?" she said.

"Oh, yes. I think so. But what did—?"

"Then will you take Wentworth with you, please? I'd like to . . . rest for a while."

"Are you sure?" said Roland, looking concerned.

"Yes. I won't be long. Please? You can drop him off at the farm. Tell my parents I'll be down soon. Tell them I'm fine."

"Weewee men," said Wentworth. "Crivens! Want bed."

Roland was still looking uncertain.

"Off you go!" Tiffany commanded, and waved him away.

When the two of the them had disappeared below the brow of the hill, with several backward glances, she sat between the four iron wheels and hugged her knees.

She could see, far off, the mound of the Nac Mac Feegle. Already they were a slightly puzzling memory, and she'd seen them only a few minutes ago. But when they'd gone, they'd left the impression of never having been there.

She could go to the mound and see if she could find the big hole. But supposing it wasn't there? Or supposing it was, but all there was down there was rabbits?

No, it's all true, she said to herself. *I must remember that, too.*

A buzzard screamed in the dawn grayness. She looked up as it circled into sunlight, and a tiny dot detached itself from the bird.

That was far too high up even for a pictsie to stand the fall.

Tiffany scrambled to her feet as Hamish tumbled through the sky. And then—something ballooned above him, and the fall became just a gentle floating, like thistledown.

The bulging shape above Hamish was Y-shaped. As it got bigger, the shape become more precise, more . . . familiar.

He landed, and a pair of Tiffany's pants, the long-legged ones with the rosebud pattern, settled down on top of him.

"That was *great!*" he said, pushing his way through the folds of fabric. "Nae more landin' on my heid for me!"

"They're my best pants," said Tiffany wearily. "You stole them off our clothesline, didn't you?"

"Oh aye. Nice and clean," said Hamish. "I had to cut the lace off 'cause it got in the way, but I put it aside and ye could easily sew it on again." He gave Tiffany the big grin of someone who, for once, has not dived heavily into the ground.

She sighed. She'd liked the lace. She didn't have many things that weren't necessary. "I think you'd better keep them," she said.

"Aye, I will, then," said Hamish. "Noo, what wuz it? Oh, yes. Ye have visitors comin'. I spotted them out over the valley. Look up there."

There were two other things up there, bigger than a buzzard, so high that they were already in full sunlight. Tiffany watched as they circled lower.

They were broomsticks.

I knew I had to wait! Tiffany thought.

Her ears bubbled. She turned and saw Hamish running across the grass. As she looked, the buzzard picked him up and sped onward. She wondered if he was frightened or, at least, didn't want to meet whoever was coming

The broomsticks descended.

The lowest one had two figures on it. As it landed, Tiffany saw that one of them was Miss Tick, clinging anxiously to a smaller figure who'd been doing the steering. She half climbed off, half fell off, and tottered over to Tiffany.

"You wouldn't believe the time I've had," she said. "It was just a nightmare! We flew through the storm! Are you all right?"

"Er . . . yes . . ."

"What happened?"

Tiffany looked at her. How did you begin to answer something like that?

"The Queen's gone," she said. That seemed to cover it.

"What? The Queen has *gone*? Oh . . . er . . . these ladies are Mrs. Ogg—"

"Mornin'," said the broomstick's other occupant, who was pulling at her long black dress, from under the folds of which came the sounds of twanging elastic. "The wind up there blows where it likes, I don't mind telling you!" She was a short fat lady with a cheerful face like an apple that had been stored too long; all the wrinkles moved into different positions when she smiled.

"And this," said Miss Tick, "is Miss—"

"Mistress," snapped the other witch.

"I'm so sorry, *Mistress* Weatherwax," said Miss Tick. "Very, *very* good witches," she whispered to Tiffany. "I was very lucky to find them. They *respect* witches up in the mountains."

Tiffany was impressed that anyone could make Miss Tick

flustered, but the other witch seemed to do it just by standing there. She was tall—except, Tiffany realized, she wasn't *that* tall, but she *stood* tall, which could easily fool you if you weren't paying attention—and like the other witch wore a rather shabby black dress. She had an elderly, thin face that gave nothing away. Piercing blue eyes looked Tiffany up and down, from head to toe.

"You've got good boots," said the witch.

"Tell Mistress Weatherwax what happened," Miss Tick began. But the witch held up a hand, and Miss Tick stopped talking immediately. Tiffany was even more impressed now.

Mistress Weatherwax gave Tiffany a look that went right through her head and about five miles out the other side. Then she walked over to the stones and waved one hand. It was an odd movement, a kind of wriggle in the air, but for a moment it left a glowing line. There was a noise, a chord, as though all sorts of sounds were happening at the same time. It snapped into silence.

"Jolly Sailor tobacco?" said the witch.

"Yes," said Tiffany.

The witch waved a hand again. There was another sharp, complicated noise. Mistress Weatherwax turned suddenly and stared at the distant pimple that was the pictsie mound.

"Nac Mac Feegle? *Kelda?*" she demanded.

"Er, yes. Only temporary," said Tiffany.

"Hmmph," said Mistress Weatherwax.

Wave. Sound.

"Frying pan?"

"Yes. It got lost, though."

"Hmm."

Wave. Sound. It was as if the woman was extracting her history from the air.

"Filled buckets?"

"And they filled up the log box, too," said Tiffany.

Wave. Sound.

"I see. Special Sheep Liniment?"

"Yes, my father says it puts—"

Wave. Sound.

"Ah. Land of snow." Wave. Sound. "A queen." Wave. Sound. "Fighting." Wave, sound. "On the sea?" Wave, sound, wave, sound . . .

Mistress Weatherwax stared at the flashing air, looking at pictures only she could see. Mrs. Ogg sat down beside Tiffany, her little legs going up in the air as she made herself comfortable.

"I've tried Jolly Sailor," she said. "Smells like toenails, don't it?"

"Yes, it does!" said Tiffany, gratefully.

"To be a kelda of the Nac Mac Feegle, you have to marry one of 'em, don't you?" said Mrs. Ogg innocently.

"Ah, yes, but I found a way around that," said Tiffany. She told her. Mrs. Ogg laughed. It was a sociable kind of laugh, the sort of laugh that makes you comfortable.

The noise and flashing stopped. Mistress Weatherwax stood staring at nothing for a moment and then said: "You beat the Queen, at the end. But you had help, I think."

"Yes, I did," said Tiffany.

"And that was—?"

"I don't ask you *your* business," said Tiffany, before she even realized she was going to say it. Miss Tick gasped. Mrs. Ogg's eyes twinkled, and she looked from Tiffany to Mistress Weatherwax like someone watching a tennis match.

"Tiffany, Mistress Weatherwax is the most famous witch in all—" Miss Tick began severely, but the witch waved a hand at her again. I really must learn how to do that, Tiffany thought.

Then Mistress Weatherwax took off her pointed hat and bowed to Tiffany.

"Well said," she said, straightening up and staring directly at Tiffany. "I didn't have no right to ask you. This is your country—we're here by your leave. I show you respect *as you in turn will respect me*." The air seemed to freeze for a moment and the skies to darken. Then Mistress Weatherwax went on, as if the moment of thunder hadn't happened: "But if one day you care to tell me more, I should be grateful to hear about it," she said, in a conversational voice. "And them creatures that look like they're made of dough, I should like to know more about them, too. Never run across them before. And your grandmother sounds the kind of person I would have liked to meet." She straightened up. "In the meantime, we'd better see if there's anything left you can still be taught."

"Is this where I learn about the witches' school?" said Tiffany.

There was a moment of silence.

"Witches' school?" said Mistress Weatherwax.

"Um," said Miss Tick.

"You were being metapahorrical, weren't you?" said Tiffany.

"Metapahorrical?" said Mrs. Ogg, wrinkling her forehead.

"She means metaphorical," mumbled Miss Tick.

"It's like stories," said Tiffany. "It's all right. I worked it out. *This* is the school, isn't it? The magic place? The world. Here. And you don't realize it until you look. Do you know the pictsies think this world is heaven? We just don't look. You can't give lessons on witchcraft. Not properly. It's all about how you are . . . you, I suppose."

"Nicely said," said Mistress Weatherwax. "You're sharp. But there's magic, too. You'll pick that up. It don't take much intelligence, otherwise wizards wouldn't be able to do it."

"You'll need a job, too," said Mrs. Ogg. "There's no money in witchcraft. Can't do magic for yourself, see? Cast-iron rule."

"I make good cheese," said Tiffany.

"Cheese, eh?" said Mistress Weatherwax. "Hmm. Yes. Cheese is good. But do you know anything about medicines? Midwifery? That's a good portable skill."

"Well, I've helped deliver difficult lambs," said Tiffany. "And I saw my brother being born. They didn't bother to turn me out. It didn't look too difficult. But I think cheese is probably easier, and less noisy."

"Cheese is good," Mistress Weatherwax repeated, nodding. "Cheese is alive."

"And what do you *really* do?" said Tiffany.

The thin witch hesitated for a moment, and then:

"We look to . . . the edges," said Mistress Weatherwax. "There's a lot of edges, more than people know. Between life and death, this world and the next, night and day, right and wrong . . . an' they need watchin'. We watch 'em, we guard the sum of things. And we never ask for any reward. That's important."

"People give us stuff, mind you. People can be very gen'rous to witches," said Mrs. Ogg happily. "On bakin' days in our village, sometimes I can't move for cake. There's ways and ways of not askin', if you get my meaning. People like to see a happy witch."

"But down here people think witches are bad!" said Tiffany, but her Second Thoughts added: *Remember how rarely Granny Aching ever had to buy her own tobacco?*

"It's amazin' what people can get used to," said Mrs. Ogg. "You just have to start slow."

"And we have to hurry," said Mistress Weatherwax. "There's a man riding up here on a farm horse. Fair hair, red face—"

"It sounds like my father!"

"Well, he's making the poor thing gallop," said Mistress Weatherwax. "Quick, now. You want to learn the skills? When can you leave home?"

"Pardon?" said Tiffany.

"Don't the girls here go off to work as maids and things?" said Mrs. Ogg.

"Oh, yes. When they're a bit older than me."

"Well, when you're a bit older than you, Miss Tick here will come and find you," said Mistress Weatherwax. Miss Tick nodded. "There're elderly witches up in the mountains who'll pass on what they know in exchange for a bit of help around the cottage. This place will be watched over while you're gone, you may depend on it. In the meantime you'll get three meals a day, your own bed, use of broomstick . . . that's the way we do it. All right?"

"Yes," said Tiffany, grinning happily. The wonderful moment was passing too quickly for all the questions she wanted to ask. "Yes! But, er . . ."

"Yes?" said Mrs. Ogg.

"I don't have to dance around with no clothes on or anything like that, do I? Only I heard rumors—"

Mistress Weatherwax rolled her eyes.

Mrs. Ogg grinned cheerfully. "Well, that procedure does have something to recommend it—" she began.

"No, you don't have to!" snapped Mistress Weatherwax. "No cottage made of sweets, no cackling, and no dancing!"

"Unless you want to," said Mrs. Ogg, standing up. "There's no harm in an occasional cackle, if the mood takes you that way. I'd teach you a good one right now, but we really ought to be going."

"But . . . but how did you manage it?" said Miss Tick to Tiffany. "This is all chalk! You've become a witch on chalk? How?"

"That's all *you* know, Perspicacia Tick," said Mistress Weatherwax. "The *bones* of the hills is flint. It's hard and sharp and useful. King of stones." She picked up her broomstick and turned back to Tiffany. "Will you get into trouble, do you think?" she said.

"I might," said Tiffany.

"Do you want any help?"

"If it's my trouble, I'll get out of it," said Tiffany. She wanted to say: Yes, yes! I'm going to need help! I don't know what's going to happen when my father gets here! The Baron's probably gotten really angry! But I don't want them to think I can't deal with my own problems. I ought to be able to cope.

"That's right," said Mistress Weatherwax.

Tiffany wondered if the witch could read minds.

"Minds? No," said Mistress Weatherwax, climbing onto her broomstick. "Faces, yes. Come here, young lady."

Tiffany obeyed.

"The thing about witchcraft," said Mistress Weatherwax, "is that it's not like school at all. *First* you get the test, and then afterward you spend years findin' out how you passed it. It's a bit like life in that respect." She reached out and gently raised Tiffany's chin so that she could look into her face.

"I see you opened your eyes," she said.

"Yes."

"Good. Many people never do. Times ahead might be a little tricky, even so. You'll need this."

She stretched out a hand and made a circle in the air around Tiffany's head, then brought her hand up over the head while making little movements with her forefinger.

Tiffany raised her hands to her head. For a moment she thought there was nothing there, and then they touched . . . something. It was more like a sensation in the air; if you weren't expecting it to be there, your fingers passed straight through.

"Is it *really* there?" she said.

"Who knows?" said the witch. "It's *virtually* a pointy hat. No one else will know it's there. It might be a comfort."

"You mean it just exists in my head?" said Tiffany.

"You've got lots of things in your head. That doesn't mean they aren't real. Best not to ask me too many questions."

"What happened to the toad?" said Miss Tick, who *did* ask questions.

"He's gone off with the Wee Free Men," said Tiffany. "It turned out he used to be a lawyer."

"You've given a clan of the Nac Mac Feegle their own lawyer?" said Mrs. Ogg. "That'll make the world tremble. Still, I always say the occasional tremble does you good."

"Come, sisters, we must away," said Miss Tick, who had climbed on the other broomstick behind Mrs. Ogg.

"There's no need for that sort of talk," said Mrs. Ogg. "That's theater talk, that is. Cheerio, Tiff. We'll see you again."

Her stick rose gently into the air. From the stick of Mistress Weatherwax, though, there was merely a sad little noise, like the *thwop* of Miss Tick's hat point. The broomstick went *kshugagugah.*

Mistress Weatherwax sighed. "It's them dwarfs," she said. "They *say* they've repaired it, oh yes, and it starts first time in their workshop—"

They heard the sound of distant hooves. With surprising speed, Mistress Weatherwax swung herself off the stick, grabbed it firmly in both hands, and ran away across the turf, skirts billowing behind her.

She was a speck in the distance when Tiffany's father came over the brow of the hill on one of the farm horses. He hadn't even stopped to put the leather shoes on it; great slices of earth flew up as hooves the size of large soup plates,* each one shod with iron, bit into the turf.

Tiffany heard a faint *kshugagugahvvvvvooom* behind her as he leaped off the horse.

She was surprised to see him laughing and crying at the same time.

◆ ◆ ◆

It was all a bit of a dream.

Tiffany found that a very useful thing to say. It's hard to remember, it was all a bit of a dream. It was all a bit of a dream, I can't be certain.

The overjoyed Baron, however, was very certain. Obviously this—this Queen woman, whoever she was, had been stealing children but Roland had beaten her, oh yes, and helped these two young children to get back as well.

Her mother had insisted on Tiffany's going to bed, even though it was broad daylight. Actually, she *didn't* mind. She was tired, and lay under the covers in that nice pink world halfway between asleep and awake.

She heard the Baron and her father talking downstairs. She heard the story being woven between them as they tried to make sense of it all. Obviously the girl had been very brave (this was the Baron speaking), but well, she was nine, wasn't she? And didn't even know how to use a sword! Whereas Roland had had fencing lessons at his school . . .

---

*Probably about eleven inches across. Tiffany didn't measure them this time.

And so it went on. There were other things she heard her parents discussing later, when the Baron had gone. There was the way Ratbag now lived on the roof, for example.

Tiffany lay in bed and smelled the ointment her mother had rubbed into her temples. Tiffany must have been hit on the head, she'd said, because of the way she kept on touching it.

So . . . Roland with the beefy face was the hero, was he? And she was just like the stupid princess who broke her ankle and fainted all the time? That was *completely* unfair!

She reached out to the little table beside her bed where she'd put the invisible hat. Her mother had put down a cup of broth right through it, but it was still there. Tiffany's fingers felt, very faintly, the roughness of the brim.

We never ask for any reward, she thought. Besides, it was her secret, all of it. No one else knew about the Wee Free Men. Admittedly Wentworth had taken to running through the house with a tablecloth around his waist shouting, "Weewee mens! I'll scone you in the boot!" but Mrs. Aching was still so glad to see him back, and so happy that he was talking about things other than sweets, that she wasn't paying too much attention to what he *was* talking about.

No, she couldn't tell anyone. They'd never believe her, and suppose that they did, and went up and poked around in the pictsies' mound? She couldn't let that happen.

What would Granny Aching have done?

Granny Aching would have said nothing. Granny Aching often said nothing. She just smiled to herself, and puffed on her pipe, and waited until the right time.

Tiffany smiled to herself.

She slept, and didn't dream.

And a day went past.

◆　　◆　　◆

And another day.

◆　　◆　　◆

On the third day it rained. Tiffany went into the kitchen when no one was about and took down the china shepherdess from the shelf. She put it in a sack, then slipped out of the house and ran up onto the downs.

The worst of the weather was going to either side of the Chalk, which cut through the clouds like the prow of a ship. But when Tiffany reached the spot where an old stove and four iron wheels stood out of the grass, and cut a square of turf, and carefully chipped out a hole for the china shepherdess, and then put the turf back . . . it was raining hard enough to soak in and give the turf a chance of surviving. It seemed the right thing to do. And she was sure she caught a whiff of tobacco.

Then she went to the pictsies' mound. She'd worried about that. She knew they were there, didn't she? So, somehow, going to check that they were there would be sort of showing that she doubted if they would be, wouldn't it? They were busy people. They had lots to do. They had the old kelda to mourn. They were probably very busy. That's what she told herself. It wasn't because she kept wondering if there *really* might be nothing down the hole but rabbits. It wasn't that at all.

She was the kelda. She had a duty.

She heard music. She heard voices. And then sudden silence as she peered into the gloom.

She carefully took a bottle of Special Sheep Liniment out of her sack and let it slide into darkness.

Tiffany walked away and heard the faint music start up again.

She did wave at a buzzard, circling lazily under the clouds, and she was sure a tiny dot waved back.

◆　◆　◆

On the fourth day Tiffany made butter and did her chores. She did have help.

"And now I want you to go and feed the chickens," she said to Wentworth. "What is it I want you to do?"

"Fee' the cluck-clucks," said Wentworth.

"Chickens," said Tiffany severely.

"Chickens," said Wentworth obediently.

"And wipe your nose *not on your sleeve*! I gave you a handkerchief. And on the way back see if you can carry a whole log, will you?"

"Ach, crivens," muttered Wentworth.

"And what is it we don't say?" said Tiffany. "We don't say the—"

"—the crivens word," Wentworth muttered.

"And we don't say it in front of—"

"—in fron' of Mummy," said Wentworth.

"Good. And then when I've finished, we'll have time to go down to the river."

Wentworth brightened up.

"Weewee mens?" he said.

Tiffany didn't reply immediately.

She hadn't seen a single Feegle since she'd been home.

"There might be," she said. "But they're probably very busy. They've got to find another kelda, and . . . well, they're very busy. I expect."

"Weewee men say hit you in the head, fish face!" said Wentworth happily.

"We'll see," said Tiffany, feeling like a parent. "Now please go and get the eggs."

When he'd wandered away, carrying the egg basket in both hands, Tiffany turned out some butter onto the marble slab and picked up the paddles to pat it into, well, a pat of butter. Then she'd stamp it with one of the wooden stamps. People appreciated a little picture on their butter.

As she began to shape the butter, she was aware of a shadow in the doorway and turned.

It was Roland.

He looked at her, his face even redder than usual. He was twiddling his very expensive hat nervously, just like Rob Anybody did.

"Yes?" she said.

"Look, about . . . well, about all that . . . about . . ." Roland began.

"Yes?"

"Look, I didn't—I mean, I didn't lie to anyone or anything," he blurted out. "But my father just sort of assumed I'd been a hero, and he just wouldn't listen to anything I said even after I told him how . . . how . . ."

"Helpful I'd been?" said Tiffany.

"Yes . . . I mean, no! He said, he said, he said it was lucky for you I was there, he said—"

"It doesn't matter," said Tiffany, picking up the butter paddles again.

"And he just kept telling everyone how brave I'd been and—"

"I said it doesn't matter," said Tiffany. The little paddles went *patpatpat* on the fresh butter.

Roland's mouth opened and shut for a moment.

"You mean you don't mind?" he said at last.

"No. I don't mind," said Tiffany.

"But it's not fair!"

"We're the only ones who know the truth," said Tiffany.

Patapatpat. Roland stared at the fat, rich butter as she calmly patted it into shape.

"Oh," he said. "Er . . . you won't tell anyone, will you? I mean, you've got every right to, but—"

Patapatapat.

"No one would believe me," said Tiffany.

"I did try," said Roland. "Honestly. I really did."

I expect you did, Tiffany thought. But you're not very clever, and the Baron certainly is a man without First Sight. He sees the world the way he wants to see it.

"One day you'll be Baron, won't you?" she said.

"Well, yes. One day. But look, are you really a witch?"

"*When you're Baron* you'll be good at it, I expect?" said Tiffany, turning the butter around. "Fair and generous and decent? You'll pay good wages and look after the old people? You wouldn't let people turn an old lady out of her house?"

"Well, I hope I—"

Tiffany turned to face him, a butter paddle in each hand.

"Because *I'll* be there, you see. You'll look up and see my eye on you. I'll be there on the edge of the crowd. All the time. I'll be watching everything, because I come from a long line of Aching people and this is my land. But you can be the Baron for us and I hope you're a good one. If you are not . . . there will be a reckoning."

"Look, I know you were . . . were . . ." Roland began, going redder in the face.

"Very helpful?" said Tiffany.

". . . but you can't talk to me like that, you know!"

Tiffany was *sure* she heard, up in the roof and on the very edge of hearing, someone say: "Ach, crivens, what a wee snotter . . ."

She shut her eyes for a moment and then, heart pounding, pointed a butter paddle at one of the empty buckets.

"Bucket, fill yourself!" she commanded.

It blurred, and then sloshed. Water dripped down the side.

Roland stared at it. Tiffany gave him one of her sweetest smiles, which could be quite scary.

"You won't tell anyone, will you?" she said.

He turned to her, face pale. "No one would believe me . . ." he stammered.

"Aye," said Tiffany. "So we understand one another. Isn't that nice? And now, if you don't mind, I've got to finish this and make a start on some cheese."

"Cheese? But you . . . you could do anything you wanted!" Roland burst out.

"And right now I want to make cheese," said Tiffany calmly. "Go away."

"My father owns this farm!" said Roland, and then realized he'd said that out loud.

There were two little but strangely *loud* clicks as Tiffany put down the butter paddles and turned around.

"That was a very brave thing you just said," she said, "but I expect you're sorry you said it, now that you've had a really good think?"

Roland, who had shut his eyes, nodded his head.

"Good," said Tiffany. "Today I'm making cheese. Tomorrow I may do something else. And in a while, maybe, I won't be here and you'll wonder: Where is she? But part of me will always be here, always. I'll always be thinking about this place. I'll have it in my eye. And I *will* be back. Now, *go away!*"

He turned and ran.

After his footsteps had died away, Tiffany said: "All right, who's there?"

"It's me, mistress. No'-as-big-as-Medium-Sized-Jock-but-bigger-than-Wee-Jock-Jock, mistress." The pictsie appeared from behind the bucket and added: "Rob Anybody said we should come tae keep an eye on ye for a wee while, and tae thank ye for the offerin'."

It's still magic even if you know how it's done, Tiffany thought.

"Only watch me in the dairy, then," she said. "No spying!"

"Ach, no, mistress," said Not-as-big-as-Medium-Sized-Jock-but-bigger-than-Wee-Jock-Jock nervously. Then he grinned. "Fion's goin' off to be the kelda for a clan over near Copperhead Mountain," he said, "an' she's asked me to go along as the gonnagle!"

"Congratulations!"

"Aye, and William says I should be fine if I just work on the mousepipes," said the pictsie. "And . . . er . . ."

"Yes?" said Tiffany.

"Er . . . Hamish says there's a girl in the Long Lake clan who's looking to become a kelda . . . er . . . it's a fine clan she's from . . . er . . ." The pictsie was going violet with embarrassment.

"Good," said Tiffany. "If I was Rob Anybody, I'd invite her over right away."

"Ye dinna mind?" asked Not-as-big-as-Medium-Sized-Jock-but-bigger-than-Wee-Jock-Jock hopefully.

"Not at all," said Tiffany. She did a little bit, she had to admit to herself, but it was a bit she could put away on a shelf in her head somewhere.

"That's grand!" said the pictsie. "The lads were a bit worried, ye ken. I'll run up and tell them." He lowered his voice. "An' would ye like me to run after that big heap o' jobbies that just left and see that he falls off his horse again?"

"No!" said Tiffany hurriedly. "No. Don't. No." She picked up the butter paddles. "You leave him to me," she added, smiling. "You can leave everything to me."

When she was alone again, she finished the butter . . . *patapata-pat*. . . .

She paused, put the paddles down, and with the tip of a very clean finger drew a curved line in the surface, with another curved line just touching it, so that together they looked like a wave. She traced a third, flat curve under it, which was the Chalk.

Land Under Wave.

She quickly smoothed the butter again and picked up the stamp she'd made yesterday; she'd carved it carefully out of a piece of apple wood that Mr. Block, the carpenter, had given her.

She stamped it onto the butter and took it off carefully.

There, glistening on the oily rich yellow surface, was a gibbous moon and, sailing in front of the moon, a witch on a broomstick.

She smiled again, and it was Granny Aching's smile. Things would be different one day.

But you had to start small, like oak trees.

Then she made cheese . . .

. . . in the dairy, on the farm, and the fields unrolling, and becoming the downlands sleeping under the hot midsummer sun, where the flocks of sheep, moving slowly, drift over the short turf like clouds on a green sky, and here and there sheepdogs speed over the grass like shooting stars. Forever and ever, wold without end.

AUTHOR'S NOTE

The picture that Tiffany "enters" in this book really exists. It's called *The Fairy-Feller's Master-Stroke*, by Richard Dadd, and is in the Tate Gallery in London. It is only about twenty-one by fifteen inches. It took the artist nine years to complete, in the middle of the nineteenth century. I cannot think of a more famous fairy painting. It is, indeed, very strange. Summer heat leaks out of it.

What people "know" about Richard Dadd is that he went mad, killed his father, was locked up in a lunatic asylum for the rest of his life, and painted a weird picture. Crudely, that's all true, but it's a dreadful summary of the life of a skilled and talented artist who developed a serious mental illness.

A Nac Mac Feegle does not appear anywhere in the painting, but I suppose it's always possible that one was removed for making an obscene gesture. It's the sort of thing they'd do.

Oh, and the tradition of burying a shepherd with a piece of raw wool in the coffin is true, too. Even gods understand that a shepherd can't neglect the sheep. A god who didn't understand that would not be worth believing in.

There is no such word as *noonlight*, but it would be nice if there was.

A HAT FULL OF SKY

CONTENTS

Introduction

꩜

From *Fairies and How to Avoid Them* by Miss Perspicacia Tick:
The Nac Mac Feegle
(also called Pictsies, The Wee Free Men, The Little Men, and
"Person or Persons Unknown, Believed to be Armed")

The Nac Mac Feegle are the most dangerous of the fairy races, particularly when drunk. They love drinking, fighting, and stealing, and will in fact steal anything that is not nailed down. If it is nailed down, they will steal the nails as well.

Nevertheless, those who have managed to get to know them and survive say that they are also amazingly loyal, strong, dogged, brave, and, in their own way, quite moral. (For example, they won't steal from people who don't have anything.)

The average Feegle man (Feegle women are rare—see later) is about six inches high, red haired, his skin turned blue with tattoos and the dye called woad, and, since you're this close, he's probably about to hit you.

He'll wear a kilt made of any old material, because among the Feegles the clan allegiance is shown by the tattoos. He may wear a rabbit-skull helmet, and a Feegle often decorates his beard and hair with feathers, beads, and anything else that takes his fancy. He will almost certainly carry a sword, although it is mainly for show, the Feegles' preferred method of fighting being with the boot and the head.

History and Religion

The origin of the Nac Mac Feegle is lost in the famous Mists of Time. They say that they were thrown out of Fairyland by the Queen of the Fairies because they objected to her spiteful and tyrannical rule. Others say they were just thrown out for being drunk.

Little is known about their religion, if any, save for one fact: They think they are dead. They like our world, with its sunshine and mountains and blue skies and things to fight. An amazing world like this couldn't be open to just anybody, they say. It must be some kind of a heaven or Valhalla, where brave warriors go when they are dead. So, they reason, they have already been alive somewhere else, and then died and were allowed to come here because they have been so good.

This is a quite incorrect and fanciful notion because, as we know, the truth is exactly the other way around.

There is not a great deal of mourning when a Feegle dies, and it's only because his brothers are sad that he's not spent more time with them before going back to the land of the living, which they also call "The Last World."

Habits and Habitat

By choice, the clans of the Nac Mac Feegle live in the burial mounds of ancient kings, where they hollow out a cozy cavern amid the gold. Generally there will be one or two thorn or elder trees growing on it—the Feegles particularly like old, hollow elder trees, which become chimneys for their fires. And there will, of course, be a rabbit hole. It will look just like a rabbit hole. There will be rabbit droppings around it, and maybe even a few bits of rabbit fur if the Feegles are feeling particularly creative.

Down below, the world of the Feegle is a bit like a beehive, but with a lot less honey and a lot more sting.

The reason for this is that females are very rare among the Feegle. And, perhaps because of this, Feegle women give birth to lots of babies, very often and very quickly. They're about the size of peas when born but grow extremely fast if they're fed well (Feegles like to live near humans so that they can steal milk from cows and sheep for this purpose).

The queen of the clan is called the kelda, who as she gets older becomes the mother of most of it. Her husband is known as the Big Man. When a girl child is born—and it doesn't often happen—she stays with her mother to learn the hiddlins, *which are the secrets of keldaring. When she is old enough to be married,* she must leave the clan, *taking a few of her brothers with her as bodyguards on her long journey.*

Often she'll travel to a clan that has no kelda. Very, very rarely, if there is no clan without a kelda, she'll meet with Feegles from several clans and form a completely new clan, with a new name and a mound of its own. She will also choose her husband. And from then on, while her word is absolute law among her clan and must be obeyed, she'll seldom go more than a little distance from the mound. She is both its queen and its prisoner.

But once, for a few days, there was a kelda who was a human girl. . . .

A Feegle Glossary,

adjusted for those of a delicate disposition

Bigjobs: Human beings.

Blethers: Rubbish, nonsense.

Carlin: Old woman.

Cludgie: The privy.

Crivens!: A general exclamation that can mean anything from "My goodness!" to "I've just lost my temper and there is going to be trouble."

Dree your/my/his/her weird: Face the fate that is in store for you/me/him/her.

Geas: A very important obligation, backed up by tradition and magic. Not a bird.

Eldritch: Weird, strange. Sometimes means oblong, too, for some reason.

Hag: A witch of any age.

Hagging/Haggling: Anything a witch does.

Hiddlins: Secrets.

Mudlin: Useless person.

Pished: I am *assured* that this means "tired."

Scunner: A generally unpleasant person.

Scuggan: A *really* unpleasant person.

Ships: Wooly things that eat grass and go baa. Easily confused with the other kind.

Spavie: *See Mudlin.*

Special Sheep Liniment: Probably moonshine whisky, I am very sorry to say. No one knows what it'd do to sheep, but it is said that a drop of it is good for shepherds on a cold winter's night and for Feegles at any time at all. Do not try to make this at home.

Waily: A general cry of despair.

CHAPTER 1

Leaving

❦

*I*t came crackling over the hills, like an invisible fog. Movement without a body tired it, and it drifted very slowly. It wasn't thinking now. It had been months since it had last thought, because the brain that was doing the thinking for it had died. They always died. So now it was naked again, and frightened.

It could hide in one of the blobby white creatures that baa'd nervously as it crawled over the turf. But they had useless brains, capable of thinking only about grass and making other things that went baa. No. They would not do. It needed, needed something better, a strong mind, a mind with power, a mind that could keep it safe.

It searched. . . .

The new boots were all wrong. They were stiff and shiny. Shiny boots! That was disgraceful. Clean boots, that was different. There was nothing wrong with putting a bit of a polish on boots to keep the wet out. But boots had to work for a living. They shouldn't *shine*.

Tiffany Aching, standing on the rug in her bedroom, shook her head. She'd have to scuff the things as soon as possible.

Then there was the new straw hat, with a ribbon on it. She had some doubts about that, too.

She tried to look at herself in the mirror, which wasn't easy because the mirror was not much bigger than her hand, and cracked and blotchy. She had to move it around to try and see as much of herself as possible and remember how the bits fitted together.

But today . . . well, she didn't usually do this sort of thing in the house, but it was important to look smart today, and since no one was around . . .

She put the mirror down on the rickety table by the bed, stood in the middle of the threadbare rug, shut her eyes, and said:

"See me."

And away on the hills something, a thing with no body and no mind but a terrible hunger and a bottomless fear, felt the power.

It would have sniffed the air if it had a nose.

It searched.

It found.

Such a strange mind, like a lot of minds inside one another, getting smaller and smaller! So strong! So close!

It changed direction slightly and went a little faster. As it moved, it made a noise like a swarm of flies.

The sheep, nervous for a moment about something they couldn't see or smell, baa'd . . . .

. . . and went back to chewing grass.

Tiffany opened her eyes. There she was, a few feet away from herself. She could see the back of her own head.

Carefully, she moved around the room, not looking down at the "her" that was moving, because she found that if she did that, then the trick was over.

It was quite difficult, moving like that, but at last she was in front of herself and looking herself up and down.

Brown hair to match brown eyes . . . well, there was nothing she could do about that. At least her hair was clean and she'd washed her face.

She had a new dress on, which improved things a bit. It was so unusual to buy new clothes in the Aching family that, of course, it was bought big so that she'd "grow into it." But at least it was pale green, and it didn't actually touch the floor. With the shiny new boots and the straw hat she looked . . . like a farmer's daughter, quite respectable, going off to her first job. It'd have to do.

From here she could see the pointy hat on her head, but she had to look hard for it. It was like a glint in the air, gone as soon as you saw it. That's why she'd been worried about the new straw hat, but it had simply gone through the pointy hat as if it wasn't there.

This was because, in a way, it wasn't. It was invisible, except in the rain. Sun and wind went straight through, but rain and snow somehow saw it, and treated it as if it was real.

She'd been given it by the greatest witch in the world, a real witch with a black dress and a black hat and eyes that could go through you like turpentine goes through a sick sheep. It had been a kind of reward. Tiffany had done magic, serious magic. Before she had done it she hadn't known that she could, when she had been doing it she hadn't known that she was, and after she had done it she hadn't known how she had. Now she had to *learn* how.

"See me not," she said. The vision of her—or whatever it was, because she was not exactly sure about this trick—vanished.

It had been a shock, the first time she'd done this. But she'd *always* found it easy to see herself, at least in her head. All her memories were like little pictures of herself doing things or watching things, rather than the view from the two holes in the front of her head. There was a part of her that was always watching her.

Miss Tick—another witch, but one who was easier to talk to than the witch who'd given Tiffany the hat—had said that a witch had to know how to "stand apart," and that she'd find out more when her talent grew, so Tiffany supposed the "see me" was part of this.

Sometimes Tiffany thought she ought to talk to Miss Tick about "see me." It felt as if she was stepping out of her body but still had a sort of ghost body that could walk around. It all worked as long as her ghost eyes didn't look down and see that she *was* just a ghost body. If that happened, some part of her panicked and she found herself back in her solid body immediately. Tiffany had, in the end, decided to keep this to herself. You didn't have to tell a teacher *everything*. Anyway, it was a good trick for when you didn't have a mirror.

Miss Tick was a sort of witch finder. That seemed to be how witchcraft worked. Some witches kept a magical lookout for girls who showed promise, and found them an older witch to help them along. They didn't teach you how to do it. They taught you how to know what you were doing.

Witches were a bit like cats. They didn't much like one another's company, but they *did* like to know where all the other witches were, just in case they needed them. And what you might need them for was to tell you, as a friend, that you were beginning to cackle.

Witches didn't fear much, Miss Tick had said, but what the powerful ones were afraid of, even if they didn't talk about it, was what they called "going to the bad." It was too easy to slip into careless little cruelties because you had power and other people hadn't, too easy to think other people didn't matter much, too easy to think that ideas like right and wrong didn't apply to *you*. At the end of that road was you drooling and cackling to yourself all alone in a gingerbread house, growing warts on your nose.

Witches needed to know other witches were watching them.

And that, Tiffany thought, was why the hat was there. She could touch it anytime, provided she shut her eyes. It was a kind of reminder. . . .

"Tiffany!" her mother shouted up the stairs. "Miss Tick's here!"

◆ ◆ ◆

Yesterday Tiffany had said good-bye to Granny Aching. . . .

The iron wheels of the old shepherding hut were half buried in the turf, high up on the hills. The potbellied stove, which still stood lopsided in the grass, was red with rust. The chalk hills were taking them, just like they'd taken the bones of Granny Aching.

The rest of the hut had been burned on the day she'd been buried. No shepherd would have dared to use it, let alone spend the night there. Granny Aching had been too big in people's minds, too hard to replace. Night and day, in all seasons, she *was* the Chalk country: its best shepherd, its wisest woman, and its memory. It was as if the green downland had a soul that walked about in old boots and a sacking apron and smoked a foul old pipe and dosed sheep with turpentine.

The shepherds said that Granny Aching had cussed the sky blue. They called the fluffy little white clouds of summer "Granny Aching's little lambs." And although they laughed when they said these things, part of them was not joking.

No shepherd would have dared presume to live in that hut, no shepherd at all.

So they had cut the turf and buried Granny Aching in the chalk, watered the turf afterward to leave no mark, then burned her hut.

Sheep wool, Jolly Sailor tobacco, and turpentine . . .

. . . had been the smells of the shepherding hut, and the smell of Granny Aching. Such things have a hold on people that goes right to the heart. Tiffany only had to smell them now to be back there, in the warmth and silence and safety of the hut. It was the place she had gone to when she was upset, and the place she had gone to when she was happy. And Granny Aching would always smile and make tea and say nothing. And nothing bad could happen in the shepherding hut. It was a fort against the world. Even now, after Granny had gone, Tiffany still liked to go up there.

Tiffany stood there, while the wind blew over the turf and sheep bells *clonk*ed in the distance.

"I've got . . ." She cleared her throat. "I've got to go away. I . . . I've got to learn proper witching, and there's no one here now to teach me, you see. I've got to . . . to look after the hills like you did. I can . . . *do* things but I don't *know* things, and Miss Tick says what you don't know can kill you. I want to be as good as you were. I will come back! I will come back soon! I promise I will come back, better than I went!"

A blue butterfly, blown off course by a gust, settled on Tiffany's shoulder, opened and shut its wings once or twice, then fluttered away.

Granny Aching had never been at home with words. She collected silence like other people collected string. But she had a way of saying nothing that said it all.

Tiffany stayed for a while, until her tears had dried, and then went off back down the hill, leaving the everlasting wind to curl around the wheels and whistle down the chimney of the pot-bellied stove. Life went on.

♦ ♦ ♦

It wasn't unusual for girls as young as Tiffany to go "into service." It meant working as a maid somewhere. Traditionally, you started by helping an old lady who lived by herself; she wouldn't be able to pay much, but since this was your first job, you probably weren't worth much either.

In fact Tiffany practically ran Home Farm's dairy by herself, if someone helped her lift the big milk churns, and her parents had been surprised she wanted to go into service at all. But as Tiffany said, it was something everyone did. You got out into the world a little bit. You met new people. You never knew what it could lead to.

That, rather cunningly, got her mother on her side. Her mother's rich aunt had gone off to be a scullery maid, and then a parlor maid, and had worked her way up until she was a housekeeper and married to a butler and lived in a fine house. It wasn't *her* fine house, and she only lived in a bit of it, but she was practically a *lady*.

Tiffany didn't intend to be a lady. This was all a ruse, anyway. And Miss Tick was in on it.

You weren't allowed to charge money for the witching, so all witches did some other job as well. Miss Tick was basically a witch disguised as a teacher. She traveled around with the other wandering teachers who went in bands from place to place teaching anything to anybody in exchange for food or old clothes.

It was a good way to get around, because people in the Chalk country didn't trust witches. They thought they danced around on moonlit nights without their drawers on. (Tiffany had made inquiries about this, and had been slightly relieved to find out that you didn't have to do this to be a witch. You could if you wanted to, but only if you were certain where all the nettles, thistles, and hedgehogs were.)

But if it came to it, people were a bit wary of the wandering teachers too. They were said to pinch chickens and steal away children (which was true, in a way), and they went from village to village with their gaudy carts and wore long robes with leather pads on the sleeves and strange flat hats and talked among themselves in some heathen lingo no one could understand, like *"alea jacta est"* and *"quid pro quo."* It was quite easy for Miss Tick to lurk among them. *Her* pointy hat was a stealth version, which looked just like a black straw hat with paper flowers on it until you pressed the secret spring.

Over the last year or so Tiffany's mother had been quite surprised, and a little worried, at Tiffany's sudden thirst for education, which people in the village thought was a good thing in moderation but if taken unwisely could lead to restlessness.

Then a month ago the message had come: *Be ready.*

Miss Tick, in her flowery hat, had visited the farm and had explained to Mr. and Mrs. Aching that an elderly lady up in the mountains had heard of Tiffany's *excellent* prowess with cheese and was willing to offer her the post of maid at four dollars a month, one day off a week, her own bed, and a week's vacation at Hogswatch.

Tiffany knew her parents. Three dollars a month was a bit low, and five dollars would be suspiciously high, but prowess with cheese was worth the extra dollar. And a bed all to yourself was a very nice perk. Before most of Tiffany's sisters had left home, sleeping two sisters to a bed had been normal. It was a *good* offer.

Her parents had been impressed and slightly scared of Miss Tick, but they had been brought up to believe that people who knew more than you and used long words were quite important, so they'd agreed.

Tiffany accidentally heard them discussing it after she had gone to bed that night. It's quite easy to accidentally overhear people talking downstairs if you hold an upturned glass to the floorboards and accidentally put your ear to it.

She heard her father say that Tiffany didn't have to go away at all.

She heard her mother say that all girls wondered what was out there in the world, so it was best to get it out of her system. Besides, she was a very capable girl with a good head on her shoulders. Why, with hard work there was no reason why one day she couldn't be a servant to someone quite important, like Aunt Hetty had been, and live in a house with an inside privy.

Her father said she'd find that scrubbing floors was the same everywhere.

Her mother said, well, in that case she'd get bored and come back home after the year was up and, by the way, what did *prowess* mean?

Superior skill, said Tiffany to herself. They did have an old dictionary in the house, but her mother never opened it because the sight of all those words upset her. Tiffany had read it all the way through.

And that was it, and suddenly here she was, a month later, wrapping her old boots, which had been worn by all her sisters before her, in a piece of clean rag and putting them in the secondhand suitcase her mother had bought her, which looked as if it was made of bad cardboard or pressed grape pips mixed with ear wax, and had to be held together with string.

There were good-byes. She cried a bit, and her mother cried a lot, and her little brother, Wentworth, cried as well just in case he would get a sweet for doing so. Tiffany's father didn't cry but gave her a silver dollar and rather gruffly told her to be sure to write home every week, which is a man's way of crying. She said goodbye to the cheeses in the dairy and the sheep in the paddock and even to Ratbag the cat.

Then everyone apart from the cheeses and the cat stood at the gate and waved to her and Miss Tick—well, except for the sheep, too—until they'd gone nearly all the way down the chalky-white lane to the village.

And then there was silence except for the sound of their boots on the flinty surface and the endless song of the skylarks overhead. It was late August and very hot, and the new boots pinched.

"I should take them off, if I was you," said Miss Tick after a while.

Tiffany sat down by the side of the lane and got her old boots out of the case. She didn't bother to ask how Miss Tick knew about the tight new boots. Witches paid attention. The old boots, even though she had to wear several pairs of socks with them, were much more comfortable and really easy to walk in. They'd been walking since long before Tiffany was born, and knew how to do it.

"And are we going to see any . . . little men today?" Miss Tick went on, once they were walking again.

"I don't know, Miss Tick," said Tiffany. "I told them a month ago I was leaving. They're very busy at this time of year. But there's always one or two of them watching me."

Miss Tick looked around quickly. "I can't see anything," she said. "Or hear anything."

"No, that's how you can tell they're there," said Tiffany. "It's always a bit quieter if they're watching me. But they won't show themselves while you're with me. They're a bit frightened of hags—that's their word for witches," she added quickly. "It's nothing personal."

Miss Tick sighed. "When I was a little girl, I'd have loved to see the pictsies," she said. "I used to put out little saucers of milk. Of course, later on I realized that wasn't quite the thing to do."

"No, you should have used strong licker," said Tiffany.

She glanced at the hedge and thought she saw, just for the snap of a second, a flash of red hair. And she smiled, a little nervously.

◆ ◆ ◆

Tiffany had been, if only for a few days, the nearest a human being can be to a queen of the fairies. Admittedly, she'd been called a kelda rather than a queen, and the Nac Mac Feegle should only be called fairies to their faces if you were looking for a fight. On the other hand the Nac Mac Feegle were *always* looking for a fight, in a cheerful sort of way, and when they had no one to fight they fought one another, and if one was all by himself he'd kick his own nose just to keep in practice.

Technically they *had* lived in Fairyland but had been thrown out, probably for being drunk. And now, because if you'd ever been their kelda they never forgot you . . .

. . . they were always there.

There was always one somewhere on the farm, or circling on a buzzard high over the chalk downs. And they watched her, to help and protect her, whether she wanted them to or not. Tiffany had been as polite as possible about this. She'd hidden her diary all the way at the back of a drawer and blocked up the cracks in the privy with wadded paper, and done her best with the gaps in her bedroom floorboards, too. They were little *men*, after all. She was sure they tried to remain unseen so as not to disturb her, but she'd got very good at spotting them.

They granted wishes—not the magical fairy-tale three wishes, the ones that always go wrong in the end, but ordinary, everyday ones. The Nac Mac Feegle were immensely strong and fearless and incredibly fast, but they weren't good at understanding that what people *said* often wasn't what they *meant*. One day, in the dairy, Tiffany had said, "I wish I had a sharper knife to cut this cheese," and her mother's sharpest knife was quivering in the table beside her almost before she'd got the words out.

"I wish this rain would clear up" was probably okay, because the Feegles couldn't do actual magic, but she had learned to be careful not to wish for anything that might be achievable by some small, determined, strong, fearless, and fast men who were also not above giving someone a good kicking if they felt like it.

Wishes needed thought. She was never likely to say out loud, "I wish that I could marry a handsome prince," but knowing that if you did you'd probably open the door to find a stunned prince, a tied-up priest, and a Nac Mac Feegle grinning cheerfully and ready to act as best man definitely made you watch what you said. But they could be helpful, in a haphazard way, and she'd taken to leaving out for them things that the family didn't need but might be useful to little people, like tiny mustard spoons, pins, a soup bowl that would make a nice bath for a Feegle, and, in case they didn't get the message, some soap. They didn't steal the soap.

Her last visit to the ancient burial mound high on the chalk down where the pictsies lived had been to attend the wedding of Rob Anybody, the Big Man of the clan, to Jeannie of the Long Lake. She was going to be the new kelda and spend most of the rest of her life in the mound, having babies like a queen bee.

Feegles from other clans had all turned up for the celebration, because if there's one thing a Feegle likes more than a party, it's a bigger party, and if there's anything better than a bigger party, it's a bigger party with someone else paying for the drink. To be honest, Tiffany had felt a bit out of place, being ten times as tall as the next tallest person there, but she'd been treated very well, and Rob Anybody had made a long speech about her, calling her "our fine big wee young hag" before falling face-first into the pudding. It had all been very hot, and very loud, but she'd joined in the cheer when Jeannie had carried Rob Anybody over a tiny broomstick that had been laid on the floor. Traditionally, both the bride and the groom should jump over the broomstick, but equally traditionally, no self-respecting Feegle would be sober on his wedding day.

She'd been warned that it would be a good idea to leave then, because of the traditional fight between the bride's clan and the groom's clan, which could take until Friday.

Tiffany had bowed to Jeannie, because that's what hags did, and had a good look at her. She was small and sweet and very pretty. She also had a glint in her eye and a certain proud lift to her chin. Nac Mac Feegle girls were very rare, and they grew up knowing they were going to be keldas one day, and Tiffany had a definite feeling that Rob Anybody was going to find married life trickier than he'd thought.

She was going to be sorry to leave them behind, but not *terribly* sorry. They were nice in a way, but they could, after a while, get on your nerves. Anyway, she was eleven now, and had a feeling that after a certain age you shouldn't slide down holes in the ground to talk to little men.

Besides, the look that Jeannie had given her, just for a moment, had been pure poison. Tiffany had read its meaning without having to try. Tiffany had been the kelda of the clan, even if it was only for a short time. She had also been engaged to be married to Rob Anybody, even if that *had* only been a sort of political trick. Jeannie knew all that. And the look had said: *He is mine. This place is mine. I do not want you here! Keep out!*

◆　　◆　　◆

A pool of silence followed Tiffany and Miss Tick down the lane, since the usual things that rustle in hedges tended to keep very quiet when the Nac Mac Feegle were around.

They reached the little village green and sat down to wait for the carrier's cart that went just a bit faster than walking pace and would take five hours to get to the village of Twoshirts, where—Tiffany's parents thought—they'd get the big coach that ran all the way to the distant mountains and beyond.

Tiffany could actually see the cart coming up the road when she heard the hoofbeats coming across the green. She turned, and her heart seemed to leap and sink at the same time.

It was Roland, the baron's son, on a fine black horse. He leaped down before the horse had stopped, and then stood there looking embarrassed.

"Ah, I see a very fine and interesting example of a . . . a . . . a big stone over there," said Miss Tick in a sticky-sweet voice. "I'll just go and have a look at it, shall I?"

Tiffany could have pinched her for that.

"Er, you're going, then," said Roland as Miss Tick hurried away.

"Yes," said Tiffany.

Roland looked as though he was going to explode with nervousness.

"I got this for you," he said. "I had it made by a man, er, over in Yelp." He held out a package wrapped in soft paper.

Tiffany took it and put it carefully in her pocket.

"Thank you," she said, and dropped a small curtsy. Strictly speaking, that's what you had to do when you met a nobleman, but it just made Roland blush and stutter.

"O-open it later on," said Roland. "Er, I hope you'll like it."

"Thank you," said Tiffany sweetly.

"Here's the cart. Er . . . you don't want to miss it."

"Thank you," said Tiffany, and curtsied again, because of the effect it had. It was a little bit cruel, but sometimes you had to be.

Anyway, it would be very hard to miss the cart. If you ran fast, you could easily overtake it. It was so slow that "stop" never came as a surprise.

There were no seats. The carrier went around the villages every other day, picking up packages and, sometimes, people. You just found a place where you could get comfortable among the boxes of fruit and rolls of cloth.

Tiffany sat on the back of the cart, her old boots dangling over the edge, swaying backward and forward as the cart lurched away on the rough road.

Miss Tick sat beside her, her black dress soon covered in chalk dust to the knees.

Tiffany noticed that Roland didn't get back on his horse until the cart was nearly out of sight.

And she knew Miss Tick. By now she would be just *bursting* to ask a question, because witches hate not knowing things. And sure enough, when the village was left behind, Miss Tick said, after a lot of shifting and clearing her throat:

"Aren't you going to open it?"

"Open what?" asked Tiffany, not looking at her.

"He gave you a present," said Miss Tick.

"I thought you were examining an interesting stone, Miss Tick," said Tiffany accusingly.

"Well, it was only *fairly* interesting," said Miss Tick, completely unembarrassed. "So . . . are you?"

"I'll wait until later," said Tiffany. She didn't want a discussion about Roland at this point or, really, at all.

She didn't actually dislike him. She'd found him in the land of the Queen of the Fairies and had sort of rescued him, although he had been unconscious most of the time. A sudden meeting with the Nac Mac Feegle when they're feeling edgy can do that to a person. Of course, without anyone actually lying, everyone at home had come to believe that *he* had rescued *her*. A nine-year-old girl armed with a frying pan couldn't possibly have rescued a thirteen-year-old boy who'd had a sword.

Tiffany hadn't minded that. It stopped people from asking too many questions she didn't want to answer or even know how to. But he'd taken to . . . hanging around. She kept accidentally running into him on walks more often than was really possible, and he always seemed to be at the same village events she went to. He was always polite, but she couldn't stand the way he kept looking like a spaniel that had been kicked.

Admittedly—and it took some admitting—he was a lot less of a twit than he had been. On the other hand, there had been such a lot of twit to begin with.

And then she thought, Horse, and wondered why until she realized that her eyes had been watching the landscape while her brain stared at the past.

"I've never seen that before," said Miss Tick.

Tiffany welcomed it as an old friend. The Chalk rose out of the plains quite suddenly on this side of the hills. There was a little valley cupped into the fall of the down, and there was a carving in the curve it made. Turf had been cut away in long flowing lines, so that the bare chalk made the shape of an animal.

"It's the White Horse," said Tiffany.

"Why do they call it that?" said Miss Tick.

Tiffany looked at her.

"Because the chalk is white?" she said, trying not to suggest that Miss Tick was being a bit dense.

"No, I meant why do they call it a horse? It doesn't *look* like a horse. It's just . . . flowing lines. . . ."

. . . that look as if they're moving, Tiffany thought.

It had been cut out of the turf way back in the old days, people said, by the folk who'd built the stone circles and buried their kin in big earth mounds. And they'd cut out the Horse at one end of this little green valley, ten times bigger than a real horse and, if you didn't look at it with your mind right, the wrong shape, too. Yet they must have known horses, owned horses, seen them every day, and they weren't stupid people just because they lived a long time ago.

Tiffany had once asked her father about the look of the Horse, when they'd come all the way over here for a sheep fair, and he told her what Granny Aching had told him when he was a little boy. He passed on what she said word for word, and Tiffany did the same now.

"'Taint what a horse *looks* like," said Tiffany. "It's what a horse *be*."

"Oh," said Miss Tick. But because she was a teacher as well as a witch, and probably couldn't help herself, she added, "The funny thing is, of course, that officially there is no such thing as a white horse. They're called gray."*

"Yes, I know," said Tiffany. "This one's white," she added, flatly.

That quietened Miss Tick down for a while, but she seemed

---

*She had to say that because she was a witch and a teacher, and that's a terrible combination. They want things to be *right*. They like things to be *correct*. If you want to upset a witch, you don't have to mess around with charms and spells—you just have to put her in a room with a picture that's hung slightly crooked and watch her squirm.

to have something on her mind.

"I expect you're upset about leaving the Chalk, aren't you?" she said as the cart rattled on.

"No," said Tiffany.

"It's okay to be," said Miss Tick.

"Thank you, but I'm not really," said Tiffany.

"If you want to have a bit of a cry, you don't have to pretend you've got some grit in your eye or anything—"

"I'm all right, actually," said Tiffany. "Honestly."

"You see, if you bottle that sort of thing up, it can cause terrible damage later on."

"I'm not bottling, Miss Tick."

In fact, Tiffany was a bit surprised at not crying, but she wasn't going to tell Miss Tick that. She'd left a sort of space in her head to burst into tears in, but it wasn't filling up. Perhaps it was because she'd wrapped up all those feelings and doubts and left them on the hill by the potbellied stove.

"And if, of course, you were feeling a bit downcast at the moment, I'm sure you could open the present he—" Miss Tick tried.

"Tell me about Miss Level," Tiffany said quickly. The name and address were all she knew about the lady she was going to stay with, but an address like "Miss Level, Cottage in the Woods Near the Dead Oak Tree in Lost Man's Lane, High Overhang, If Out Leave Letters in Old Boot by Door" sounded promising.

"Miss Level, yes," said Miss Tick, defeated. "Er, yes. She's not really very old, but she says she'll be happy to have a third pair of hands around the place."

You couldn't slip words past Tiffany, not even if you were Miss Tick.

"So there's someone else there already?" she said.

"Er . . . no. Not exactly," said Miss Tick.

"Then she's got four arms?" said Tiffany. Miss Tick sounded like someone trying to avoid a subject.

Miss Tick sighed. It was difficult to talk to someone who paid attention all the time. It put you off.

"It's best if you wait until you meet her," she said. "Anything I tell you will only give you the wrong idea. I'm sure you'll get along with her. She's very good with people, and in her spare time she's a research witch. She keeps bees—and goats, the milk of which, I believe, is very good indeed, owing to homogenized fats."

"What does a research witch do?"

"Oh, it's a very ancient craft. She tries to find new spells by learning how old ones were really done. You know all that stuff about 'ear of bat and toe of frog'? They never work, but Miss Level thinks it's because we don't know exactly what *kind* of frog, or which toe—"

"I'm sorry, but I'm not going to help anyone chop up innocent frogs and bats," said Tiffany firmly.

"Oh, no, she never kills any!" said Miss Tick hurriedly. "She only uses creatures that have died naturally or been run over or committed suicide. Frogs can get quite depressed at times."

The cart rolled on down the white, dusty road, until it was lost from view.

Nothing happened. Skylarks sang, so high up they were invisible. Grass seeds filled the air. Sheep *baa*'d, high up on the Chalk.

And then something came along the road. It moved like a little slow whirlwind, so it could be seen only by the dust it stirred up. As it went past, it made a noise like a swarm of flies.

Then it, too, disappeared down the hill. . . .

After a while a voice, low down in the long grass, said: "Ach, *crivens!* And it's on her trail, right enough!"

A second voice said: "Surely the old hag will spot it?"

"Whut? The teachin' hag? She's nae a proper hag!"

"She's got the pointy hat under all them flowers, Big Yan," said the second voice a bit reproachfully. "I seen it. She presses a wee spring an' the point comes up!"

"Oh, aye, Hamish, an' I daresay she does the readin' and the writin' well enough, but she disna ken aboot stuff that's no' in books. An' I'm no' showin' meself while she's aroond. She's the kind of a body that'd write things doon about a man! C'mon, let's go and find the kelda!"

◆　◆　◆

The Nac Mac Feegle of the Chalk hated writing for all kinds of reasons, but the biggest one was this: Writing *stays*. It fastens words down. A man can speak his mind and some nasty wee *scuggan* will write it down and who knows what he'll do with those words? Ye might as weel nail a man's shadow tae the wall!

But now they had a new kelda, and a new kelda brings new ideas. That's how it's supposed to *work*. It stopped a clan getting too set in its ways. Kelda Jeannie was from the Long Lake clan, up in the mountains—and they *did* write things down.

She didn't see why her husband shouldn't too. And Rob Anybody was finding out that Jeannie was definitely a kelda.

Sweat was dripping off his forehead. He'd once fought a wolf all by himself, and he'd cheerfully do it again with his eyes shut and one hand tied behind him rather than do what he was doing now.

He had mastered the first two rules of writing, as he understood them.

    1. Steal some paper.

    2. Steal a pencil.

Unfortunately there was more to it than that.

Now he held the stump of pencil in front of him in both hands and leaned backward as two of his brothers pushed him toward the piece of paper pinned up on the chamber wall (it was an old bill for sheep bells, stolen from the farm). The rest of the clan watched, in fascinated horror, from the galleries around the walls.

"Mebbe I could kind o' *ease* my way inta it gently," he protested as his heels left little grooves in the packed-earth floor of the mound. "Mebbe I could just do one o' they commeras or full stoppies—"

"You're the Big Man, Rob Anybody, so it's fittin' ye should be the first tae do the writin'," said Jeannie. "I canna hae a husband who canna even write his ain name. I showed you the letters, did I not?"

"Aye, wumman, the nasty, loopy, bendy things!" growled Rob. "I dinna trust that Q, that's a letter than has it in for a man. That's a letter with a sting, that one!"

"You just hold the pencil on the paper and I'll tell ye what marks to make," said Jeannie, folding her arms.

"Aye, but 'tis a bushel of trouble, writin'," said Rob. "A word writ doon can hang a man!"

"Wheest, now, stop that! 'Tis easy!" snapped Jeannie. "Bigjob babies can do it, and you're a full-growed Feegle!"

"An' writin' even goes on sayin' a man's wurds after he's *deid*!" said Rob Anybody, waving the pencil as if trying to ward off evil spirits. "Ye canna tell me that's right!"

"Oh, so you're *afeared* o' the letters, is that it?" said Jeannie artfully. "Ach, that's fine. All big men fear something. Take the pencil off 'f him, Wullie. Ye canna ask a man to face his fears."

There was silence in the mound as Daft Wullie nervously took the pencil stub from his brother. Every beady eye was turned to Rob Anybody. His hands opened and shut. He started to breathe heavily, still glaring at the blank paper. He stuck out his chin.

"Ach, ye're a harrrrd wumman, Jeannie Mac Feegle!" he said at last. He spat on his hands and snatched back the pencil stub from Daft Wullie. "Gimme that tool o' perdition! Them letters won't know whut's hit them!"

"There's my brave lad!" said Jeannie, as Rob squared up to the paper. "Right, then. The first letter is an R. That's the one that looks like a fat man walking, remember?"

The assembled pictsies watched as Rob Anybody, grunting fiercely and with his tongue sticking out of the corner of his mouth, dragged the pencil through the curves and lines of the letters. He looked at the kelda expectantly after each one.

"That's it," she said at last. "A bonny effort!"

Rob Anybody stood back and looked critically at the paper.

"That's it?" he asked.

"Aye," said Jeannie. "Ye've writ your ain name, Rob Anybody!"

Rob stared at the letters again. "I'm gonna go to pris'n noo?" he asked.

There was a polite cough from beside Jeannie. It belonged to the toad. He had no other name, because toads don't go in for names. Despite sinister forces that would have people think differently, no toad has ever been called Tommy the Toad, for example. It's just not something that happens.

This toad had once been a lawyer (a human lawyer; toads manage without them) who'd been turned into a toad by a fairy godmother who'd *intended* to turn him into a frog but had been a bit hazy on the difference. Now he lived in the Feegle mound, where he ate worms and helped them out with the difficult thinking.

"I've told you, Mr. Anybody, that *just* having your name written down is no problem at all," he said. "There's nothing illegal about the words *Rob Anybody*. Unless, of course"—and the toad gave a little legal laugh—"it's meant as an instruction!"

None of the Feegles laughed. They liked their humor to be a bit, well, funnier.

Rob Anybody stared at his very shaky writing. "That's my name, aye?"

"It certainly is, Mr. Anybody."

"An' nothin' bad's happenin' at a'," Rob noted. He looked closer. "How can you *tell* it's my name?"

"Ah, that'll be the readin' side o' things," said Jeannie.

"That's where the lettery things make a sound in yer heid?" asked Rob.

"Exactly so," said the toad. "But we thought you'd like to start with the more *physical* aspect of the procedure."

"Could I no' mebbe just learn the writin' and leave the readin' to someone else?" Rob asked, without much hope.

"No, my man's got to do both," said Jeannie, folding her arms. When a female Feegle does that, there's no hope left.

"Ach, it's a terrible thing for a man when his wumman gangs up on him wi' a toad," said Rob, shaking his head. But when he turned to look at the grubby paper, there was just a hint of pride in his face.

"Still, that's my name, right?" he said, grinning.

Jeannie nodded.

"Just there, all by itself and no' on a WANTED poster or anything. My name, drawn by me."

"Yes, Rob," said the kelda.

"*My* name, under my thumb. No scunner can do anythin' aboot it? *I've* got my name, nice and safe?"

Jeannie looked at the toad, who shrugged. It was generally held by those who knew them that most of the brains in the Nac Mac Feegle clans ended up in the women.

"A man's a man o' some standin' when he's got his own name where no one can touch it," said Rob Anybody. "That's serious magic, that is—"

"The R is the wrong way roond and you left the A and a Y out of Anybody," said Jeannie, because it is a wife's job to stop her husband actually exploding with pride.

"Ach, wumman, I didna' ken which way the fat man wuz walkin'," said Rob, airily waving a hand. "Ye canna trust the fat man. That's the kind of thing us nat'ral writin' folk knows about. One day he might walk this way, next day he might walk *that* way."

He beamed at his name:

ЯOB NybO D

"And I reckon you got it wrong wi' them Y's," he went on. "I reckon it should be N E Bo D. That's Enn . . . eee . . . bor . . . dee, see? That's *sense*!"

He stuck the pencil into his hair and gave her a defiant look.

Jeannie sighed. She'd grown up with seven hundred brothers and knew how they thought, which was often quite fast while being totally in the wrong direction. And if they couldn't bend their thinking around the world, they bent the world around their thinking. Usually, her mother had told her, it was best not to argue.

Actually, only half a dozen Feegles in the Long Lake clan could read and write very well. They were considered odd, strange hobbies. After all, what—when you got out of bed in the morning—

were they good for? You didn't need to know them to wrestle a trout or mug a rabbit or get drunk. The wind couldn't be read and you couldn't write on water.

But things written down lasted. They were the voices of Feegles who'd died long ago, who'd seen strange things, who'd made strange discoveries. Whether you approved of that depended on how creepy you thought it was. The Long Lake clan approved. Jeannie wanted the best for her new clan, too.

It wasn't easy, being a young kelda. You came to a new clan, with only a few of your brothers as bodyguards, where you married a husband and ended up with hundreds of brothers-in-law. It could be troubling if you let your mind dwell on it. At least back on the island in the Long Lake she had her mother to talk to, but a kelda never went home again.

A kelda was all alone.

Jeannie was homesick and lonely and frightened of the future, which is why she was about to get things wrong.

"Rob!"

Hamish and Big Yan came tumbling through the fake rabbit hole that was the entrance to the mound.

Rob Anybody glared at them. "We wuz engaged in a lit'try enterprise," he said.

"Yes, Rob, but we watched the big wee young hag safe awa', like you said, but there's a hiver after her!" Hamish blurted out.

"Are ye sure?" said Rob, dropping his pencil. "I never heard o' one of them in this world!"

"Oh, aye," said Big Yan. "Its buzzin' fair made my teeths ache!"

"So did you no' tell her, ye daftie?" said Rob.

"There's that other hag wi' her, Rob," said Big Yan. "The educatin' hag."

"Miss Tick?" said the toad.

"Aye, the one wi' a face like a yard o' yogurt," said Big Yan. "An' you said we wuzna' to show ourselves, Rob."

"Aye, weel, this is different—" Rob Anybody began, but stopped.

He hadn't been a husband for very long, but upon marriage men get a whole lot of extra senses bolted into their brain, and one is there to tell a man that he's suddenly neck deep in real trouble.

Jeannie was tapping her foot. Her arms were still folded. She had the special smile women learn about when they marry too which seems to say "Yes, you're in big trouble but I'm going to let you dig yourself in even more deeply."

"What's this about the big wee hag?" she said, her voice as small and meek as a mouse trained at the Rodent College of Assassins.

"Oh, ah, ach, weel, aye . . ." Rob began, his face falling. "Do ye not bring her to mind, dear? She was at oor wedding, aye. She was oor kelda for a day or two, ye ken. The Old One made her swear to that just afore she went back to the Land o' the Livin'," he added, in case mentioning the wishes of the last kelda would deflect whatever storm was coming. "It's as well tae keep an eye on her, ye ken, her being oor hag and all. . . ."

Rob Anybody's voice trailed away in the face of Jeannie's look.

"A true kelda has tae marry the Big Man," said Jeannie. "Just like I married ye, Rob Anybody Feegle, and am I no' a good wife tae ye?"

"Oh, fine, fine," Rob burbled. "But—"

"And ye canna be married to two wives, because that would be bigamy, would it not?" said Jeannie, her voice dangerously sweet.

"Ach, it wasna *that* big," said Rob Anybody, desperately looking around for a way of escape. "And it wuz only temp'ry, an' she's but a lass, an' she wuz good at thinkin'—"

"*I'm* good at thinking, Rob Anybody, and I am the kelda o' this clan, am I no'? There can only be one, is that not so? And I am thinking that there will be no more chasin' after this big wee girl. Shame on ye, anyway. She'll no' want the like o' Big Yan a-gawpin' at her all the time, I'm sure."

Rob Anybody hung his head.

"Aye . . . but," he said.

"But what?"

"A hiver's chasin' the puir wee lass."

There was a long pause before Jeannie said, "Are ye sure?"

"Aye, kelda," said Big Yan. "Once you hear that buzzin', ye never forget it."

Jeannie bit her lip. Then, looking a little pale, she said, "Ye said she's got the makin's o' a powerful hag, Rob?"

"Aye, but nae one in his'try has survived a hiver! Ye canna kill it, ye canna stop it, ye canna—"

"But wuz ye no' tellin' me how the big wee girl even fought the Quin and won?" said Jeannie. "Wanged her wi' a skillet, ye said. That means she's good, aye? If she is a true hag, she'll find a way hersel'. We all ha' to dree our weird. Whatever's out there, she's got to face it. If she canna, she's no true hag."

"Aye, but a hiver's worse than—" Rob began.

"She's off to learn hagglin' from other hags," said Jeannie. "An' I must learn keldarin' all by myself. Ye must hope she learns as fast as me, Rob Anybody."

CHAPTER 2

Twoshirts and Two Noses

Twoshirts was just a bend in the road with a name. There was
nothing there but an inn for the coaches, a blacksmith's shop, and
a small store with the word SOUVENIRS written optimistically on a
scrap of cardboard in the window. And that was it. Around the
place, separated by fields and scraps of woodland, were the houses
of people for whom Twoshirts was, presumably, the big city. Every
world is full of places like Twoshirts. They are places for people to
come from, not go to.

It sat and baked silently in the hot afternoon sunlight. Right in
the middle of the road an elderly spaniel, mottled brown and
white, dozed in the dust.

Twoshirts was bigger than the village back home, and Tiffany
had never seen souvenirs before. She went into the store and spent
half a penny on a small wood carving of two shirts on a washing
line, and two postcards entitled "View of Twoshirts," which
showed the souvenir shop and what was quite probably the same
dog sleeping in the road. The little old lady behind the counter
called her "young lady" and said that Twoshirts was very popular
later in the year, when people came from up to a mile around for
the Cabbage Macerating Festival.

When Tiffany came out, she found Miss Tick standing next to the sleeping dog, frowning back the way they'd come.

"Is there something the matter?" said Tiffany.

"What?" said Miss Tick, as if she'd forgotten that Tiffany existed. "Oh . . . no. I just . . . I thought I . . . look, shall we go and have something to eat?"

It took a while to find someone in the inn, but Miss Tick wandered into the kitchens and found a woman who promised them some scones and a cup of tea. She was actually quite surprised she'd promised that, since she hadn't intended to, it strictly speaking being her afternoon free until the coach came, but Miss Tick had a way of asking questions that got the answers she wanted.

Miss Tick also asked for a fresh egg, not cooked, in its shell. Witches were also good at asking questions that weren't followed by the other person saying, "Why?"

They sat and ate in the sun, on the bench outside the inn. Then Tiffany took out her diary.

She had one in the dairy too, but that was for cheese and butter records. This one was personal. She'd bought it off a peddler, cheap, because it was last year's. But, as he said, it had the same number of days.

It also had a lock, a little brass thing on a leather flap. It had its own tiny key. It was the lock that had attracted Tiffany. At a certain age you see the point of locks.

She wrote down "Twoshirts," and spent some time thinking before adding "a bend in the road."

Miss Tick kept staring at the road.

"Is there something wrong, Miss Tick?" Tiffany asked again, looking up.

"I'm . . . not sure. Is anyone watching us?"

Tiffany looked around. Twoshirts slept in the heat. There was no one watching.

"No, Miss Tick."

The teacher removed her hat and took from inside it a couple pieces of wood and a spool of black thread. She rolled up her sleeves, looking around quickly in case Twoshirts had sprouted a population, then broke off a length of the thread and picked up the egg.

Egg, thread, and fingers blurred for a few seconds and then there was the egg, hanging from Miss Tick's fingers in a neat little black net.

Tiffany was impressed.

But Miss Tick hadn't finished. She began to draw things from her pockets, and a witch generally has a lot of pockets. There were some beads, a couple of feathers, a glass lens, and one or two strips of colored paper. These all got threaded into the tangle of wood and cotton.

"What is that?" said Tiffany.

"It's a shamble," said Miss Tick, concentrating.

"Is it magic?"

"Not exactly. It's *trickery*."

Miss Tick lifted her left hand. Feathers and beads and egg and pocket junk spun in the web of threads.

"Hmm," she said. "Now let me see what I can see. . . ."

She pushed the fingers of her right hand into the spiderwork of threads and pulled.

Egg and glass and beads and feathers danced through the tangle, and Tiffany was sure that at one point one thread had passed straight through another.

"Oh," she said. "It's like cat's cradle!"

"You've played that, have you?" said Miss Tick vaguely, still concentrating.

"I can do all the common shapes," said Tiffany. "The Jewels and the Cradle and the House and the Flock and the Three Old Ladies, One With a Squint, Carrying the Bucket of Fish to Market When They Meet the Donkey, although you need two people for that one, and I only ever did it once, and Betsy Tupper scratched her nose at the wrong moment and I had to get some scissors to cut her loose...."

Miss Tick's fingers worked like a loom.

"Funny it should be a children's toy now," she said. "Aha . . ." She stared into the complex web she had created.

"Can you see anything?" said Tiffany.

"If I may be allowed to concentrate, child? *Thank* you. . . ."

Out in the road the sleeping dog woke, yawned, and pulled itself to its feet. It ambled over to the bench the two of them were sitting on, gave Tiffany a reproachful look, and then curled up by her feet. It smelled of old damp carpets.

"There's . . . *something* . . ." said Miss Tick very quietly.

Panic gripped Tiffany.

Sunlight reflected off the white dust of the road and the stone wall opposite. Bees hummed between the little yellow flowers that grew on top of the wall. By Tiffany's feet the spaniel snorted and farted occasionally.

But it was all *wrong*. She could feel the pressure bearing down on her, pushing at her, pushing at the landscape, *squeezing* it under the bright light of day. Miss Tick and her cradle of threads were motionless beside her, frozen in the moment of bright horror.

Only the threads moved, by themselves. The egg danced, the glass glinted, the beads slid and jumped from string to string—

The egg burst.

The coach rolled in.

It arrived dragging the world behind it, in a cloud of dust and noise and hooves. It blotted out the sun. Doors opened. Harnesses jingled. Horses steamed. The spaniel sat up and wagged its tail hopefully.

The pressure went—no, it *fled*.

Beside Tiffany, Miss Tick pulled out a handkerchief and started to wipe egg off her dress. The rest of the shamble had disappeared into a pocket with remarkable speed.

She smiled at Tiffany but kept the smile as she spoke, making herself look slightly mad.

"Don't get up, don't do anything, just be as quiet as a little mouse," she said. Tiffany felt in no state to do anything but sit still; she felt like you feel when you wake up after a nightmare.

The richer passengers got out of the coach, and the poorer ones climbed down from the roof. Grumbling and stamping their feet, trailing road dust behind them, they disappeared.

"Now," said Miss Tick, when the inn door had swung shut, "we're . . . we're going to go for a, a stroll. See that little woods up there? That's where we're heading. And when Mr. Crabber, the carter, sees your father tomorrow, he'll say he—he dropped you off here just before the coach arrived and—and, and everyone will be happy and no one will have lied. That's important."

"Miss Tick?" said Tiffany, picking up the suitcase.

"Yes?"

"What happened just now?"

"I don't know," said the witch. "Do you feel all right?"

"Er . . . yes. You've got some yolk on your hat." And you're very nervous, Tiffany thought. That was the most worrying part. "I'm sorry about your dress," she added.

"It's seen a lot worse," said Miss Tick. "Let's go."

"Miss Tick?" said Tiffany again as they trudged away.

"Er, yes?"

"You are *very* nervous," said Tiffany. "If you told me why, that means there's two of us, which is only half the nervousness each."

Miss Tick sighed. "It was probably nothing," she said.

"Miss Tick, the egg exploded!"

"Yes. Um. A shamble, you see, can be used as a simple magic detector and amplifier. It's actually very crude, but it's always useful to make one in times of distress and confusion. I think I . . . probably didn't make it right. And sometimes you do get big discharges of random magic."

"You made it because you were worried," said Tiffany.

"Worried? Certainly not. I am *never* worried!" snapped Miss Tick. "However, since you raise the subject, I *was* concerned. Something was making me uneasy. Something close, I think. It was probably nothing. In fact, I feel a lot better now we're leaving."

But you don't look it, Tiffany thought. And I was wrong. Two people means *twice* as much nervousness each.

But she was sure there was nothing magical about Twoshirts. It was just a bend in the road.

Twenty minutes later the passengers came out to get into the coach. The coachman did notice that the horses were sweating, and wondered why he could hear a swarm of flies when there were no flies to be seen.

The dog that had been lying in the road was found later cowering in one of the inn's stables, whimpering.

The woods was about half an hour's walk away, with Miss Tick and Tiffany taking turns to carry the suitcase. It was nothing special, as woods go, being mostly full-grown beech, although once you know that beech drips unpleasant poisons on the ground beneath it to keep it clear, it's not quite the timber you thought it was.

They sat on a log and waited for sunset. Miss Tick told Tiffany about shambles.

"They're not magical then?" said Tiffany.

"No. They're something to be magical through."

"You mean like spectacles help you see but don't see for you?"

"That's right, well done! Is a telescope magical? Certainly not. It's just glass in a tube, but with one you could count the dragons on the moon. And . . . well, have you ever used a bow? No, probably not. But a shamble can act like a bow, too. A bow stores up muscle power as the archer draws it, and sends a heavy arrow much farther than the archer could actually *throw* it. You can make one out of anything, so long as it . . . looks right."

"And then you can tell if magic is happening?"

"Yes, if that's what you're looking for. When you're good at it, you can use it to help you do magic yourself, to really focus on what you have to do. You can use it for protection, like a curse net, or to send a spell, or . . . well, it's like those expensive pen-knives, you know? The ones with the tiny saw and the scissors and the toothpick? Except that I don't think any witch has ever used a shamble as a toothpick, ha ha. All young witches should learn how to make a shamble. Miss Level will help you."

Tiffany looked around the woods. The shadows were growing longer, but they didn't worry her. Bits of Miss Tick's teachings floated through her head: *Always face what you fear. Have just enough money, never too much, and some string. Even if it's not your fault, it's your responsibility. Witches deal with things. Never stand between two mirrors. Never cackle. Do what you must do. Never lie, but you don't always have to be honest. Never wish. Especially don't wish upon a star, which is astro-nomically stupid. Open your eyes, and then open your eyes again.*

"Miss Level has got long gray hair, has she?" she said.

"Oh, yes."

"And she's quite a tall lady, just a bit fat, and she wears quite a lot of necklaces," Tiffany went on. "And glasses on a chain. And surprisingly high-heeled boots."

Miss Tick wasn't a fool. She looked around the clearing.

"Where is she?" she said.

"Standing by the tree over there," said Tiffany.

Even so, Miss Tick had to squint. What Tiffany had noticed was that witches filled space. In a way that was almost impossible to describe, they seemed to be more real than others around them. They just showed more. But if they didn't want to be seen, they became amazingly hard to notice. They didn't hide, they didn't magically fade away, although it might seem like that; but if you had to describe the room afterward, you'd swear there hadn't been a witch in it. They just seemed to let themselves get lost.

"Ah yes, well done," said Miss Tick. "I was wondering when you'd notice."

Ha! thought Tiffany.

Miss Level got realer as she walked toward them. She was all in black, but clattered slightly as she walked because of all the black jewelry she wore, and she did have glasses, too, which struck Tiffany as odd for a witch. Miss Level reminded Tiffany of a happy hen. And she had two arms, the normal number.

"Ah, Miss Tick," she said. "And you must be Tiffany Aching."

Tiffany knew enough to bow; witches don't curtsy (unless they want to embarrass Roland).

"I'd just like to have a word with Miss Level, Tiffany, if you *don't* mind," said Miss Tick, meaningfully. "Senior witch business."

Ha! thought Tiffany again, because she liked the sound of it.

"I'll just go and have a look at a tree then, shall I?" she said with what she hoped was withering sarcasm.

"I should use the bushes if I was you, dear," Miss Level called after her. "I don't like stopping once we're airborne."

There *were* some holly bushes that made a decent screen, but after being talked to as though she was ten years old, Tiffany would rather have allowed her bladder to explode.

I beat the Queen of the Fairies! she thought as she wandered into the woods. All right, I'm not sure how, because it's all like a dream now, but I did do it!

She was angry at being sent away like that. A *little* respect wouldn't hurt, would it? That's what the old witch Mistress Weatherwax had said, wasn't it? "I show you respect, *as you in turn will respect me.*" Mistress Weatherwax, the witch who all the other witches secretly wanted to be like, had shown her *respect*, so you'd think the others could make a bit of effort in that department.

She said: "See me."

. . . and stepped out of herself and walked away toward Miss Tick and Miss Level, in her invisible ghost body. She didn't dare look down, in case she saw her feet weren't there. When she turned and looked back at her solid body, she saw it standing demurely by the holly bushes, clearly too far away to be listening to anyone's conversation.

As Tiffany stealthily drew nearer, she heard Miss Tick say:

"*—but quite frighteningly precocious.*"

"*Oh dear. I've never got on very well with clever people,*" said Miss Level.

"*Oh, she's a good child at heart,*" said Miss Tick, which annoyed

Tiffany rather more than "frighteningly precocious" had.

"*Of course, you know my situation,*" said Miss Level, as the invisible Tiffany inched closer.

"*Yes, Miss Level, but your work does you great credit. That's why Mistress Weatherwax suggested you.*"

"*But I am afraid I'm getting a bit absentminded,*" Miss Level worried. "*It was terrible flying down here, because like a big silly I left my long-distance spectacles on my other nose. . . .*"

Her *other* nose? thought Tiffany.

Both witches froze, exactly at the same time.

"I'm without an egg!" said Miss Tick.

"I have a beetle in a matchbox against just such an emergency!" squeaked Miss Level.

Their hands flew to their pockets and pulled out string and feathers and bits of colored cloth—

They know I'm here! thought Tiffany, and whispered, "See me not!"

She blinked and rocked on her heels as she arrived back in the patient little figure by the holly bushes. In the distance Miss Level was frantically making a shamble and Miss Tick was staring around the woods.

"Tiffany, come here at once!" she shouted.

"Yes, Miss Tick," said Tiffany, trotting forward like a good girl.

They spotted me somehow, she thought. Well, they *are* witches, after all, even if in my opinion they're not very good ones—

Then the pressure came. It seemed to squash the woods flat and filled it with the horrible feeling that something is standing right behind you. Tiffany sank to her knees with her hands over her ears and a pain like the worst earache squeezing her head.

"Finished!" shouted Miss Level. She held up a shamble. It was quite different from Miss Tick's, made up of string and crow feathers and glittery black beads and, in the middle, an ordinary matchbox.

Tiffany yelled. The pain was like red-hot needles and her ears filled with the buzz of flies.

The matchbox exploded.

And then there was silence, and birdsong, and nothing to show that anything had happened apart from a few pieces of matchbox spiraling down, along with iridescent fragments of wing case.

"Oh dear," said Miss Level. "He was quite a good beetle, as beetles go. . . ."

"Tiffany, are you all right?" said Miss Tick. Tiffany blinked. The pain had gone as fast as it has arrived, leaving only a burning memory. She scrambled to her feet.

"I think so, Miss Tick!"

"Then a word, if you please!" said Miss Tick. She marched over to a tree and stood there looking stern.

"Yes, Miss Tick?" said Tiffany.

"Did you . . . *do* anything?" said Miss Tick. "You haven't been summoning things, have you?"

"No! Anyway, I don't know how to!" said Tiffany.

"It's not your little men then, is it?" said Miss Tick doubtfully.

"They're not mine, Miss Tick. And they don't do that sort of thing. They just shout 'Crivens!' and then start kicking people on the ankle. You definitely know it's them."

"Well, whatever it was, it seems to have gone," said Miss Level. "And we should go too—otherwise we'll be flying all night." She reached behind another tree and picked up a bundle of firewood. At least, it looked exactly like that, because it was supposed to. "My own invention," she said, modestly. "One never knows down here on the plains, does one? And the handle shoots out by means of this button—oh, I'm so sorry, it sometimes does that. Did anyone see where it went?"

The handle was located in a bush and screwed back in.

Tiffany, a girl who *listened* to what people said, watched Miss Level closely. She definitely had only one nose on her face, and it was sort of uncomfortable to imagine where anyone might have another one and what'd they use it for.

Then Miss Level pulled some rope out of her pocket and passed it to someone who wasn't there.

That's what she did, Tiffany was sure. She didn't drop it, she didn't throw it, she just held it out and let go, as though she'd thought she was hanging it on an invisible hook.

It landed in a coil on the moss. Miss Level looked down, then saw Tiffany staring at her and laughed nervously.

"Silly me," she said. "I thought I was over there! I'll forget my own head next!"

"Well . . . if it's the one on top of your neck," said Tiffany cautiously, still thinking about the other nose, "you've still got it."

The old suitcase was roped to the bristle end of the broomstick, which now floated calmly a few feet above the ground.

"There, that'll make a nice comfy seat," said Miss Level, now the bag of nerves that most people turned into when they felt Tiffany staring at them. "If you'd just hang on behind me. Er. That's what I normally do."

"You normally hang on *behind* you?" said Tiffany. "How can—"

"Tiffany, I've always encouraged your forthright way of asking questions," said Miss Tick loudly. "And now, please, I would love to congratulate you on your mastery of silence! Do climb on behind Miss Level. I'm sure she'll want to leave while you've still got some daylight."

The stick bobbed a little as Miss Level climbed onto it. She patted it invitingly.

"You're not frightened of heights, are you, dear?" she asked as Tiffany climbed on.

"No," said Tiffany.

"I shall drop in when I come up for the Witch Trials," said Miss Tick as Tiffany felt the stick rise gently under her. "Take care!"

It turned out that when Miss Level had asked Tiffany if she was scared of heights, it had been the wrong question. Tiffany was not afraid of heights at all. She could walk past tall trees without batting an eyelid. Looking up at huge towering mountains didn't bother her a bit.

What she *was* afraid of, although she hadn't realized it until this point, was depths. She was afraid of dropping such a long way out of the sky that she'd have time to run out of breath screaming before hitting the rocks so hard that she'd turn to a sort of jelly and all her bones would break into dust. She was, in fact, afraid of the ground. Miss Level should have thought before asking the question.

Tiffany clung to Miss Level's belt and stared at the cloth of her dress.

"Have you ever flown before, Tiffany?" asked the witch as they rose.

"Gnf!" squeaked Tiffany.

"If you like, I could take us round in a little circle," said Miss Level. "We should have a fine view of your country from up here."

The air was rushing past Tiffany now. It was a lot colder. She kept her eyes fixed firmly on the cloth.

"Would you like that?" said Miss Level, raising her voice as the wind grew louder. "It won't take a moment!"

Tiffany didn't have time to say no and, in any case, was sure she'd be sick if she opened her mouth. The stick lurched under her, and the world went sideways.

She didn't want to look but remembered that a witch is always inquisitive to the point of nosiness. To stay a witch, she *had* to look.

She risked a glance and saw the world under her. The red-gold light of sunset was flowing across the land, and down there were the long shadows of Twoshirts and, farther away, the woods and villages all the way back to the long curved hill of the Chalk—

—which glowed red, and the white carving of the chalk Horse burned gold like some giant's pendant. Tiffany stared at it; in the fading light of the afternoon, with the shadows racing away from the sliding sun, it looked alive.

At that moment she wanted to jump off, fly back, get there by closing her eyes and clicking her heels together, do *anything*—

No! She'd bundled those thoughts away, hadn't she? She had to learn, and there was no one on the hills to teach her!

But the Chalk was her world. She walked on it every day. She could feel its ancient life under her feet. The land was in her bones, just as Granny Aching had said. It was in her name, too; in the old language of the Nac Mac Feegle, her name sounded like "Land Under Wave," and in the eye of her mind she'd walked in those deep prehistoric seas when the Chalk had been formed, in a million-year rain made of the shells of tiny creatures. She trod a land made of life, and breathed it in, and listened to it, and thought its thoughts for it. To see it now, small, alone, in a land-scape that stretched to the end of the world, was too much. She had to go back to it—

For a moment the stick wobbled in the air.

No! I know I must go!

It jerked back, and there was a sickening feeling in her stomach as the stick curved away toward the mountains.

"A little bit of turbulence there, I think," said Miss Level over her shoulder. "By the way, did Miss Tick warn you about the thick wooly pants, dear?"

Tiffany, still shocked, mumbled something that managed to sound like "no." Miss Tick had mentioned the pants, and how a sensible witch wore at least three pairs to stop ice forming, but she had forgotten about them.

"Oh dear," said Miss Level. "Then we'd better hedgehop."

The stick dropped like a stone.

Tiffany never forgot that ride, though she often tried to. They flew just above the ground, which was the blur just below her feet. Every time they came to a fence or a hedge, Miss Level would jump it with a cry of "Here we go!" or "Ups-a-daisy!" which was probably meant to make Tiffany feel better. It didn't. She threw up twice.

Miss Level flew with her head bent so far down as to be almost level with the stick, thus getting the maximum aerodynamic advantage from the pointy hat. It was quite a stubby one, only about nine inches high, rather like a clown hat without the bobbles; Tiffany found out later that this was so that she didn't have to take it off when entering low-ceilinged cottages.

After a while—an eternity from Tiffany's point of view—they left the farmlands behind and started to fly through foothills. Before long they'd left trees behind, too, and the stick was flying above the fast white waters of a wide river studded with boulders. Spray splashed over their boots.

She heard Miss Level yell above the roar of the river and the rush of the wind: "Would you mind leaning back? This bit's a little tricky!"

Tiffany risked peeking over the witch's shoulder and gasped.

There was not much water on the Chalk, except for the little streams that people called bournes, which flowed down the valleys in late winter and dried up completely in the summer. Big rivers flowed around it, of course, but they were slow and tame.

The water ahead wasn't slow and tame. It was *vertical*.

The river ran up into the dark-blue sky, soared up to the early stars. The broom followed it.

Tiffany leaned back and screamed, and went on screaming as the broomstick tilted in the air and climbed up the waterfall. She'd known the *word*, certainly, but the word hadn't been so big, so wet, and above all it hadn't been so *loud*.

The mist of it drenched her. The noise pounded in her ears. She held on to Miss Level's belt as they climbed though spray and thunder and felt that she'd slip at any minute—

—and then she was thrown forward, and the noise of the falls died away behind her as the stick, now once again going "along" rather than "up," sped across the surface of a river that, while still leaping and foaming, at least had the decency to do it on the ground.

There was a bridge high above, and walls of cold rock hemmed the river in on either side, but the walls got lower and the river got slower and the air got warmer again until the broomstick skimmed across calm fat water that probably didn't know what was going to happen to it. Silver fish zigzagged away as they passed over the surface.

After a while Miss Level sent them curving up across new fields, smaller and greener than the ones at home. There were trees again, and little woods in deep valleys. But the last of the sunlight was draining away, and soon all there was below was darkness.

Tiffany must have dozed off, clinging to Miss Level, because she felt herself jerk awake as the broomstick stopped in midair. The ground was some way below, but someone had set out a ring of what turned out to be candle ends, burning in old jars.

Delicately, turning slowly, the stick settled down until it stopped just above the grass.

At this point Tiffany's legs decided to untwist, and she fell off.

"Up we get!" said Miss Level cheerfully, picking her up. "You did very well!"

"Sorry about screaming and being sick," Tiffany mumbled, tripping over one of the jars and knocking the candle out. She tried to make out anything in the dark, but her head was spinning. "Did you light these candles, Miss Level?"

"Yes. Let's get inside, it's getting chilly—" Miss Level began.

"Oh, by magic," said Tiffany, still dizzy.

"Well, it *can* be done by magic, yes," said Miss Level. "But I prefer matches, which are of course a lot less effort and quite magical in themselves, when you come to think about it." She untied the suitcase from the stick and said: "Here we are, then! I do hope you'll like it here!"

There was that cheerfulness again. Even when she felt sick and dizzy, and quite interested in knowing where the privy was as soon as possible, Tiffany still had ears that worked and a mind that, however much she tried, wouldn't stop thinking. And it thought: That cheerfulness has got cracks around the edges. Something isn't right here. . . .

CHAPTER 3

A Single-Minded Lady

T here was a cottage, but Tiffany couldn't see much in the gloom. Apple trees crowded in around it. Something hanging from a branch brushed against her as, walking unsteadily, she followed Miss Level. It swung away with a tinkling sound. There was the sound of rushing water, too, some way away.

Miss Level was opening a door. It led into a small, brightly lit, and amazingly tidy kitchen. A fire was burning briskly in the iron stove.

"Um . . . I'm supposed to be the apprentice," said Tiffany, still groggy from the flight. "I'll make something to drink if you show me where things are—"

"No!" Miss Level burst out, raising her hands. The shout seemed to have shocked her, because she was shaking when she lowered them. "No, I, I wouldn't dream of it," she said in a more normal voice, trying to smile. "You've had a long day. I'll show you to your room and where things are, and I'll bring you up some stew, and you can be an apprentice tomorrow. No rush."

Tiffany looked at the bubbling pot on the iron stove, and the loaf on the table. It was freshly baked bread, she could smell that.

The trouble with Tiffany was her Third Thoughts.* They thought: She lives by herself. Who lit the fire? A bubbling pot needs stirring from time to time. Who stirred it? And someone lit the candles. Who?

"Is there anyone else staying here, Miss Level?" she said.

Miss Level looked desperately at the pot and the loaf and back to Tiffany.

"No, there's only me," she said, and somehow Tiffany knew she was telling the truth. Or *a* truth, anyway.

"In the morning?" said Miss Level, almost pleading. She looked so forlorn that Tiffany actually felt sorry for her.

She smiled. "Of course, Miss Level," she said.

There was a brief tour by candlelight. There was a privy not far from the cottage; it was a two-holer, which Tiffany thought was a bit odd—but of course maybe other people had lived here once. There was also a room just for a bath, a terrible waste of space by the standards of Home Farm. It had its own pump and a big boiler for heating the water. This was definitely posh.

Her bedroom was a . . . nice room. *Nice* was a very good word. Everything had frills. Anything that could have a cover on it was covered. Some attempt had been made to make the room . . . jolly, as if being a bedroom was a jolly wonderful thing to be. Tiffany's room back on the farm had a rag rug on the floor, a water jug and basin on a stand, a big wooden box for clothes, an ancient dolls' house, and some old calico curtains, and that was pretty much it. On the farm, bedrooms were for shutting your eyes in.

The room had a chest of drawers. The contents of Tiffany's

---

*First Thoughts are the everyday thoughts. Everyone has those. Second Thoughts are the thoughts you think about the *way* you think. People who enjoy thinking have those. Third Thoughts are thoughts that watch the world and think all by themselves. They're rare, and often troublesome. Listening to them is part of witchcraft.

suitcase filled one drawer easily.

The bed made no sound when Tiffany sat on it. Her bed at home had a mattress so old that it had a comfy hollow in it, and the springs all made different noises; if she couldn't sleep, she could move various parts of her body and play "The Bells of St. Ungulants" on the springs—*cling twing glong, gling ping bloyinnng, dlink plang dyonnng, ding* ploink.

This room smelled different too. It smelled of spare rooms and other people's soap.

At the bottom of her suitcase was a small box that Mr. Block, the farm's carpenter, had made for her. He did not go in for delicate work, and it was quite heavy. In it, she kept . . . keepsakes. There was a piece of chalk with a fossil in it, which was quite rare, and her personal butter stamp (which showed a witch on a broomstick) in case she got a chance to make butter here, and a dobby stone, which was supposed to be lucky because it had a hole in it. (She'd been told that when she was seven, and had picked it up. She couldn't quite see how the hole made it lucky, but since it had spent a lot of time in her pocket, and then safe and sound in the box, it probably *was* more fortunate than most stones, which got kicked around and run over by carts and so on.)

There was also a blue-and-yellow wrapper from an old packet of Jolly Sailor tobacco, and a buzzard feather, and an ancient flint arrowhead wrapped up carefully in a piece of sheep's wool. There were plenty of these on the Chalk. The Nac Mac Feegle used them for spear points.

She lined these up neatly on the top of the chest of drawers, alongside her diary, but they didn't make the place look more homey. They just looked lonely.

Tiffany picked up the old wrapper and the sheep wool and

sniffed them. They weren't *quite* the smell of the shepherding hut, but they were close enough to it to bring tears to her eyes.

She had never spent a night away from the Chalk before. She knew the word *homesickness* and wondered whether this cold, thin feeling growing inside her was what it felt like—

Someone knocked at the door.

"It's me," said a muffled voice.

Tiffany jumped off the bed and opened the door. Miss Level came in with a tray that held a bowl of beef stew and some bread. She put it down on the little table by the bed.

"If you put it outside the door when you're finished, I'll take it down later," she said.

"Thank you very much," said Tiffany.

Miss Level paused at the door. "It's going to be so nice having someone to talk to, apart from myself," she said. "I do hope you won't want to leave, Tiffany."

Tiffany gave her a happy little smile, then waited until the door had shut and she'd heard Miss Level's footsteps go downstairs before tiptoeing to the window and checking there were no bars in it.

There had been something scary about Miss Level's expression. It was sort of hungry and hopeful and pleading and frightened, all at once.

Tiffany also checked that she could bolt the bedroom door on the inside.

The beef stew tasted, indeed, just like beef stew and not, just to take an example *completely* and *totally* at random, stew made out of the last poor girl who'd worked here.

To be a witch, you have to have a very good imagination. Just now, Tiffany was wishing that hers wasn't *quite* so good. But

Mistress Weatherwax and Miss Tick wouldn't have let her come here if it was dangerous, would they? Well, would they?

They might. They just might. Witches didn't believe in making things too easy. They assumed you used your brains. If you didn't use your brains, you had no business being a witch. The world doesn't make things easy, they'd say. Learn how to learn fast.

But . . . they'd give her a chance, wouldn't they?

Of course they would.

Probably.

She'd nearly finished the not-made-of-people-at-all-honestly stew when something tried to take the bowl out of her hand. It was the gentlest of tugs, and when she automatically pulled it back, the tugging stopped immediately.

O-kay, she thought. Another strange thing. Well, this *is* a witch's cottage.

Something pulled at the spoon but, again, stopped as soon as she tugged back.

Tiffany put the empty bowl and spoon back on the tray.

"All right," she said, hoping she sounded not scared at all. "I've finished."

The tray rose into the air and drifted gently toward the door, where it landed on the floor with a faint tinkle.

Up on the door, the bolt slid back.

The door opened.

The tray rose up and sailed through the doorway.

The door shut.

The bolt slid across.

Tiffany heard the rattle of the spoon as, somewhere on the dark landing, the tray moved on.

It seemed to Tiffany that it was vitally important that she *thought* before doing anything. And so she thought: It would be stupid to run around screaming because your tray had been taken away. After all, whatever had done it had even had the decency to bolt the door after itself, which meant that it respected her privacy, even while it ignored it.

She cleaned her teeth at the washstand, got into her nightgown, and slid into the bed. She blew out the candle.

After a moment she got up, relit the candle, and with some effort dragged the chest of drawers in front of the door. She wasn't quite certain why, but she felt better for doing it.

She lay back in the dark again.

Tiffany was used to sleeping while, outside on the downland, sheep baaed and sheep bells occasionally went *tonk*.

Up here, there were no sheep to *baa* and no bells to *tonk*, and every time one didn't, she woke up thinking, What was that?

But she did get to sleep eventually, because she remembered waking up in the middle of the night to hear the chest of drawers very slowly slide back to its original position.

◆　◆　◆

Tiffany woke up, still alive and not chopped up, when the dawn was just turning gray. Unfamiliar birds were singing.

There were no sounds in the cottage, and she thought: I'm the apprentice, aren't I? *I'm* the one who should be cleaning up and getting the fire lit. I know how this is supposed to go.

She sat up and looked around the room.

Her old clothes had been neatly folded on top of the chest of drawers. The fossil and the lucky stone and the other things had gone, and it was only after a frantic search that she found them back in the box in her suitcase.

"Now *look*," she said to the room in general. "I *am* a hag, you know. If there are any Nac Mac Feegle here, step out this minute!"

Nothing happened. She hadn't expected anything to happen. The Nac Mac Feegle weren't particularly interested in tidying things up, anyway.

As an experiment she took the candlestick off the bedside table, put it on the chest of drawers, and stood back. More nothing happened.

She turned to look out of the window and, as she did so, there was a faint *blint* noise.

When she spun around, the candlestick was back on the table.

Well . . . today was going to be a day when she got *answers*. Tiffany enjoyed the slightly angry feeling. It stopped her thinking about how much she wanted to go home.

She went to put her dress on and realized that there was something soft yet crackly in a pocket.

Oh, how could she have forgotten? But it had been a busy day, a very busy day, and maybe she'd wanted to forget, anyway.

She pulled out Roland's present and opened the white tissue paper carefully.

It was a necklace.

It was the Horse.

Tiffany stared at it.

Not what a horse looks like, but what a horse be. . . . It had been carved in the turf back before history began, by people who had managed to convey in a few flowing lines everything a horse was: strength, grace, beauty, and speed, straining to break free of the hill.

And now someone—someone clever and, therefore, probably also someone expensive—had made it out of silver. It was flat, just like it was on the hillside, and just like the Horse on the hillside, some parts of it were not joined to the rest of the body. The crafts-man, though, had joined these carefully together with tiny silver chain, so when Tiffany held it up in astonishment, it was all there, moving-while-standing-still in the morning light.

She had to put it on. And . . . there was no mirror, not even a tiny hand one. Oh, well . . .

"See me," said Tiffany.

And far away, down on the plains, something that had lost the trail awoke. Nothing happened for a moment, and then the mist on the fields parted as something invisible started to move, making a noise like a swarm of flies. . . .

Tiffany shut her eyes, took a couple of small steps sideways and a few steps forward, turned around, and carefully opened her eyes again. There she stood, in front of her, as still as a picture. The Horse looked very good on the new dress, silver against green.

She wondered how much it must have cost Roland. She won-dered *why*.

"See me not," she said. Slowly she took the necklace off, wrapped it up again in its tissue paper, and put it in the box with the other things from home. Then she found one of the postcards from Twoshirts and a pencil, and with care and attention, she wrote Roland a short thank-you note. After a flash of guilt she carefully used the other postcard to tell her parents that she was completely still alive.

Then, thoughtfully, she went downstairs.

It had been dark last night, so she hadn't noticed the posters stuck up all down the stairs. They were from circuses, and were covered with clowns and animals and that old-fashioned poster lettering where no two lines of type are the same.

They said things like:

THRILLS GALORE! HURRY! HURRY! HURRY!

**PROFESSOR MONTY BLADDER'S THREE-RING CIRCUS AND
CABINET OF CURIOSITIES!!**

SEE THE HORSE WITH HIS HEAD WHERE HIS TAIL SHOULD BE!

**SEE THE AMAZING DISLOCATING JACK PUT A LION'S HEAD IN HIS
ACTUAL MOUTH!!!**

SEE THE EGRESS!!!!!

CLOWNS! CLOWNS! CLOWNS!

**THE FLYING PASTRAMI BROTHERS WILL DEFY
GRAVITY, THE GREATEST FORCE IN THE UNIVERSE
*WITHOUT A NET!***

SEE CLARENCE THE TAP-DANCING MULE!

**WONDER AT
TOPSY AND TIPSY**
*THE ASTOUNDING MIND-READING ACT *

And so it went on, right down to tiny print. They were strange, bright things to find in a little cottage in the woods.

She found her way into the kitchen. It was cold and quiet, except for the ticking of a clock on the wall. Both the hands had fallen off the clock face and lay at the bottom of the glass cover, so while the clock was still measuring time, it wasn't inclined to tell anyone about it.

As kitchens went, it was very tidy. In the cupboard drawer under the sink, forks, spoons, and knives were all in neat sections, which was a bit worrying. Every kitchen drawer Tiffany had ever seen might have been *meant* to be neat but over the years had been crammed with things that didn't quite fit, like big ladles and bent bottle openers, which meant that they always stuck unless you knew the trick of opening them.

Experimentally she took a spoon out of the spoon section, dropped it among the forks, and shut the drawer. Then she turned her back.

There was a sliding noise and a tinkle exactly like the tinkle a spoon makes when it's put back among the other spoons, who have missed it and are anxious to hear its tales of life among the frighteningly pointy people.

This time she put a knife in with the forks, shut the drawer—and leaned on it.

Nothing happened for a while, and then she heard the cutlery rattling. The noise got louder. The drawer began to shake. The whole sink began to tremble—

"All right," said Tiffany, jumping back. "Have it your way!"

The drawer burst open, the knife jumped from section to section like a fish, and the drawer slammed back.

Silence.

"Who *are* you?" said Tiffany. No one replied. But she didn't like the feeling in the air. Someone was upset with her now. It had been a silly trick, anyway.

She went out into the garden quickly. The rushing noise she had heard last night was made by a waterfall not far from the cottage. A little waterwheel pumped water into a big stone cistern, and there was a pipe that led into the house.

The garden was full of ornaments. They were rather sad, cheap ones—bunny rabbits with crazy grins, pottery deer with big eyes, gnomes with pointy red hats and expressions that suggested they were on bad medication.

Things hung from the apple trees or were tied to posts all around the place. There were some dream catchers and curse nets, which she sometimes saw hanging up outside cottages at home. Other things looked like big shambles, spinning and tinkling gently. Some . . . well, one looked like a bird made out of old brushes, but most looked like piles of junk. Odd junk, though. It seemed to Tiffany that some of it moved slightly as she went past.

When she went back into the cottage, Miss Level was sitting at the kitchen table.

So was Miss Level. There were, in fact, two of her.

"Sorry," said the Miss Level on the right. "I thought it was best to get it over with right now."

The two women were exactly alike. "Oh, I see," said Tiffany. "You're twins."

"No," said the Miss Level on the left, "I'm not. This might be a little difficult—"

"—for you to understand," said the other Miss Level. "Let me see, now. You know—"

"—how twins are sometimes said to be able to share thoughts and feelings?" said the first Miss Level.

Tiffany nodded.

"Well," said the second Miss Level, "I'm a bit more complicated than that, I suppose, because—"

"—I'm one person with two bodies," said the first Miss Level, and now they spoke like players in a tennis match, slamming the words back and forth.

"I wanted to break this to you—"

"—gently, because some people get upset by the—"

"—idea and find it creepy or—"

"—just plain—"

"—weird."

The two bodies stopped.

"Sorry about that last sentence," said the Miss Level on the left. "I only do that when I'm really nervous."

"Er, do you mean that you both—" Tiffany began, but the Miss Level on the right said quickly, "There is no both. There's just me, do you understand? I know it's hard. But I have a right right hand and a right left hand and a left right hand and a left left hand. It's all me. I can go shopping and stay home at the same time, Tiffany. If it helps, think of me as one—"

"—person with four arms and—"

"—four legs and—"

"—four eyes."

All four of those eyes now watched Tiffany nervously.

"And two noses," said Tiffany.

"That's right. You've got it. My right body is slightly clumsier than my left body, but I have better eyesight in my right pair of eyes. I'm human, just like you, except that there's more of me."

"But one of you—that is, one half of you—came all the way to Twoshirts for me," said Tiffany.

"Oh yes, I can split up like that," said Miss Level. "I'm quite good at it. But if there's a gap of more than twenty miles or so, I get rather clumsy. And now a cup of tea would do us both good, I think."

Before Tiffany could move, both the Miss Levels stood up and crossed the kitchen.

Tiffany watched one person make a cup of tea using four arms.

There are quite a few things that need to be done to make a cup of tea, and Miss Level did them all at once. The bodies stood side by side, passing things from hand to hand to hand, moving kettle and cups and spoon in a sort of ballet.

"When I was a child, they thought I was twins," she said over one of her shoulders. "And then . . . they thought I was evil," she said, over another shoulder.

"Are you?" said Tiffany.

Both of Miss Level turned around, looking shocked.

"What kind of question is that to ask anyone?" she said.

"Um . . . the obvious one?" said Tiffany. "I mean, if they said, 'Yes I am! Mwahahaha!' that would save a lot of trouble, wouldn't it?"

Four eyes narrowed.

"Mistress Weatherwax was right," said Miss Level. "She said you were a witch to your boots."

Inside, Tiffany beamed with pride.

"Well, the thing about the obvious," said Miss Level, "is that it so often isn't. . . . Did Mistress Weatherwax *really* take off her hat to you?"

"Yes."

"One day perhaps you'll know how much honor she did you," said Miss Level. "Anyway . . . no, I'm not evil. But I nearly became evil, I think. Mother died not long after I was born, my father was at sea and never came back—"

"Worse things happen at sea," said Tiffany. It was something Granny Aching had told her.

"Yes, right, and probably they did, or possibly he never wanted to come back in any case," said Miss Level dryly. "And I was put in a charity home, bad food, horrible teachers, blah, blah, and I fell into the worst company possible, which was my own. It's *amazing* the tricks you can get up to when you've got two bodies. Of course, everyone thought I was twins. In the end I ran away to join the circus. Me! Can you imagine that?"

"Topsy and Tipsy, The Astounding Mind-Reading Act?" said Tiffany.

Miss Level stood stock-still, her mouths open.

"It was on the posters over the stairs," Tiffany added.

Now Miss Level relaxed.

"Oh, yes. Of course. Very . . . quick of you, Tiffany. Yes. You *do* notice things, don't you. . . ."

"I know I wouldn't pay money to see the egress," said Tiffany. "It just means 'the way out.'"*

"Clever!" said Miss Level. "Monty put that on a sign to keep people moving though the Believe-It-or-Not tent. *'This way to the Egress!'* Of course, people thought it was a female eagle or something, so Monty had a big man with a dictionary outside to show them they got exactly what they paid for! Have you ever been to a circus?"

Once, Tiffany admitted. It hadn't been much fun. Things that try too hard to be funny often aren't. There had been a moth-eaten lion with practically no teeth, a tightrope walker who was never more than a few feet above the ground, and a knife thrower who threw a lot of knives at an elderly woman in pink tights on a big spinning wooden disc and completely failed to hit her every time.

---

*Knowing the dictionary all the way through does have *some* uses.

The only real amusement was afterward, when a cart ran over the clown.

"My circus was a lot bigger," said Miss Level, when Tiffany mentioned this. "Although, as I recall, our knife thrower was also very bad at aiming. We had elephants and camels and a lion so fierce it bit a man's arm nearly off."

Tiffany had to admit that this sounded a lot more entertaining.

"And what did *you* do?" she said.

"Well, I just bandaged him up while I shooed the lion off him—"

"Yes, Miss Level, but I meant in the circus. Just reading your own mind?"

Miss Level beamed at Tiffany. "That, yes, and nearly everything else, too," she said. "With different wigs on I was the Stupendous Bohunkus Sisters. I juggled plates, you know, and wore costumes covered in sequins. And I helped with the high-wire act. Not walking the wire, of course, but generally smiling and glittering at the audience. Everyone assumed I was twins, and circus people don't ask too many personal questions in any case. And then what with one thing and another, this and that . . . I came up here and became a witch."

Both of Miss Level watched Tiffany carefully.

"That was quite a long sentence, that last sentence," said Tiffany.

"Yes, it was, wasn't it," said Miss Level. "I can't tell you *everything*. Do you still want to stay? The last three girls didn't. Some people find me slightly . . . odd."

"Um . . . I'll stay," said Tiffany slowly. "The thing that moves things about is a bit strange, though."

Miss Level looked surprised and then said, "Oh, do you mean Oswald?"

"There's an invisible man called Oswald who can get into my *bedroom*?" said Tiffany, horrified.

"Oh, no. That's just a name. Oswald isn't a man, he's an *ondageist*. Have you heard of poltergeists?"

"Er . . . invisible spirits that throw things around?"

"Good," said Miss Level. "Well, an ondageist is the opposite. They're obsessive about tidiness. He's quite handy around the house, but he's absolutely dreadful if he's in the kitchen when I'm cooking. He keeps putting things away. I think it makes him happy. Sorry, I should have warned you, but he normally hides if anyone comes to the cottage. He's shy."

"And he's a man? I mean, a male spirit?"

"How would you tell? He's got no body and he doesn't speak. I just called him Oswald because I always picture him as a worried little man with a dustpan and brush." The left Miss Level giggled when the right Miss Level said this. The effect was odd and, if you thought that way, also creepy.

"Well, we *are* getting on well," said the right Miss Level nervously. "Is there anything more you want to know, Tiffany?"

"Yes, please," said Tiffany. "What do you want me to do? What do *you* do?"

◆ ◆ ◆

And mostly, it turned out, what Miss Level did was chores. Endless chores. You could look in vain for much broomstick tuition, spelling lessons, or pointy-hat management. They were, mostly, the kind of chores that are just . . . chores.

There was a small flock of goats, technically led by Stinky Sam, who had a shed of his own and was kept on a chain, but really led by Black Meg, the senior nanny, who patiently allowed Tiffany to milk her and then, carefully and deliberately, put a hoof in the milk bucket. That's a goat's idea of getting to know you. A goat is a worrying thing if you're used to sheep, because a goat is a sheep with *brains*. But Tiffany had met goats before, because a few people in the village kept them for their milk, which was very nourishing. And she knew that with goats you had to use persicology.* If you got excited, and shouted, and hit them (hurting your hand, because it's like slapping a sack full of coat hangers), then they had Won and sniggered at you in goat language, which is almost all sniggering anyway.

By day two Tiffany learned that the thing to do was reach out and grab Black Meg's hind leg just as she lifted it up to kick the bucket, *and lift it up farther.* That made her unbalanced and nervous and the other goats sniggered at *her*, and Tiffany had Won.

Next there were the bees. Miss Level kept a dozen hives, for the wax as much as the honey, in a little clearing that was loud with buzzing. She made Tiffany wear a veil and gloves before she opened a hive. She wore some too.

"Of course," she observed, "if you are careful and sober and well centered in your life, the bees won't sting. Unfortunately, not all the bees have heard about this theory. Good morning, Hive Three, this is Tiffany. She will be staying with us for a while. . . ."

Tiffany half expected the whole hive to pipe up, in some horrible high-pitched buzz, *"Good morning, Tiffany!"* It didn't.

"Why did you tell them that?" she asked.

"Oh, you have to talk to your bees," said Miss Level. "It's very bad luck not to. I generally have a little chat with them most evenings. News and gossip, that sort of thing. Every beekeeper knows about 'telling the bees.'"

---

*Tiffany knew what psychology was, but it hadn't been a *pronunciation* dictionary.

"And who do the bees tell?" asked Tiffany.

Both of Miss Level smiled at her.

"Other bees, I suppose," she said.

"So . . . if you knew how to *listen* to the bees, you'd know everything that was going on, yes?" Tiffany persisted.

"You know, it's funny you should say that," said Miss Level. "There have been a few rumors . . . But you'd have to learn to think like a swarm of bees. One mind with *thousands* of little bodies. Much too hard to do, even for me." She exchanged a thoughtful glance with herself. "Maybe not *impossible*, though."

Then there were the herbs. The cottage had a big herb garden, although it contained very little that you'd stuff a turkey with, and at this time of year there was still a lot of work to be done collecting and drying, especially the ones with important roots. Tiffany quite enjoyed that. Miss Level was big on herbs.

There is something called the Doctrine of Signatures. It works like this: When the Creator of the Universe made helpful plants for the use of people, he (or in some versions, she) put little clues on them to give people hints. A plant useful for toothache would look like teeth, one to cure earache would look like an ear, one good for nose problems would drip green goo, and so on. Many people believed this.

You had to use a certain amount of imagination to be good at it (but not much in the case of Nose Dropwort), and in Tiffany's world the Creator had got a little more . . . creative. Some plants had writing on them, if you knew where to look. It was often hard to find and usually difficult to read, because plants can't spell. Most people didn't even know about it and just used the traditional method of finding out whether plants were poisonous or useful by testing them on some elderly aunt they didn't need, but Miss Level was pioneering new techniques that she hoped would mean life would be better for everyone (and, in the case of the aunts, often longer, too).

"This one is False Gentian," she told Tiffany when they were in the long, cool workroom behind the cottage. She was holding up a weed triumphantly. "Everyone thinks it's another toothache cure, but just look at the cut root by stored moonlight, using my blue magnifying glass. . . ."

Tiffany tried it, and read: "GoOD F4r Colds May cors drowsniss Do nOt oprate heavE mashinry."

"Terrible spelling, but not bad for a daisy," said Miss Level.

"You mean plants *really* tell you how to use them?" said Tiffany.

"Well, not all of them, and you have to know where to look," said Miss Level. "Look at this, for example, on the common walnut. You have to use the green magnifying glass by the light of a taper made from red cotton, thus. . . ."

Tiffany squinted. The letters were small and hard to read.

"'May contain Nut'?" she ventured. "But it's a nutshell. Of *course* it'll contain a nut. Er . . . won't it?"

"Not necessarily," said Miss Level. "It may, for example, contain an exquisite miniature scene wrought from gold and many colored precious stones depicting a strange and interesting temple set in a far-off land. Well, it *might*," she added, catching Tiffany's expression. "There's no actual law against it. As such. The world is full of surprises."

That night Tiffany had a lot more to put in her diary. She kept it on top of her chest of drawers with a large stone on it. Oswald seemed to get the message about this, but he had started to polish the stone.

◆　◆　◆

And pull back, and rise above the cottage, and fly the eye across the night-time. . . .

Miles away, pass invisibly across something that is itself invisible, but which buzzes like a swarm on flies as it drags itself over the ground. . . .

Continue, the roads and towns and trees rushing behind you with *zip-zip* noises, until you come to the big city, and near the center of the city the high old tower, and beneath the tower the ancient magical university, and in the university the library, and in the library the bookshelves, and . . . the journey has hardly begun.

Bookshelves stream past. The books are on chains. Some snap at you as you pass.

And here is the section of the more dangerous books, the ones that are kept chained in cages or in vats of iced water or simply clamped between lead plates.

But here is a book, faintly transparent and glowing with thaumic radiation, under a glass dome. Young wizards about to engage in research are *encouraged* to go and read it.

The title is *Hivers: A Dissertation Upon a Device of Amazing Cunning* by Sensibility Bustle, D.M. Phil., B. El L., Patricius Professor of Magic. Most of the handwritten book is about how to construct a large and powerful magical apparatus to capture a hiver without harm to the user, but on the very last pages Dr. Bustle writes, or wrote:

According to the ancient and famous volume Res Centum et Una Quas Magus Facere Potet,* *hivers are a type of demon (indeed, Professor Poledread classifies them as such in* I Spy

---

*One Hundred and One Things a Wizard Can Do

Demons, *and Cuvee gives them a section under "wandering spirits" in* Liber Immanis Monstrorum.* *However, ancient texts discovered in the Cave of Jars by the ill-fated First Expedition to the Loko Region give quite a different story, which bears out my own not inconsiderable research.*

Hivers were formed in the first seconds of Creation. They are not alive but they have, as it were, the shape *of life. They have no body, brain, or thoughts of their own, and a naked hiver is a sluggish thing indeed, tumbling gently though the endless night between the worlds. According to Poledread, most end up at the bottoms of deep seas, or in the bellies of volcanoes, or drifting through the hearts of stars. Poledread was a very inferior thinker compared to myself, but in this case he is right.*

Yet a hiver does have the ability to fear and to crave. We cannot guess what frightens a hiver, but they seem to take refuge in bodies that have power of some sort—great strength, great intellect, great prowess with magic. In this sense they are like the common hermit elephant of Howondaland, Elephas solitarius, *which will always seek the strongest mud hut as its shell.*

There is no doubt in my mind that hivers have advanced the cause of life. Why did fish crawl out of the sea? Why did humanity grasp such a dangerous thing as fire? Hivers, I believe, have been behind this, firing outstanding *creatures of various species with the flame of necessary ambition, which drove them onward and upward! What is it that a hiver seeks? What is it that drives them forward? What is it they want? This I shall find out!*

Oh, lesser wizards warn us that a hiver distorts the mind of its host, curdling it and inevitably causing an early death through brain fever. I say poppycock! People have always been afraid of what

---

*The Monster Book of Monsters

they do not understand!

But I have understanding!

This morning, at two o'clock, I captured a hiver with my device! And now it is locked inside my head. I can sense its memories, the memories of every creature it has inhabited. Yet because of my superior intellect, I control the hiver. It does not control me. I do not feel that it has changed me in any way. My mind is as extraordinarily powerful as it always has been!

At this point the writing is smudgy, apparently because Bustle was beginning to drool.

Oh, how they have held me back over the years, those worms and cravens that have through sheer luck been allowed to call themselves my superiors! They laughed at me! BUT THEY ARE NOT LAUGHING NOW!!! Even those who called themselves my friends, OH YES, they did nothing but hinder me. What about the warnings? they said. Why did the jar you found the plans in have the words "Do Not Open Under Any Circumstances!" engraved in fifteen ancient languages on the lid? they said. Cowards! So-called "chums"! Creatures inhabited by a hiver become paranoid and insane, they said! Hivers cannot be controlled, they squeaked!! DO ANY OF US BELIEVE THIS FOR ONE MINUTE? Oh, what glories AWAIT! Now I have cleansed my life of such worthlessness! And as for those even now having the DISRESPECT YES DISRESPECT to hammer on my door because of what I did to the so-called Archchancellor and the College Council . . . HOW DARE THEY JUDGE ME! Like all insects they have NO CONCEPT OF GREATNESS!!!!! I WILL SHOW THEM!!! But . . . I insoleps . . . blit !!!!! hammeringggg dfgujf blort . . .

. . . And there the writing ends. On a little card beside the book some wizard of former times has written: *All that could be found of Professor Bustle was buried in a jar in the old Rose Garden. We advise all research students to spend some time there, and reflect upon the manner of his death.*

◆　◆　◆

The moon was on the way to being full. A gibbous moon, it's called. It's one of the duller phases of the moon and seldom gets illustrated. The full moon and the crescent moon get all the publicity.

Rob Anybody sat alone on the mound just outside the fake rabbit hole, staring at the distant mountains where the snow on the peaks gleamed in the moonlight.

A hand touched him lightly on the shoulder.

"'Tis not like ye to let someone creep up on ye, Rob Anybody," said Jeannie, sitting down beside him.

Rob Anybody sighed.

"Daft Wullie was telling me ye havena been eatin' your meals," said Jeannie carefully.

Rob Anybody sighed.

"And Big Yan said when ye wuz out huntin' today, ye let a fox go past wi'out gieing it a good kickin'?"

Rob sighed again.

There was a faint *pop* followed by a glugging noise. Jeannie held out a tiny wooden cup. In her other hand was a small leather bottle.

Fumes from the cup wavered in the air.

"This is the last o' the Special Sheep Liniment your big wee hag gave us at our wedding," said Jeannie. "I put it safely by for emergencies."

"She's no' *my* big wee hag, Jeannie," said Rob, without looking at the cup. "She's *oor* big wee hag. An' I'll tell ye, Jeannie, she has it in her tae be the hag o' hags. There's power in her she doesna dream of. But the hiver smells it."

"Aye, well, a drink's a drink, whomsoever ye call her," said Jeannie soothingly. She waved the cup under Rob's nose.

He sighed and looked away.

Jeannie stood up quickly. "Wullie! Big Yan! Come quick!" she yelled. "He willna tak' a drink! I think he's *deid*!"

"Ach, this is no' the time for strong licker," said Rob Anybody. "My heart is heavy, wumman."

"Quickly now!" Jeannie shouted down the hole. *"He's deid and still talkin'!"*

"She's the hag o' these hills," said Rob, ignoring her. "Just like her granny. She tells the hills what they are, every day. She has them in her bones. She holds 'em in her heart. Wi'out her, I dinna like tae think o' the future."

The other Feegles had come scurrying out of the hole and were looking uncertainly at Jeannie.

"Is somethin' wrong?" said Daft Wullie.

"Aye!" snapped the kelda. "Rob willna tak' a drink o' Special Sheep Liniment!"

Wullie's little face screwed up in instant grief. "Ach, the Big Man's *deid*!" he sobbed. "Oh waily waily waily—"

"Will ye hush yer gob, ye big mudlin!" shouted Rob Anybody, standing up. "I am no' deid! I'm trying to have a moment o' existential dreed here, right? Crivens, it's a puir lookout if a man canna feel the chilly winds o' fate lashing aroound his nethers wi'out folks telling him he's deid, eh?"

"Ach, and I see ye've been talking to the toad again, Rob," said

Big Yan. "He's the only one aroound here that used them lang words that tak' all day to walk the length of. . . ." He turned to Jeannie. "It's a bad case o' the thinkin' he's caught, missus. When a man starts messin' wi' the readin' and the writin', then he'll come doon with a dose o' the thinkin' soon enough. I'll fetch some o' the lads and we'll hold his heid under water until he stops doin' it—'tis the only cure. It can kill a man, the thinkin'.'"

"I'll wallop ye and ten like ye!" yelled Rob Anybody in Big Yan's face, raising his fists. "I'm the Big Man in this clan and—"

"And I am the kelda," said their kelda, and one of the hiddlins of keldaring is to use your voice like that: hard, cold, sharp, cutting the air like a dagger of ice. "And I tell you men to go back doon the hole and dinna show your faces back up here until I say. *Not you, Rob Anybody Feegle!* You stay here until I tell ye!"

"Oh waily waily—" Daft Wullie began, but Big Yan clapped a hand over his mouth and dragged him away quickly.

When they were alone, and scraps of cloud were beginning to mass around the moon, Rob Anybody hung his head.

"I willna go, Jeannie, if you say," he said.

"Ach, Rob, *Rob*," said Jeannie, beginning to cry. "Ye dinna *understand*. I want no harm to come to the big wee girl, truly I don't. But I canna face thinkin' o' you out there fightin' this monster that canna be killed! It's you I'm worried aboot, can ye no' *see*?"

Rob put his arm around her. "Aye, I see," he said.

"I'm your wife, Rob, askin' ye not to go!"

"Aye, aye. I'll stay," said Rob.

Jeannie looked up to him. Tears shone in the moonlight. "Ye mean it?"

"I never braked my word yet," said Rob. "Except to polis'men and other o' that kidney, ye ken, and they dinna count."

"Ye'll stay? Ye'll abide by my word?" said Jeannie, sniffing.

Rob sighed. "Aye. I will."

Jeannie was quiet for a while and then said, in the sharp cold voice of a kelda: "Rob Anybody Feegle, I'm tellin' ye now to go and save the big wee hag."

"Whut?" said Rob Anybody, amazed. "Jus' noo ye said I was tae stay—"

"That was as your wife, Rob. Now I'm telling you as your kelda." Jeannie stood up, chin out and looking determined. "If ye dinna heed the world o' yer kelda, Rob Anybody Feegle, ye can be banished fra' the clan. Ye ken that. So you'll listen t' me guid. Tak' what men you need afore it's too late, and go to the mountains, and see that the big wee girl comes tae nae harm. And come back safe yoursel'. That is an order! Nay, 'tis more'n an order. 'Tis a geas I'm laying on ye! That cannae be brake!"

"But I—" Rob began, completely bewildered.

"I'm the *kelda*, Rob," said Jeannie. "I canna run a clan with the Big Man pinin'. And the hills of our children need their hag. Everyone knows the land needs someone tae tell it whut it is."

There was something about the way Jeannie had said "children." Rob Anybody was not the fastest of thinkers, but he always got there in the end.

"Aye, Rob," said Jeannie, seeing his expression. "Soon I'll be birthing seven sons."

"Oh," said Rob Anybody. He didn't ask how she knew the number. Keldas just knew.

"That's *great*!" he said.

"And one daughter, Rob."

Rob blinked.

"A daughter? This soon?"

"Aye," said Jeannie.

"That's wonderful good luck for a clan!" said Rob.

"Aye. So you've got something to come back safe to me for, Rob Anybody. An' I beg ye to use your heid for somethin' other than nuttin' folk."

"I thank ye, Kelda," said Rob Anybody. "I'll do as ye bid. I'll tak' some lads and find the big wee hag, for the good o' the hills. It canna be a good life for the puir wee big wee thing, all alone and far fra' home, among strangers."

"Aye," said Jeannie, turning her face away. "I ken that, too."

CHAPTER 4

The PLN

At dawn Rob Anybody, watched with awe by his many brothers, wrote the word:

PLN

. . . on a scrap of paper bag. Then he held it up.

"Plan, ye ken," he said to the assembled Feegles. "Now we have a Plan, all we got tae do is work out what tae *do*. Yes, Wullie?"

"Whut was that about this geese Jeannie hit ye with?" said Daft Wullie, lowering his hand.

"Not geese, geas," said Rob Anybody. He sighed. "I *told* yez. That means it's serious. It means I got tae bring back the big wee hag, an' no excuses, otherwise my soul gaes slam-bang intae the big cludgie in the sky. It's like a magical order. 'Tis a heavy thing, tae be under a geas."

"Well, they're big birds," said Daft Wullie.

"Wullie," said Rob, patiently, "ye ken I said I would tell ye when there wuz times you should've kept your big gob shut?"

"Aye, Rob."

"Weel, that wuz one o' them times." He raised his voice. "Now, lads, ye ken all aboot hivers. They cannae be killed! But 'tis oor duty to save the big wee hag, so this is, like, a sooey-side mission and ye'll probably all end up back in the land o' the living doin' a borin' wee job. So . . . I'm askin' for volunteers!"

Every Feegle over the age of four automatically put his hand up.

"Oh, come *on*," said Rob. "You canna *all* come! Look, I'll tak' . . .
Daft Wullie, Big Yan, and . . . you, Awf'ly Wee Billy Bigchin. An'
I'm takin' no weans, so if yez under three inches high, ye're not
comin'! Except for ye, o'course, Awf'ly Wee Billy. As for the rest
of youse, we'll settle this the traditional Feegle way. I'll tak' the last
fifty men still standing!"

He beckoned the chosen three to a place in the corner of the
mound while the rest of the crowd squared up cheerfully. A Feegle
liked to face enormous odds all by himself, because it meant you
didn't have to look where you were hitting.

"She's more'n a hundret miles awa'," said Rob as the big fight
started. "We canna run it—'tis too far. Any of youse scunners got
any ideas?"

"Hamish can get there on his buzzard," said Big Yan, stepping
aside as a cluster of punching, kicking Feegles rolled past.

"Aye, and he'll come wi' us, but he canna tak' more'n one passenger," shouted Rob over the din.

"Can we swim it?" said Daft Wullie, ducking as a stunned Feegle
hurtled over his head.

The others looked at him. "Swim it? How can we swim there
fra' here, yer daftie?" said Rob Anybody.

"It's just worth consid'ring, that's all," said Wullie, looking hurt.
"I wuz just tryin' to make a contribution, ye ken? Just wanted to
show willin'."

"The big wee hag left in a cart," said Big Yan.

"Aye, so what?" said Rob.

"Weel, mebbe we could?"

"Ach, no!" said Rob. "Showin' oursels tae hags is one thing, but
not to other folks! You remember what happened a few years back

when Daft Wullie got spotted by that lady who wuz painting the pretty pichoors doon in the valley? I dinna want to have them Folklore Society bigjobs pokin' aroound again!"

"I have an idea, Mister Rob. It's me, Awf'ly Wee Billy Bigchin Mac Feegle. We could disguise oursels."

Awf'ly Wee Billy Bigchin Mac Feegle always announced himself in full. He seemed to feel that if he didn't tell people who he was, they'd forget about him and he'd disappear. When you're half the size of most grown pictsies, you're *really* short; much shorter and you'd be a hole in the ground.

He was the new gonnagle. A gonnagle is the clan's bard and battle poet, but they don't spend all their lives in the same clan. In fact, they're a sort of clan all by themselves. Gonnagles move around among the other clans, making sure the songs and stories get spread around all the Feegles. Awf'ly Wee Billy had come with Jeannie from the Long Lake clan, which often happens. He was very young for a gonnagle, but as Jeannie had said, there was no age limit to gonnagling. If the talent was in you, you gonnagled. And Awf'ly Wee Billy knew all the songs and could play the mousepipes so sadly that outside it would start to rain.

"Aye, lad?" said Rob Anybody, kindly. "Speak up, then."

"Can we get hold o' some human clothes?" said Awf'ly Wee Billy. "Because there's an old story about the big feud between the Three Peaks clan and the Windy River clan and the Windy River boys escaped by making a tattie-bogle walk, and the men o' Three Peaks thought it was a bigjob and kept oot o' its way."

The others looked puzzled, and Awf'ly Wee Billy remembered that they were men of the Chalk and had probably never seen a tattie-bogle.

"A scarecrow?" he said. "It's like a bigjob made o' sticks, wi' clothes on, for to frighten away the birdies fra' the crops? Now, the song says the Windy River's kelda used magic to make it walk, but I reckon it was done by cunnin' and strength."

He sang about it. They listened.

He explained how to make a human that would walk. They looked at one another. It was a mad, desperate plan, which was very dangerous and risky and would require tremendous strength and bravery to make it work.

Put like that, they agreed to it instantly.

◆　◆　◆

Tiffany found that there was more than chores and the research, though. There was what Miss Level called "filling what's empty and emptying what's full."

Usually only one of Miss Level's bodies went out at a time. People thought Miss Level was twins, and she made sure they continued to do so, but she found it a little bit safer all around to keep the bodies apart. Tiffany could see why. You only had to watch both of Miss Level when she was eating. The bodies would pass plates to one another without saying a word, sometimes they'd eat off one another's forks, and it was rather strange to see one person burp and the other one say "Oops, pardon me."

"Filling what's empty and emptying what's full" meant wandering around the local villages and the isolated farms and, mostly, doing medicine. There were always bandages to change or expectant mothers to talk to. Witches did a lot of midwifery, which is a kind of "emptying what's full," but Miss Level wearing her pointy hat had only to turn up at a cottage for other people to suddenly come visiting, by sheer accident. And there was an awful lot of gossip and tea drinking. Miss Level moved in a twitching, living world of gossip, although Tiffany noticed that she picked up a lot more than she passed on.

It seemed to be a world made up entirely of women, but occasionally, out in the lanes, a man would strike up a conversation about the weather and somehow, by some sort of code, an ointment or a potion would get handed over.

Tiffany couldn't quite work out how Miss Level got paid. Certainly the basket she carried filled up more than it emptied. They'd walk past a cottage and a woman would come scurrying out with a fresh-baked loaf or a jar of pickles, even though Miss Level hadn't stopped there. But they'd spend an hour somewhere else, stitching up the leg of a farmer who'd been careless with an axe, and get a cup of tea and a stale biscuit. It didn't seem fair.

"Oh, it evens out," said Miss Level, as they walked on through the woods. "You do what you can. People give what they can, when they can. Old Slapwick there, with the leg, he's as mean as a cat, but there'll be a big cut of beef on my doorstep before the week's end, you can bet on it. His wife will see to it. And pretty soon people will be killing their pigs for the winter, and I'll get more lard, ham, bacon, and sausages turning up than a family could eat in a year."

"You will? What do you do with all that food?"

"Store it," said Miss Level.

"But you—"

"I store it in other people. It's amazing what you can store in other people." Miss Level laughed at Tiffany's expression. "I mean, I take what I don't need around to those who don't have a pig, or who're going through a bad patch, or who don't have anyone to remember them."

"But that means they'll owe *you* a favor!"

"Right! And so it just keeps on going around. It all works out."

"I bet some people are too mean to pay—"

"Not *pay*," said Miss Level, severely. "A witch never expects payment and never asks for it and just hopes she never needs to. But sadly, you are right."

"And then what happens?"

"What do you mean?"

"You stop helping them, do you?"

"Oh, no," said Miss Level, genuinely shocked. "You can't *not* help people just because they're stupid or forgetful or unpleasant. Everyone's poor around here. If I don't help them, who will?"

"Granny Aching . . . that is, my grandmother said someone has to speak up for them as has no voices," Tiffany volunteered after a moment.

"Was she a witch?"

"I'm not sure," said Tiffany. "I think so, but she didn't know she was. She mostly lived by herself in an old shepherding hut up on the downs."

"She wasn't a cackler, was she?" said Miss Level, and when she saw Tiffany's expression she said hurriedly, "Sorry, sorry. But it can happen, when you're a witch who doesn't know it. You're like a ship with no rudder. But obviously she wasn't like that, I can tell."

"She lived on the hills and talked to them, and she knew more about sheep than anybody!" said Tiffany hotly.

"I'm sure she did, I'm sure she did—"

"She *never* cackled!"

"Good, good," said Miss Level soothingly. "Was she clever at medicine?"

Tiffany hesitated. "Um . . . only with sheep," she said, calming down. "But she was very good. Especially if it involved turpentine.

Mostly if it involved turpentine, actually. But always she . . . was . . . just . . . there. Even when she wasn't *actually* there. . . ."

"Yes," said Miss Level.

"You know what I mean?" said Tiffany.

"Oh, yes," said Miss Level. "Your Granny Aching lived down on the uplands—"

"No, up on the downland," Tiffany corrected her.

"Sorry, up on the downland, with the sheep, but people would look up sometimes, look up at the hills, knowing she was there somewhere, and say to themselves, 'What would Granny Aching do?' or 'What would Granny Aching say if she found out?' or 'Is this the sort of thing Granny Aching would be angry about?'" said Miss Level. "Yes?"

Tiffany narrowed her eyes. It was true. She remembered when Granny Aching had hit a peddler who'd overloaded his donkey and was beating it. Granny usually used only words, and not many of them. The man had been so frightened by her sudden rage that he'd stood there and taken it.

It had frightened Tiffany, too. Granny, who seldom said anything without thinking about it for ten minutes beforehand, had struck the wretched man twice across the face in a brief blur of movement. And then news had got around, all along the Chalk. For a while, at least, people were a little more gentle with their animals. For months after that moment with the peddler, carters and drovers and farmers all across the downs would hesitate before raising a whip or a stick, and think: Suppose Granny Aching is watching?

But—

"How did you *know* that?" Tiffany asked.

"Oh, I guessed. She sounds like a witch to me, whatever she thought she was. A good one, too."

Tiffany inflated with inherited pride.

"Did she help people?" Miss Level added.

The pride deflated a bit. The instant answer "yes" jumped onto her tongue, and yet . . . Granny Aching hardly ever came down off the hills, except for Hogswatch and the early lambing. You seldom saw her in the village unless the peddler who sold Jolly Sailor tobacco was late on his rounds, in which case she'd be down in a hurry and a flurry of greasy black skirts to cadge a pipeful off one of the old men.

But there wasn't a person on the Chalk, from the Baron down, who didn't owe something to Granny. And what they owed to her, she made them pay to others. She always knew who was short of a favor or two.

"She made them help one another," she said. "She made them help themselves."

In the silence that followed, Tiffany heard the birds singing by the road. You got a lot of birds here, but she missed the high scream of the buzzards.

Miss Level sighed. "Not many of us are *that* good," she said. "If *I* was that good, we wouldn't be going to visit old Mr. Weavall again."

Tiffany said "Oh dear" inside.

Most days included a visit to Mr. Weavall. Tiffany dreaded them.

Mr. Weavall's skin was paper-thin and yellowish. He was always in the same old armchair, in a tiny room in a small cottage that smelled of old potatoes and was surrounded by a more or less over-grown garden. He'd be sitting bolt upright, his hands on two walking sticks, wearing a suit that was shiny with age, staring at the door.

"I make sure he has something hot every day, although he eats

357

like a bird," Miss Level had said. "And old Widow Tussy down the lane does his laundry, such as it is. He's ninety-one, you know."

Mr. Weavall had very bright eyes and chatted away to and at them as they tidied up the room. The first time Tiffany had met him, he'd called her Mary. Sometimes he still did so. And he'd grabbed her wrist with surprising force as she walked past. . . . It had been a real shock, that claw of a hand suddenly gripping her. You could see blue veins under the skin.

"I shan't be a burden on anyone," he'd said urgently. "I got money put by for when I go. My boy, Toby, won't have nothin' to worry about. I can pay my way! I want the proper funeral show, right? With the black horses and the plumes and the mutes and a knife-and-fork tea for everyone afterward, I've written it all down, fair and square. Check in my box to make sure, will you? That witch woman's always hanging around here!"

Tiffany had given Miss Level a despairing look. She'd nodded and pointed to an old wooden box tucked under Mr. Weavall's chair.

It had turned out to be full of coins, mostly copper, but there were quite a few silver ones. It looked like a fortune, and for a moment Tiffany'd wished she had as much money.

"There's a lot of coins in here, Mr. Weavall," she'd said.

Mr. Weavall relaxed. "Ah, that's right," he'd said. "Then I won't be a burden."

Today Mr. Weavall was asleep when they called on him, snoring with his mouth open and his yellow-brown teeth showing. But he awoke in an instant, stared at them, and then said, "My boy Toby's coming to see I Sat'day."

"That's nice, Mr. Weavall," said Miss Level, plumping up his cushions. "We'll get the place nice and tidy."

"He's done very well for hisself, you know," said Mr. Weavall proudly. "Got a job indoors with no heavy lifting. He said he'll see I all right in my old age, but I told him, I *told* him I'd pay my way when I go, the whole thing, the salt and earth and tuppence for the ferryman, too!"

Today Miss Level gave him a shave. His hands shook too much for him to do it himself. (Yesterday she'd cut his toenails, because he couldn't reach them; it was not a safe spectator sport, especially when one smashed a windowpane.)

"It's all in a box under my chair," he said as Tiffany nervously wiped the last bits of foam off him. "Just check for me, will you, Mary?"

Oh, yes. That was the ceremony, every day.

There was the box, and there was the money. He asked every time. There was always the same amount of money.

"Tuppence for the ferryman?" said Tiffany, as they walked home.

"Mr. Weavall remembers all the old funeral traditions," said Miss Level. "Some people believe that when you die, you cross the River of Death and have to pay the ferryman. People don't seem to worry about that these days. Perhaps there's a bridge now."

"He's always talking about . . . his funeral."

"Well, it's important to him. Sometimes old people are like that. They'd hate people to think that they were too poor to pay for their own funeral. Mr. Weavall'd die of shame if he couldn't pay for his own funeral."

"It's very sad, him being all alone like that. Something should be done for him," said Tiffany.

"Yes. We're doing it," said Miss Level. "And Mrs. Tussy keeps a friendly eye on him."

"Yes, but it shouldn't have to be us, should it?"

"Who should it *have* to be?" said Miss Level.

"Well, what about this son he's always talking about?" said Tiffany.

"Young Toby? He's been dead for fifteen years. And Mary was the old man's daughter, she died quite young. Mr. Weavall is very shortsighted, but he sees better in the past."

Tiffany didn't know what to reply except: "It shouldn't be like this."

"There isn't a way things *should* be. There's just what happens, and what we do."

"Well, couldn't you help him by magic?"

"I see to it that he's in no pain, yes," said Miss Level.

"But that's just herbs."

"It's still magic. Knowing things is magical, if other people don't know them."

"Yes, but *you* know what I mean," said Tiffany, who felt she was losing this argument.

"Oh, you mean make him young again?" said Miss Level. "Fill his house with gold? That's not what witches do."

"We see to it that lonely old men get a cooked dinner and cut their toenails?" said Tiffany, just a little sarcastically.

"Well, yes," said Miss Level. "We do what can be done. Mistress Weatherwax said you've got to learn that witchcraft is mostly about doing quite ordinary things."

"And you have do what she says?" said Tiffany.

"I listen to her advice," said Miss Level coldly.

"Mistress Weatherwax is the head witch, then, is she?"

"Oh no!" said Miss Level, looking shocked. "Witches are all equal. We don't have things like head witches. That's *quite* against the spirit of witchcraft."

"Oh, I see," said Tiffany.

"Besides," Miss Level added, "Mistress Weatherwax would never allow that sort of thing."

◆ ◆ ◆

Suddenly, things were going missing from the households around the Chalk. This wasn't the occasional egg or chicken. Clothes were vanishing off washing lines. A pair of boots mysteriously disappeared from under the bed of Nosey Hinds, the oldest man in the village—"And they was damn good boots, they could walk home from the pub all by themselves if I but pointed they in the right direction," he complained to anyone who would listen. "And they marched off wi' my old hat, too. And I'd got he just as I wanted he, all soft and floppy!"

A pair of trousers and a long coat vanished from a hook belonging to Abiding Swindell, the ferret keeper, and the coat still had ferrets living in the inside pockets. And who, *who* climbed through the bedroom window of Clem Doins and shaved off his beard, which had been so long that he could tuck it into his belt? Not a hair was left. He had to go around with a scarf over his face, in case the sight of his poor pink chin frightened the ladies.

It was probably witches, people agreed, and made a few more curse nets to hang in their windows.

However . . .

On the far side of the Chalk, where the long green slopes came down to the flat fields of the plain, there were big thickets of bramble and hawthorn. Usually, these were alive with birdsong, but this particular one, the one just here, was alive with cussing.

"*Ach, crivens! Will ye no' mind where ye're puttin' yer foot, ye spavie!*"

"*I canna help it! It's nae easy, bein' a knee!*"

"*Ye think ye got troubles? Ye wanna be doon here in the boots! That old man Swindell couldnae ha' washed his feet in years! It's fair reekin' doon here!*"

"Reekin', izzit? Well, you try bein' in this pocket! Them ferrets ne'er got oot to gae to the lavie, if you get my meanin'!"

"Crivens! Will ye dafties no' shut up?"

"Oh, aye? Hark at him! Just 'cuz ye're up in the heid, you think you know everythin'? Fra' doon here ye're nothing but deid weight, pal!"

"Aye, right! I'm wi' the elbows on this one! Where'd you be if it wuzn't for us carryin' ye aroound? Who's ye think ye are?"

"I'm Rob Anybody Feegle, as you ken well enough, an' I've had enough o' the lot o' yez!"

"Okay, Rob, but it's real stuffy in here!"

"Ach, an' I'm fed up wi' the stomach complainin', too!"

"Gentlemen." This was the voice of the toad; no one else would dream of calling the Nac Mac Feegle gentlemen. "Gentlemen, time is of the essence. The cart will be here soon! You must *not* miss it!"

"We need more time to practice, Toad! We're walkin' like a feller wi' nae bones and a serious case o' the trots!" said a voice a little higher up than the rest.

"At least you *are* walking. That's good enough. I wish you luck, gentlemen."

There was a cry from farther along the thickets, where a lookout had been watching the road.

"The cart's comin' doon the hill!"

"Okay, lads!" shouted Rob Anybody. "Toad, you look after Jeannie, y'hear? She'll need a thinkin' laddie to rely on while I'm no' here! Right, ye scunners! It's do or die! Ye ken what to do! Ye lads on the ropes, pull us up noo!" The bushes shook. "Right! Pelvis, are ye ready?"

"Aye, Rob!"

"Knees? Knees? I said, *knees*?"

"Aye, Rob, but—"

"Feets?"

"Aye, Rob!"

The bushes shook again.

"Right! Remember: right, left, right, left! Pelvis, knee, foot on the grround! Keep a spring in the step, feets! Are you ready? All together, boys . . . walk!"

It was a big surprise for Mr. Crabber, the carter. He'd been staring vaguely at nothing, thinking only of going home, when *something* stepped out of the bushes and into the road. It looked human or, rather, it looked slightly more human than it looked like anything else. But it seemed to be having trouble with its knees, and walked as though they'd been tied together.

However, the carter didn't spend too much time thinking about that because, clutched in one gloved hand that was waving vaguely in the air, was something gold.

This *immediately* identified the stranger, as far as the carter was concerned. He was not, as first sight might suggest, some old tramp to be left by the roadside, but an obvious gentleman down on his luck, and it was practically the carter's *duty* to help him. He slowed the horse to a standstill.

The stranger didn't really have a face. There was nothing much to see between the droopy hat brim and the turned-up collar of the coat except a lot of beard. But from somewhere within the beard a voice said:

". . . *Shudupshudup . . . will ye all shudup while I'm talkin'*. . . . Ahem. Good day ta' ye, carter fellow my ol' fellowy fellow! If ye'll gie us—me a lift as far as yer are goin', we—I'll gie ye this fine shiny golden coin!"

The figure lurched forward and thrust its hand in front of Mr. Crabber's face.

It was quite a large coin. And it was certainly gold. It had come from the treasure of the old dead king who was buried in the main part of the Feegles' mound. Oddly enough, the Feegles weren't hugely interested in gold once they'd stolen it, because you couldn't drink it and it was difficult to eat. In the mound, they mostly used the old coins and plates to reflect candlelight and give the place a nice glow. It was no hardship to give some away.

The carter stared at it. It was more money than he had ever seen in his life.

"If . . . sir . . . would like to . . . hop on the back of the cart, sir," he said, carefully taking it.

"Ach, right you are, then," said the bearded mystery man after a pause. "Just a moment, this needs a wee bitty organizin' . . . Okay, youse hands, you just grab the side o' the cart, and you leftie leg, ye gotta kinda sidle along . . . ach, crivens! Ye gotta bend! Bend! C'mon, get it right!" The hairy face turned to the carter. "Sorry aboot this," it said. "I talk to my knees, but they dinna listen to me."

"Is that right?" said the carter weakly. "I have trouble with my knees in the wet weather. Goose grease works."

"Ah, weel, these knees is gonna get more'n a greasin' if I ha' to get doon there an' sort them oot!" snarled the hairy man.

The carter heard various bangs and grunts behind him as the man hauled himself onto the tail of the cart.

"Okay, let's gae," said a voice. "We havena got all day. And youse knees, you're sacked! Crivens, I'm walkin' like I got a big touch of the stoppies! You gae up to the stomach and send doon a couple of good knee men!"

The carter bit the coin thoughtfully as he urged the horse into a walk. It was such pure gold that he left toothmarks. That meant his passenger was very, very rich. That was becoming very important at this point.

"Can ye no' go a wee bitty faster, my good man, my good man?" said the voice behind him, after they had gone a little way.

"Ah, well, sir," said the carter, "see them boxes and crates? I've got a load of eggs, and those apples mustn't be bruised, sir, and then there's those jugs of—"

There were some bangs and crashes behind him, including the *sploosh* that a large crate of eggs makes when it hits a road.

"Ye can gae faster noo, eh?" said the voice.

"Hey, that was my—" Mr. Crabber began.

"I've got another one o' they big wee gold coins for ye!" And a heavy and smelly arm landed on the carter's shoulder. Dangling from the glove on the end of it was, indeed, another coin. It was ten times what the load had been worth.

"Oh, well . . ." said the carter, carefully taking the coin. "Accidents do happen, eh, sir?"

"Aye, especially if I dinna think I'm goin' fast enough," said the voice behind him. "We—I mean I'm a big hurry tae get tae yon mountains, ye ken!"

"But I'm not a stagecoach, sir," said the carter reproachfully as he urged his old horse into a trot.

"Stagecoach, eh? What's one o' them things?"

"That's what you'll need to catch to take you up into the mountains, sir. You can catch one in Twoshirts, sir. I never go any farther than Twoshirts, sir. But you won't be able to get the stage today, sir."

"Why not?"

"I've got to make stops at the other villages, sir, and it's a long way, and on Wednesdays it runs early, sir, and this cart can only go so fast, sir, and—"

"If we—I dinna catch yon coach today I'll gie' ye the hidin' o' yer life," growled the passenger. "But if I *do* catch yon coach today, I'll gie ye five o' them gold coins."

Mr. Crabber took a deep breath, and yelled:

"*Hi! Hyah! Giddyup, Henry!*"

◆　　◆　　◆

All in all, it seemed to Tiffany, most of what witches did really *was* very similar to work. Dull work. Miss Level didn't even use her broomstick very much.

That was a bit depressing. It was all a bit . . . well, goody-goody. Obviously that was better than being baddy-baddy, but a little more . . . excitement would be nice. Tiffany wouldn't like anyone to think she'd expected to be issued with a magic wand on Day One but, well, the way Miss Level talked about magic, the whole *point* of witchcraft lay in not using any.

Mind you, Tiffany thought she would be depressingly good at not using any. It was doing the simplest magic that was hard.

Miss Level patiently showed her how to make a shamble, which could more or less be made of anything that seemed a good idea at the time provided it also contained something alive, like a beetle or a fresh egg.

Tiffany couldn't get the hang of it. That was . . . annoying. Didn't she have the virtual hat? Didn't she have First Sight and Second Thoughts? Miss Tick and Miss Level could throw a shamble together in seconds, but Tiffany just got a tangle, dripping with egg. Over and over again.

"I know I'm doing it right, but it just twists up!" Tiffany complained. "What can I do?"

"We could make an omelette?" said Miss Level cheerfully.

"Oh, please, Miss Level!" Tiffany wailed.

Miss Level patted her on the back. "It'll happen. Perhaps you're trying too hard. One day it'll come. The power does come, you know. You just have to put yourself in its path."

"Couldn't you make one that I could use for a while, to get the hang of it?"

"I'm afraid I can't," said Miss Level. "A shamble is a very tricky thing. You can't even carry one around, except as an ornament. You have to make it for yourself, there and then, right where and when you want to use it."

"Why?" said Tiffany.

"To catch the moment," said the other part of Miss Level, coming in. "The way you tie the knots, the way the string runs—"

"—the freshness of the egg, perhaps, and the moisture in the air—" said the first Miss Level.

"—the tension of the twigs and the kinds of things that you just happen to have in your pocket at that moment—"

"—even the way the wind is blowing," the first Miss Level concluded. "All these things make a kind of . . . of picture of the here and now when you move them right. And I can't tell you how to move them, because I don't know."

"But you *do* move them," said Tiffany, getting lost. "I saw you—"

"I do it but I don't know *how* I do," said Miss Level, picking up a couple of twigs and taking a length of thread. Miss Level sat down at the table opposite Miss Level, and all four hands started to put a shamble together.

"This reminds me of when I was in the circus," she said. "I was—"

"—walking out for a while with Marco and Falco, the Flying Pastrami Brothers," the other part of Miss Level went on. "They would do—"

"—triple somersaults fifty feet up with no safety net. What lads they were! As alike as two—"

"—peas, and Marco could catch Falco blindfolded. Why, for a moment I wondered if they were just like me—"

She stopped, went a bit red on both faces, and coughed. *"Anyway,"* she went on, "one day I asked them how they managed to stay on the high wire, and Falco said, 'Never ask the tightrope walker how he keeps his balance. If he stops to think about it, he falls off.' Although actually—"

"—he said it like this, 'Nev-ah aska tightaropa walkera . . .' because the lads pretended they were from Brindisi, you see, because that sounds foreign and impressive and they thought no one would want to watch acrobats called the Flying Sidney and Frank Cartwright. Good advice, though, wherever it came from."

The hands worked. This was not a lone Miss Level, a bit flustered, but the full Miss Level, all twenty fingers working together.

"Of course," she said, "it can be helpful to have the right sort of things in your pocket. I always carry a few sequins—"

"—for the happy memories they bring back," said Miss Level from the other side of the table, blushing again.

She held up the shamble. There were sequins, and a fresh egg in a little bag made of thread, and a chicken bone and many other things hanging or spinning in the threads.

Each part of Miss Level put both its hands into the threads and pulled. . . .

The threads took up a pattern. Did the sequins jump from one thread to another? It looked like it. Did the chicken bone pass *through* the egg? So it seemed.

Miss Level peered into it.

She said: "Something's coming. . . ."

◆　◆　◆

The stagecoach left Twoshirts half full and was well out over the plains when one of the passengers sitting on the rooftop tapped the driver on the shoulder.

"Excuse me, did you know there's something trying to catch up to us?" he said.

"Bless you, sir," said the driver, because he hoped for a good tip at the end of the run, "there's nothing that can catch up to *us*."

Then he heard the screaming in the distance, getting louder.

"Er, I think he means to," said the passenger as the carter's wagon caught up to them.

"Stop! Stop, for pity's sake, *stop!*" yelled the carter as he sailed past.

But there was no stopping Henry. He'd spent years pulling the carrier's cart around the villages, very slowly, and he'd always had this idea in his big horse head that he was cut out for faster things. He'd plodded along, being overtaken by coaches and carts and three-legged dogs, and now he was having the time of his life.

Besides, the cart was a lot lighter than usual, and the road was slightly downhill here. All he was really having to do was gallop fast enough to stay in front. And finally he'd nearly overtaken the stagecoach. Him, Henry!

He only stopped because the stagecoach driver stopped first. Besides, the blood was pumping through Henry now, and there were a couple of mares in the team of horses pulling the coach who he felt he'd really like to get to know—find out when was their day off, what kind of hay they liked, that kind of thing.

The carter, white in the face, got down carefully and then lay on the ground and held on tight to the dirt.

His one passenger, who looked to the coach driver like some sort of scarecrow, climbed unsteadily down from the back and lurched toward the coach.

"I'm sorry, we're full up," the driver lied. They weren't full, but there was certainly no room for a thing that looked like that.

"Ach, and there wuz me willin' to pay wi' gold," said the creature. "Gold such as this here," it added, waving a ragged glove in the air.

Suddenly there was plenty of space for an eccentric millionaire. Within a few seconds he was seated inside, and to the annoyance of Henry, the coach set off again.

◆　◆　◆

Outside Miss Level's cottage a broomstick was heading through the trees. A young witch—or at least, someone dressed as a witch; it never paid to jump to conclusions—was sitting on it sidesaddle.

She wasn't flying it very well. It jerked sometimes, and it was clear the girl was no good at making it turn corners, because sometimes she stopped, jumped off, and pointed the stick in a new direction by hand. When she reached the garden gate, she got off again quickly and tethered the stick to it with string.

"Nicely done, Petulia!" said Miss Level, clapping with all four hands. "You're getting quite good!"

"Um, thank you, Miss Level," said the girl, bowing. She stayed bowed, and said, "Um, oh dear . . ."

Half of Miss Level stepped forward.

"Oh, I can see the problem," she said, peering down. "Your amulet with the little owls on it is tangled up with your necklace of silver bats, and they've both got caught around a button. Just hold still, will you?"

"Um, I've come to see if your new girl would like come to the sabbat tonight," said the bent Petulia, her voice a bit muffled.

Tiffany couldn't help noticing that Petulia had jewelry everywhere; later she found that it was hard to be around Petulia for any length of time without having to unhook a bangle from a necklace or, once, an earring from an ankle bracelet (nobody ever found out how that one happened). Petulia couldn't resist occult jewelry. Most of the stuff was to magically protect her from things, but she hadn't found anything to protect her from looking a bit silly.

She was short and plump and permanently red-faced and slightly worried.

"Sabbat? Oh, one of your meetings," said Miss Level. "That would be nice, wouldn't it, Tiffany?"

"Yes?" said Tiffany, not quite sure yet.

"Some of the girls meet up in the woods in the evenings," said Miss Level. "For some reason the craft is getting popular again. That's very welcome, of course."

She said it as if she wasn't quite sure. Then she added: "Petulia here works for Old Mother Blackcap, over in Sidling Without. Specializes in animals. Very good woman with pig diseases. I mean, with pigs that've got diseases, I don't mean she *has* pig diseases. It'll be nice for you to have friends here. Why don't you go? There, everything's unhooked."

Petulia stood up and gave Tiffany a worried smile.

"Um, Petulia Gristle," she said, holding out a hand.

"Tiffany Aching," said Tiffany, shaking it gingerly in case the sound of all the bangles and bracelets jangling together deafened everyone.

"Um, you can ride with me on the broomstick, if you like," said Petulia.

"I'd rather not," said Tiffany. Petulia looked relieved but said: "Um, do you want to get dressed?"

Tiffany looked down at her green dress. "I am."

"Um, don't you have any gems or beads or amulets or anything?"

"No, sorry," said Tiffany.

"Um, you must at least have a shamble, surely?"

"Um, can't get the hang of them," said Tiffany. She hadn't meant the "um," but around Petulia it was catching.

"Um . . . a black dress, perhaps?"

"I don't really like black. I prefer blue or green," said Tiffany. "Um . . ."

"Um. Oh well, you're just starting," said Petulia generously. "I've been crafty for three years."

Tiffany looked desperately at the nearest half of Miss Level.

"In the craft," said Miss Level helpfully. "Witchcraft."

"Oh." Tiffany knew she was being very unfriendly, and Petulia with her pink face was clearly a nice person, but she felt awkward in front of her and she couldn't work out why. It was stupid, she knew. She could do with a friend. Miss Level was nice enough, and she managed to get along with Oswald, but it would be good to have someone around her own age to talk to.

"Well, I'd love to come," she said. "I know I've got a lot to learn."

◆   ◆   ◆

The passengers inside the stagecoach had paid good money to be inside on the soft seats and out of the wind and the dust, and therefore it was odd that so many got out at the next stop and went and sat on the roof.

The few who didn't want to ride up there or couldn't manage the climb sat huddled together on the seat opposite, watching the new traveler like a group of rabbits watching a fox and trying not to breathe.

The problem wasn't that he smelled of ferrets. Well, that *was* a problem, but compared to the *big* problem it wasn't much of one.

He talked to himself. That is, bits of him talked to other bits of him. *All the time.*

"Ah, it's fair boggin' doon here. Ah'm tellin ye! Ah'm sure it's my turn to be up inna heid!"

"Hah, at leas' youse people are all cushy in the stomach—it's us in the legs that has tae do all the work!"

At which the right hand said: *"Legs? Youse dinna know the meanin' of the word 'work'! Ye ought tae try being stuck in a glove! Ach, blow this for a game o' sojers! Ah'm gonna stretch ma legs!"*

In horrified silence the other passengers watched one of the man's gloved hands drop off and walk around on the seat.

"Aye, weel, it's nae picnic doon here inna troosers, neither. A'm gonna let some fresh air in right noo!"

"Daft Wullie, don't you dare do that—"

The passengers, squeezing even closer together, watched the trousers with terrible fascination. There was some movement, some swearing under the breath in a place where nothing should be breathing, and then a couple of buttons popped and a very small red-headed blue man stuck his head out, blinking in the light.

He froze when he saw the people.

He stared.

They stared.

Then his face widened into a mad smile.

"Youse folks all right?" he said, desperately. "That's greaaat! Dinna worry aboout me—I'm one o' they opper-tickle aloosyon's, ye ken?"

He disappeared back into the trousers, and they heard him whisper: "I'm thinkin' I fooled 'em easily, no problemo!"

A few minutes later the coach stopped to change horses. When it set off again, it was minus the inside passengers. They got off, and asked for their luggage to be taken off, too. No thank you, they did not want to continue their ride. They'd catch the coach tomorrow, thank you. No, there was no problem in waiting here in this delightful little, er, town of Dangerous Corner. Thank you. Good-bye.

The coach set off again, somewhat lighter and faster. It didn't stop that night. It should have done so, and the rooftop passengers were still eating their dinner in the last inn when they heard it set off without them. The reason probably had something to do with the big heap of coins now in the driver's pocket.

CHAPTER 5

The Circle

❦

Tiffany walked through the woods while Petulia flew unsteadily alongside in a series of straight lines. Tiffany learned that Petulia *was* nice, had three brothers, wanted to be a midwife for humans as well as pigs when she grew up, and was afraid of pins. She also learned that Petulia hated to disagree about *anything*.

So parts of the conversation went like this:

Tiffany said, "I live down on the Chalk."

And Petulia said, "Oh, where they keep all those sheep? I don't like sheep much—they're so kind of . . . baggy."

Tiffany said, "Actually, we're very proud of our sheep."

And then you could stand back as Petulia reversed her opinions like someone trying to turn a cart around in a very narrow space: "Oh, I didn't really mean I *hate* them. I expect some sheep are all right. We've got to *have* sheep, obviously. They're better than goats, and woolier. I mean I actually like sheep, really. Sheep are nice."

Petulia spent a lot of time trying to find out what other people thought so that she could think the same way. It would be impossible to have an argument with her. Tiffany had to stop herself from saying "the sky is green" just to see how long it would take for Petulia to agree. But she liked her. You couldn't *not* like her. She was restful company. Besides, you couldn't help liking someone who couldn't make a broomstick turn corners.

It was a long walk through the woods. Tiffany had always wanted to see a forest so big that you couldn't see daylight through the other side, but now that she'd lived in one for a couple of weeks, it got on her nerves. It was quite open woodland here, at least around the villages, and not hard to walk through. She'd had to learn what maples and birches were, and she'd never before seen the spruces and firs that grew higher up the slopes. But she wasn't happy in the company of trees. She missed the horizons. She missed the sky. Everything was too close.

Petulia chattered nervously. Old Mother Blackcap was a pig borer, cow shouter, and all-around veterinary witch. Petulia liked animals, especially pigs, because they had wobbly noses. Tiffany quite liked animals too, but no one except other animals liked animals as much as Petulia.

"So . . . what's this meeting about?" she said, to change the subject.

"Um? Oh, it's just to keep in touch," said Petulia. "Annagramma says it's important to make contacts."

"Annagramma's the leader, then, is she?" said Tiffany.

"Um, no. Witches don't have leaders, Annagramma says."

"Hmm," said Tiffany.

They arrived at last at a clearing in the woods, just as the sun was setting. There were the remains of an old cottage there, now covered mostly in brambles. You might miss it completely if you didn't spot the rampant growth of lilac and the gooseberry bushes, now a forest of thorns. Someone had lived here once, and had had a garden.

Someone else, now, had lit a fire. Badly. And they had found that lying down flat to blow on a fire because you hadn't started it with enough paper and dry twigs was not a good idea, because it would then cause your pointy hat, which you had forgotten to take off, to fall into the smoking mess and then, because it was dry, catch fire.

A young witch was now flailing desperately at her burning hat, watched by several interested spectators.

Another one, sitting on a log, said: "Dimity Hubbub, that is *literally* the most stupid thing anyone has ever done anywhere in the whole world, ever." It was a sharp, not very nice voice, the sort most people used for being sarcastic with.

"Sorry, Annagramma!" said Miss Hubbub, pulling off the hat and stamping on the point.

"I mean, just look at you, will you? You really are letting everyone down."

"Sorry, Annagramma!"

"Um," said Petulia.

Everyone turned to look at the new arrivals.

"You're *late*, Petulia Gristle!" snapped Annagramma. "And who's this?"

"Um, you *did* ask me to stop in at Miss Level's to bring the new girl, Annagramma," said Petulia, as if she'd been caught doing something wrong.

Annagramma stood up. She was at least a head taller than Tiffany and had a face that seemed to be built backward from her nose, which she held slightly in the air. To be looked at by Annagramma was to know that you'd already taken up too much of her valuable time.

"Is this her?"

"Um, yes, Annagramma."

"Let's have a look at you, new girl."

Tiffany stepped forward. It was amazing. She hadn't really meant to. But Annagramma had the kind of voice that you obeyed.

"What is your name?"

"Tiffany Aching?" said Tiffany, and found herself saying her name as if she was asking permission to have it.

"Tiffany? That's a funny name," said the tall girl. "*My* name is Annagramma Hawkin."

"Um, Annagramma works for—" Petulia began.

"—works *with*," said Annagramma sharply, still looking Tiffany up and down.

"Um, sorry, works *with* Mrs. Earwig," said Petulia. "But she—"

"I intend to leave next year," said Annagramma. "Apparently, I'm doing *extremely* well. So you're the girl who's joined Miss Level, are you? She's weird, you know. The last three girls all left very quickly. They said it was just too strange trying to keep track of which one of her was which."

"Which witch was which," said one of the girls cheerfully.

"Anyone can do that pun, Lucy Warbeck," said Annagramma, without looking around. "It's not funny, and it's not clever."

She turned her attention back to Tiffany, who felt that she was being examined as critically and thoroughly as Granny Aching would check a ewe she might be thinking of buying. She wondered if Annagramma would actually try to open her mouth and make sure she had all her teeth.

"They say you can't breed good witches on chalk," said Annagramma.

All the other girls looked from Annagramma to Tiffany, who thought: Hah, so witches don't have leaders, do they? But she was in no mood to make enemies.

"Perhaps they do," she said quietly. This did not seem to be what Annagramma wanted to hear.

"You haven't even dressed the part," said Annagramma.

"Sorry," said Tiffany.

"Um, Annagramma says that if you want people to treat you

like a witch, you should look like one," Petulia said.

"Hmm," said Annagramma, staring at Tiffany as if she'd failed a simple test. Then she nodded her head. "Well, we all had to start somewhere." She stood back. "Ladies, this is Tiffany. Tiffany, you know Petulia. She crashes into trees. Dimity Hubbub is the one with the smoke coming out of her hat, so that she looks like a chimney. That's Gertruder Tiring, that's the hilariously funny Lucy Warbeck, that's Harrieta Bilk, who can't seem to do anything about the squint, and then that's Lulu Darling, who can't seem to do anything about the name. You can sit in for this evening . . . Tiffany, wasn't it? I'm sorry you've been taken on by Miss Level. She's rather sad. Complete amateur. Hasn't really got a clue. Just bustles about and hopes. Oh, well, it's too late now. Gertruder, Summon the World's Four Corners and Open the Circle, please."

"Er . . ." said Gertruder nervously. It was amazing how many people around Annagramma became nervous.

"Do I have to do everything around here?" said Annagramma. "*Try* to remember, please! We must have been through this *literally* a million times!"

"I've never heard of the World's Four Corners," said Tiffany.

"Really? There's a surprise," said Annagramma. "Well, they're the directions of power, Tiffany, and I *would* advise you to do something about that name, too, please."

"But the world's round, like a plate," said Tiffany.

"Um, you have to imagine them," Petulia whispered.

Tiffany wrinkled her forehead.

"Why?" she said.

Annagramma rolled her eyes. "Because that's the way to do things *properly*."

"Oh."

"You *have* done *some* kind of magic, haven't you?" Annagramma demanded.

Tiffany was a bit confused. She wasn't used to people like Annagramma.

"Yes," she said. All the other girls were staring at her, and Tiffany couldn't help thinking about sheep. When a dog attacks a sheep, the other sheep run away to a safe distance and then turn and watch. They don't gang up on the dog. They're just happy it's not them.

"What are you best at, then?" snapped Annagramma.

Tiffany, her mind still full of sheep, spoke without thinking. "Soft Nellies," she said. "It's a sheep cheese. It's quite hard to make. . . ."

She looked around at the circle of blank faces and felt embarrassment rise inside her like hot jelly.

"Um, Annagramma meant what magic can you do best," said Petulia kindly.

"Although Soft Nellies is good," said Annagramma with a cruel little smile. One or two of the girls gave that little snort that meant they were trying not to laugh out loud but didn't mind showing that they were trying.

Tiffany looked down at her boots again.

"I don't know," she mumbled, "but I did throw the Queen of the Fairies out of my country."

"Really?" said Annagramma. "The Queen of the Fairies, eh? How did you do that?"

"I'm . . . not sure. I just got angry with her." And it was hard to remember exactly what had happened that night. Tiffany recalled the anger, the terrible anger, and the world . . . changing. She'd seen it clearer than a hawk sees, heard it better than a dog hears, felt its age beneath her feet, felt the hills still living. And she remembered thinking that no one could do this for long and still be human.

"Well, you've got the right boots for stamping your foot," said Annagramma. There were a few more half-concealed giggles. "A Queen of the Fairies," she added. "I'm *sure* you did. Well, it helps to dream."

"I don't tell lies," mumbled Tiffany, but no one was listening.

Sullen and upset, she watched the girls Open the Corners and Summon the Circle, unless she'd got that the wrong way around. This went on for some time. It would have gone better if they'd all been sure what to do, but it was probably hard to *know* what to do when Annagramma was around, since she kept correcting everyone. She was standing with a big book open in her arms.

". . . now you, Gertruder, go widdershins, *no, that's the other way, I must have told you literally a thousand times*, and Lulu—where's Lulu? Well, you shouldn't have been there! Get the shriven chalice, not that one, no, the one without handles . . . yes. Harrieta, hold the Wand of the Air a bit higher, I mean, it must *be* in the air, d'you understand? And for goodness' sake, Petulia, *please* try to look a little more stately, will you? I appreciate that it doesn't come naturally to you, but you might at least show you're making an effort. By the way, I've been meaning to tell you, no invocation ever written starts with 'um,' unless I'm very much mistaken. Harrieta, is that the Cauldron of the Sea? Does it even *look* like a Cauldron of the Sea? I don't think so, do you? *What was that noise?*"

The girls looked down. Then someone mumbled: "Dimity trod on the Circlet of Infinity, Annagramma."

"Not the one with the genuine seed pearls on it?" said Annagramma in a tight little voice.

"Um, yes," said Petulia. "But I'm sure she's very sorry. Um . . . shall I make a cup of tea?"

The book slammed shut.

"What is the point?" said Annagramma to the world in general. "What. Is. The. *Point?* Do you want to spend the rest of your lives as village witches, curing boils and warts for a cup of tea and a biscuit? Well? Do you?"

There was a shuffling among the huddled witches, and a general murmur of "No, Annagramma."

"You did all *read* Mrs. Earwig's book, didn't you?" she demanded. "Well, did you?"

Petulia raised a hand nervously. "Um—" she began.

"Petulia, I've told you literally a million times not to start. Every. Single. Sentence. With 'Um'—haven't I?"

"Um—" said Petulia, trembling with nervousness.

"Just speak up, for goodness' sake! Don't hesitate all the time!"

"Um—"

"Petulia!"

"Um—"

"Really, you might make an *effort.* Honestly, I don't know what's the matter with all of you!"

I do, Tiffany thought. You're like a dog worrying sheep all the time. You don't give them time to obey you, and you don't let them know when they've done things right. You just keep barking.

Petulia had lapsed into tongue-tied silence.

Annagramma put the book down on the log. "Well, we've *completely* lost the moment," she said. "We may as well have that cup of tea, Petulia. Do hurry up."

Petulia, relieved, grabbed the kettle. People relaxed a little.

Tiffany looked at the cover of the book. It read:

The Higher MagiK
by Letice Earwig, Witch

"Magic with a K?" she said aloud. "Magik*kkk*?"

"That's deliberate," said Annagramma coldly. "Mrs. Earwig says that if we are to make any progress at all we *must* distinguish the higher MagiK from the everyday sort."

"The *everyday* sort of magic?" said Tiffany.

"Exactly. None of that mumbling in hedgerows for *us*. Proper sacred circles, spells written down. A proper hierarchy, not everyone running around doing whatever they feel like. Real wands, not bits of grubby stick. Professionalism, with respect. Absolutely no warts. That's the only way forward."

"Well, I think—" Tiffany began.

"I don't really care what you think, because you don't know enough yet," said Annagramma sharply. She turned to the group in general. "Do we all at least have something for the Trials this year?" she asked. There were general murmurs and nods on the theme of "yes."

"What about you, Petulia?" said Annagramma.

"I'm going to do the pig trick, Annagramma," said Petulia meekly.

"Good. You're nearly good at that," said Annagramma, and pointed around the circle, from one girl to another, nodding at their answers, until she came to Tiffany.

"Soft Nellies?" she said, to sniggering amusement.

"What are Witch Trials?" said Tiffany. "Miss Level mentioned them, but I don't know what they are."

Annagramma gave one of her noisy sighs.

"You tell her, Petulia," she said. "*You* brought her, after all."

Hesitantly, with lots of "um"s and glances at Annagramma, Petulia explained about the Witch Trials. Um, it was a time when witches from all over the mountains could meet up and um see old friends and um pick up the latest news and gossip. Ordinary people could come along too, and there was a fair and um sideshows.

It was quite an um big event. And in the afternoon all the witches that um wanted to could show off a spell or um something they'd been working on, which was very um popular.

To Tiffany they sounded like sheepdog trials, without the dogs or the sheep. They were in Sheercliff this year, which was quite close.

"And is there a prize?" she asked.

"Um, oh no," said Petulia. "It's all done in the spirit of fun and good fellow—um, good sistership."

"Hah!" said Annagramma. "Not even she will believe that! It's all a fix, anyway. They'll all applaud Mistress Weatherwax. She always wins, whatever she does. She just messes up people's minds. She just fools them into thinking she's good. She wouldn't last five minutes against a wizard. They do *real* magic. And she dresses like a scarecrow, too! It's ignorant old women like her who keep witch-craft rooted in the past, as Mrs. Earwig points out in Chapter One!"

One or two girls looked uncertain. Petulia even looked over her shoulder.

"Um, people do say she's done amazing things, Annagramma," she said. "And, um, they say she can spy on people miles away—"

"Yes, they *say* that," said Annagramma. "That's because they're all frightened of her! She's such a bully! That's all she does, bully people and mess up their heads! That's *old* witchcraft, that is. Just one step away from cackling, in *my* opinion. She's half cracked now, they say."

"She didn't seem cracked to me."

"Who said that?" snapped Annagramma.

Everyone looked at Tiffany, who wished she hadn't spoken. But now there was nothing for it but to go on.

"She was just a bit old and stern," she said. "But she was quite . . . polite. She didn't cackle."

"You've met her?"

"Yes."

"*She* spoke to *you*, did she?" snarled Annagramma. "Was that before or after you kicked out the Fairy Queen?"

"Just after," said Tiffany, who was not used to this sort of thing. "She turned up on a broomstick," she added. "I *am* telling the truth."

"Of course you are," said Annagramma, smiling grimly. "And she congratulated you, I expect."

"Not really," said Tiffany. "She seemed pleased, but it was hard to tell."

And then Tiffany said something really, really stupid. Long afterward, and long after all sorts of things had happened, she'd go "la la la!" to blot out the memory whenever something reminded her of that evening.

She said: "She did give me this hat."

And they said, all of them, with one voice: *"What hat?"*

◆　◆　◆

Petulia took her back to the cottage. She did her best, and assured Tiffany that *she* believed her, but Tiffany knew she was just being nice. Miss Level tried to talk to her as she ran upstairs, but she bolted her door, kicked off her boots, and lay down on the bed with the pillow over her head to drown out the laughter echoing inside.

Downstairs there was some muffled conversation between Petulia and Miss Level and then the sound of the door closing as Petulia left.

After a while there was a scraping noise as Tiffany's boots were dragged across the floor and arranged neatly under the bed. Oswald was never off duty.

After another while the laughter died down, although she was sure it'd never go completely.

Tiffany could feel the hat. At least, she *had* been able to feel it. The virtual hat, on her real head. But no one could see it, and Petulia had even waved a hand back and forth over Tiffany's head and encountered a complete absence of hat.

The worst part—and it was hard to find the worst part, so humiliatingly bad had it been—was hearing Annagramma say, "No, don't laugh at her. That's too cruel. She's just foolish, that's all. I told you the old woman messes with people's heads!"

Tiffany's First Thoughts were running around in circles. Her Second Thoughts were caught up in the storm. Only her Third Thoughts, which were very weak, came up with: *Even though your world is completely and utterly ruined and can never be made better, no matter what, and you're completely inconsolable, it would be nice if you heard someone bringing some soup upstairs. . . .*

The Third Thoughts got Tiffany off the bed and over to the door, where they guided her hand to slide the bolt back. Then they let her fling herself on the bed again.

A few minutes later there was a creak of footsteps on the landing. It's nice to be right.

Miss Level knocked, then came in after a decent pause. Tiffany heard the tray go down on the table, then felt the bed move as a body sat down on it.

"Petulia is a capable girl, I've always thought," said Miss Level after a while. "She'll make some village a very serviceable witch one day."

Tiffany stayed silent.

"She told me all about it," said Miss Level. "Miss Tick never mentioned the hat, but if I was you, I wouldn't have told her about it anyway. It sounds the sort of thing Mistress Weatherwax would do. You know, sometimes it helps to talk about these things."

More silence from Tiffany.

"Actually, that's not true," Miss Level added. "But as a witch I am incredibly inquisitive and would love to know more."

That had no effect either. Miss Level sighed and stood up. "I'll leave the soup, but if you let it get too cold, Oswald will try to take it away."

She went downstairs.

Nothing stirred in the room for about five minutes. Then there was faintest of tinkles as the soup began to move.

Tiffany's hand shot out and gripped the tray firmly. That's the job of Third Thoughts: First and Second Thoughts might understand your current tragedy, but *something* has to remember that you haven't eaten since lunchtime.

Afterward, and after Oswald had speedily taken the empty bowl away, Tiffany lay in the dark, staring at nothing.

The novelty of this new country had taken all her attention in the past few days, but now that had drained away in the storm of laughter, and homesickness rushed to fill in the empty spaces.

She missed the sounds and the sheep and the silences of the Chalk. She missed seeing the blackness of the hills from her bedroom window, outlined against the stars. She missed . . . part of herself. . . .

But they'd laughed at her. They'd said "What hat?" and they'd laughed even more when she'd raised her hand to touch the invisible brim and hadn't found it. . . .

She'd touched it every day for eighteen months, and now it had gone. And she couldn't make a shamble. And she just had a green dress, while all the other girls wore black ones. Annagramma had a lot of jewelry, too, in black and silver. *All* the other girls had shambles, too, beautiful ones. Who cared if they were just for show?

Perhaps she wasn't a witch at all. Oh, she'd defeated the Queen, with the help of the little men and the memory of Granny Aching, but she hadn't used magic. She wasn't sure, now, what she *had* used. She'd felt something go down through the soles of her boots, down through the hills and through the years, and come back loud and roaring in a rage that shook the sky:

. . . *How dare you invade* my *world*, my *land*, my *life* . . .

But what had the virtual hat done for her? Perhaps the old woman had tricked her, had just made her *think* there was a hat there. Perhaps she was a bit cracked, like Annagramma had said, and had just got things wrong. Perhaps Tiffany should go home and make Soft Nellies for the rest of her life.

Tiffany turned around and crawled down the bed and opened her suitcase. She pulled out the rough box, opened it in the dark, and closed a hand around the lucky stone.

She'd hoped that there'd be some kind of spark, some kind of friendliness in it. There was none. There was just the roughness of the outside of the stone, the smoothness on the face where it had split, and the sharpness between the two. And the piece of sheep's wool did nothing but make her fingers smell of sheep, and this made her long for home and feel even more upset. The silver Horse was cold.

Only someone quite close would have heard the sob. It was quite faint, but it was carried on the dark red wings of misery. She wanted, *longed for*, the hiss of wind in the turf and the feel of centuries under her feet. She wanted that sense, which had never left her before, of being where Achings had lived for thousands of years. She needed blue butterflies and the sounds of sheep and the big empty skies.

Back home, when she'd felt upset, she'd gone up to the remains of the old shepherding hut and sat there for a while. That had always worked.

It was a long way away now. Too far. Now she was full of a horrible, heavy, dead feeling, and there was nowhere to leave it. And it wasn't how things were supposed to go.

Where was the *magic*? Oh, she understood that you had learn about the basic, everyday *craft*, but when did the "witch" part turn up? She'd been trying to learn, she really had, and she was turning into . . . well, a good worker, a handy girl with potions and a reliable person. Dependable, like Miss Level.

She'd expected—well, what? Well . . . to be doing serious witch stuff, you know, broomsticks, magic, guarding the world against evil forces in a noble yet modest way, and then *also* doing good for poor people because she was a really nice person. And the people she'd seen in the picture had had rather less messy ailments and their children didn't have such runny noses. Mr. Weavall's flying toenails weren't in it *anywhere*. Some of them *boomeranged*.

She got *sick* on broomsticks. *Every time.* She couldn't even make a shamble. She was going to spend her days running around after people who, to be honest, could sometimes be doing a bit more for themselves. No magic, no flying, no secrets . . . just toenails and bogeys.

She belonged to the Chalk. Every day she'd told the hills what they were. Every day they'd told her who she was. But now she couldn't hear them.

Outside, it began to rain, quite hard, and in the distance Tiffany heard the mutter of thunder.

What would Granny Aching have done? But even folded in the

wings of despair she knew the answer to that.

Granny Aching never gave up. She'd search all night for a lost lamb. . . .

She lay looking at nothing for a while, and then lit the candle by the bed and swiveled her legs onto the floor. This couldn't wait until morning.

Tiffany had a little trick for seeing the hat. If you moved your hand behind it quickly, there was a slight, brief blurriness to what you saw, as though the light coming through the invisible hat took a little more time.

It *had* to be there.

Well, the candle should give enough light to be sure. If the hat was there, everything would be fine, and it wouldn't matter what other people thought.

She stood in the middle of the carpet, while lightning danced across the mountains outside, and closed her eyes.

Down in the garden the apple-tree branches flayed in the wind, the dream catchers and curse nets clashing and jangling. . . .

"See me," she said.

The world went quiet, totally silent. It hadn't done that before. But Tiffany tiptoed around until she knew she was opposite herself, and opened her eyes again . . .

And there she was, and so was the hat, as clear as it had ever been.

And the image of Tiffany below, a young girl in a green dress, opened its eyes and smiled at her and said:

"We see you. Now we are you."

Tiffany tried to shout, "See me not!" But there was no mouth to shout. . . .

Lightning struck somewhere nearby. The window blew in. The candle flame flew out in a streamer of fire and died.

And then there was only darkness, and the hiss of the rain.

CHAPTER 6

The Hiver

*T*hunder rolled *across the Chalk.*

Jeannie carefully opened the package that her mother had given her on the day she'd left the Long Lake mound. It was a traditional gift, one that every young kelda got when she went away, never to return. Keldas could never go home. Keldas *were* home.

The gift was this: memory.

Inside the bag were a triangle of tanned sheepskin, three wooden stakes, a length of string twisted out of nettle fibers, a tiny leather bottle, and a hammer.

She knew what to do, because she'd see her mother do it many times. The hammer was used to bang in the stakes around the smoldering fire. The string was used to tie the three corners of the leather triangle to the stakes so that it sagged in the center, just enough to hold a small bucketful of water, which Jeannie had drawn herself from the deep well.

She knelt down and waited until the water very slowly began to seep though the leather, then built up the fire.

She was aware of all the eyes of the Feegles in the shadowy galleries around and above her. None of them would come near her while she was boiling the cauldron. They'd rather chop their own legs off. This was *pure* hiddlins.

And this was what a cauldron really was, back in the days before humans had worked copper or poured iron. It looked like magic. It was supposed to. But if you knew the trick, you could see how the cauldron would boil dry before the leather burned.

When the water in the skin was steaming, she damped down the fire and added to the water the contents of the little leather bottle, which contained some of the water from her mother's cauldron. That's how it had always gone, from mother to daughter, since the very beginning.

Jeannie waited until the cauldron had cooled some more, then took up a cup, filled it, and drank. There was a sigh from the shadowy Feegles.

She lay back and closed her eyes, waiting. Nothing happened except that the thunder rattled the land and the lightning turned the world black and white.

And then, so gently that it had already happened before she realized that it was starting to happen, the past caught up with her. There, around her, were all the old keldas, starting with her mother, her grandmothers, their mothers . . . back until there was no one to remember . . . one big memory, carried for a while by many, worn and hazy in parts but old as a mountain.

But all the Feegles knew about that. Only the kelda knew about the real hiddlin, which was this: The river of memory wasn't a river, it was a sea.

Keldas yet to be born would remember, one day. On nights yet to come, they'd lie by their cauldron and become, for a few minutes, part of the eternal sea. By listening to unborn keldas remembering their past, you remember your future. . . .

You needed skill to find those faint voices, and Jeannie did not have all of it yet, but *something* was there.

As lightning turned the world to black and white again, she sat bolt upright.

"It's found her," she whispered. "Oh, the puir wee thing!"

◆ ◆ ◆

Rain had soaked into the rug when Tiffany woke up. Damp daylight spilled into the room.

She got up and closed the window. A few leaves had blown in. *O-kay.*

It hadn't been a dream. She was certain of that. Something . . . strange had happened. The tips of her fingers were tingling. She felt . . . different. But not, now that she took stock, in a bad way. No. Last night she'd felt awful, but now, *now* she felt . . . full of life.

Actually, she felt happy. She was going to take charge. She was going to take control of *her* life. Get-up-and-go had got up and come.

The green dress was rumpled, and really it needed a wash. She had her old blue one in the chest of drawers, but somehow it didn't seem right to wear it now. She'd have to make do with the green until she could get another one.

She went to put on her boots, then stopped and stared at them.

They just wouldn't do, not now. She got the new shiny ones out of her case and wore them instead.

She found both of Miss Level was out in the wet garden in her nightie, sadly picking up bits of dream catcher and fallen apples. Even some of the garden ornaments had been smashed, although the madly grinning gnomes had unfortunately escaped destruction.

Miss Level brushed her hair out of one pair of her eyes and said: "Very, very strange. All the curse nets seem to have exploded. Even the boredom stones are discharged! Did you notice anything?"

"No, Miss Level," said Tiffany meekly.

"And all the old shambles in the workroom are in pieces! I mean, I know they are really only ornamental and have next to no power left, but something really *strange* must have happened."

Both of her gave Tiffany a look that Miss Level probably thought was very sly and cunning, but it made her look slightly ill.

"The storm seemed a touch magical to me. I suppose you girls weren't doing anything . . . odd last night, were you, dear?" she said.

"No, Miss Level. I thought they were a bit silly."

"Because, you see, Oswald seems to have gone," said Miss Level. "He's very sensitive to atmospheres. . . ."

It took Tiffany a moment to understand what she was talking about. Then she said: "But he's always here!"

"Yes, ever since I can remember!" said Miss Level.

"Have you tried putting a spoon in the knife section?"

"Yes, of course! Not so much as a rattle!"

"Dropped an apple core? He always—"

"That was the first thing I tried!"

"How about the salt and sugar trick?"

Miss Level hesitated. "Well, no . . ." She brightened up. "He does love that one, so he's *bound* to turn up, yes?"

Tiffany found the big bag of salt and another of sugar, and poured both of them into a bowl. Then she stirred up the fine white crystals with her hand.

She'd found this was the ideal away of keeping Oswald occupied while they did the cooking. Sorting the salt and sugar grains back into the right bags could take him an entire happy afternoon. But now the mixture just lay there, Oswaldless.

"Oh, well . . . I'll search the house," said Miss Level, as if that was a good way of finding an invisible person. "Go and see to the goats, will you, dear? And then we'll have to try to remember how to do the dishes!"

Tiffany let the goats out of the shed. Usually Black Meg imme-diately went and stood on the milking platform and gave her an expectant look as if to say, I've thought up a *new* trick.

But not today. When Tiffany looked inside the shed, the goats were huddled in the dark at the far end. They panicked, nostrils flaring, and scampered around as she went toward them, but she managed to grab Black Meg by her collar. The goat twisted and fought her as she dragged her out toward the milking stand. Meg climbed up because it was either that or have her head pulled off, then stood there snorting and bleating.

Tiffany stared at the goat. Her bones felt as though they were itching. She wanted to . . . do things, climb the highest mountain, leap into the sky, run around the world. And she thought: This is *silly*. I start every day with a battle of wits with an *animal*!

Well, let's show this creature who is in charge.

She picked up the broom that was used for sweeping out the milking parlor. Black Meg's slot eyes widened in fear, and *wham!* went the broom.

It hit the milking stand. Tiffany hadn't intended to miss like that. She'd wanted to give Meg the wallop the creature richly deserved, but somehow, the stick had twisted in her hand. She raised it again, but the look in her eye and the whack on the wood had achieved the right effect. Meg cowered.

"No more games!" hissed Tiffany, lowering the stick.

The goat stood as still as a log. Tiffany milked her out, took the pail back into the dairy, weighed it, chalked up the amount on the slate by the door, and tipped the milk into a big bowl.

The rest of the goats were nearly as bad, but a herd learns fast.

All together they gave three gallons, which was pretty pitiful for ten goats. Tiffany chalked this up without enthusiasm and stood staring at it, fiddling with the chalk. What was the point of this?

Yesterday she'd been full of plans for experimental cheeses, but now cheese was *dull*.

Why was she here, doing silly chores, helping people too stupid to help themselves? She could be doing . . . *anything!*

She looked down at the scrubbed wooden table.

HElp Me

Someone had written on the wood in chalk. And the piece of chalk was still in her hand—

"Petulia's come to see you, dear," said Miss Level, behind her.

Tiffany quickly shifted a milking bucket over the words and turned around guiltily.

"What?" she said. "Why?"

"Just to see if you're all right, I think," said Miss Level, watching Tiffany carefully.

The dumpy girl stood very nervously on the doorstep, her pointy hat in her hands.

"Um, I just thought I ought to see how you, um, are . . ." she muttered, looking Tiffany squarely in the boots. "Um, I don't think anyone really wanted to be unkind. . . ."

"You're not very clever and you're too fat," said Tiffany. She stared at the round pink face for a moment and *knew* things. "And you still have a teddy bear help me and you believe in fairies."

She slammed the door, went back to the dairy, and stared at the bowls of milk and curds as if she was seeing them for the first time.

Good with Cheese. That was one of the things everyone remembered about her: Tiffany Aching, brown hair, Good with Cheese. But now the dairy looked all wrong and unfamiliar.

She gritted her teeth. Good with Cheese. Was that *really* what she wanted to be? Of all the things people could be in the world, did she want to be known just as a dependable person to have around rotted milk? Did she *really* want to spend all day scrubbing slabs and washing pails and plates and . . . and . . . and that weird wire thing just there, that—

. . . cheese cutter . . .

—that cheese cutter? Did she want her whole life to—

Hold on . . .

"Who's there?" said Tiffany. "Did someone just say 'cheese cutter'?"

She peered around the room, as if someone could be hiding behind the bundles of dried herbs. It couldn't have been Oswald. He'd gone, and he never spoke in any case.

Tiffany grabbed the pail, spat on her hand, and rubbed out the chalked HElp Me.

—*tried* to rub it out. But her hand gripped the edge of the table and held it firmly, no matter how much she pulled. She flailed with her left hand, managing to knock over a pail of milk, which washed across the letters . . . and her right hand let go suddenly.

The door was pushed open. Both of Miss Level was there. When she pulled herself together like that, standing side by side, it was because she felt she had something important to say.

"I have to say, Tiffany, that I think—"

"—you were very nasty to Petulia just—"

"—now. She went off crying."

She stared at Tiffany's face. "Are you all right, child?"

Tiffany shuddered.

"Er . . . yes. Fine. Feel a bit odd. Heard a voice in my head. Gone now."

Miss Level looked at her with her heads on one side, right

and left in different directions.

"If you're sure, then. I'll get changed. We'd better leave soon. There's a lot to do today."

"A lot to do," said Tiffany weakly.

"Well, yes. There's Slapwick's leg, and I've got to see to the Grimly baby, and it's been a week since I've visited Surleigh Bottom, and, let's see, Mr. Plover's got gnats again, and I'd better just find a moment to have a word with Mistress Slopes . . . then there's Mr. Weavall's lunch to cook. I think I'll have to do that here and run down with it for him, and of course Mrs. Fanlight is near her time, and"—she sighed—"so is Miss Hobblow, *again*. . . . It's going to be a full day. It's really hard to fit it all in, really it is."

Tiffany thought: You stupid woman, standing there looking worried because you just haven't got time to give people everything they demand! Do you think you could ever give them *enough* help? Greedy, lazy, dumb people, always *wanting* all the time! The Grimly baby? Mrs. Grimly's got eleven children! Who'd miss one?

Mr. Weavall's dead already! He just won't go! You think they're grateful, but all they're doing is making sure you come around again! That's not gratitude, that's just insurance!

The thought horrified part of her, but it had turned up and it flamed there in her head, just itching to escape from her mouth.

"Things need tidying up here," she muttered.

"Oh, I can do that while we're gone," said Miss Level cheerfully. "Come on, let's have a smile! There's lots to do!"

There was *always* lots to do, Tiffany growled in her head as she trailed after Miss Level to the first village. Lots and lots. And it never made any difference. There was no end to the *wanting*.

They went from one grubby, smelly cottage to another, ministering to people too stupid to use soap, drinking tea from cracked cups, gossiping with old women with fewer teeth than toes. It made her feel ill.

It was a bright day, but it seemed to darken as they walked on. The feeling was like a thunderstorm inside her head.

Then the daydreams began. She was helping to splint the broken arm of some dull child when she glanced up and saw her reflection in the glass of the cottage window.

She was a tiger, with huge fangs.

She yelped and stood up.

"Oh, do be careful," said Miss Level, and then saw her face. "Is there something wrong?" she asked.

"I . . . I . . . something bit me!" lied Tiffany. That was a safe bet in these places. The fleas bit the rats and the rats bit the children.

She managed to get out into the daylight, her head spinning. Miss Level came out a few minutes later and found her leaning against the wall, shaking.

"You look *dreadful*," she said.

"Ferns!" said Tiffany. "Everywhere! Big ferns! And big things, like cows made out of lizards!" She turned a wide, mirthless smile onto Miss Level, who took a step back. "You can *eat* them!" She blinked. "What's happening?" she whispered.

"I don't know, but I'm coming right down here this minute to fetch you," said Miss Level. "I'm on the broomstick right now!"

"They laughed at me when I said I could trap one. Well, who's laughing now, tell me that, eh?"

Miss Level's expression of concern turned into something close to panic.

"That didn't sound like your voice. That sounded like a man! Do you *feel* all right?"

"Feel . . . crowded," murmured Tiffany.

"Crowded?" said Miss Level.

"Strange . . . memories . . . help me . . ."

Tiffany looked at her arm. It had scales on it. Now it had hair on it. Now it was smooth and brown, and holding—

"A scorpion sandwich?" she said.

"Can you hear me?" asked Miss Level, her voice a long way away. "You're delirious. Are you sure you girls haven't been playing with potions or anything like that?"

The broomstick dropped out of the sky and the other part of Miss Level nearly fell off. Without speaking, both of Miss Level got Tiffany onto the stick and part of Miss Level got on behind her.

It didn't take long to fly back to the cottage. Tiffany spent the flight with her mind full of hot cotton wool and wasn't at all certain where she was, although her body did know and threw up again.

Miss Level helped her off the stick and sat her on the garden seat just outside the cottage door.

"Now just you wait there," said Miss Level, who dealt with emergencies by talking incessantly and using the word "just" too often because it's a calming word, "and I'll just get you a drink and then we'll just see what the matter is. . . ." There was a pause, and then the stream of words came out of the house again, dragging Miss Level after them. ". . . And I'll just check on . . . things. Just drink this, please!"

Tiffany drank the water and, out of the corner of her eye, saw Miss Level weaving string around an egg. She was trying to make a shamble without Tiffany noticing.

Strange images were floating around Tiffany's mind. There were scraps of voices, fragments of memories . . . and one little voice that was her own, small and defiant and getting fainter:

You're not me. You just think you are! Someone help me!

"Now, then," said Miss Level, "let's just see what we can see—"

The shamble exploded, not just into pieces but into fire and smoke.

"Oh, Tiffany," said Miss Level, frantically waving smoke away. "Are you all right?"

Tiffany stood up slowly. It seemed to Miss Level that she was slightly taller than she remembered.

"Yes, I think I am," said Tiffany. "I think I've been all wrong, but *now* I'm all right. And I've been wasting my time, Miss Level."

"What—" Miss Level began.

Tiffany pointed a finger at her.

"I *know* why you had to leave the circus, Miss Level," she said. "It had to do with the clown Floppo, the trick ladder, and . . . some *custard*. . . ."

Miss Level went pale. "How could you possibly know that?"

"Just by looking at you!" said Tiffany, pushing past her into the dairy. "Watch this, Miss Level!"

She pointed a finger. A wooden spoon rose an inch from the table. Then it began to spin, faster and faster, until with a cracking sound it broke into splinters. They whirled away across the room.

"And I can do *this*!" Tiffany shouted. She grabbed a bowl of curds, tipped them out onto the table, and waved a hand at them. They turned into a cheese.

"Now *that's* what cheese making should be!" she said. "To think that I spent stupid *years* learning the hard way! That's how a *real* witch does it! Why do we crawl in the dirt, Miss Level? Why do we amble around with herbs and bandage smelly old men's legs? Why do we get paid with eggs and stale cakes? Annagramma is as stupid as a hen, but even she can see it's wrong. Why don't we *use* magic? Why are you so *afraid*?"

Miss Level tried to smile.

"Tiffany, dear, we all go through this," she said, and her voice was shaking. "Though not as . . . explosively as you, I have to say. And the answer is . . . well, it's dangerous."

"Yes, but that's what people always say to scare children," said Tiffany. "We get told stories to frighten us, to keep us scared! Don't go into the big bad woods help me because it's full of scary things, that's what we're told. But really, the big bad woods should be scared of *us*! I'm going out!"

"I think that would be a good idea," said Miss Level weakly. "Until you behave."

"I *don't* have to do things your way," snarled Tiffany, slamming the door behind her.

Miss Level's broomstick was leaning against the wall a little way away. Tiffany stopped and stared at it, her mind on fire.

She'd tried to keep away from it. Miss Level had wheedled her into a trial flight with Tiffany clinging on tightly with arms and legs while both of Miss Level ran alongside her, holding on to ropes and making encouraging noises. They had stopped when Tiffany threw up for the fourth time.

Well, that was then!

She grabbed the stick, swung a leg over it—and found that her other foot stuck to the ground as though nailed there. The broomstick swung around wildly as she tried to pull it up, and, when the boot was finally tugged off the ground, the stick turned over so that Tiffany was upside down. This is not the best position in which to make a grand exit.

She said, quietly, "I am not going to learn you, *you* are going to learn *me*. Or the next lesson will involve an axe!"

The broomstick turned upright, then gently rose.

"Right," said Tiffany. There was no fear this time. There was just impatience. The ground dropping away below her didn't worry her at all. If it didn't have the sense to stay away from her, she'd *hit it. . . .*

◆　◆　◆

As the stick drifted away, there was whispering in the long grass of the garden.

"*Ach, we're too late, Rob. That wuz the hiver, that wuz.*"

"*Aye, but did ye see that foot? It's nae won yet—oour hag's in there somewhere! She's fighting it! It canna win until it's taken the last scrap o' her! Wullie, will ye stop tryin' to grab them apples!*"

"*It's sorry I am tae say this, Rob, but no one can fight a hiver. 'Tis like fightin' yoursel. The more you fight, the more it'll tak' o' ye. And when it has all o' ye—*"

"*Wash oot yer mouth wi' hedgehog pee, Big Yan! That isna gonna happen—*"

"*Crivens! Here comes the big hag!*"

Half of Miss Level stepped out into the ruined garden.

She stared up at the departing broomstick, shaking her head.

Daft Wullie was stuck out in the open, where he'd been trying to snag a fallen apple. He turned to flee and would have got clean away if he hadn't run straight into a pottery garden gnome. He bounced off, stunned, and staggered wildly, trying to focus on the big, fat, chubby-cheeked figure in front of him. He was far too angry to hear the click of the garden gate and the soft tread of approaching footsteps.

When it comes to choosing between running and fighting, a Feegle doesn't think twice. He doesn't think at all.

"What're ye grinnin' at, pal?" he demanded. "Oh aye, you reckon you're the big man, eh, jus' 'cos yez got a fishin' rod?" He grabbed a pink pointy ear in each hand and aimed his head at what turned out be quite a hard pottery nose. It smashed anyway, as things tend to in these circumstances, but it did slow the little man down and cause him to stagger in circles.

Too late, he saw Miss Level bearing down on him from the doorway. He turned to flee, right into the hands of *also* Miss Level.

Her fingers closed around him.

"I'm a witch, you know," she said. "And if you don't stop struggling this minute, I will subject you to the most dreadful torture. Do you know what that is?"

Daft Wullie shook his head in terror. Long years of juggling had given Miss Level a grip like steel. Down in the long grass the rest of the Feegles listened so hard it hurt.

Miss Level brought him a little closer to her mouth.

"I'll let you go right now *without* giving you a taste of the twenty-year-old MacAbre single malt I have in my cupboard," she said.

Rob Anybody leaped up.

"Ach, crivens, mistress, what a thing to taunt a body wi'! D'ye no' have a drop of mercy in you?" he shouted. "Ye're a cruel hag indeed tae—" He stopped. Miss Level was smiling. Rob Anybody looked around, flung his sword on the ground and said: "Ach, *crivens!*"

◆　　◆　　◆

The Nac Mac Feegle respected witches, even if they did call them hags. And this one had brought out a big loaf and a whole bottle of whisky on the table for the taking. You had to respect someone like that.

"Of course, I'd *heard* of you, and Miss Tick mentioned you," she said, watching them eat, which is not something to be done lightly. "But I always thought you were just a myth."

"Aye, weel, we'll stay that way if ye dinna mind," said Rob Anybody, and belched. "'Tis bad enough wi' them arky-olly-gee men wantin' to dig up oour mounds wi'oot them folklore ladies wantin' to tak' pichoors o' us an' that."

"And you watch over Tiffany's farm, Mr. Anybody?"

"Aye, we do that, an' we dinna ask for any reward," said Rob Anybody stoutly.

"Aye, we just tak' a few wee eiggs an' fruits an' old clothes and—" Daft Wullie began.

Rob gave him a look.

"Er . . . wuz that one o' those times when I shouldna open my big fat mouth?" said Wullie.

"Aye. It wuz," said Rob. He turned back to both of Miss Level. "Mebbe we tak' the odd bitty thing lyin' aboot—"

"—in locked cupboards an' such—" added Daft Wullie happily.

"—but it's no' missed, an' we keeps an eye on the ships in payment," said Rob, glaring at his brother.

"You can see the sea from down there?" said Miss Level, entering that state of general bewilderment that most people fell into when talking to the Feegles.

"Rob Anybody means the sheep," said Awf'ly Wee Billy. Gonnagles know a bit more about language.

"Aye, I said so, ships," said Rob Anybody. "Anywa' . . . aye, we watch her farm. She's the hag o' oor hills, like her granny." He added proudly, "It's through her the hills knows they are alive."

"And a hiver is . . . ?"

Rob hesitated. "Dunno the proper haggin' way o' talking aboot it," he said. "Awf'ly Wee Billy, you know them lang words."

Billy swallowed. "There's old poems, mistress. It's like a, a mind wi'oot a body, except it disna think. Some say it's nothing but a fear, and never dies. And what it does . . ." His tiny face wrinkled. "It's like them things you get on sheep," he decided.

The Feegles who weren't eating and drinking came to his aid.

"Horns?"

"Wools?"

"Tails?"

"Legs?"

"Chairs?" This was Daft Wullie.

"Sheep ticks," said Billy thoughtfully.

"A parasite, you mean?" said Miss Level.

"Aye, that could be the word," said Billy. "It creeps in, ye ken. It looks for folks wi' power and strength. Kings, ye ken, magicians, leaders. They say that way back in time, afore there *wuz* people, it lived in beasts. The strongest beasts, ye ken, the ones wi' big, big teeths. An' when it finds ye, it waits for a chance tae creep intae your head and it *becomes* ye."

The Feegles fell silent, watching Miss Level.

"Becomes you?" she said.

"Aye. Wi' your memories an' all. Only . . . it changes ye. It gives ye a lot o' power, but it takes ye over, makes ye its own. An' the last wee bit of ye that still *is* ye . . . well, that'll fight and fight, mebbe, but it will dwindle and dwindle until it's a' gone an' ye're just a memory. . . ."

The Feegles watched both of Miss Level. You never knew what a hag would do at a time like this.

"Wizards used to summon demons," she said. "They may still do so, although I think that's considered so fifteen-centuries-ago these days. But that takes a lot of magic. And you could talk to demons, I believe. And there were rules."

"Never heard o' a hiver talkin'," said Billy. "Or obeyin' rules."

"But why would it want Tiffany?" said Miss Level. "She's not powerful!"

"She has the power o' the land in her," said Rob Anybody stoutly. "'Tis a power that comes at need, not for doin' wee conjurin' tricks. We seen it, mistress!"

"But Tiffany doesn't do *any* magic," said Miss Level helplessly. "She's very bright, but she can't even make a shamble. You must be wrong about that."

"Any o' youse lads *seen* the hag do any hagglin' lately?" Rob Anybody demanded. There were a lot of shaken heads, and a shower of beads, beetles, feathers, and miscellaneous head items.

"Do you spy— I mean, do you watch over her *all* the time?" said Miss Level, slightly horrified.

"Oh, aye," said Rob, airily. "No' in the privy, o' course. An' it's getting harder in her bedroom 'cuz she's blocked up a lot o' the cracks, for some reason."

"I can't imagine why," said Miss Level carefully.

"No' us, neither," said Rob. "We reckon it was 'cuz o' the drafts."

"Yes, I expect that's why it was," said Miss Level.

"So mostly we get in through a mousehole and hides out in her old dolly house until she guz tae sleep," said Rob. "Dinna look at me like that, mistress—all the lads is perrrfect gentlemen an' keeps their eyes tight shut when she's gettin' intae her nightie. Then there's one guarding her window and another at the door."

"Guarding her from what?"

"Everything."

For a moment Miss Level had a picture in her mind of a silent, moonlit bedroom with a sleeping child. She saw, by the window, lit by the moon, one small figure on guard, and another in the shadows by the door. What were they guarding her from? *Everything* . . .

But now something, this *thing*, has taken her over and she's locked inside somewhere. But she never used to do magic! I could understand it if it was one of the other girls messing around, but . . . Tiffany?

One of the Feegles was slowly raising a hand.

"Yes?" she said.

"It's me, mistress, Big Yan. I dinna know if it wuz proper hagglin', mistress," he said nervously, "but me an' Nearly Big Angus saw her doin' something odd a few times, eh, Nearly Big Angus?" The Feegle next to him nodded and the speaker went on. "It was when she got her new dress and her new hat . . ."

"And verra bonny she looked, too," said Nearly Big Angus.

"Aye, she did that. But she'd put 'em on, and then standing in the middle o' the floor she said—whut wuz it she said, Nearly Big Angus?"

"'See me,'" Nearly Big Angus volunteered.

Miss Level looked blank. The speaker, now looking a bit sorry that he'd raised this, went on: "Then after a wee while we'd hear her voice say, 'See me not,' and then she'd adjust the hat, ye know, mebbe to a more fetchin' angle."

"Oh, you mean she was looking at herself in what we call a *mirror*," said Miss Level. "That's a kind of—"

"We ken well what them things are, mistress," said Nearly Big Angus. "She's got a tiny one, all cracked and dirty. But it's nae good for a body as wants tae see herself properly."

"Verra good for the stealin', mirrors," said Rob Anybody. "We got oour Jeannie a silver one wi' garnets in the frame."

"And she'd say 'See me'?" said Miss Level.

"Aye, an' then 'See me not,'" said Big Yan. "An' betweentimes she'd stand verra still, like a stachoo."

"Sounds like she was trying to invent some kind of invisibility spell," Miss Level mused. "They don't work like that, of course."

"We reckoned she was just tryin' to throw her voice," said Nearly Big Angus. "So it sounds like it's comin' fra' somewhere else, ye ken? Wee Iain can do that a treat when we're huntin'."

"Throw her voice?" said Miss Level, her brow wrinkling. "Why did you think that?"

"'Cuz when she said, 'See me not,' it sounded like it wuz no' comin fra' her, and her lips didnae move."

Miss Level stared at the Feegles. When she spoke next, her voice was a little strange.

"Tell me," she said, "when she was just standing there, was she moving at *all*?"

"Just breathin' verra slow, mistress," said Big Yan.

"Were her eyes shut?"

"Aye!"

Miss Level started to breathe very fast.

"She walked out of her own body! There's not one—"

"—witch in a hundred who can do that!" she said. "That's Borrowing, that is! It's better than any circus trick! It's putting—"

"—your mind somewhere else! You have to—"

"—learn how to protect yourself before you ever *try* it! And *she* just invented it because she didn't have a mirror? The little fool, why didn't she—"

"—*say*? She walked out of her own body and left it there for anything to take over! I wonder what—"

"—she *thought* she was—"

"—doing?"

After a while Rob Anybody gave a polite cough.

"We're better at questions about fightin', drinkin', and stealin'," he mumbled. "We dinna have the knowin' o' the hagglin'."

CHAPTER 7

The Matter of Brian

❧

*S*omething *that called itself Tiffany flew across the treetops.*

It thought it was Tiffany. It could remember everything—nearly every-thing—about being Tiffany. It looked like Tiffany. It even thought like Tiffany, more or less. It had everything it needed to be Tiffany . . .

. . . except Tiffany. Except the tiny part of her that was . . . her.

It peered from her own eyes, tried to hear with her own ears, think with her own brain.

A hiver took over its victim not by force, exactly, but simply by moving into any space, like the hermit elephant.* It just took you over because that was what it did, until it was in all the places and there was no room left . . .

. . . except . . .

. . . it was having trouble. It had flowed through her like a dark tide but there was a place, tight and sealed, that was still closed. If it had had the brains of a tree, it would have been puzzled.

If it had had the brains of a human, it would have been frightened. . . .

---

*The hermit elephant of Howondaland has a very thin hide, except on its head, and young ones will often move into a small mud hut while the owners are out. It is far too shy to harm anyone, but most people quit their huts pretty soon after an elephant moves in. For one thing, it lifts the hut off the ground and carries it away on its back across the veldt, settling it down over any patch of nice grass that it finds. This makes housework very unpredictable. Nevertheless, an entire village of hermit elephants moving across the plains is one of the finest sights on the continent.

Tiffany brought the broomstick in low over the trees and landed it neatly in Mrs. Earwig's garden. There really was nothing to it, she decided. You just had to *want* it to fly.

Then she was sick again, or at least tried to be, but since she'd thrown up twice in the air, there wasn't much left to be sick with. It was ridiculous! She wasn't frightened of flying anymore, but her stupid stomach was!

She wiped her mouth carefully and looked around.

She'd landed on a lawn. She'd heard of them, but had never seen a real one before. There was grass all around Miss Level's cottage, but that was just, well, the grass of the clearing. Every other garden she'd seen was used for growing vegetables, with perhaps just a little space for flowers if the wife had gotten tough about it. A lawn meant you were posh enough to afford to give up valuable potato space.

This lawn had stripes.

Tiffany turned to the stick and said, "Stay!" and then marched across the lawn to the house. It was a lot grander than Miss Level's cottage, but from what Tiffany had heard, Mrs. Earwig was a more senior witch. She'd also married a wizard, although he didn't do any wizarding these days. It was a funny thing, Miss Level said, but you didn't often meet a poor wizard.

She knocked at the door and waited.

There was a curse net hanging in the porch. You'd have thought that a witch wouldn't need such a thing, but Tiffany supposed they used them as decoration. There was also a broomstick leaning against the wall, and a five-pointed silver star on the door. Mrs. Earwig *advertised*.

Tiffany knocked on the door again, much harder.

It was instantly opened by a tall, thin woman, all in black. But it was a very decorative, rich, deep black, all lacy and ruffled, and set off with more silver jewelry than Tiffany imagined could exist. She didn't just have rings on her fingers. Some fingers had sort of silver finger gloves, designed to look like claws. She gleamed like the night sky.

And she was wearing her pointy hat, which Miss Level never did at home. It was taller than any hat that Tiffany had ever seen. It had stars on it, and silver hatpins glittered.

All of this should have added up to something pretty impressive. It didn't. Partly it was because there was just too much of *everything*, but mostly it was because of Mrs. Earwig. She had a long, sharp face and looked very much as though she was about to complain about the cat from next door widdling on her lawn. And she looked like that all the time. Before she spoke, she very pointedly looked at the door to see if the heavy knocking had made a mark.

"Well?" she said, haughtily, or what she probably thought was haughtily. It sounded a bit strangled.

"Bless all in this house," said Tiffany.

"What? Oh, yes. Favorable runes shine on this our meeting," said Mrs. Earwig hurriedly. "Well?"

"I've come to see Annagramma," said Tiffany. There really *was* too much silver.

"Oh, are you one of her girls?" said Mrs. Earwig.

"Not . . . exactly," said Tiffany. "I work with Miss Level."

"Oh, *her*," said Mrs. Earwig, looking her up and down. "Green is a very dangerous color. What is your name, child?"

"Tiffany."

"Hmm," said Mrs. Earwig, not approving at all. "Well, you had better come in." She glanced up and made a *tch!* sound. "Oh, will you look at that? I bought that at the craft fair over in Slice, too. It was *very* expensive!"

The curse net was hanging in tatters.

"You didn't do that, did you?" Mrs. Earwig demanded.

"It's too high, Mrs. Earwig," said Tiffany.

"It's pronounced Ah-wij," said Mrs. Earwig coldly.

"Sorry, Mrs. Earwig."

"Come."

It was a strange house. You couldn't doubt that a witch lived in it, and not just because every doorframe had a tall pointy bit cut out of the top of it to allow Mrs. Earwig's hat to pass through. Miss Level had nothing on her walls except circus posters, but Mrs. Earwig had proper big paintings everywhere and they were all . . . witchy. There were lots of crescent moons and young women with quite frankly not enough clothes on, and big men with horns and, ooh, not just horns. There were suns and moon on the tiles of the floor, and the ceiling of the room Tiffany was led into was high, blue, and painted with stars. Mrs. Earwig (pronounced *Ah-wij*) pointed to a chair with gryphon feet and crescent-shaped cushions.

"Sit there," she said. "I will tell Annagramma you are here. Do not kick the chair legs, please."

She went out via another door.

Tiffany looked around—

—the hiver looked around—

—and thought: I've got to be the strongest. When I am strongest, I shall be safe. *That* one is weak. She thinks you can buy magic.

"Oh, it really *is* you," said a sharp voice behind her. "The cheese girl."

Tiffany stood up.

—the hiver had been many things, including a number of wizards, because wizards sought power all the time and sometimes found, in their

treacherous circles, not some demon that was so stupid that it could be tricked with threats and riddles, but the hiver, which was so stupid that it could not be tricked at all. And the hiver remembered—

Annagramma was drinking a glass of milk. Once you'd seen Mrs. Earwig, you understood something about Annagramma. There was an air about her that she was taking notes on the world in order to draw up a list of suggestions for improvements.

"Hello," said Tiffany.

"I suppose you came along to beg to be allowed to join after all, have you? I suppose you might be fun."

"No, not really. But I might let you join *me*," said Tiffany. "Are you enjoying that milk?"

The glass of milk turned into a bunch of thistles and grass. Annagramma dropped it hurriedly. When it hit the floor, it became a glass of milk again, and shattered and splashed.

Tiffany pointed at the ceiling. The painted stars flared, filling the room with light. But Annagramma stared at the spilled milk. "You know they say the power comes?" said Tiffany. "Well, it's come to *me*. Do you want to be my friend? Or do you want to be ... in my way? I should clean up that milk, if I was you."

She concentrated. She didn't know where this was coming from, but it seemed to know exactly what to do.

Annagramma rose a few inches off the floor. She struggled and tried to run, but that only made her spin. To Tiffany's dreadful delight, the girl started to cry.

"*You* said we ought to use our power," said Tiffany, walking around her as Annagramma tried to break free. "*You* said if we had the gift, people ought to know about it. You're a girl with her head screwed on right." Tiffany bent down a bit to look her in the eye. "Wouldn't be *awful* if it got screwed on wrong?"

She waved a hand and her prisoner dropped to the ground. But while Annagramma was unpleasant, she wasn't a coward, and she rose up with her mouth open to yell and a hand upraised—

"Careful," said Tiffany. "I can do it again."

Annagramma wasn't stupid, either. She lowered her hand and shrugged.

"Well, you *have* been lucky," she said grudgingly.

"But I still need your help," said Tiffany.

"Why would you need my help?" asked Annagramma sulkily.

—*We need allies,* the hiver thought with Tiffany's mind. *They can help protect us. If necessary, we can sacrifice them. Other creatures will always want to be friends with the powerful, and this one loves power—*

"To start with," said Tiffany, "where can I get a dress like yours?"

Annagramma's eyes lit up. "Oh, you want Zakzak Stronginthe-arm, over in Sallett Without," she said. "He sells *everything* for the modern witch."

"Then I want everything," said Tiffany.

"*He'll* want paying," Annagramma went on. "He's a dwarf. They know real gold from illusion gold. Everyone tries it out on him, of course. He just laughs. If you try it twice, he'll make a complaint to your mistress."

"Miss Tick said a witch should have just enough money," said Tiffany.

"That's right," said Annagramma. "Just enough to buy every-thing she wants! Mrs. Earwig says that just because we're witches, we don't have to live like peasants. But Miss Level is old-fashioned, isn't she? Probably hasn't got any money in the house."

And Tiffany said, "Oh, I know where I can get some money. I'll meet you please help me! here this afternoon, and you can show me where his place is."

"What was that?" said Annagramma sharply.

"I just said I'd stop me! meet you here this—" Tiffany began.

"There it was again! There was a sort of . . . odd echo in your voice," said Annagramma. "Like two people trying to talk at once."

"Oh, that," said the hiver. "That's nothing. It'll stop soon."

◆　◆　◆

It was an interesting mind, and the hiver enjoyed using it—but always there was that one place, that little place that was closed; it was annoying, like an itch that wouldn't go away. . . .

It did not think. The mind of the hiver was just what remained of all the other minds it had once lived in. They were like echoes after the music is taken away. But even echoes, bouncing off one another, can produce new harmonies.

They clanged now. They rang out things like: fit in. Not strong enough yet to make enemies. Have friends. . . .

Zakzak's low-ceilinged, dark shop had plenty to spend your money on. Zakzak was indeed a dwarf, and they're not traditionally interested in using magic, but he certainly knew how to display merchandise, which is what they are very good at.

There were wands, mostly of metal, some of rare woods. Some had shiny crystals stuck on them, which of course made them more expensive. There were bottles of colored glass in the potions section, and oddly enough, the smaller the bottle, the more expensive it was.

"That's because there's often very rare ingredients, like the tears of some rare snake or something," said Annagramma.

"I didn't know snakes cried," said Tiffany.

"Don't they? Oh, well, I expect that's why it's expensive."

There was plenty of other stuff. Shambles hung from the ceiling, much prettier and more interesting than the working ones that

Tiffany had seen. Since they were made up complete, then surely they were dead, just like the ones Miss Level kept for ornamentation. But they looked good—and looking was important.

There were even stones for looking *into*.

"Crystal balls," said Annagramma as Tiffany picked one up. "Careful! They're *very* expensive!" She pointed to a sign, which had been placed thoughtfully among the glittering globes. It said:

LOVELY TO LOOK AT
NICE TO HOLD
IF YOU DROP IT
YOU GET TORN APART BY WILD HORSES

Tiffany held the biggest one in her hand and saw how Mr. Stronginthearm moved slightly away from his counter, ready to rush forward with a bill if she dropped it.

"Miss Tick uses a saucer of water with a bit of ink poured into it," she said. "And she usually borrows the water and cadges the ink, at that."

"Oh, a *fundamentalist*," said Annagramma. "Letice—that's Mrs. Earwig—says they let us down terribly. Do we really want people to think witches are just a bunch of mad old women who look like crows? That's *so* gingerbread-cottagey! We really ought to be professional about these things."

"Hmm," said Tiffany, throwing the crystal ball up into the air and catching it again with one hand. "People should be made to *fear* witches."

"Well, er, certainly they should respect us," said Annagramma. "Um . . . I should be careful with that, if I was you. . . ."

"Why?" said Tiffany, tossing the ball over her shoulder.

"That was finest quartz!" shouted Zakzak, rushing around his counter.

"Oh, *Tiffany*," said Annagramma, shocked and trying not to giggle.

Zakzak rushed past them to where the shattered ball lay in hundreds of very expensive fragmen—

—did *not* lie in very expensive fragments.

Both he and Annagramma turned to Tiffany.

She was spinning the crystal globe on the tip of her finger.

"Quickness of the hand deceives the eye," she said.

"But I heard it smash!" said Zakzak.

"Deceives the ear, too," said Tiffany, putting the ball back on its stand. "I don't want this, *but*"—and she pointed a finger—"I'll take that necklace and that one and the one with the cats and that ring and a set of *those* and two, no, three of those and—what are these?"

"Um, that's a Book of Night," said Annagramma nervously. "It's a sort of magical diary. You write down what you've been working on. . . ."

Tiffany picked up the leather-bound book. It had an eye set in heavier leather on the cover. The eye rolled to look at her. This was a real witch's diary, and much more impressive than some shamefully cheap old book bought off a peddler.

"Whose eye was it?" said Tiffany. "Anyone interesting?"

"Er, I get the books from the wizards at Unseen University," said Zakzak, still shaken. "They're not real eyes, but they're clever enough to swivel around until they see another eye."

"It just blinked," said Tiffany.

"Very clever people, wizards," said the dwarf, who knew a sale when he saw one. "Shall I wrap it up for you?"

"Yes," said Tiffany. "Wrap everything up. And now can anyone hear me? show me the clothes department . . ."

. . . where there were hats. There are fashions in witchery, just like everything else. Some years the slightly concertina'd look is in, and you'll even see the point twisting around so much it's nearly pointing at the ground. There are varieties even in the most traditional hat (Upright Cone, Black), such as the Countrywoman (inside pockets, waterproof), the Cloudbuster (low-drag coefficient for broomstick use), and, quite importantly, the Safety (guaranteed to survive 80 percent of falling farmhouses).

Tiffany chose the tallest upright cone. It was more than two feet high and had big stars sewn on it.

"Ah, the Sky Scraper. Very much your look," said Zakzak, bustling around and opening drawers. "It's for the witch on the way up, who knows what she wants and doesn't care how many frogs it takes, aha. Incidentally, many ladies like a cloak with that. Now, we have the Midnight, pure wool, fine knit, very warm, but"—he gave Tiffany a knowing look—"we currently have *very* limited supplies of the Zephyr Billow, just in, very rare, black as coal and thin as a shadow. Completely useless for keeping you warm or dry, but it looks *fabulous* in even the slightest breeze. Observe."

He held up the cloak and blew gently. It billowed out almost horizontally, flapping and twisting like a sheet in a gale.

"Oh, *yes*," breathed Annagramma.

"I'll take it," said Tiffany. "I shall wear it to the Witch Trials on Saturday."

"Well, if you win, be sure to tell everyone you bought it here," said Zakzak.

"*When* I win, I shall tell them I got it at a considerable discount," said Tiffany.

"Oh, I don't do discounts," said Zakzak, as loftily as a dwarf can manage.

Tiffany stared at him, then picked up one of the most expensive wands from the display. It glittered.

"That's a Number Six," whispered Annagramma. "Mrs. Earwig has one of those!"

"I see it's got runes on it," said Tiffany, and something about the way she said it made Zakzak go pale.

"Well, of *course*," said Annagramma. "You've got to have *runes*."

"These are in Oggham," said Tiffany, smiling nastily at Zakzak. "It's a very ancient language of the dwarfs. Shall I tell you what they *say*? They say 'Oh What a Wally Is Waving This.'"

"Don't you take that nasty lying tone with me, young lady!" said the dwarf. "Who's your mistress? I know your type! Learn one spell and you think you're Mistress Weatherwax! I'm not standing for this kind of behavior! *Brian!*"

There was a rustling from the bead curtains that led to the back of the shop, and a wizard appeared.

You could tell he was a wizard. Wizards never want you to have to guess. He had long flowing robes with stars and magical symbols on them; there were even some sequins. His beard would have been long and flowing if indeed he'd been the kind of young man who could really grow a beard. Instead, it was ragged and wispy and not very clean. And the general effect was also spoiled by the fact that he was smoking a cigarette, and had a mug of tea in his hand and a face that looked a bit like something that lives under damp logs.

The mug was chipped, and on it were the jolly words YOU DON'T HAVE TO BE MAGIC TO WORK HERE BUT IT HELPS!

"Yeah?" he asked, adding reproachfully, "I *was* on my tea break, you know."

"This young . . . lady is being awkward," said Zakzak. "Throwing magic about. Talking back and being smart at me. The usual stuff."

Brian looked at Tiffany. She smiled.

"Brian's been to Unseen University," said Zakzak with a "so there" smirk. "Got a *degree*. What he doesn't know about magic could fill a book! These ladies need showing the way out, Brian."

"Now then, ladies," said Brian nervously, putting down his mug. "Do what Mr. Stronginthearm says and push off, right? We don't want trouble, do we? Go on, there's good kids."

"Why do you need a wizard to protect you, with all these magical amulets around the place, Mr. Stronginthearm?" said Tiffany sweetly.

Zakzak turned to Brian. "What're you standing there for?" he demanded. "She's doing it again! I pay you, don't I? Put a 'fluence on 'em or something!"

"Well, er . . . that one could be a bit of an awkward customer . . ." Brian said, nodding toward Tiffany.

"If you studied wizardry, Brian, then you know about conservation of mass, don't you?" she said. "I mean, you know what *really* happens when you try to turn someone into a frog?"

"Well, er . . ." the wizard began.

"Ha! That's just a figure of speech!" snapped Zakzak. "I'd like to see *you* turn someone into a frog!"

"Wish granted," said Tiffany, and waved the wand.

Brian started to say, "Look, when I said I'd been to Unseen University, I meant—"

But he ended up saying, *"Erk."*

◆　◆　◆

Take the eye away from Tiffany, up through the shop, high, high above the village until the landscape spreads out in a patchwork of fields, woods, and mountains.

The magic spreads out like the ripples made when a stone is

dropped in water. Within a few miles of the place it makes shambles spin and breaks the threads of curse nets. As the ripples widen, the magic gets fainter, although it never dies and still can be felt by things far more sensitive than any shamble. . . .

Let the eye move and fall now on *this* woods, *this* clearing, *this* cottage. . . .

There is nothing on the walls but whitewash, nothing on the floor but cold stone. The huge fireplace doesn't even have a cooking stove. A black teakettle hangs on a black hook over what can hardly be called a fire at all; it's just a few little sticks huddling together.

This is the house of a life peeled to the core.

Upstairs, an old woman, all in faded black, is lying on a narrow bed. But you wouldn't think she was dead, because there is a big card on a string around her neck that reads:

I ATE'NT DEAD

. . . and you have to believe it when it's written down like that.

Her eyes are shut, her hands are crossed on her chest, her mouth is open.

And bees crawl into her mouth, and over her ears, and all over her pillow. They fill the room, flying in and out of the open window, where someone has put a row of saucers filled with sugary water on the sill.

None of the saucers match, of course. A witch never has matching crockery. But the bees work on, coming and going . . . busy as bees.

When the ripple of magic passes through, the buzz rises to a roar. Bees pour in through the window urgently, as though driven by a gale. They land on the still old woman until her head and shoulders are a boiling mass of tiny brown bodies.

And then, as one insect, they rise in a storm and pour away into the outside air, which is full of whirling seeds from the sycamore trees outside.

Mistress Weatherwax sat bolt upright and said, "Bzzzt!" Then she stuck a finger into her mouth, rootled around a bit, and pulled out a struggling bee. She blew on it and shooed it out of the window.

For a moment her eyes seemed to have many facets, just like a bee's.

"So," she said. "She's learned how to Borrow, has she? Or she's been Borrowed!"

◆ ◆ ◆

Annagramma fainted. Zakzak stared, too *afraid* to faint.

"You see," said Tiffany, while something in the air went *gloop, gloop* above them, "a frog weighs only a few ounces, but Brian weighs, oh, about a hundred and twenty pounds, yes? *So* to turn someone big into a frog, you've got to find something to do with all the bits you can't fit into a frog, right?"

She bent down and lifted up the pointy wizard's hat on the floor.

"Happy, Brian?" she asked. A small frog, squatting in a heap of clothes, looked up and said, *"Erk!"*

Zakzak didn't look at the frog. He was looking at the thing that went *gloop, gloop.* It was like a large pink balloon full of water, quite pretty really, wobbling gently against the ceiling.

"You've killed him!" he mumbled.

"What? Oh, no. That's just the stuff he doesn't need right now. It's sort of . . . *spare* Brian."

"Erk," said Brian. *Gloop* went the rest of him.

"About this discount—" Zakzak began hurriedly. "Ten percent would be—"

Tiffany waved the wand. Behind her, the whole display of crystals rose in the air and began to orbit one another in a glittering and, above all, *fragile* way.

"That wand shouldn't do that!" he said.

"Of course it can't. It's rubbish. But *I* can," said Tiffany. "Ninety percent discount, did I hear you say? Think quickly, I'm getting tired. And the spare Brian is getting . . . heavy."

"You can keep it all!" Zakzak screamed. "For free! Just don't let him splash! Please!"

"No, no, I'd like you to stay in business," said Tiffany. "A ninety percent discount would be fine. I'd like you to think of me as . . . a friend. . . ."

"Yes! Yes! I *am* your friend! I'm a very friendly person! Now please put him baaack! Please!" Zakzak dropped to his knees, which wasn't very far. *"Please!* He's not really a wizard! He just did evening classes there in fretwork! They hire out classrooms, that sort of thing. He thinks I don't know! But he read a few of the magic books on the quiet and he pinched the robes and he can talk wizard lingo so's you'd hardly know the difference! Please! I'd never get a *real* wizard for the money I pay him! Don't hurt him, *please!"*

Tiffany waved a hand. There was a moment even more unpleasant than the one that had ended up with the spare Brian bumping against the ceiling, and then the whole Brian stood there, blinking.

"Thank you! Thank you! Thank you!" gasped Zakzak.

Brian blinked. "What just happened?" he asked.

Zakzak, beside himself with horror and relief, patted him frantically.

"You're all there?" he said. "You're not a balloon?"

"Here, get off!" said Brian, pushing him away.

There was a groan from Annagramma. She opened her eyes, saw Tiffany, and tried to scramble to her feet *and* back-away, which meant that she went backward like a spider.

"Please don't do that to me! Please don't!" she shouted.

Tiffany ran after her and pulled her to her feet.

"I wouldn't do anything to *you*, Annagramma," she said happily. "You're my friend! We're *all* friends! Isn't that *nice* please please stop me . . ."

◆ ◆ ◆

You had to remember that pictsies weren't brownies. In theory brownies would do the housework for you if you left them a saucer of milk.

The Nac Mac Feegle . . . wouldn't.

Oh, they'd try, if they liked you and you didn't insult them with *milk* in the saucer. They *were* helpful. They just weren't good at it. For example, you shouldn't try to remove a stubborn stain from a plate by repeatedly hitting it with your head.

And you didn't want to see a sink full of them and your best china. Or a precious pot rolling backward and forward across the floor while the Feegles inside simultaneously fought the ground-in dirt *and* each other.

But Miss Level, once she'd got the better china out of the way, found she rather liked the Feegles. There was something unsquashable about them. And they were entirely unamazed by a woman with two bodies too.

"Ach, that's nothin'," Rob Anybody had said. "When we wuz raidin' for the Quin, we once found a world where there wuz people wi' five bodies each. All sizes, ye ken, for doin' a' kinds of jobs."

"Really?" said both of Miss Level.

"Aye, and the biggest body had a huge left hand, just for openin' pickle jars."

"Those lids can get very tight, it's true," Miss Level had agreed.

"Oh, we saw some muckle eldritch places when we wuz raiding for the Quin," said Rob Anybody. "But we gave that up, for she wuz a schemin', greedy, ill-fared carlin, that she was!"

"Aye, and it wuz no' because she threw us oout o' Fairyland for being completely pished at two in the afternoon, whatever any scunner might mphf mphf . . ." said Daft Wullie.

"Pished?" said Miss Level.

"Aye . . . oh, aye, it means . . . tired. Aye. Tired. That's whut it means," said Rob Anybody, holding his hands firmly over his brother's mouth. "An' ye dinna ken how to talk in front o' a lady, yah shammerin' wee scunner!"

"Er . . . thank you for doing the dishes," said Miss Level. "You really didn't need to . . ."

"Ach, it wasna any trouble," said Rob Anybody cheerfully, letting Daft Wullie go. "An' I'm sure all them plates an' stuff will mend fine wi' a bit o' glue."

Miss Level looked up at the clock with no hands.

"It's getting late," she said. "What exactly is it you propose to do, Mr. Anybody?"

"Whut?"

"Do you have a plan?"

"Oh, aye!"

Rob Anybody rummaged around in his spog, which is a leather bag most Feegles have hanging from their belt. The contents are usually a mystery but sometimes include interesting teeth.

He flourished a much-folded piece of paper.

Miss Level carefully unfolded it.

"'PLN'?" she said.

"Aye," said Rob proudly. "We came prepared! Look, it's *written doon*. Pee El Ner. Plan."

"Er . . . how can I put this . . ." Miss Level mused. "Ah, yes. You came rushing all this way to save Tiffany from a creature that can't be seen, touched, smelled, or killed. What did you intend to do when you found it?"

Rob Anybody scratched his head, to a general shower of objects.

"I think mebbe you've put yer finger on the one weak spot, mistress," he admitted.

"Do you mean you charge in regardless?"

"Oh, aye. That's the plan, sure enough," said Rob Anybody, brightening up.

"And then what happens?"

"Weel, gen'raly people are tryin' tae wallop us by then, so we just make it up as we gae along."

"Yes, Robert, but the creature is inside her head!"

Rob Anybody gave Billy a questioning look.

"Robert is a heich-heidit way o' sayin' Rob," said the gonnagle, and to save time he said to Miss Level: "That means kinda posh."

"Ach, we can get inside her heid, if we have to," said Rob. "I'd hoped tae get here afore the thing got to her, but we can chase it."

Miss Level's face was a picture. Two pictures.

"*Inside* her *head*?" she said.

"Oh, aye," said Rob, as if that sort of thing happened every day. "No problemo. We can get in or oout o' anywhere. Except maybe pubs, which for some reason we ha' trouble leavin'. A heid? Easy."

"Sorry, we're talking about a real head here, are we?" said Miss Level, horrified. "What do you do, go in through the ears?"

Once again, Rob stared at Billy, who looked puzzled.

"No, mistress. They'd be too small," he said patiently. "But we can move between worlds, ye ken. We're fairy folk."

Miss Level nodded both heads. It was true, but it was hard to look at the assembled ranks of the Nac Mac Feegle and remember that they were, technically, fairies. It was like watching penguins swimming underwater and having to remember that they were birds.

"And?" she said.

"We can get intae dreams, ye see. . . . And what's a mind but another world o' dreamin'?"

"No, I must forbid that!" said Miss Level. "I can't have you running around inside a young girl's head! I mean, look at you! You're fully grow . . . well, you're men! It'd be like, like . . . well, it'd be like you looking at her diary!"

Rob Anybody looked puzzled.

"Oh, aye?" he said. "We looked at her diary loads o' times. Nae harm done."

"You *looked* at her *diary?*" said Miss Level, horrified. "Why?"

Really, she thought later, she should have expected the answer.

"'Cuz it wuz locked," said Daft Wullie. "If she didna want anyone tae look at it, why'd she keep it at the back o' her sock drawer? Anyway, all there wuz wuz a load o' words we couldna unnerstan' an' wee drawings o' hearts and flowers an' that."

"Hearts? Tiffany?" said Miss Level. *"Really?"* She shook herself. "But you shouldn't have done that! And going into someone's mind is even worse!"

"The hiver is in there, mistress," said Awf'ly Wee Billy meekly.

"But you said you can't do anything about it!"

"*She* might. If we can track her doon," said the gonnagle. "If we can find the wee bitty bit o' her that's still *her*. She's a bonny fighter when she's roused. Ye see, mistress, a mind's like a world itself. She'll be hidin' in it somewhere, lookin' oout though her own eyes, listenin' wi' her own ears, tryin' to make people hear, tryin' no' to let yon beast find her . . . and it'll be hunting her all the time, trying tae break her doon. . . ."

Miss Level began to look hunted herself. Fifty small faces, full of worry and hope and broken noses, looked up at her. And she knew she didn't have a better plan. Or even a PLN.

"All right," she said. "But at least you ought to have a bath. I know that's silly, but it will make me feel better about the whole thing."

There was a general groan.

"A bath? But we a' had one no' a year ago," said Rob Anybody. "Up at the big dew pond for the ships!"

"Ach, crivens!" said Big Yan. "Ye canna ask a man tae take a bath again this soon, mistress! There'll be nothin' left o' us!"

"With hot water and soap!" said Miss Level. "I mean it! I'll run the water and I . . . I'll put some rope over the edge so you can climb in and out, but you *will* get clean. I'm a wi—a hag, and you'd better do what I say!"

"Oh, all reet!" said Rob. "We'll do it for the big wee hag. But ye're no' tae peek, okay?"

"Peek?" said Miss Level. She pointed a trembling finger. "Get into that bathroom now!"

◆　◆　◆

Miss Level did, however, listen at the door. It's the sort of thing a witch does.

There was nothing to hear at first but the gentle splash of water, and then:

"This is no' as bad as I thought!"

"Aye, very pleasin'."

"Hey, there's a big yellow duck here. Who're ye pointin' that beak at, yer scunner—"

There was a wet quack and some bubbling noises as the rubber duck sank.

"Rob, we oughta get one o' these put in back in the mound. Verra warmin' in the wintertime."

"Aye, it's no' that good for the ship, havin' tae drink oout o' that pond after we've been bathin'. It's terrible, hearin' a ship try tae spit."

"Ach, it'll make us softies! It's nae a guid wash if ye dinna ha' the ice formin' on yer heid!"

"Who're you callin' a softie?"

There followed a lot more splashing, and water started to seep under the door.

Miss Level knocked.

"Come on out now, and dry yourselves off!" she commanded. "She could be back at any minute!"

In fact, it wasn't for another two hours, by which time Miss Level had got so nervous that her necklaces jingled all the time.

She'd come to witching later than most, being naturally qualified by reason of the two bodies, but she'd never been very happy about magic. In truth, most witches could get through their whole lives without having to do serious, undeniable magic (making shambles and curse nets and dream catchers didn't really count, being rather more like arts and crafts, and most of the rest of it was practical medicine, common sense, and the ability to look stern in a pointy hat). But being a witch and wearing the big black hat was like being a policeman. People saw the uniform, not you. When the mad axeman was running down the street, you weren't allowed to back away, muttering, "Could you find someone else? Actually,

I mostly just do, you know, stray dogs and road safety. . . ." You were there, you had the hat, you did the job. That was a basic rule of witchery: *It's up to you.*

She was two bags of nerves when Tiffany arrived back, and stood side by side holding hands with herself to give herself confidence.

"Were have you been, dear?"

"Out," said Tiffany.

"And what have you been doing?"

"Nothing."

"I see you've been shopping."

"Yes."

"Who with?"

"Nobody."

"Ah, yes," Miss Level trilled, completely adrift. "I remember when I used to go out and do nothing. Sometimes you can be your own worst company. Believe me, I know—"

But Tiffany had already swept upstairs.

Without anyone actually seeming to move, Feegles started to appear everywhere in the room.

"Well, that could ha' gone better," said Rob Anybody.

"She looked so different!" Miss Level burst out. "She moved differently! I just didn't know what to do! And those clothes!"

"Aye. Sparklin' like a young raven," said Rob.

"Did you see all those bags? Where could she have got the money? *I* certainly don't have that kind of—"

She stopped, and both of Miss Level spoke.

"Oh, no—"

"—surely not! She wouldn't—"

"—have, would she?"

"I dinna ken whut ye're talkin' aboot," said Awf'ly Wee Billy, "but whut *she* would dae isna the point. That's the hiver doin' the thinkin'!"

Miss Level clasped all four hands together in distress. "Oh dear . . . I *must* go down to the village and check!"

One of her ran toward the door.

"Well, at least she's brought the broomstick back," muttered the Miss Level who stayed. She started to wear the slightly unfocused expression she got when both her bodies weren't in the same place.

They could hear noises from upstairs.

"I vote we just tap her gently on the heid," said Big Yan. "It canna give us any trouble if it's gone sleepies, aye?"

Miss Level clenched and unclenched her fists nervously. "No," she said. "I'll go up there and have a *serious* talk with her!"

"I told yez, mistress, it's not her," said Awf'ly Wee Billy wearily.

"Well at least I'll wait until I've visited Mr. Weavall," said Miss Level, standing in her kitchen. "I'm nearly there . . . ah . . . he's asleep. I'll just *eease* the box out quietly. . . . If she's taken his money, I'm going to be *so* angry—"

◆   ◆   ◆

It was a *good* hat, Tiffany thought. It was at least as tall as Mrs. Earwig's hat, and it shone darkly. The stars gleamed.

The other packages covered the floor and the bed. She pulled out another one of the black dresses, the one covered in lace, and the cloak, which spread out in the air. She really liked the cloak. In anything but a complete dead calm, it floated and billowed as if whipped by a gale. If you were going to be a witch, you had to start by looking like one.

She twirled in it once or twice and then said something without thinking, so that the hiver part of her was caught unawares.

"See me."

The hiver was suddenly thrust outside her body. Tiffany was free. She hadn't expected it. . . .

She felt herself to the tips of her fingers. She dived toward the bed, grabbed one of Zakzak's best wands, and waved it desperately in front of her like a weapon.

"You stay out!" she said. "Stay away! It's my body, not yours! You've made it do dreadful things! You *stole* Mr. Weavall's money! Look at these stupid clothes! And don't you know about eating and drinking? You stay away! You're not coming back! Don't you dare! I've got power, you know!"

So have we, said her own voice in her own head. *Yours.*

They fought. A watcher would have seen only a girl in a black dress, spinning around the room and flailing her arms as if she'd been stung, but Tiffany fought for every toe, every finger. She bounced off a wall, banged against the chest of drawers, slammed into another wall—

—and the door was flung open.

One of Miss Level was there, no longer nervous but trembling with rage. She pointed a shaking finger.

"Listen to me, whoever you are! Did you steal Mr.—" she began.

The hiver turned.

The hiver struck.

The hiver . . . killed.

CHAPTER 8

The Secret Land

❧

It's bad enough being dead. Waking up and seeing a Nac Mac Feegle standing on your chest and peering intently at you from an inch away only makes things worse.

Miss Level groaned. It felt as though she was lying on the floor.

"Ach, this one's alive, right enough," said the Feegle. "Told yez! That's a weasel skull ye owe me!"

Miss Level blinked one set of eyes and then froze in horror.

"What happened to me?" she whispered.

The Feegle in front of her was replaced by the face of Rob Anybody. It was not an improvement.

"How many fingers am I holdin' up?" he said.

"Five," whispered Miss Level.

"Am I? Ah, well, ye could be right, ye'd have the knowin' o' the countin'," said Rob, lowering his hand. "Ye've had a wee bittie accident, ye ken. You're a wee bittie dead."

Miss Level's head slumped back. Through the mist of something that wasn't exactly pain, she heard Rob Anybody say to someone she couldn't see:

"Hey, I *wuz* breakin' it tae her gently! I did say 'wee bittie' twice, right?"

"It's as though part of me is . . . a long way off," murmured Miss Level.

"Aye, you're aboout right there," said Rob, champion of the bedside manner.

Some memories bobbed to the surface of the thick soup in Miss Level's mind.

"Tiffany killed me, didn't she?" she said. "I remember seeing that black figure turn around, and her expression was horrible—"

"That wuz the hiver," said Rob Anybody. "That was no 'Tiffany! She was fightin' it! She still is, inside! But it didna remember you ha' *two* bodies! We got tae help her, mistress!"

Miss Level pushed herself upright. It *wasn't* pain she felt, but it was the . . . ghost of pain.

"What happened to me?" she said, weakly.

"There was like, an explosion, an' smoke an' that," said Rob. "Not messy, really."

"Oh, well, that's a small mercy, anyway," said Miss Level, sagging back.

"Aye, there was just this, like, big purple cloud o', like, dust," said Daft Wullie.

"Where's my . . . I can't feel . . . Where's my other body?"

"Aye, that was what got blown up in that big cloud, right enough," said Rob. "Good job ye hae a spare, eh?"

"She's all mithered in her heid," whispered Awf'ly Wee Billy. "Take it gently, eh?"

"How do you manage, seeing only one side of things?" said Miss Level dreamily to the world in general. "How will I get everything done with only one pair of hands and feet? Being in just one place all the time . . . how do people manage? It's impossible. . . ."

She shut her eyes.

"Mistress Level, we *need* ye!" shouted Rob Anybody into her ear.

"Need, need, need," murmured Miss Level. "Everyone needs a witch. No one cares if a witch *needs*. *Giving* and *giving* always . . . a fairy godmother never gets a wish, let me tell you . . ."

"Mistress Level!" Rob screamed. "Ye cannae pass oout on us noo!"

"I'm weary," whispered Miss Level. "I'm very, very pished."

"Mistress Level!" Rob Anybody yelled. "The big wee hag is lying on the floor like a dead person, but she's cold as ice and sweatin' like a horse! She's fightin' the beast inside her, mistress! And she's losin'!" Rob peered into Miss Level's face and shook his head. "Auchtahelweit! She's swooned! C'mon, lads, let's move her!"

Like many small creatures, Feegles are immensely strong for their size. It still took ten of them to carry Miss Level up the narrow stairs without banging her head more than necessary, although they did use her feet to push open the door to Tiffany's room.

Tiffany lay on the floor. Sometimes a muscle twitched.

Miss Level was propped up like a doll.

"How're we gonna bring the big hag roound?" said Big Yan.

"I heard where ye has to put someone's heid between their legs," said Rob doubtfully.

Daft Wullie sighed and drew his sword. "Sounds a wee bit drastic tae me," he said, "but if someone will help me hold her steady—"

Miss Level opened her eyes, which was just as well. She focused unsteadily on the Feegles and smiled a strange, happy little smile.

"Ooo, fairies!" she mumbled.

"Ach, noo she's ramblin'," said Rob Anybody.

"She means fairies like bigjobs *think* they are," said Awf'ly Wee Billy. "Tiny wee tinkly creatures that live in flowers an' fly aroound cuddlin' butterflies an' that."

"What? Have they no' *seen* real fairies? They're worse'n wasps!" said Big Yan.

"We havna got *time* for this!" snapped Rob Anybody. He jumped onto Miss Level's knee.

"Aye, ma'am, we's fairies from the land o'—" He stopped and looked imploringly at Billy.

"Tinkle?" Billy suggested.

"Aye, the land o' Tinkle, ye ken, and we found this puir wee—"

"—princess," said Billy.

"Aye, princess, who's been attacked by a bunch o' scunners—"

"—wicked goblins," said Billy.

"—yeah, wicked goblins, right, an' she's in a bad way, so we wuz wonderin' if ye could kinda tell us how tae look after her—"

"—until the handsome prince turns up on a big white horse wi' curtains roound it an' wakes her with a magical kiss," said Billy.

Rob gave him a desperate look and turned back to the bemused Miss Level.

"Aye, what ma friend Fairy Billy just said," he managed.

Miss Level tried to focus.

"You're very *ugly* for fairies," she said.

"Aye, well, the ones you gen'rally see are for the *pretty* flowers, ye ken," said Rob Anybody, inventing desperately. "We're more for the stingin' nettles and bindweed an' Old Man's Troosers an' thistles, okay? It wouldna be fair for only the bonny flowers tae have fairies noo, would it? It'd prob'ly be against the law, eh? Noo, can ye *please* help us wi' this princess here before them scunners—"

"—wicked goblins—" said Billy.

"Aye, before they come back," said Rob.

Panting, he watched Miss Level's face. There seemed to be a certain amount of thinking going on.

"Is her pulse rapid?" murmured Miss Level. "You say her skin is cold but she's sweating? Is she breathing rapidly? It sounds like shock. Keep her warm. Raise her legs. Watch her carefully. Try to remove . . . the cause. . . ." Her head slumped.

Rob turned to Awf'ly Wee Billy.

"A horse wi' *curtains* roound it?" he said. "Where did ye get all that blethers?"

"There's a big hoouse near the Long Lake, an' they read stories tae their wee bairn an' I got along an' listened fra' a mousehole," said Awf'ly Wee Billy. "One day I snuck in and looked at the pichoors, and there was bigjobs called k'nits wi' shields and armor and horses wi' curtains—"

"Weel, it worked, blethers though it be," said Rob Anybody. He looked at Tiffany. She was lying down, so he was about as high as her chin. It was like walking around a small hill. "Crivens, it does me nae guid at all ta see the puir wee thing like this," he said, shaking his head. "C'mon, lads, get that cover off the bed and put that cushion under her feet."

"Er, Rob?" said Daft Wullie.

"Aye?" Rob was staring up at the unconscious Tiffany.

"How are we goin' tae get *inta* her heid? There's got tae be somethin' tae guide us in."

"Aye, Wullie, an' I ken whut it's gonna be, 'cuz I've been usin' mah heid for thinkin'!" said Rob. "Ye've seen the big wee hag often enough, right? Well, see this necklet?"

He reached up. The silver horse had slipped around Tiffany's neck as she lay on the floor. It hung there, amid the amulets and dark glitter.

"Aye?" said Wullie.

"It was a present from that son o' the Baron," said Rob. "An' she's kept it. She's tried tae turn hersel' intae some kind of creature o' the night, but somethin' made her keep this. It'll be in her heid, too. 'Tis important tae her. All we need tae do is frannit a wheelstone on it and it'll tak' us right where she is."*

Daft Wullie scratched his head.

"But I thought *she* thought he was just a big pile of jobbies?" he said. "I seen her ooot walkin', an' when he comes ridin' past, she sticks her nose in th' air and looks the other wa'. In fact, sometimes I seen her wait aroound a full five-and-twenty minutes for him tae come past, just so's she can do that."

"Ah, weel, no man kens the workin's o' the female mind," said Rob Anybody loftily. "We'll follow the Horse."

From *Fairies and How to Avoid Them* by Miss Perspicacia Tick:

No one knows exactly how the Nac Mac Feegle step from one world to another. Those who have seen Feegles actually travel this way say that they apparently throw back their shoulders and thrust out one leg straight ahead of them. Then they wiggle their foot and are gone. This is known as "the crawstep," and the only comment on the subject by a Feegle is "It's all in the ankle movement, ye ken." They appear to be able to travel magically between worlds of all kinds but not within a world. For this purpose, they assure people, they have "feets."

◆   ◆   ◆

The sky was black, even though the sun was high. It hung at just past noon, lighting the landscape as brilliantly as a hot summer day, but the sky was midnight black, shorn of stars.

This was the landscape of Tiffany Aching's mind.

The Feegles looked around them. There seemed to be downland underfoot, rolling and green.

---

*If anyone knew what this meant, they'd know a lot more about the Nac Mac Feegle's way of traveling.

"She tells the land what it is. The land tells her who she is," whispered Awf'ly Wee Billy. "She really *does* hold the soul o' the land in her *heid*. . . ."

"Aye, so 'tis," muttered Rob Anybody. "But there's nae creatures, ye ken. Nae ships. Nae burdies."

"Mebbe . . . mebbe somethin's scared them awa'?" said Daft Wullie.

There was, indeed, no life. Stillness and silence ruled here. In fact Tiffany, who cared a lot about getting words right, would have said it was a hush, which is not the same as silence. A hush is what you get in cathedrals at midnight.

"Okay, lads," Rob Anybody whispered. "We dinna ken what we're goin' tae find, so ye tread as light as e'er foot can fall, unnerstan'? Let's find the big wee hag."

They nodded, and stepped forward like ghosts.

The land rose slightly ahead of them, to some kind of earthworks. They advanced on it carefully, wary of ambush, but nothing stopped them as they climbed two long mounds in the turf that made a sort of cross.

"Manmade," said Big Yan, when they reached the top. "Just like in the old days, Rob." The silence sucked his speech away.

"This is deep inside o' the big wee hag's head," said Rob Anybody, looking around warily. "We dinna know *whut* made 'em."

"I dinna like this, Rob," said a Feegle. "It's too quiet."

"Aye, Slightly Sane Georgie, it is that—"

"You are my sunshine, my only su—"

"Daft Wullie!" snapped Rob, without taking his eyes off the strange landscape.

The singing stopped. "Aye, Rob?" said Daft Wullie from behind him.

"Ye ken I said I'd tell ye when ye wuz guilty o' stupid and inna-pro-pree-ate behavior?"

"Aye, Rob," said Daft Wullie. "That wuz another one o' those times, wuz it?"

"Aye."

They moved on again, staring around them. And still there was the hush. It was the pause before an orchestra plays, the quietness before thunder. It was as if all the small sounds of the hills had shut down to make room for one big sound to happen.

And then they found the Horse.

They'd seen it, back on the Chalk. But here it was not carved into the hillside but spread out before them. They stared at it.

"Awf'ly Wee Billy?" said Rob, beckoning the young gonnagle toward him. "You're a gonnagle, ye ken aboout poetry and dreams. What's this? Why's it up here? It shouldna be on the *top* o' the hills!"

"Serious hiddlins, Mr. Rob," said Billy. "This is *serious* hiddlins. I canna work it out yet."

"She knows the Chalk. Why'd she get this wrong?"

"I'm thinkin' aboout it, Mr. Rob."

"You wouldna care tae think a bit faster, would ye?"

"Rob?" said Big Yan, hurrying up. He'd been scouting ahead.

"Aye?" said Rob gloomily.

"Ye'd better come and see this."

On top of a round hill was a four-wheeled shepherding hut, with a curved roof and a chimney for the potbellied stove. Inside, the walls were covered with the yellow and blue wrappers from hundreds of packets of Jolly Sailor tobacco. There were old sacks hanging up there, and the back of the door was covered with chalk marks where Granny Aching had counted sheep and days. And there was a narrow iron bedstead, made comfortable with old fleeces and feed sacks.

"D'ye have the unnerstandin' of this, Awf'ly Wee Billie?" said Rob. "Can ye tell us where the big wee hag is?"

The young gonnagle looked worried. "Er, Mister Rob, ye ken I've only just been made a gonnagle? I mean, I know the songs an' a', but I'm no' verra experienced at this. . . ."

"Aye?" said Rob Anybody. "An' just how many gonnagles afore ye ha' walked through the dreams o' a hag?"

"Er . . . none I've ever heard of, Mister Rob," Billy confessed.

"Aye. So you already know more aboout it than any o' them big men," said Rob. He gave the boy a smile. "Do yer best, laddie. I dinna expect any more of you than that."

Billy looked out of the shed door and took a deep breath: "Then I'll tell ye I think she's hidin' somewhere close, like a hunted creature, Mr. Rob. This is a wee bit o' her memory, the place o' her granny, the place where she's always felt safe. I'll tell ye I think that we're in the soul and center o' her. The bit o' her that *is* her. And I'm frightened for her. Frightened to mah boots."

"Why?"

"Because I've been watchin' the shadows, Mr. Rob," said Billy. "The sun is movin'. It's slippin' doon the sky."

"Aye, weel, that's whut the sun does—" Rob began.

Billy shook his head. "*Nay*, Mr. Rob. Ye dinna understand! I'm tellin' ye that's no' the sun o' the big wide world. That's the sun o' the soul o' her."

The Feegles looked at the sun, and at the shadows, then back at Billy. He'd stuck his chin out bravely, but he was trembling.

"She'll die when night comes?" Rob said.

"There's worser things than death, Mr. Rob. The hiver will have her, head tae toe . . ."

"That is *nae* gonna happen!" shouted Rob Anybody, so suddenly

442

that Billy backed away. "She's a strong big wee lass! She fought the Quin wi' no more than a fryin' pan!"

Awf'ly Wee Billy swallowed. There were a lot of things he'd rather do than face Rob Anybody now. But he pressed on.

"Sorry, Mr. Rob, but I'm telling ye she had iron then, an' she wuz on her ain turf. She's a lang, lang way fra' hame here. An' it'll squeeze this place when it finds it, leave no more room for it, and the night will come, an' . . ."

"'Scuse me, Rob. I ha' an idea."

It was Daft Wullie, twisting his hands nervously. Everyone turned to look at him.

"*Ye* ha' an idea?" said Rob.

"Aye, an' if I tell youse, I dinna want you ta' say it's inna-pro-pree-ate, okay, Rob?"

Rob Anybody sighed. "Okay, Wullie ye ha' my word on it."

"Weel," said Wullie, his fingers knotting and unknotting, "what is *this* place if it's not truly her ain place? What is it if not her ain turf? If she canna fight the creature here, she canna fight it any-where!"

"But it willna come here," said Billy. "It doesna need to. As she grows weaker, this place will fade away."

"Oh, crivens," mumbled Daft Wullie. "Weel, it was a good idea, right? Even if it doesna work?"

Rob Anybody wasn't paying any attention. He stared around the shepherding hut. *My man's got to use his heid for something other than nuttin' folk,* Jeannie had said.

"Daft Wullie is right," he said quietly. "This is her safe place. She holds the land, she has it in her eye. The creature can ne'er touch her here. *Here* she has power. But 'twill be a jailhoouse for her here unless she fights the monster. She'd be locked in here and watch her life gae doon the cludgie. She'll look oot at the world like a pris'ner at a tiny window, and see hersel' hated and feared. So we'll fetch the beast in here against its will, and here it will die!"

The Feegles cheered. They weren't sure what was going on, but they liked the sound of it.

"How?" said Awf'ly Wee Billy.

"Ye had to gae and ask that, eh?" said Rob Anybody bitterly. "An' I wuz doin' sae weel wi' the thinkin'. . ."

He turned. There was a scratching noise on the door above him.

Up there, across the rows and rows of half-rubbed-out markings, freshly chalked letters were appearing one by one, as if an invisible hand was writing them.

"Worrds," said Rob Anybody. "She's tryin' tae tell us somethin'!"

"Yes, they say—" Billy began.

"I ken weel what they say!" snapped Rob Anybody. "I ha' the knowin' of the readin'! They say . . ."

He looked up again. "Okay, they say . . . that's the snake, an' that's the kinda like a gate letter, an' the comb on its side, two o' that, an' the fat man standin' still, an' the snake again, and then there's whut we calls a 'space,' and then there's the letter like a saw's teeth, and two o' the letters that's roound like the sun, and the letter that's a man sittin' doon. And onna next line we ha' . . . the man wi' his arms oot, and the letter that's you, an' ha, the fat man again but noo he's walkin, an' next he's standin' still again, an' next is the comb, an' the up-an'-doon ziggy-zaggy letter, and the man's got his arms oot, and then there's me, and that ziggy-zaggy and we end the line with the comb again. . . . An' on the *next* line we starts wi' the bendy hook, that's the letter roound as the sun, them's twa' men sittin' doon, there's the letter reaching oout tae the sky, then there's a space 'cuz there's nae letter, then there's the snaky again, an' the letter like a hoouse frame, and then there's the letter that's me, aye, an' another fella sitting doon, an' another big roound letter, and, ha, oour ol' friend, the fat man walkin'! The End!"

He stood back, hands on hips, and demanded:

"There! Is that readin' I just did, or wuz it no'?" There was a cheer from the Feegles, and some applause.

Awf'ly Wee Billy looked up at the chalked words:

SHEEPS WOOL
TURPENTINE
JOLLY SAILOR

And then he looked at Rob Anybody's expression.

"Aye, aye," he said. "Ye're doin great, Mr. Rob. Sheep's wool, turpentine, and Jolly Sailor tobacco."

"Ach, weel, anyone can read it all in one go," said Rob Anybody dismissively. "But youse gotta be *guid* to break it doon intae all the tricksie letters. And *veera* guid to have the knowin' o' the meanin' o' the whole."

"What is that?" asked Awf'ly Wee Billy.

"The meaning, gonnagle, is that you are gonna go *stealin'*!" There was a cheer from the rest of the Feegles. They hadn't been keeping up very well, but they recognized *that* word all right.

"An' it's gonna be a stealin' tae remember!" Rob yelled, to another cheer. "Daft Wullie!"

"Aye!"

"Ye'll be in charge! Ye ha' not got the brains o' a beetle, brother o' mine, but when it comes tae the thievin', ye hae no equal in this wurld! Ye've got tae fetch turpentine and fresh sheep wool and some o' the Jolly Sailor baccy! Ye got tae get them to the big hag wi' twa' bodies! Tell her she must mak' the hiver *smell* them, right? It'll bring it here! And ye'd best be quick, because that sun is movin' down the sky. Ye'll be stealin' fra' Time itself—aye? Ye have a question?"

Daft Wullie had raised a finger.

"Point o' order, Rob," he said, "but it was a wee bittie hurtful there for you to say I dinna hae the brains of a beetle . . ."

Rob hesitated, but only for a moment. "Aye, Daft Wullie, ye are right in whut ye say. It was unricht o' me to say that. It was the heat o' the moment, an' I am full sorry for it. As I stand here before ye now, I will say: Daft Wullie, ye *do* hae the brains o' a beetle, an' I'll fight any scunner who says different!"

Daft Wullie's face broke into a huge smile, then crinkled into a frown.

"But ye are the leader, Rob," he said.

"No' on this raid, Wullie. A'm staying here. I have every confidence that ye'll be a fiiinne leader on this raid an' not totally mess it up like ye did the last seventeen times!"

There was a general groan from the crowd.

"Look at the sun, will ye!" said Rob, pointing. "It's moved since we've been talkin'! Someone's got tae stay wi' her! I will no' ha' it said we left her tae die alone! Now, get movin', ye scunners, or feel the flat o' my blade!"

He raised his sword and growled. They fled.

Rob Anybody laid his sword down with care, then sat on the step of the shepherding hut to watch the sun.

After a while he was aware of something else. . . .

◆　◆　◆

Hamish the aviator gave Miss Level's broomstick a doubtful look. It hung a few feet above the ground, and it worried him.

He hitched up the bundle on his back that contained his parachute, although it was technically the "paradrawers," since it was made of string and an old pair of Tiffany's best Sunday drawers, well washed. They still had flowers on them, but there was nothing like them for getting a Feegle safely to the ground. He had a feeling it (or they) were going to be needed.

"It's no' got feathers," he complained.

"Look, we dinna ha' time to argue!" said Daft Wullie. "We're in a hurry, ye ken, an' you're the only one who knows how tae fly!"

"A broomstick isna *flyin'*," said Hamish. "It's magic. It hasna any wings! I dinna ken that stuff!"

But Big Yan had already thrown a piece of string over the bristle end of the stick and was climbing up. Other Feegles followed.

"Besides, how do they steer these things?" Hamish went on.

"Weel, how do ye do it with wi' the birdies?" Daft Wullie demanded.

"Oh, that's easy. Ye just shift your weight, but—"

"Ach, ye'll learn as we go," said Wullie. "Flying canna be that difficult. Even *ducks* can do it, and they have nae brains at a'."

And there was really no point in arguing, which is why, a few minutes later, Hamish inched his way along the stick's handle. The rest of the Feegles clung to the bristles at the other end, chattering.

Firmly tied to the bristles was a bundle of what looked like sticks and rags, with a battered hat and the stolen beard on top of it.

At least this extra weight meant that the stick end was pointing up, toward a gap in the fruit trees. Hamish sighed, took a deep breath, pulled his goggles over his eyes, and put a hand on a shiny area of stick just in front of him.

Gently, the stick began to move through the air. There was a cheer from the Feegles.

"See? Told yez ye'd be okay," Daft Wullie called out. "But can ye no' make it go a wee bit faster?"

Carefully, Hamish touched the shiny area again.

The stick shuddered, hung motionless for a moment, and then shot upward trailing a noise very like:

Arrrrrrrrrrggggggggggggggghhhhhhhhhhhhhhhh. . . .

◆　◆　◆

In the silent world of Tiffany's head, Rob Anybody picked up his sword again and crept across the darkening turf.

There was something there, small but moving.

It was a tiny thornbush, growing so fast that its twigs visibly moved. Its shadow danced on the grass.

Rob Anybody stared at it. It had to mean something. He watched it carefully. Little bush, growing . . .

And then he remembered what the old kelda had told them when he'd been a wee boy.

Once, the land had been all forest, heavy and dark. Then men came and cut down trees. They let the sun in. The grass grew up in the clearings. The bigjobs brought in sheep, which ate the grass, and also what grew in the grass: *tree seedlings*. And so the dark forests died. There hadn't been much life in them, not once the tree trunks closed in behind you; it had been dark as the bottom of the sea in there, the leaves far above keeping out the light. Sometimes there was the crash of a branch, or the rattle and patter as acorns the squirrels had missed bounced down, from branch to branch, into the gloom. Mostly it was just hot and silent. Around the edges of the forest were the homes of many creatures. Deep inside the forest, the everlasting forest, was the home of wood.

But the turf *lived* in the sun, with its hundreds of grasses and flowers and birds and insects. The Nac Mac Feegle knew that better than most, being so much closer to it. What looked like a green desert at a distance was a tiny, thriving, roaring *jungle*. . . .

"Ach," said Rob Anybody. "So that's yer game, izzit? Weel, ye're no' takin' over in here too!"

He chopped at the spindly thing with his sword and stood back.

The rustling of leaves behind him made him turn.

There were two more saplings unfolding. And a third. He looked across the grass and saw a dozen, a hundred tiny trees beginning their race for the sky.

Worried though he was, and he was worried to his boots, Rob Anybody grinned. If there's one thing a Feegle likes, it's knowing that wherever you strike, you're going to hit an enemy.

The sun was going down and the shadows were moving and the turf was dying.

Rob *charged*.

Arrrrrrrrrgggggggggggggghhhhhhhhhhhhhhh . . .

What happened during the Nac Mac Feegle's search for the right smell was remembered by several witnesses (quite apart from all the owls and bats who were left spinning in the air by a broomstick being navigated by a bunch of screaming little blue men).

One of them was Number 95, a ram owned by a not very imaginative farmer. But all he remembered was a sudden noise in the night and a draughty feeling on his back. That was about as exciting as it got for Number 95, so he went back to thinking about grass.

Arrrrrrrrrgggggggggggggghhhhhhhhhhhhhhh . . .

Then there was Mildred Pusher, age seven, who was the daughter of the shepherd who owned Number 95. One day, when she'd grown up and become a grandmother, she told her grandchildren about the night she came downstairs by candlelight for a drink of water and heard the noises under the sink. . . .

"And there were these little voices, you see, and one said, 'Ach, Wullie, you canna drink that, look, it says "Poison!" on the bottle,' and another voice said, 'Aye, gonnagle, they put that on tae frighten a man from havin' a wee drink,' and the *first* voice said, 'Wullie, it's rat poison!' and the second voice said, 'That's fine, then, 'cuz I'm no' a rat!' And then I opened the cupboard under the sink, and what do you think—it was full of fairies! And they looked at me and I looked at them and one of them said, 'Hey, this is a dream you're having, big wee girl!' and immediately they all agreed! And the first one said, 'So, in this *dream* ye're having, big wee girl, you wouldna mind telling us where the turpentine is, wouldya?' And so I told them it was outside in the barn, and he said, 'Aye? Then we're offski. But here's a wee gift fra' the fairies for a big wee girl who's gonna go right back tae sleep!' And then they were gone!"

One of her grandchildren, who'd been listening with his mouth open, said, "What did they give you, Grandma?"

"This!" Mildred held up a silver spoon. "And the strange thing is, it's just like the ones my mother had, which vanished mysteriously from the drawer the very same night! I've kept it safe ever since!"

This was admired by all. Then one of the grandchildren asked: "What were the fairies *like*, Grandma?"

Grandma Mildred thought about this. "Not as pretty as you might expect," she said at last. "But definitely more smelly. And just after they'd gone there was a sound like—"

Arrrrrrrrrggggggggggggghhhhhhhhhhhhhh . . .

People in The King's Legs (the owner had noticed that there were lots of inns and pubs called The King's Head or The King's Arms, and spotted a gap in the market) looked up when they heard the noise outside.

After a minute or two the door burst open.

"Good night to ye, fellow bigjobs!" roared a figure in the doorway.

The room fell horribly silent. Awkwardly, legs going in every direction, the scarecrow figure wove unsteadily toward the bar and grabbed it thankfully, hanging on as it sagged to its knees.

"A big huge wee drop o' yer finest whisky, me fine fellow barman fellow," it said from somewhere under the hat.

"It seems to me that you've already had enough to drink, friend," said the barman, whose hand had crept to the cudgel he kept under the bar for special customers.

"Who're ye calling 'friend,' pal?" roared the figure, trying to pull itself up. "That's fightin' talk, that is! And I havena had enough to drink, pal, 'cuz if I have, why've I still got all this money, eh? Answer me that!"

A hand sagged into a coat pocket, came out jerkily, and slammed down onto the top of the bar. Ancient gold coins rolled in every direction, and a couple of silver spoons dropped out of the sleeve.

The silence of the bar became a lot deeper. Dozens of eyes watched the shiny discs as they spun off the bar and rolled across the floor.

"An' I want an ounce o' Jolly Sailor baccy," said the figure.

"Why, certainly, sir," said the barman, who had been brought up to be respectful to gold coins. He felt under the bar and his expression changed.

"Oh. I'm sorry, sir, we've sold out. Very popular, Jolly Sailor. But we've got plenty of—"

The figure had already turned around to face the rest of the room.

"Okay, I'll gie a handful o' gold to the first scunner who gi'es me a pipeful o' Jolly Sailor!" it yelled.

The room erupted. Tables scraped. Chairs overturned.

The scarecrow man grabbed the first pipe and threw the coins into the air. As fights immediately broke out, he turned back to the bar and said: "And I'll ha' that wee drop o' whisky before I go, barman. Ach, no you willna, Big Yan! *Shame on ye!* Hey, youse legs can shut up right noo! A wee pint of whisky'll do us no harm! Oh, aye? *Who deid and made ye Big Man, eh?* Listen, ye scunner, oour Rob is in there! *Aye, and he'd have a wee drink, too!*"

The customers stopped pushing one another out the way to get at the coins, and got up to face a whole body arguing with itself.

"Anywa', I'm in the heid, right? The heid's in charge. I dinna ha' tae listen to a bunch o' knees! *I said this wuz a bad idea, Wullie. Ye ken we ha' trouble getting oout of pubs!* Well, speaking on behalf o' the legs, we're not gonna stand by and watch the heid get pished, thank ye so veerae much!"

To the horror of the customers the entire bottom half of the figure turned around and started to walk toward the door, causing the top half to fall forward. It gripped the edge of the bar desperately, managed to say, "Okay! Is a deep-fried pickled egg totally oout o' the question?" and then the figure—

—tore itself in half. The legs staggered a few steps toward the door and fell over.

In the shocked silence a voice from somewhere in the trousers said: "Crivens! Time for offski!"

The air blurred for a moment and the door slammed.

After a while one of the customers stepped forward cautiously and prodded the heap of old clothes and sticks that was all that remained of the visitor. The hat rolled off, and he jumped back.

A glove that was still hanging on to the bar fell to the floor with a *thwap!* that sounded very loud.

"Well, look at it this way," said the barman. "Whatever it was, at least it's left its pockets."

From outside came the sound of:

Arrrrrrrrrggggggggggggghhhhhhhhhhhhhh . . .

The broomstick hit the thatched roof of Miss Level's cottage hard and stuck in it. Feegles fell off, still fighting.

In a struggling, punching mass they rolled into the cottage, conducted guerrilla warfare all the way up the stairs, and ended up in a head-butting, kicking heap in Tiffany's bedroom, where those who'd been left behind to guard the sleeping girl and Miss Level joined in out of interest.

Gradually the fighters became aware of a sound. It was the skirl of the mousepipes, cutting through the battle like a sword. Hands stopped gripping throats, fists stopped in mid punch, kicks hovered in midair.

Tears ran down Awf'ly Wee Billy's face as he played "The Bonny Flowers," the saddest song in the world. It was about home, and mothers, and good times gone past, and faces no longer there. The Feegles let go of one another and stared down at their feet as the forlorn notes wound about them, speaking of betrayal and treachery and the breaking of promises—

"Shame on ye!" screamed Awf'ly Wee Billy, letting the pipe drop out of his mouth. "Shame on ye! Traitors! Betrayers! Ye shame hearth and hame! Your hag is fightin' for her verra soul! Have ye no honor?" He flung down the mousepipes, which wailed into silence. "I curse my feets that let me stand here in front o' ye! Ye shame the verrae sun shinin' on ye! Ye shame the kelda that birthed ye! Traitors! Scuggans! What ha' I done to be among this parcel o' rogues? Any man here want tae fight? Then fight me! Aye, *fight me!* An' I swear by the harp o' bones I'll tak' him tae the deeps o' the sea an' then kick him tae the craters o' the moon an' see him ride tae the Pit o' Heel itself on a saddle made o' hedgehogs! I tell ye, my rage is the strength of the storm that tears mountains intae sand! Who among ye will stand agin me?"

Big Yan, who was almost three times the size of Awf'ly Wee Billy, cowered back as the little gonnagle stood in front of him. Not a Feegle would have raised a hand at that moment, for fear of his life. The rage of a gonnagle was a dreadful thing to see. A gonnagle could use words like swords.

Daft Wullie shuffled forward.

"I can see ye're upset, gonnagle," he mumbled. "'Tis me that's at fault, on account o' being daft. I shoulda remembered aboout us and pubs."

He looked so dejected that Awf'ly Wee Billie calmed down a little.

"Very well then," he said, but rather coldly because you can't lose that much anger all at once. "We'll not talk aboout this again. But we *will* remember it, right?" He pointed to the sleeping shape of Tiffany. "Now pick up that wool, and the tobacco, and the turpentine, understand? Someone tak' the top off the turpentine bottle and pour a wee drop onto a bit o' cloth. And no one, let me mak' myself clear, is tae drink *any* of it!"

The Feegles fell over themselves to obey. There was a ripping noise as the "bit o' cloth" was obtained from the bottom of Miss Level's dress.

"Right," said Awf'ly Wee Billy. "Daft Wullie, you tak' all the three things and put them up on the big wee hag's chest, where she can smell them."

"How can she smell them when she's oout cold like that?" asked Wullie.

"The nose disna sleep," said the gonnagle flatly.

The three smells of the shepherding hut were laid reverentially just below Tiffany's chin.

"Noo we wait," said Awf'ly Wee Billy. "We wait, and hope."

◆ ◆ ◆

It was hot in the little bedroom with the sleeping witches and a crowd of Feegles. It wasn't long before the smells of sheep's wool, turpentine, and tobacco rose and twined and filled the air. . . .

Tiffany's nose twitched.

The nose is a big thinker. It's good at memory—very good. So good that a smell can take you back in memory so hard that it hurts. The brain can't stop it. The brain has nothing to do with it. The hiver could control brains, but it couldn't control a stomach that threw up when it was flown on a broomstick. And it was *useless* at noses. . . .

The smell of sheeps' wool, turpentine, and Jolly Sailor tobacco could carry a mind away, all the way to a silent place that was warm and safe and free from harm...

The hiver opened its eyes and looked around.

"The shepherding hut?" it said.

It sat up. Red light shone in through the open door, and between the trunks of the saplings growing everywhere. Many of them were quite big now and cast long shadows, putting the setting sun behind bars. Around the shepherding hut, though, they had been cut down.

"This is a trick," it said. "It won't work. We are you. We think like you. We're better at thinking like you than you are."

Nothing happened.

The hiver looked like Tiffany, although here it was slightly taller because Tiffany thought she was slightly taller than she really was. It stepped out of the hut and onto the turf.

"It's getting late," it said to the silence. "Look at the trees! This place is dying. We don't have to escape. Soon all of this will be part of us. Everything that you really could be. You're proud of your little piece of ground. We can remember when there were no worlds! We—you could change things with a wave of your hand! You could make things right or make things wrong, and *you* could decide which is which! You will never die!"

"Then why are ye sweatin', ye big heap o' jobbies? Ach, what a scunner!" said a voice behind it.

For a moment the hiver wavered. Its shape changed, many times in the fractions of a second. There were bits of scales, fins, teeth, a pointy hat, claws . . . and then it was Tiffany again, smiling.

"Oh, Rob Anybody, we are glad to see you," it said. "Can you help us?"

"Dinna gi' me all that swiddle!" shouted Rob, bouncing up and down in rage. "I know a hiver when I sees one! Crivens, but ye're due a kickin'!"

The hiver changed again, became a lion with teeth the size of swords and roared at him.

"Ach, it's like that, is it?" said Rob Anybody. "Dinna go awa'!" He ran a few steps and vanished.

The hiver changed back to its Tiffany shape again.

"Your little friend has gone," it said. "Come out now. Come out *now*. Why fear us? We *are* you. You won't be like the rest, the dumb animals, the stupid kings, the greedy wizards. Together—"

Rob Anybody returned, followed by . . . well, everyone.

"Ye canna die," he yelled. "But we'll make ye wish ye could!"

They charged.

The Feegles had the advantage in most fights because they were small and fought big enemies. If you're small and fast, you're hard to hit. The hiver fought back by changing shape, all the time. Swords clanged on scales, heads butted fangs—it whirled across the turf, growling and screaming, calling up past shapes to counter every attack. But Feegles were hard to kill. They bounced when thrown, sprang back when trodden on, and easily dodged teeth and claws. They fought—

—and the ground shook so suddenly that even the hiver lost its footing.

The shepherding hut creaked and began to settle into the turf, which opened up around it as easily as butter. The saplings trembled and began to fall over, one after the other, as if their roots were being cut under the grass.

The land . . . rose.

Rolling down the shifting slope, the Feegles saw the hills cimbing toward the sky. What was there, what had always been there, become more plain.

Rising into the dark sky was a head, shoulders, a chest. Someone who had been lying down, growing turf, their arms and legs the hills and valleys of the downland, was sitting up. They moved with great stony slowness, millions of tons of hill shifting and creaking around them. What had looked like two long mounds in the shape of a cross became giant green arms, unfolding.

A hand with fingers longer than houses reached down, picked up the hiver, and lifted it up into the air.

Far off, something thumped three times. The sound seemed to be coming from outside the world. The Feegles, turning and watching from the small hill that was one of the knees of the giant girl, ignored it.

"She tells the land whut it is, and it tells her who she is," said Awf'ly Wee Billy, tears running down his face. "I canna write a song aboot this! I'm nae good enough!"

"Is that the big wee hag dreamin' she's the hills or the hills dreamin' they're the big wee hag?" said Daft Wullie.

"Both, mebbe," said Rob Anybody. They watched the huge hand close and winced.

"But ye canna kill a hiver," said Daft Wullie.

"Aye, but ye can frit it awa'," said Rob Anybody. "It's a big wee universe oout there. If I was it, I'd no' think o' tryin' *her* again!"

There were three more booms in the distance, louder this time.

"I think," he went on, "that's it's time we were offski."

In Miss Level's cottage someone was knocking heavily on the front door. *Thump. Thump. Thump.*

CHAPTER 9

Soul and Center

◈

Tiffany opened her eyes, remembered, and thought: Was that a dream, or was that real?

And the next thought was: How do I know I'm me? Suppose I'm not me but just think I'm me? How can I tell if I'm me or not? Who's the "me" who's asking the question? Am I thinking these thoughts? How would I know if I wasn't?

"Dinna ask me," said a voice by her head. "Is this one of them tricksie ones?"

It was Daft Wullie. He was sitting on her pillow.

Tiffany squinted down. She was in bed in Miss Level's cottage. A green quilt stretched out in front of her. A quilt. Green. Not turf, not hills . . . but it looked like the downland from here.

"Did I say all that aloud?" she asked.

"Oh, aye."

"Er . . . it did all happen, didn't it?" said Tiffany.

"Oh, aye," said Daft Wullie cheerfully. "The big hag o' hags wuz up here till just noo, but she said ye probably wasna gonna wake up a monster."

More bits of memory landed in Tiffany's head like red-hot rocks landing on a peaceful planet.

"Are you all right?"

"Oh, aye," said Daft Wullie.

"And Miss Level?"

And this rock of memory was huge, a flaming mountain that'd make a million dinosaurs flee for their lives. Tiffany's hands flew to her mouth.

"I killed her!" she said.

"Noo, then, ye didna—"

"I did! I felt my mind thinking it. She made me angry! I just waved my hand like this"—a dozen Nac Mac Feegle dived for cover—"and she just exploded into nothing! It was *me*! I remember!"

"Aye, but the hag o' hags said it wuz usin' your mind tae think with—" Daft Wullie began.

"I've got the memories! It was *me*, with this hand!" The Feegles who had raised their heads ducked back down again. "And . . . the memories I've got . . . I remember dust, turning into stars . . . things . . . the heat . . . blood . . . the taste of blood . . . I remember . . . I remember the see-me trick! Oh, no! I practically *invited* it in! I killed Miss Level!"

Shadows were closing in around her vision, and there was a ringing in her ears. Tiffany heard the door swing open, and hands picked her up as though she was as light as a bubble. She was slung over a shoulder and carried swiftly down the stairs and out into the bright morning, where she was swung down onto the ground.

". . . And all of us . . . we killed her . . . take one crucible of silver . . ." she mumbled.

A hand slapped her sharply across the face. She stared through inner mists at the tall dark figure in front of her. A bucket handle was pressed firmly into her hand.

"Milk the goats now, Tiffany! Now, Tiffany, d'you hear! The

trusting creatures look to you! They wait for you! Tiffany milks the goats. Do it, Tiffany! The hands know how, the mind *will* remember and grow stronger, Tiffany!"

She was thrust down into the milking stall and, through the mist in her head, made out the cowering shape of . . . of . . . Black Meg.

The hands remembered. They placed the pail, grasped a teat, and then, as Meg raised a leg to play the foot-in-the-bucket game, grabbed it and forced it safely back down onto the milking platform.

She worked slowly, her head full of hot fog, letting her hands have their way. Buckets were filled and emptied, milked goats got a bucket of feed from the bin. . . .

Sensibility Bustle was rather puzzled that his hands were milking a goat. He stopped.

"What is your name?" said a voice behind him.

"Bustle. Sensibil—"

"No! That was the wizard, Tiffany! He was the strongest echo, but you're not him! Get into the dairy, Tiffany!"

She stumbled into the cool room under the command of that voice, and the world focused. There was a foul cheese on the slab, sweating and stinking.

"Who put this here?" she asked.

"The hiver did, Tiffany. Tried to make a cheese by magic, Tiffany. Hah! And you are not it, Tiffany! You *know* how to make cheese the right way, don't you, Tiffany? Indeed you do! What is your name?"

. . . all was confusion and strange smells. In panic, she roared—

Her face was slapped again.

"No, that was the saber-toothed tiger, Tiffany! They're all just old memories the hiver left behind, Tiffany! It's worn a lot of creatures, but they are not you! Come forward, Tiffany!"

She heard the words without really understanding them. They were just out there somewhere, between people who were just shadows. But it was unthinkable to disobey them.

"Drat!" said the hazy tall figure, "where's that little blue feller? Mr. Anyone?"

"Here, mistress. It's Rob Anybody, mistress. I beg o' ye not tae turn me intae somethin' unnatural, mistress!"

"You said she had a box of keepsakes. Fetch it down here this minute. I feared this might happen. I *hates* doin' it this way!"

Tiffany was turned around and once again looked into the blurry face while strong hands gripped her arms. Two blue eyes stared into hers. They shone in the mist like sapphires.

"What's your name, Tiffany?" said the voice.

"Tiffany!"

The eyes bored into her. "Is it? Really? Sing me the first song you ever learned, Tiffany! *Now!*"

"Hzan, hzana, m'taza—"

"Stop! That was never learned on a chalk hill! You ain't Tiffany! I reckon you're that desert queen who killed twelve of her husbands with scorpion sandwiches! Tiffany is the one I'm after! Back into the dark with you!"

Things went blurry again. She could hear whispered discussions through the fog, and the voice said: "Well, that might work. What's your name, pictsie?"

"Awf'ly Wee Billy Bigchin Mac Feegle, mistress."

"You're *very* small, aren't you?"

"Only for my height, mistress."

The grip tightened on Tiffany's arms again. The blue eyes glinted.

"What does your name mean in the Old Speech of the Nac

Mac Feegle, Tiffany? Think . . ."

It rose from the depths of her mind, trailing the fog behind it. It came up through the clamoring voices and lifted her beyond the reach of ghostly hands. Ahead, the clouds parted.

"My name is Land Under Wave," said Tiffany, and slumped forward.

"No, no, none of that, we can't have that," said the figure holding her. "You've slept enough. Good, you know who you are! Now you must be up and doing! You must *be* Tiffany as hard as you may, and the other voices *will* leave you alone, depend on it. Although it might be a good idea if you don't make sandwiches for a while."

She did feel better. She'd said her name. The clamoring in her head had calmed down, although it was still a chatter that made it hard to think straight. But now at least she could see clearly. The black-dressed figure holding her wasn't tall, but she was so good at acting as if she was that it tended to fool most people.

"Oh . . . you're . . . *Mistress Weatherwax?*"

Mistress Weatherwax pushed her down gently into a chair. From every flat surface in the kitchen, the Nac Mac Feegles watched Tiffany.

"I am. And a fine mess we have here. Rest for a moment, and then we must be up and doing—"

"Good morning, ladies. Er, how is she?"

Tiffany turned her head. Miss Level stood in the door. She looked pale, and she was walking with a stick.

"I was lying in bed and I thought, well, there's no reason to stay up here feeling sorry for myself," she said.

Tiffany stood up. "I'm so sor—" she began, but Miss Level waved a hand vaguely.

"Not your fault," she said, sitting down heavily at the table. "How are you? And, for that matter, *who* are you?"

Tiffany blushed. "Still me, I think," she mumbled.

"I got here last night and saw to Miss Level," said Mistress Weatherwax. "Watched over you, too, girl. You talked in your sleep, or rather, Sensibility Bustle did, what's left of him. That ol' wizard was quite helpful, for something that's nothing much more'n a bunch of memories and habits."

"I don't understand about the wizard," said Tiffany. "Or the desert queen."

"Don't you?" said the witch. "Well, a hiver collects people. Tries to add them to itself, you might say, use them to think with. Dr. Bustle was studying them hundreds of years ago, and set a trap to catch one. It got him instead, silly fool. It killed him in the end. It gets 'em all killed in the end. They go mad, one way or the other—they stop remembering what they shouldn't do. But it keeps a sort of . . . pale copy of them, a sort of living memory. . . ." She looked at Tiffany's puzzled expression and shrugged. "Something like a ghost," she said.

"And it's left *ghosts* in my head?"

"More like ghosts of ghosts, really," said Mistress Weatherwax. "Something we don't have a word for, maybe."

Miss Level shuddered. "Well, thank goodness you've got rid of the thing, at least," she quavered. "Would anyone like a nice cup of tea?"

"Ach, leave that tae us!" shouted Rob Anybody, leaping up. "Daft Wullie, you an' the boys mak' some tea for the ladies!"

"Thank you," said Miss Level weakly, as a clattering began behind her. "I feel so clum—*what?* I thought you broke all the teacups when you did the dishes!"

"Oh, aye," said Rob cheerfully. "But Wullie found a whole load o' old ones shut awa' in a cupboard—"

"That very valuable bone china was left to me by a very dear friend!" shouted Miss Level. She sprang to her feet and turned toward the sink. With amazing speed for someone who was partly dead, she snatched teapot, cup, and saucer from the surprised pictsies and held them up as high as she could.

"Crivens!" said Rob Anybody, staring at the crockery. "Now that's what I *call* hagglin'!"

"I'm sorry to be rude, but they're of great sentimental value!" said Miss Level.

"Mr. Anybody, you and your men will kindly get away from Miss Level and *shut up!*" said Mistress Weatherwax quickly. "Pray do not disturb Miss Level while she's making tea!"

"But she's holding—" Tiffany began in amazement.

"And let her get on with it without your chatter either, girl!" the witch snapped.

"Aye, but she picked up yon teapot wi'oot—" a voice began.

The old witch's head spun around. Feegles backed away like trees bending to a gale.

"Daft William," she said coldly, "there's room in my well for one more frog, except that you don't have the brains of one!"

"Ahahaha, that's wholly correct, mistress," said Daft Wullie, sticking out his chin with pride. "I fooled you there! I ha' the brains o' a beetle!"

Mistress Weatherwax glared at him, then turned back to Tiffany.

"*I* turned someone into a frog!" Tiffany said. "It was dreadful! He didn't all fit in, so there was this sort of huge pink—"

"Never mind that right now," said Mistress Weatherwax in a voice that was suddenly so nice and ordinary that it tinkled like a bell. "I expect you finds things a bit different here than they were at home, eh?"

"What? Well, yes, at home I never turned—" Tiffany began in surprise, then saw that just above her lap the old woman was making frantic circular hand motions that somehow meant *keep going as if nothing has happened*.

So they chatted madly about sheep, and Mistress Weatherwax said they were very wooly, weren't they, and Tiffany said that they were, extremely so, and Mistress Weatherwax said extremely wooly was what she'd heard ... while every eye in the room watched Miss Level—

—making tea using four arms, two of which did not exist, and not realizing it.

The black kettle sailed across the room and apparently tipped itself into the pot. Cups and saucers and spoons and the sugar bowl floated with a purpose.

Mistress Weatherwax leaned across to Tiffany.

"I hope you're still feeling ... alone?" she whispered.

"Yes, thank you. I mean, I can ... sort of ... feel them there, but they're not getting in the way ... er ... sooner or later she's going to realize ... I mean, isn't she?"

"Very funny thing, the human mind," whispered the old woman. "I once had to see to a poor young man who had a tree fall on his legs. Lost both legs from the knee down. Had to have wooden legs made. Still, they were made out of that tree, which I suppose was some comfort, and he gets about pretty well. But I remember him saying, 'Mistress Weatherwax, I can still feel my toes sometimes.' It's like the head don't accept what's happened. And it's not like she's ... your everyday kind of person to start with. I mean, she's used to havin' arms she can't see—"

"Here we are," said Miss Level, bustling over with three cups and saucers and the sugar bowl. "One for you, one for you, and one for—oh . . ."

The sugar bowl dropped from an invisible hand and spilled its sugar onto the table. Miss Level stared at it in horror while, in the other hand that wasn't there, a cup and saucer wobbled without visible means of support.

"Shut your eyes, Miss Level!" And there was something in the voice, some edge or strange tone, that made Tiffany shut her eyes too.

"Right! Now, you *know* the cup's there, you can *feel* your arm," said Mistress Weatherwax, standing up. "Trust it! Your eyes are not in possession of all the facts! Now put the cup down gently . . . thaaat's right. You can open your eyes now, but what I wants you to do, right, as a favor to me, is *put the hands that you can see flat down on the table.* Right. Good. Now, without takin' those hands away, just go over to the dresser and fetch me that blue biscuit tin, will you? I'm always partial to a biscuit with my tea. Thank you very much."

"But . . . but I can't do that now—"

"Get past 'I can't,' Miss Level," Mistress Weatherwax snapped. "Don't think about it, just do it! My tea's getting cold!"

So *this* is witchcraft too, Tiffany thought. It's like Granny Aching talking to animals. It's in the voice! Sharp and soft by turns, and you use little words of command and encouragement and you *keep* talking, making the words fill the creature's world, so that the sheepdogs obey you and the nervous sheep are calmed. . . .

The biscuit tin floated away from the dresser. As it neared the old woman, the lid unscrewed and hovered in the air beside it. She reached in delicately.

"Ooh, store-bought Teatime Assortment," she said, taking four biscuits and quickly putting three of them in her pocket. "Very posh."

"It's terribly difficult to do this!" Miss Level moaned. "It's like trying not to think of a pink rhinoceros!"

"Well?" said Mistress Weatherwax. "What's so special about not thinking of a pink rhinoceros?"

"It's impossible to think of one if someone tells you mustn't," Tiffany explained.

"No it ain't," said Mistress Weatherwax firmly. "I ain't thinking of one right now, and I gives you my word on that. You want to take control of that brain of yours, Miss Level. So you've lost a spare body? What's another body when all's said and done? Just a lot of upkeep, another mouth to feed, wear and tear on the furniture . . . in a word, *fuss*. Get your mind right, Miss Level, and the world is your . . ." The old witch leaned down to Tiffany and whispered: "What's that thing, lives in the sea, very small, folks eat it?"

"Shrimp?" Tiffany suggested, a bit puzzled.

"Shrimp? All right. The world is your shrimp, Miss Level. Not only will there be a great saving on clothes and food, which is not to be sneezed at in these difficult times, but when people see you moving things through the air, well, they'll say, 'There's a witch and a half, and no mistake! and they will be right. You just hold on to that skill, Miss Level. You maintain. Think on what I've said. And now you stay and rest. We'll see to what needs doing today. You just make a little list for me, and Tiffany'll know the way."

"Well, indeed, I do feel . . . somewhat shaken," said Miss Level, absentmindedly brushing her hair out of her eyes with an invisible hand. "Let me see . . . you could just drop in on Mr. Umbril, and Mistress Turvy, and the young Raddle boy, and check on Mrs. Towney's bruise, and take some Number 5 ointment to Mr. Drover, and pay a call on old Mrs. Hunter at Saucy Corner, and . . . now, who have I forgotten?"

Tiffany realized she was holding her breath. It had been a horrible day, and a dreadful night, but what was looming and lining up for its place on Miss Level's tongue was, somehow, going to be worse than either.

". . . Ah, yes, have a word with Miss Quickly at Uttercliff, and then probably you'll need to talk to Mrs. Quickly, too, and there're a few packages to be dropped off on the way, they're in my basket, all marked up. And I think that's it. . . . Oh, no, silly me, I almost forgot . . . and you need to drop in on Mr. Weavall, too."

Tiffany breathed out. She really didn't want to. She'd rather not breathe ever again than face Mr. Weavall and open an empty box.

"Are you sure you're . . . totally yourself, Tiffany?" said Miss Level, and Tiffany leaped at this lifesaving excuse not to go.

"Well, I do feel a bit—" she began, but Mistress Weatherwax interrupted with, "She's fine, Miss Level, apart from the echoes. The hiver has gone away from this house, I can assure you."

"Really?" said Miss Level. "I don't mean to be rude, but how can you be so certain?"

Mistress Weatherwax pointed down.

Grain by grain, the spilled sugar was rolling across the tabletop and leaping into the sugar bowl.

Miss Level clasped her hands together.

"Oh, *Oswald*," she said, her face one huge smile, "you've come back!"

◆　◆　◆

Miss Level, and possibly Oswald, watched them go from the gate.

"She'll be fine with your little men keeping her company," said Mistress Weatherwax as she and Tiffany turned away and took the lane through the woods. "It could be the making of her, you know, being half dead."

Tiffany was shocked. "How can you be so cruel?"

"She'll get some respect when people see her moving stuff through the air. Respect is meat and drink to a witch. Without respect, you ain't got a thing. She doesn't get much respect, our Miss Level."

That was true. People didn't respect Miss Level. They liked her, in an unthinking sort of way, and that was it. Mistress Weatherwax was right, and Tiffany wished she wasn't.

"Why did you and Miss Tick send me to her, then?" she said.

"Because she likes people," said the witch, striding ahead. "She cares about 'em. Even the stupid, mean, drooling ones, the mothers with the runny babies and no sense, the feckless and the silly and the fools who treat her like some kind of a servant. Now *that's* what *I* call magic—seein' all that, dealin' with all that, and still goin' on. It's sittin' up all night with some poor old man who's leavin' the world, taking away such pain as you can, comfortin' their terror, seein' 'em safely on their way . . . and then cleanin' 'em up, layin' 'em out, making 'em neat for the funeral, and helpin' the weeping widow strip the bed and wash the sheets—which is, let me tell you, no errand for the fainthearted—and stayin' up the *next* night to watch over the coffin before the funeral, and then going home and sitting down for five minutes before some shouting *angry* man comes bangin' on your door 'cuz his wife's havin' difficulty givin' birth to their first child and the midwife's at her wits' end and then getting up and fetching your bag and going out again. . . . We all do that, in our own way, and she does it better'n me, if I was to put my hand on my heart. *That* is the root and heart and soul and center of witchcraft, that is. The soul and center!"

Mistress Weatherwax smacked her fist into her hand, hammering out her words. "The . . . soul . . . and . . . *center!*"

Echoes came back from the trees in the sudden silence. Even the grasshoppers by the side of the track had stopped sizzling.

"And Mrs. Earwig," said Mistress Weatherwax, her voice sinking to a growl, "*Mrs. Earwig* tells her girls it's about cosmic balances and stars and circles and colors and wands and . . . and toys, nothing but *toys!*" She sniffed. "Oh, I daresay they're all very well as *decoration*, somethin' nice to look at while you're workin', somethin' for show, but the start and finish, *the start and finish*, is helpin' people when life is on the edge. Even people you don't like. Stars is easy, people is hard."

She stopped talking. It was several seconds before birds began to sing again.

"Anyway, that's what I think," she added in the tones of someone who suspects that she might have gone just a bit further than she meant to.

She turned around when Tiffany said nothing, and saw that she had stopped and was standing in the lane looking like a drowned hen.

"Are you all right, girl?" she said.

"It was me!" wailed Tiffany. "The hiver *was* me! It wasn't thinking with my brain, it was using my thoughts! It was using what it found in my head! All those insults, all that . . ." She gulped. "That . . . nastiness. All it was was me with—"

"—*without* the bit of you that was locked away," said Mistress Weatherwax sharply. "Remember that."

"Yes, but supposing—" Tiffany began, struggling to get all the woe out.

"The locked-up bit was the important bit," said Mistress

Weatherwax. "Learnin' how not to do things is as hard as learning *how* to do them. Harder, maybe. There'd be a sight more frogs in this world if I didn't know how *not* to turn people into them. And big pink balloons, too."

"Don't," said Tiffany, shuddering.

"That's why we do all the tramping around and doctorin' and stuff," said Mistress Weatherwax. "Well, and because it makes people a bit better, of course. But doing it moves you into your center, so's you don't wobble. It anchors you. Keeps you human, stops you cackling. Just like your granny with her sheep, which are to my mind as stupid and wayward and ungrateful as humans. You think you've had a sight of yourself and found out you're bad? Hah! I've seen bad, and you don't get near it. Now, are you going to stop grizzling?"

"What?" snapped Tiffany.

Mistress Weatherwax laughed, to Tiffany's sudden fury.

"Yes, you're a witch to your boots," she said. "You're sad, and behind that you're watching yourself being sad and thinking, Oh, poor me, and behind *that* you're angry with *me* for not going 'There, there, poor dear.' Let me talk to those Third Thoughts then, because I want to hear from the girl who went to fight a fairy queen armed with nothin' but a fryin' pan, not some child feelin' sorry for herself and wallowing in misery!"

"What? I am *not* wallowing in misery!" Tiffany shouted, striding up to her until they were inches apart. "And what was all that about being nice to people, eh?" Overhead, leaves fell off the trees.

"That doesn't count when it's another witch, especially one like you!" Mistress Weatherwax snapped, prodding her in the chest with a finger as hard as wood.

"Oh? Oh? And what's that supposed to mean?" A deer galloped

off through the woods. The wind got up.

"One who's not paying attention, child!"

"Why, what I have I missed that *you've* seen . . . old woman?"

"Old woman I may be, but I'm tellin' you the hiver is still around! You only threw it out!" Mistress Weatherwax shouted. Birds rose from the trees in panic.

"I know!" screamed Tiffany.

"Oh yes? Really? And how do you know that?"

"Because there's a bit of me still in it! A bit of me I'd rather not know about, thank you! I can *feel* it out there! Anyway, how do *you* know?"

"Because I'm a bloody good witch, that's why," snarled Mistress Weatherwax, as rabbits burrowed deeper to get out of the way. "And what do you want me to do about the creature while you sit there snivelin', eh?"

"How dare you! How *dare* you! It's my responsibility! I'll deal with it, thank you so very much!"

"You? A hiver? It'll take more than a frying pan! They can't be killed!"

"I'll find a way! A witch deals with things!"

"Hah! I'd like to see you try!"

"I will!" shouted Tiffany. It started to rain.

"Oh? So you know how to attack it, do you?"

"Don't be silly! I can't! It can always keep out of my way! It can even sink into the ground! But it'll come looking for me, understand? *Me*, not anyone else! I *know* it! And this time I'll be ready!"

"Will you, indeed?" said Mistress Weatherwax, folding her arms.

"Yes!"

"When?"

"Now!"

"No!"

The old witch held up a hand.

"Peace be on this place," she said quietly. The wind dropped. The rain stopped. "No, not yet," she went on as peace once again descended. "It's not attackin' yet. Don't you think that's odd? It'd be licking its wounds, if it had a tongue. And you're not ready yet, whatever you thinks. No, we've got somethin' else to do, haven't we?"

Tiffany was speechless. The tide of outrage inside her was so hot that it burned her ears. But Mistress Weatherwax was smiling. The two facts did not work well together.

Her First Thoughts were: I've just had a blazing row with Mistress Weatherwax! They say that if you cut her with a knife, she wouldn't bleed until she wanted to! They say that when some vampires bit *her*, they all started to crave tea and sweet biscuits. She can do anything, be anywhere! And I called her an old woman!

Her Second Thoughts were: Well, she is.

Her Third Thoughts were: Yes, she *is* Mistress Weatherwax. And she's keeping you angry. If you're full of anger, there's no room left for fear.

"You hold that anger," Mistress Weatherwax said, as if reading all of her mind. "Cup it in your heart, remember where it came from, remember the shape of it, save it until you need it. But now the wolf is out there somewhere in the woods, and you need to see to the flock."

It's the voice, Tiffany thought. She really does talk to people like Granny Aching talked to sheep, except she hardly cusses at all. But I feel . . . better.

"Thank you," she said.

"And that includes Mr. Weavall."

"Yes," said Tiffany. "I know."

CHAPTER 10

The Late Bloomer

❦

I t was an . . . interesting day. *Everyone* in the mountains had heard of Mistress Weatherwax. If you didn't have respect, she said, you didn't have anything. Today she had it all. Some of it even rubbed off on Tiffany.

They were treated like royalty—not the sort who get dragged off to be beheaded or have something nasty done with a red-hot poker, but the other sort, when people walk away dazed saying, "She actually said hello to me, very graciously! I will never wash my hand again!"

Not that many people they dealt with washed their hands at all, Tiffany thought with the primness of a dairy worker. But people crowded around outside the cottage doors, watching and listening, and they sidled up to Tiffany to say things like "Would she like a cup of tea? I've cleaned our cup!" And in the garden of every cottage they passed, Tiffany noticed, the beehives were suddenly bustling with activity.

She worked away, trying to stay calm, trying to think about what she was doing. You did the doctoring work as neatly as you could, and if it was on something oozy, then you just thought about how nice things would be when you'd stopped doing it. She felt

Mistress Weatherwax wouldn't approve of this attitude. But Tiffany didn't much like hers either. She lied all the— She *didn't tell the truth* all the time.

For example, there was the Raddles' privy. Miss Level had explained carefully to Mr. and Mrs. Raddle several times that it was far too close to the well, and so the drinking water was full of tiny, tiny creatures that were making their children sick. They'd listened very carefully, every time they heard the lecture, and still they never moved the privy. But Mistress Weatherwax told them it was caused by goblins who were attracted to the smell, and by the time they left that cottage, Mr. Raddle and three of his friends were already digging a new well the other end of the garden.

"It really *is* caused by tiny creatures, you know," said Tiffany, who'd once handed over an egg to a traveling teacher so she could line up and look through his "**ASTOUNDING MIKROSCOPICAL DEVICE! A ZOO IN EVERY DROP OF DITCHWATER!**" She'd almost collapsed the next day from not drinking. Some of those creatures were *hairy*.

"Is that so?" said Mistress Weatherwax sarcastically.

"Yes. It is. And Miss Level believes in telling them the truth!"

"Good. She's a fine, honest woman," said Mistress Weatherwax. "But what *I* say is you have to tell people a story they can understand. Right now I reckon you'd have to change quite a lot of the world, and maybe bang Mr. Raddle's stupid fat head against the wall a few times, before he'd believe that you can be sickened by drinking tiny invisible beasts. And while you're doing that, those kids of theirs will get sicker. But goblins, now, they makes sense *today*. A story gets things done. And when I see Miss Tick tomorrow, I'll tell her it's about time them wandering teachers started coming up here."

"All right," said Tiffany reluctantly, "but you told Mr. Umbril the shoemaker that his chest pains will clear up if he walks to the waterfall at Tumble Crag every day for a month and throws three shiny pebbles into the pool for the water sprites! That's not doctoring!"

"No, but he thinks it is. The man spends too much time sitting hunched up. A five-mile walk in the fresh air every day for a month will see him as right as rain," said Mistress Weatherwax.

"Oh," said Tiffany. "Another story?"

"If you like," said Mistress Weatherwax, her eyes twinkling. "And you never know, maybe the water sprites will be grateful for the pebbles."

She glanced sidelong at Tiffany's expression and patted her on the shoulder.

"Never mind, miss," she said. "Look at it this way. Tomorrow, your job is to change the world into a better place. Today, my job is to see that everyone gets there."

"Well, I think—" Tiffany began, then stopped. She looked up at the line of woods between the small fields of the valleys and the steep meadows of the mountains.

"It's still there," she said.

"I know," said Mistress Weatherwax.

"It's moving around, but it's keeping away from us."

"I know," said Mistress Weatherwax.

"What does it think it's doing?"

"It's got a bit of you in it. What do *you* think it's doing?"

Tiffany tried to think. Why wouldn't it attack? Oh, she'd be better prepared this time, but it was strong.

"Maybe it's waiting until I'm upset again," she said. "But I keep having a thought. It makes no sense. I keep thinking about . . . three wishes."

"Wishes for what?"

"I don't know. It sounds silly."

Mistress Weatherwax stopped. "No, it's not," she said. "It's a deep part of you trying to send yourself a message. Just remember it. Because now—"

Tiffany sighed. "Yes, I know. Mr. Weavall."

◆　◆　◆

No dragon's cave was ever approached as carefully as the cottage in the overgrown garden.

Tiffany paused at the gate and looked back, but Mistress Weatherwax had diplomatically vanished. Probably she's found someone to give her a cup of tea and a sweet biscuit, she thought. She lives on them!

She opened the gate and walked up the path.

You couldn't say: It's not my fault. You couldn't say: It's not my responsibility.

You could say: I will deal with this.

You didn't have to want to. But you had to do it.

Tiffany took a deep breath and stepped into the dark cottage.

Mr. Weavall, in his chair, was just inside the door and fast asleep, showing the world an open mouth full of yellow teeth.

"Um . . . hello, Mr. Weavall," Tiffany quavered, but perhaps not quite loudly enough. "Just, er, here to see that you, that everything is . . . is all right. . . ."

There was a snort nonetheless, and he woke, smacking his lips to get the sleep out of his mouth.

"Oh, 'tis you," he said. "Good afternoon to ye." He eased himself more upright and started to stare out of the doorway, ignoring her.

Maybe he won't ask, she thought as she did the dishes and

dusted and plumped the cushions and, not to put too fine a point on it, emptied the commode. But she nearly yelped when the arm shot out and grabbed her wrist and the old man gave her his pleading look.

"Just check the box, Mary, will you? Before you go? Only I heard clinking noises last night, see. Could be one o' the sneaky thieves got in."

"Yes, Mr. Weavall," said Tiffany, all the while thinking: *Idon'twanttobehereIdon'twanttobehere!*

She pulled out the box. There was no choice.

It felt heavy. She stood up and lifted the lid.

After the creak of the hinges, there was silence.

"Are you all right, girl?" said Mr. Weavall.

"Um . . ." said Tiffany.

"It's all there, ain't it?" said the old man anxiously.

Tiffany's mind was a puddle of goo.

"Um . . . it's all here," she managed. "Um . . . and now it's all *gold*, Mr. Weavall."

"Gold? Hah! Don't you pull my leg, girl. No gold ever came my way!"

Tiffany put the box on the old man's lap, as gently as she could, and he stared into it.

Tiffany recognized the worn coins. The pictsies ate off them in the mound. There had been pictures on them, but they were too worn to make out now.

But gold was gold, pictures or not.

She turned her head sharply and was certain she saw something small and redheaded vanish into the shadows.

"Well now," said Mr. Weavall. "Well now." And that seemed to exhaust his conversation for a while. Then he said, "Far too much money here to pay for a buryin'. I don't recall savin' all this. I reckon you could bury a *king* for this amount of money."

Tiffany swallowed. She couldn't leave things like this. She just couldn't.

"Mr. Weavall, I've got something I must tell you," she said. And she told him. She told him all of it, not just the good bits. He sat and listened carefully.

"Well, now, isn't that interesting," he said when she'd finished.

"Um . . . I'm sorry," said Tiffany. She couldn't think of anything else to say.

"So what you're *saying*, right, is 'cuz that creature made you take my burying money, right, you think these fairy friends o' yourn filled my ol' box with gold so's you wouldn't get into trouble, right?"

"I think so," said Tiffany.

"Well, it looks like I should thank you, then," said Mr. Weavall. *"What?"*

"Well, it seems to I, if you hadn't ha' took the silver and copper, there wouldn't have been any room for all this gold, right?" said Mr. Weavall. "And I shouldn't reckon that ol' dead king up on yon hills needs it now."

"Yes, but—"

Mr. Weavall fumbled in the box and held up a gold coin that would have bought his cottage.

"A little something for you, then, girl," he said. "Buy yourself some ribbons or something. . . ."

"No! I can't! That wouldn't be fair!" Tiffany protested desperately. This was *completely* going wrong!

"Wouldn't it, now?" said Mr. Weavall, and his bright eyes gave her a long, shrewd look. "Well, then, let's call it payment for this little errand you're gonna run for I, eh? You're gonna run up they stairs, which I can't quite manage anymore, and bring down the black suit that's hanging behind the door, and there's a clean shirt in the chest at the end of the bed. And you'll polish my boots and help I up, but I'm thinking I could prob'ly make it down the lane on my own. 'Cuz, y'see, this is far too much money to buy a man's funeral, but I reckon it'll do fine to marry him off, so I am proposin' to propose to the Widow Tussy that she engages in matrimony with I!"

The last sentence took a little working out, and then Tiffany said, "You *are?*"

"That I am," said Mr. Weavall, struggling to his feet. "She's a fine woman who bakes a very reasonable steak-and-onion pie, and she has all her own teeth. I know that because she showed I. Her youngest son got her a set of fancy store-bought teeth all the way from the big city, and very handsome she looks in 'em. She was kind enough to loan 'em to I one day when I had a difficult piece of pork to tackle, and a man doesn't forget a kindness like that."

"Er . . . you don't think you ought to think about this, do you?" said Tiffany.

Mr. Weavall laughed. "Think? I got no business to be *thinking* about it, young lady! Who're you to tell an old 'un like I that he ought to be thinking? I'm ninety-one, I am! Got to be up and doing! Besides, I have reason to believe by the twinkle in her eye that the Widow Tussy will not turn up her nose at my suggestion. I've seen a fair number of twinkles over the years, and that was a good 'un. And I daresay that suddenly having a box of gold will fill in the corners, as my ol' dad would say."

It took ten minutes for Mr. Weavall to get changed, with a lot of struggling and bad language and no help from Tiffany, who was told to turn her back and put her hands over her ears. Then she had to help him out into the garden, where he threw away one walking stick and waggled a finger at the weeds.

"And I'll be chopping down the lot of you tomorrow!" he shouted triumphantly.

At the garden gate he grasped the post and pulled himself nearly vertical, panting.

"All right," he said, just a little anxiously. "It's now or never. I look okay, does I?"

"You look fine, Mr. Weavall."

"Everything clean? Everything done up?"

"Er . . . yes," said Tiffany.

"How's my hair look?"

"Er . . . you don't have any, Mr. Weavall," she reminded him.

"Ah, right. Yes, 'tis true. I'll have to buy one o' they whatdyoucallem's, like a hat made of hair? Have I got enough money for that, d'you think?"

"A wig? You could buy thousands, Mr. Weavall!"

"Hah! Right." His gleaming eyes looked around the garden. "Any flowers out? Can't see too well. . . . Ah . . . speckatickles, I saw 'em once, made of glass, makes you see good as new. That's what I need. . . . Have I got enough for speckatickles?"

"Mr. Weavall," said Tiffany, "you've got enough for *anything*."

"Why, bless you!" said Mr. Weavall. "But right now I need a bow-kwet of flowers, girl. Can't go courtin' without flowers and I can't see none. Anythin' left?"

A few roses were hanging on among the weeds and briars in the garden. Tiffany fetched a knife from the kitchen and made them up into a bouquet.

"Ah, good," he said. "Late bloomers, just like I!" He held them tightly in his free hand and suddenly frowned, and fell silent, and stood like a statue.

"I wish my Toby and my Mary was goin' to be able to come to the weddin'," he said quietly. "But they're dead, you know."

"Yes," said Tiffany. "I know, Mr. Weavall."

"And I could wish that my Nancy was alive, too, although bein' as I hopes to be marryin' another lady, that ain't a sensible wish, maybe. Hah! Nearly everyone one I knows is dead." Mr. Weavall stared at the bunch of flowers for a while, and then straightened up again. "Still, can't do nothin' about that, can we? Not even for a box full of gold!"

"No, Mr. Weavall," said Tiffany hoarsely.

"Oh, don't cry, girl! The sun is shinin', the birds is singin', and what's past can't be mended, eh?" said Mr. Weavall jovially. "And the Widow Tussy is waitin'!"

For a moment he looked panicky, and then he cleared his throat.

"Don't *smell* too bad, do I?" he said.

"Er . . . only of mothballs, Mr. Weavall."

"Mothballs? Mothballs is okay. Right, then! Time's a-wastin'!"

Using only the one stick, waving his other arm with the flowers in the air to keep his balance, Mr. Weavall set off with surprising speed.

"Well," said Mistress Weatherwax as, with jacket flying, he rounded the corner. "That was nice, wasn't it?"

Tiffany looked around quickly. Mistress Weatherwax was still nowhere to be seen, but she was somewhere to be unseen. Tiffany squinted at what was definitely an old wall with some ivy growing up it, and it was only when the old witch moved that she spotted her. She hadn't done anything to her clothes, hadn't done any magic as far as Tiffany knew, but she'd simply . . . faded in.

"Er, yes," said Tiffany, taking out a handkerchief and blowing her nose.

"But it worries you," said the witch. "You think it *shouldn't* have ended like that, right?"

"No!" said Tiffany hotly.

"It would have been better if he'd been buried in some ol' cheap coffin paid for by the village, you think?"

"No!" Tiffany twisted up her fingers. Mistress Weatherwax was sharper than a field of pins. "But . . . all right, it just doesn't seem . . . fair. I mean, I wish the Feegles hadn't done that. I'm sure I could have . . . sorted it out somehow, saved up . . ."

"It's an unfair world, child. Be glad you have friends."

Tiffany looked up at the treeline.

"Yes," said Mistress Weatherwax. "But not up there."

"I'm going away," said Tiffany. "I've been thinking about it, and I'm going away."

"Broomstick?" said Mistress Weatherwax. "It don't move fast—"

"No! Where would I fly to? Home? I don't want to take it there! Anyway, I can't just fly off with it roaming around! When it . . . when I meet it, I don't want to be near people, you understand? I know what I . . . what *it* can do if it's angry! It half killed Miss Level!"

"And if it follows you?"

"Good! I'll take it up there somewhere!" Tiffany waved at the mountains.

"All alone?"

"I don't have a choice, do I?"

Mistress Weatherwax gave her a look that went on too long.

"No," she said. "You don't. But neither have I. That's why I *will* come with you. Don't argue, miss. How would you stop me, eh?

Oh, that reminds me . . . them mysterious bruises Mrs. Towny gets is because Mr. Towny beats her, and the father of Miss Quickly's baby is young Fred Turvey. You might mention that to Miss Level."

As she spoke, a bee flew out of her ear.

◆　◆　◆

Bait, thought Tiffany a few hours later, as they walked away from Miss Level's cottage and up toward the high moors. I wonder if I'm bait, just like in the old days when the hunters would tether a lamb or a baby goat to bring the wolves nearer.

She's got a plan to kill the hiver. I *know* it. She's worked something out. It'll come for me and she'll just wave a hand.

She must think I'm stupid.

They had argued, of course. But Mistress Weatherwax had come up with a deeply unfair one. It was: *You're eleven*. Just like that. You're eleven, and what is Miss Tick going to tell your parents? Sorry about Tiffany, but we let her go off by herself to fight an ancient monster that can't be killed and what's left of her is in this jar?

Miss Level had joined in at that part, almost in tears.

If Tiffany hadn't been a witch, she would have whined about everyone being so *unfair*!

In fact they were being fair. She knew they were being fair. They were not thinking just of her but of other people, and Tiffany hated herself—well, slightly—because she hadn't. But it was sneaky of them to choose *this* moment to be fair. *That* was unfair.

No one had told her she was only nine when she went into Fairyland armed with just a frying pan. Admittedly, no one else had known she was going, except the Nac Mac Feegle, and she was much taller than they were. Would she have gone if she'd known what was in there, she wondered?

Yes. I would have.

And you're going to face the hiver even though you don't know how to beat it?

Yes. I am. There's part of me still in it. I might be able to do something—

But aren't you just ever so slightly glad that Mistress Weatherwax and Miss Level won the argument and now you're going off very bravely but you happen to be accompanied, *completely* against your will, by the most powerful witch alive?

Tiffany sighed. It was dreadful when your own thoughts tried to gang up on you.

The Feegles hadn't objected to her going to find the hiver. They *did* object to not being allowed to come with her. They'd been insulted, she knew. But, as Mistress Weatherwax had said, this was true haggling and there was no place in it for Feegles. If the hiver came, out there, not in a dream but for real, it'd have nothing about it that could be kicked or head butted.

Tiffany had tried to make a little speech, thanking them for their help, but Rob Anybody had folded his arms and turned his back. It had all gone wrong. But the old witch had been right. They could get hurt. The trouble was, explaining to Feegles how dangerous things were going to be only got them more enthusiastic.

She left them arguing with one another. It had not gone well.

But now that was all behind her, in more ways than one. The trees beside the track were less bushy and more pointy—or, if Tiffany had known more about trees, she would have said that the oaks were giving way to evergreens.

She could feel the hiver. It was following them, but a long way back.

If you had to imagine a head witch, you wouldn't imagine Mistress Weatherwax. You might imagine Mrs. Earwig, who glided across the floor as though she was on wheels, and had a dress as black as the darkness in a deep cellar, but Mistress Weatherwax was just an old woman with a lined face and rough hands in a dress as black as night, which is never as black as people think. It was dusty and ragged around the hem, too.

On the other hand, thought her Second Thoughts, *you once bought Granny Aching a china shepherdess, remember? All blue and white and sparkly?*

Her First Thoughts thought: Well, yes, but I was a lot younger then.

Her Second Thoughts thought: *Yes, but which one was the real shepherdess? The shiny lady in the nice clean dress and buckled shoes, or the old lady who stumped around in the snow with boots filled with straw and a sack across her shoulders?*

At which point Mistress Weatherwax stumbled. She caught her balance very quickly.

"Dangerously loose stones on this path," she said. "Watch out for them."

Tiffany looked down. There weren't that many stones, and they didn't seem very dangerous or particularly loose.

How old was Mistress Weatherwax? That was another question she wished she hadn't asked. She was skinny and wiry, just like Granny Aching, the kind of person who goes on and on—but one day Granny Aching had gone to bed and had never got up again, just like that. . . .

The sun was setting. Tiffany could feel the hiver in the same way that you can sense that someone is looking at you. It was still in the woods that hugged the mountain like a scarf.

At last the witch stopped at a spot where rocks like pillars sprouted out of the turf. She sat down with her back to a big rock.

"This'll have to do," she said. "It'll be dark soon, and you could turn an ankle on all this loose stone."

There were huge boulders around them, house sized, that had rolled down from the mountains in the past. The rock of the peaks began not far away, a wall of stone that seemed to hang above Tiffany like a wave. It was a desolate place. Every sound echoed.

She sat down by Mistress Weatherwax and opened the bag that Miss Level had packed for the journey.

Tiffany wasn't very experienced at things like this but, according to the book of fairy tales, the typical food for taking on an adventure was bread and cheese. Hard cheese, too.

Miss Level had made them ham sandwiches, with pickles, and she'd included napkins. That was kind of a strange thought to keep in your head: We're trying to find a way of killing a terrible creature, but at least we won't be covered in crumbs.

There was a bottle of cold tea, too, and a bag of biscuits. Miss Level knew Mistress Weatherwax.

"Shouldn't we light a fire?" Tiffany suggested.

"Why? It's a long way down to the treeline to get the firewood, and there'll be a fine half-moon up in twenty minutes. Your friend's keeping its distance, and there's nothing else that'll attack us up here."

"Are you sure?"

"I walk safely in *my* mountains," said Mistress Weatherwax.

"But aren't there trolls and wolves and things?"

"Oh, yes. Lots."

"And they don't try to attack you?"

"Not anymore," said a self-satisfied voice in the dark. "Pass me the biscuits, will you?"

"Here you are. Would you like some pickles?"

"Pickles gives me the wind something awful."

"In that case—"

"Oh, I wasn't saying *no*," Mistress Weatherwax said, taking two large pickled cucumbers.

Oh, *good*, Tiffany thought.

She'd brought three fresh eggs with her. Getting the hang of a shamble was taking too long. It was stupid. All the other girls were able to use them. She was sure she was doing everything right.

She'd filled her pocket with random things. Now she pulled them out without looking, wove the thread around the egg as she'd done a hundred times before, grasped the pieces of wood, and moved them so that . . .

Poc!

The egg cracked and oozed.

"I told you," said Mistress Weatherwax, who'd opened one eye. "They're toys. Sticks and stones."

"Have you ever *used* one?" said Tiffany.

"No. Couldn't get the hang of them. They got in the way." Mistress Weatherwax yawned, wrapped the blanket around her, made a couple of *mnup, mnup* noises as she tried to get comfortable against the rock; and after a while, her breathing became deeper.

Tiffany waited in silence, her blanket around her, until the moon came up. She'd expected that to make things better, but it didn't. Before, there had just been darkness. Now there were shadows.

There was a snore beside her. It was one of those good solid ones, like ripping canvas.

Silence happened. It came across the night on silver wings, noiseless as the fall of a feather, silence made into a bird, which alighted on a rock close by. It swiveled its head to look at Tiffany.

There was more than just the curiosity of a bird in that look.

The old woman snored again. Tiffany reached out, still staring at the owl, and shook her gently. When that didn't work, she shook her hardly.

There was a sound like three pigs colliding and Mistress Weatherwax opened one eye and said, "Whoo?"

"There's an owl watching us! It's right up close!"

Suddenly the owl blinked, looked at Tiffany as if amazed to see her, spread its wings, and glided off into the night.

Mistress Weatherwax gripped her throat, coughed once or twice, and then said hoarsely, "Of course it was an owl, child! It took me ten minutes to lure it this close! Now just you be quiet while I starts again—otherwise I shall have to make do with a bat, and when I goes out on a bat for any time at all, I ends up thinkin' I can see with my ears, which is no way for a decent woman to behave!"

"But you were snoring!"

"I was *not* snoring! I was just resting gently while I tickled an owl closer! If you hadn't shaken me and scared it away, I'd have been up there with this entire moor under my eye."

"You . . . take over its *mind*?" said Tiffany nervously.

"No! I'm not one of your hivers! I just . . . borrows a lift from it, I just . . . nudges it now and again, it don't even know I'm there. Now try to rest!"

"But what if the hiver—?"

"If it comes anywhere near, it'll be *me* that tells *you*!" Mistress Weatherwax hissed, and lay back. Then her head jerked up one more time. "And I do *not* snore!" she added.

After half a minute she started to snore again.

Minutes after that the owl came back, or perhaps it was a different owl. It glided onto the same rock, settled there for a while, and then sped away. The witch stopped snoring. In fact, she stopped breathing.

Tiffany leaned closer and finally lowered an ear to the skinny chest to see if there was a heartbeat.

Her own heart felt as if it was clenched like a fist—

—*because of the day she'd found Granny Aching in the hut. She was lying peacefully on the narrow iron bed, but Tiffany had known something was wrong as soon as she had stepped inside*—

Boom.

Tiffany counted to three.

Boom.

Well, it *was* a heartbeat.

Very slowly, like a twig growing, a stiff hand moved. It slid like a glacier into a pocket and came up holding a large piece of card on which was written:

I ATE'NT DEAD

Tiffany decided she wasn't going to argue. But she pulled the blanket over the old woman and wrapped her own around herself.

By moonlight she tried again with her shamble. Surely she should be able to make it do *something*. Maybe if—

By moonlight she very, very carefully—

Poc!

The egg cracked. The egg *always* cracked, and now there was only one left. Tiffany didn't dare try it with a beetle, even if she could have found one. It would be too cruel.

She sat back and looked across the landscape of silver and black, and her Third Thoughts thought: *It's not going to come near.*

Why?

She thought: *I'm not sure why I know. But I know. It's keeping away. It knows Mistress Weatherwax is with me.*

She thought: How can it know that? It'd not got a mind. It doesn't know what a Mistress Weatherwax *is*!

Still thinking, thought her Third Thoughts.

Tiffany slumped against the rock.

Sometimes her head was too . . . crowded. . . .

And then it was morning, and sunlight, and dew on her hair, and mist coming off the ground like smoke . . . and an eagle sitting on the rock where the owl had been, eating something furry. She could see every feather on its wing.

It swallowed, glared at Tiffany with its crazy bird eyes, and flapped away, making the mist swirl.

Beside her, Mistress Weatherwax began to snore again, which Tiffany took to mean that she was in her body. She gave the old woman a nudge, and the sound that had been a regular *gnaaaar-grgrgrgrg* suddenly became *blort.*

The old woman sat up coughing and waved a hand irritably at Tiffany to pass her the tea bottle. She didn't speak until she'd gulped half of it.

"Ah, say what you like, but rabbit tastes a lot better cooked," she gasped, shoving the cork back in. "And *without* the fur on!"

"You took—*borrowed* the eagle?" said Tiffany.

"O' course. I couldn't expect the poor ol' owl to fly around after daybreak, just to see who's about. It was hunting voles all night, and believe me, raw rabbit's better'n voles. Don't eat voles."

"I won't," said Tiffany, and meant it. "Mistress Weatherwax, I *think* I know what the hiver's doing. It's thinking."

"I thought it had no brains!"

Tiffany let her thoughts speak for themselves.

"But there's an echo of me in it, isn't there? There must be. It has an echo of everyone it's . . . been. There *must* be a bit of me in it. I know it's out there, and it knows I'm here with you. And it's keeping away."

"Oh? Why's that, then?"

"Because it's frightened of you, I think."

"Huh! And why's that?"

"Yes," said Tiffany simply. "It's because *I* am. A bit."

"Oh dear. Are you?"

"Yes," said Tiffany. "It's like a dog that's been beaten but won't run away. It doesn't understand what it's done wrong. But . . . there's something about it that . . . there's a thought that I'm nearly having. . . ."

Mistress Weatherwax said nothing. Her face went blank.

"Are you all right?" said Tiffany.

"I was just leavin' you time to have that thought," said Mistress Weatherwax.

"Sorry. It's gone now. But . . . we're thinking about the hiver in the wrong way."

"Oh, yes? And why's that?"

"Because . . ." Tiffany struggled with the idea. "I think it's because we don't want to think about it the right way. It's something to do with . . . the third wish. And I don't know what that means."

The witch said, "Keep picking at that thought," and then looked up and added, "We've got company."

It took Tiffany several seconds to spot what Mistress Weatherwax had seen—a shape at the edge of the woods, small and dark. It was coming closer, but rather uncertainly.

It resolved itself into the figure of Petulia, flying slowly and nervously a few feet above the heather. Sometimes she jumped down and wrenched the stick in a slightly different direction.

She got off again when she reached Tiffany and Mistress Weatherwax, grabbed the broom hastily, and aimed it at a big rock. It hit it gently and hung there, trying to fly through stone.

"Um, sorry," she panted. "But I can't always stop it, and this is better than having an anchor . . . um."

She started to bob a curtsy to Mistress Weatherwax, remembered she was a witch, and tried to turn it into a bow halfway down, which was an event you'd pay money to see. She ended up bent double, and from somewhere in there came the little voice, "Um, can someone help, please? I think my Octogram of Trimontane has got caught up on my Pouch of Nine Herbs. . . ."

There was a tricky minute while they untangled her, with Mistress Weatherwax muttering, "Toys, just toys," as they unhooked bangles and necklaces.

Petulia stood upright, red in the face. She saw Mistress Weatherwax's expression, whipped off her pointy hat, and held it in front on her. This was a mark of respect, but it did mean that a two-foot, sharp, pointy thing was being aimed at them.

"Um . . . I went to see Miss Level and she said you'd come up here after some horrible thing," she said. "Um . . . so I thought I'd better see how you were."

"Um . . . that was very kind of you," said Tiffany, but her treacherous Second Thoughts thought: And what would you have done if it had attacked us? She had a momentary picture of Petulia standing in front of some horrible raging thing, but it wasn't as funny as she'd first thought. Petulia *would* stand in front of it, shaking with terror, her useless amulets clattering, scared almost out of her mind . . . but not backing away. She'd thought there might be people facing something horrible here, and she'd come *anyway*.

"What's your name, my girl?" said Mistress Weatherwax.

"Um, Petulia Gristle, mistress. I'm learning with Gwinifer Blackcap."

"Old Mother Blackcap?" said Mistress Weatherwax. "Very sound. A good woman with pigs. You did well to come here."

Petulia looked nervously at Tiffany.

"Um, are you all right? Miss Level said you'd been . . . ill."

"I'm much better now, but thank you very much for asking anyway," said Tiffany wretchedly. "Look, I'm sorry about—"

"Well, you were ill," said Petulia.

And that was another thing about Petulia. She always wanted to think the best of everybody. This was sort of worrying if you knew that the person she was doing her best to think nice thoughts about was you.

"Are you going to go back to the cottage before the Trials?" Petulia went on.

"Trials?" said Tiffany, suddenly lost.

"The Witch Trials," said Mistress Weatherwax.

"Today," said Petulia.

"I'd forgotten all about them!" said Tiffany.

"I hadn't," said the old witch calmly. "I never miss a Trial. Never missed a Trial in sixty years. Would you do a poor old lady a favor, Miss Gristle, and ride that stick of yours back to Miss Level's place and tell her that Mistress Weatherwax presents her compliments and intends to head directly to the Trials. Was she well?"

"Um, she was juggling balls *without using her hands!*" said Petulia in wonderment. "And d'you know what? I saw a *fairy* in her garden! A blue one!"

"Really?" said Tiffany, her heart sinking.

"Yes! It was rather scruffy, though. And when I asked it if it really was a fairy, it said it was . . . um . . . 'the big stinky horrible spiky iron stinging nettle fairy from the Land o' Tinkle,' and called me a 'scunner.' Do you know what that means?"

Tiffany looked into that round, hopeful face. She opened her mouth to say, "It means someone who likes fairies," but stopped in time. That just wouldn't be fair. She sighed.

"Petulia, you saw a Nac Mac Feegle," she said. "It *is* a kind of fairy, but they're not the sweet kind. I'm sorry. They're good . . . well, more or less . . . but they're not entirely nice. And 'scunner' is a kind of swear word. I don't think it's a particularly bad one, though."

Petulia's expression didn't change for a while. Then she said: "So it *was* a fairy, then?"

"Well, yes. Technically."

The round pink face smiled.

"Good, I did wonder, because it was, um, you know . . . having a wee up against one of Miss Level's garden gnomes?"

"*Definitely* a Feegle," said Tiffany.

"Oh well, I suppose the big stinky horrible spiky iron stinging nettle needs a fairy, just like every other plant," said Petulia.

CHAPTER 11

Arthur

When Petulia had gone, Mistress Weatherwax stamped her feet and said, "Let's go, young lady. It's about eight miles to Sheercliff. They'll have started before we get there."

"What about the hiver?"

"Oh, it can come if it likes." Mistress Weatherwax smiled. "Oh, don't frown like that. There'll be more'n three hundred witches at the Trials, and they're way out in the country. It'll be as safe as anything. Or do you want to meet the hiver *now*? We could probably do that. It don't seem to move fast."

"No!" said Tiffany, louder than she'd intended. "No, because . . . things aren't what they seem. We'd do things wrong. Er . . . I can't explain it. It's because of the third wish."

"Which you don't know what it is?"

"Yes. But I will soon, I hope."

The witch stared at her. "Yes, I hope so, too," she said. "Well, no point in standing around. Let's get moving." And with that the witch picked up her blanket and set off as though being pulled by a string.

"We haven't even had anything to eat!" said Tiffany, running after her.

"I had a lot of voles last night," said Mistress Weatherwax over her shoulder.

"Yes, but *you* didn't actually eat them, did you?" said Tiffany. "It was the owl that *actually* ate them."

"Technic'ly, yes," Mistress Weatherwax admitted. "But if you think you've been eating voles all night, you'd be amazed how much you don't want to eat anything the next morning. Or ever again."

She nodded at the distant, departing figure of Petulia.

"Friend of yours?" she said, as they set out.

"Er . . . if she is, I don't deserve it," said Tiffany.

"Hmm," said Mistress Weatherwax. "Well, sometimes we get what we don't deserve."

For an old woman Mistress Weatherwax could move quite fast. She strode over the moors as if distance was a personal insult. But she was good at something else too.

She knew about silence. There was the swish of her long skirt as it snagged the heathers, but somehow that became part of the background noise.

In the silence, as she walked, Tiffany could still hear the memories. There were hundreds of them left behind by the hiver. Most of them were so faint that they were nothing more than a slight uncomfortable feeling in her head, but the ancient tiger still burned brightly in the back of her brain, and behind that was the giant lizard. They'd been killing machines, the most powerful creatures in their world—once. The hiver had taken them both. And then they'd died fighting.

Always taking fresh bodies, always driving the owners mad with the urge for power, which would always end with getting them killed . . . and just as Tiffany wondered *why*, a memory said: *Because it is frightened.*

Frightened of what? Tiffany thought. It's so powerful!

Who knows? But it's mad with terror. Completely binkers!

"You're Sensibility Bustle, aren't you?" said Tiffany, and then her ears informed her that she'd said this aloud.

"Talkative, ain't he," said Mistress Weatherwax. "He talked in your sleep the other night. Used to have a very high opinion of himself. I reckon that's why his memories held together for so long."

"He doesn't know binkers from bonkers, though," said Tiffany.

"Well, memory fades," said Mistress Weatherwax. She stopped and leaned against a rock. She sounded out of breath.

"Are you all right, mistress?" said Tiffany.

"Sound as a bell," said Mistress Weatherwax, wheezing slightly. "Just getting my second wind. Anyway, it's only another six miles."

"I notice you're limping a bit," said Tiffany.

"Do you, indeed? Then stop noticing!"

The shout echoed off the cliffs, full of command.

Mistress Weatherwax coughed when the echo had died away. Tiffany had gone pale.

"It seems to me," said the old witch, "that I might just've been a shade on the sharp side there. It was prob'ly the voles." She coughed again. "Them as knows me, or has earned it one way or the other, calls me Granny Weatherwax. I shall not take it amiss if you did the same."

"*Granny* Weatherwax?" said Tiffany, shocked out of her shock by this new shock.

"Not *technic'ly*," said Mistress Weatherwax quickly. "It's what they call a honorific, like Old Mother So-and-so, or Goodie Thingy, or Nanny Whatshername. To show that a witch has . . . is fully . . . has been—"

Tiffany didn't know whether to laugh or burst into tears.

"I *know*," she said.

"You do?"

"Like Granny Aching," said Tiffany. "She *was* my granny, but everyone on the Chalk called her Granny Aching." "Mrs. Aching" wouldn't have worked, she knew. You needed a big, warm, billowing open kind of word. Granny Aching was there for everybody.

"It's like being everyone's grandmother," she added. And didn't add: *who tells them stories!*

"Well, then. Perhaps so. Granny Weatherwax it is," said Granny Weatherwax, and added quickly, "but not *technic'ly*. Now we'd best be moving."

She straightened up and set off again.

Granny Weatherwax. Tiffany tried it out in her head. She'd never known her other grandmother, who'd died before she was born. Calling someone else granny was strange, but oddly, it seemed right. And you *could* have two.

The hiver followed them. Tiffany could feel it. But it was still keeping its distance. Well, there's a trick to take to the Trials, she thought. Granny—her brain tingled as she thought the word—Granny has got a plan. She must have.

But . . . things weren't right. There was another thought she wasn't quite having; it ducked out of sight every time she thought she had it. The hiver wasn't acting right.

She made sure she kept up with Granny Weatherwax.

As they got nearer to the Trials, there were clues. Tiffany saw at least three broomsticks in the air, heading the same way. They reached a proper track, too, and groups of people were traveling in the same direction; there were a few pointy hats among them, which was a definite clue. The track dropped on down through some woods, came up in a patchwork of little fields, and headed for a tall hedge from behind which came the sound of a brass band playing a medley of Songs from the Shows, although by the sound of it no two musicians could agree on what Song or which Show.

Tiffany jumped when she saw a balloon sail up above the trees, catch the wind, and swoop away, but it turned out to be just a balloon and not a lump of excess Brian. She could tell this because it was followed by a long scream of rage mixed with a roar of complaint: "AAaargwannawannaaaagongongonaargggaaaaBLOON!" which is the traditional sound of a very small child learning that with balloons, as with life itself, it is important to know *when not to let go of the string.* The whole point of balloons is to teach small children this.

However, on this occasion a broomstick with a pointy-hatted passenger rose above the trees, caught up with the balloon, and towed it back down to the Trials ground.

"Didn't use to be like this," Granny Weatherwax grumbled as they reached a gate. "When I was a girl, we just used to meet up in some meadow somewhere, all by ourselves. But now, oh no, it has to be a Grand Day Out for All the Family. Hah!"

There had been a crowd around the gate leading into the field, but there was something about that "Hah!" The crowd parted, as if by magic, and the women pulled their children a little closer to them as Granny walked right up to the gate.

There was a boy there selling tickets and wishing, now, that he'd never been born.

Granny Weatherwax stared at him. Tiffany saw his ears go red.

"Two tickets, young man," said Granny. Little bits of ice tinkled off her words.

"That'll, er, be, er . . . one child and one senior citizen?"

the young man quavered.

Granny leaned forward and said: "*What* is a senior citizen, young man?"

"It's like . . . you know . . . old folks," the boy mumbled. Now his hands were shaking.

Granny leaned farther forward. The boy really, really wanted to step back, but his feet were rooted to the ground. All he could do was bend backward.

"Young man," said Granny, "I am not now, nor shall I ever be, an 'old folk.' We'll take two tickets, which I see on that board there is a penny apiece." Her hand shot out, fast as an adder. The boy made a noise like *gneeee* as he leaped back.

"Here's tuppence," said Granny Weatherwax.

Tiffany looked at Granny's hand. The first finger and thumb were held together, but there did not appear to be any coins between them.

Nevertheless, the young man, grinning horribly, took the total absence of coins very carefully between *his* thumb and finger. Granny twitched two tickets out of his other hand.

"Thank you, young man," she said, and walked into the field. Tiffany ran after her.

"What did—?" she began, but Granny Weatherwax raised a finger to her lips, grasped Tiffany's shoulder, and swiveled her around.

The ticket seller was still staring at his fingers. He even rubbed them together. Then he shrugged, held them over his leather moneybag, and let go.

Clink, clink . . .

The crowd around the gate gave a gasp, and one or two of them started to applaud. The boy looked around with a sick kind of grin, as if *of course* he'd expected that to happen.

"Ah, right," said Granny Weatherwax happily. "And now I could just do with a cup of tea and maybe a sweet biscuit."

"Granny, there are children here! Not just witches!"

People were looking at them. Granny Weatherwax jerked Tiffany's chin up so that she could look into her eyes.

"Look around, eh? Down here you can't move for amulets and wands and whatnot! It'll be *bound* to keep away, eh?"

Tiffany turned to look. There were sideshows all around the field. A lot of them were fun fair stuff that she'd seen before at agricultural shows around the Chalk: Roll-a-Penny, Lucky Dip, Bobbing for Piranhas, that sort of thing. The Ducking Stool was very popular among young children on such a hot day. There wasn't a fortune-telling tent, because no fortune teller would turn up at an event where so many visitors were qualified to argue and answer back, but there were a number of witch stalls. Zakzak's had a huge tent, with a display dummy outside wearing a Sky Scraper hat and a Zephyr Billow cloak, which had drawn a crowd of admirers. The other stalls were smaller, but they were thick with things that glittered and tinkled, and they were doing a brisk trade among the younger witches. There were whole stores full of dream catchers and curse nets, including the new self-emptying ones. It was odd to think of witches buying them, though. It was like fish buying umbrellas.

Surely a hiver wouldn't come here, with all these witches?

She turned to Granny Weatherwax.

Granny Weatherwax wasn't there.

It is hard to find a witch at the Witch Trials. That is, it is too *easy* to find a witch at the Witch Trials, but very hard to find the one you're looking for, especially if you suddenly feel lost and all alone and you can feel panic starting to open inside you like a fern.

Most of the older witches were sitting at trestle tables in a huge roped-off area. They were drinking tea. Pointy hats bobbed as tongues wagged. Every woman seemed capable of talking while listening to all the others at the table at the same time, although this talent isn't confined to witches. It was no place to search for an old woman in black with a pointy hat.

The sun was quite high in the sky now. The field was filling up. Witches were circling to land at the far end, and more and more people were pouring in through the gateway. The noise was intense. Everywhere Tiffany turned, black hats were scurrying.

Pushing her way through the throng, she looked desperately for a friendly face, like Miss Tick or Miss Level or Petulia. If it came to it, an unfriendly one would do—even Mrs. Earwig.

And she tried not to think. She tried not to think that she was terrified and alone in this huge crowd, and that up on the hill, invisible, the hiver now knew this because just a tiny part of it was her.

She felt the hiver stir. She felt it begin to move.

Tiffany stumbled through a chattering group of witches, their voices sounding shrill and unpleasant. She felt ill, as though she'd been in the sun too long. The world was spinning.

A remarkable thing about a hiver, a reedy voice began, somewhere in the back of her head, *is that its hunting pattern mimics that of the common shark, among other creatures—*

"I do not want a lecture, Mr. Bustle," Tiffany mumbled. "I do not want you in my head!"

But the memory of Sensibility Bustle had never taken much notice of other people when he was alive and it wasn't going to begin now. It went on in its self-satisfied squeak: *—in that, once it* *has selected its prey, it will completely ignore other attractive targets—*

She could see all the way across the Trials field, and something *was* coming. It moved through the crowd like the wind through a field of grass. You could plot its progress by the people. Some fainted, some yelped and turned around, some ran. Witches stopped their gossip, chairs were overturned, and the shouting started. But it wasn't attacking anything. It was only interested in Tiffany.

Like a shark, thought Tiffany. The killer of the sea, where worse things happen.

Tiffany backed away, the panic filling her up. She bumped into witches hurrying toward the commotion and shouted at them:

"You can't stop it! You don't know what it is! You'll flail at it and wave glittery sticks and it will keep coming! It will keep coming!"

She put her hands into her pockets and touched the lucky stone. And the string. And the piece of chalk.

If this was a story, she thought bitterly, I'd trust in my heart and follow my star and all that other stuff and it would all turn out all right, right now, by tinkly Magikkkk. But you're never in a story when you need to be.

Story, story, story . . .

The third wish. The Third Wish. The Third Wish is the important one.

In stories the genie or the witch or the magic cat . . . offers you three wishes.

Three wishes . . .

She grabbed a hurrying witch and looked into the face of Annagramma, who stared at her in terror and tried to cower away.

"Please don't do anything to me! Please!" she cried. "I'm your *friend*, aren't I?"

"If you like, but that wasn't me and I'm better now," said Tiffany, knowing she was lying. It *had* been her, and that was important. She had to remember that. "Quick, Annagramma! What's the third wish? Quickly! When you get three wishes, what's the third wish!"

Annagramma's face screwed up into the affronted frown she wore when something had the nerve not to be understandable. "But why do—?"

"Don't think about it, please! Just answer!"

"Well, er . . . it could be anything . . . being invisible or . . . or blond, or anything—" Annagramma burbled, her mind coming apart at the seams.

Tiffany shook her head and let her go. She ran to an old witch who was staring at the commotion.

"Please, mistress, this is important! In stories, what's the third wish? Don't ask me why, please! Just remember!"

"Er . . . happiness. It's happiness, isn't it?" said the old lady. "Yes, definitely. Health, wealth, and happiness. Now if I was you, I'd—"

"Happiness? Happiness . . . thank you," said Tiffany, and looked around desperately for someone else. It wasn't happiness, she knew that in her boots. You couldn't get happiness by magic, and *that* was another clue right there.

There was Miss Tick, hurrying between the tents. There was no time for half measures. Tiffany pulled her around and shouted: "HelloMissTickYesI'mFineIHopeYouAreWellTooWhatIsTheThird WishQuicklyThisIsImportantPleaseDon'tArgueOrAskQuestion ThereIsn'tTime!"

Miss Tick, to her credit, hesitated only for a moment or two. "To have a hundred more wishes, isn't it?" she said.

Tiffany stared at her and then said, "Thank you. It isn't, but that's a clue, too."

"Tiffany, there's a—" Miss Tick began.

But Tiffany had seen Granny Weatherwax.

She was standing in the middle of the field, in a big square that had been roped off for some reason. No one seemed to notice her. She was watching the frantic witches around the hiver, where there was an occasional flash and sparkle of magic. She had a calm, faraway look.

Tiffany brushed Miss Tick's arm away, ducked under the rope, and ran up to her.

"Granny!"

The blue eyes turned to her.

"Yes?"

"*In stories*, where the genie or the magic frog or the fairy godmother gives you three wishes . . . what's the third wish?"

"Ah, *stories*," said Granny. "That's easy. In any story worth the tellin', that knows about the way of the world, *the third wish is the one that undoes the harm the first two wishes caused.*"

"Yes! That's it! That's it!" shouted Tiffany, and the words piling up behind the question poured out. "It's not evil! It can't be! It hasn't got a mind of its own! This is all about wishes! *Our* wishes! It's like in the stories, where they—"

"Calm down. Take a deep breath," said Granny. She took Tiffany by the shoulders so that she faced the panicking crowd.

"You got frightened for a moment, and now it's comin' and it's not going to turn back, not now, 'cuz it's desperate. It don't even *see* the crowd. They don't mean a thing to it. It's you it wants. It's you it's after. You should be the one who faces it. Are you ready?"

"But supposing I lose—"

"I never got where I am today by supposin' I was goin' to lose, young lady. You beat it once—you can do it again!"

"But I could turn into something terrible!"

"Then you'll face me," said Granny. "You'll face me, on my ground. But that won't happen, will it? You were fed up with grubby babies and silly women? Then this is . . . the other stuff. It's noon now. They should've started the Trials proper, but, hah, it looks as though people have forgotten. Now, then . . . do you have it in you to be a witch by noonlight, far away from your hills?"

"Yes!" There was no other answer, not to Granny Weatherwax.

Granny Weatherwax bowed low and then took a few steps back.

"In your own time, then, madam," she said.

Wishes, wishes, wishes, thought Tiffany, distracted, fumbling in her pockets for the bits to make a shamble. It's not evil. *It gives us what we think we want!* And what do people ask for? More wishes!

You couldn't say: A monster got into my head and made me do it. She'd wished the money was hers. The hiver just took her at her thought.

You couldn't say: Yes, but I'd *never* have really taken it! The hiver used what it found—the little secret wishes, the desires, the moments of rage, all the things that real humans knew how to ignore! It didn't let you ignore them!

Then, as she fumbled to tie the pieces together, the egg flipped out of her hands, trusted in gravity, and smashed on the toe of her boot.

She stared at it, the blackness of despair darkening the noonlight. Why did I try this? I've never made a shamble that worked, so why did I try? Because I believed it had to work this time, that's why. Like in a story. Suddenly it would all be . . . all right.

But this isn't a story, and there are no more eggs. . . .

There was a scream, but it was high up and the sound of it took Tiffany home in the bounce of a heartbeat. It was a buzzard, in the eye of the sun, getting bigger in its plunge toward the field.

It soared up again as it passed over Tiffany's head, fast as an arrow, and as it did so, something small let go its hold on the buzzard's talons with a cry of "Crivens!"

Rob Anybody dropped like a stone, but there was a *thwap!* and suddenly a balloon of cloth snapped open above him. Two balloons, in fact, or to put it another way, Rob Anybody had "borrowed" Hamish's parachute.

He let go of them as soon as they'd slowed him down, and dropped neatly into the shamble.

"Did ye think we'd leave ye?" he shouted, holding on to the strings. "I'm under a geas, me! Get on wi' it, right noo!"

"What? I can't!" said Tiffany, trying to shake him off. "Not with you! I'll kill you! I always crack the eggs! What goose?"

"Dinna argue!" shouted Rob, bouncing up and down in the strings. "Do it! Or ye're no' the hag of the hills! An' I know ye are!"

People were running past now. Tiffany glanced up. She thought she could *see* the hiver now as a moving shape in the dust.

She looked at the tangle in her hands and at Rob's grinning face.

The moment twanged.

A witch deals with things, said her Second Thoughts. Get past the "I can't."

O-kay . . .

Why hasn't it ever worked before? Because there was no reason for it to work. I didn't *need* it to work.

I need it to help me now. No. I need *me* to help me.

So *think* about it. Ignore the noise, ignore the hiver rolling toward me over the trodden grass . . .

She'd used the things she'd had, so that was right. Calm down. Slow down. Look at the shamble. Think about the moment. There were all the things from home . . .

No. Not all the things. Not all the things at all. This time she felt the shape of what wasn't there—

—and tugged at the silver Horse around her neck, breaking its chain, then hanging it in the threads.

Suddenly her thoughts were as cool and clear as ice, as bright and shiny as they needed to be. Let's see . . . that looks better there . . . and that needs to be pulled *this* way . . .

The movement jerked the silver Horse into life. Then it spun gently, passing through the threads *and* Rob Anybody, who said "Didna hurt a bit! Keep goin'!"

Tiffany felt a tingle in her feet. The Horse gleamed as it turned.

"I dinna want to hurry ye!" said Rob Anybody. "But hurry!"

I'm far from home, thought Tiffany, in the same clear way, but I have it in my eye. Now I open my eyes. Now I open my eyes again—

Ahh . . .

Can I be a witch away from my hills? Of course I can. I never really leave you, Land Under Wave. . . .

◆　　◆　　◆

Shepherds on the Chalk felt the ground shake, like thunder under the turf. Birds scattered from the bushes. The sheep looked up.

Again, the ground trembled.

Some people said a shadow crossed the sun. Some people said they heard the sound of hooves.

And a boy trying to catch hares in the little valley of the Horse said the hillside had burst and a horse had leaped out like a wave as high as the sky, with a mane like the surf of the sea and a coat as white as chalk. He said it had galloped into the air like rising mist, and flown toward the mountains like a storm.

He got punished for telling stories, of course, but he thought it was worth it.

◆　◆　◆

The shamble glowed. Silver coursed along the threads. It was coming from Tiffany's hands, sparking like stars.

In that light she saw the hiver reach her and spread out until it was all around her, invisibility made visible. It rippled and reflected the light oddly. In those glints and sparkles there were faces, wavering and stretching like reflections in water.

Time was going slowly. She could see, beyond of the wall of hiver, witches staring at her. One had lost her hat in the commotion, but it was hanging in the air. It hadn't had time to fall yet.

Tiffany's fingers moved. The hiver shimmered in the air, disturbed like a pond when a pebble has been dropped into it. Tendrils of it reached toward her. She felt its panic, felt its terror as it found itself caught—

"Welcome," said Tiffany.

Welcome? said the hiver in Tiffany's own voice.

"Yes. You are welcome in this place. You are safe here."

No! We are never safe!

"You are safe here," Tiffany repeated.

Please! said the hiver. *Shelter us!*

"The wizard was nearly right about you," said Tiffany. "You hid in other creatures. But he didn't wonder *why*. What are you hiding from?"

Everything, said the hiver.

"I *think* I know what you mean," said Tiffany.

Do you? Do you know what it feels like to be aware of every star, every blade of grass? Yes. You do. You call it "opening your eyes again." But you do it for a moment. We have done it for eternity. No sleep, no rest, just endless . . . endless experience, endless awareness. Of everything. All the time. *How we envy you,* envy *you! Lucky humans, who can close your minds to the endless cold deeps of space! You have this thing you call . . . boredom? That is the rarest talent in the universe! We heard a song—it went "Twinkle twinkle little star. . . ." What power! What wondrous power! You can take a billion trillion tons of flaming matter, a furnace of unimaginable strength, and turn it into a little song for children! You build little worlds, little stories, little shells around your minds, and that keeps infinity at bay and allows you to wake up in the morning without screaming!*

Completely binkers! said a cheerful voice at the back of Tiffany's memory. You just couldn't keep Dr. Bustle down.

Pity us, yes, pity us, said the voices of the hiver. *No shield for us, no rest for us, no sanctuary. But you, you withstood us. We saw that in you. You have minds within minds. Hide us!*

"You want silence?" said Tiffany.

Yes, and more than silence, said the voice of the hiver. *You humans are so good at ignoring things. You are almost blind and almost deaf. You look at a tree and see . . . just a tree, a stiff weed. You don't see its history, feel the pumping of the sap, hear every insect in the bark, sense the chemistry of the leaves, notice the hundred shades of green, the tiny movements to follow the sun, the subtle growth of the wood . . .*

"But you don't understand us," said Tiffany. "I don't think any human could survive you. You give us what you think we want, as soon as we want it, just like in fairy stories. And the wishes always go wrong."

Yes. We know that now. We have an echo of you now. We have . . . understanding, said the hiver. *So now we come to you with a wish. It is the wish that puts the others right.*

"Yes," said Tiffany. "That's always the last wish, the third wish. It's the one that says 'Make this not have happened.'"

Teach us the way to die, said the voices of the hiver.

"I don't know it!"

All humans know the way, said the voices of the hiver. *You walk it every day of your short, short lives. You know it. We envy you your knowledge. You know how to end. You are very talented.*

I *must* know how to die, Tiffany thought. Somewhere deep down. Let me think. Let me get past the "I can't." . . .

She held up the glittering shamble. Shafts of light still spun off it, but she didn't need it anymore. She could hold the power in the center of herself. It was all a matter of balance.

The light died. Rob Anybody was still hanging in the threads, but all his hair had come unplaited and stood out from his head in a great red ball. He looked stunned.

"I could just *murrrder* a kebab," he said.

Tiffany lowered him to the ground, where he swayed slightly; then she put the rest of the shamble in her pocket.

"Thank you, Rob," she said. "But I want you to go now. It could get . . . serious."

It was, of course, the wrong thing to say.

"I'm no' leavin'!" he snapped. "I promised Jeannie to keep ye safe! Let's get on wi' it!"

There was no arguing. Rob was standing in that half crouch of his, fists bunched, chin out, ready for anything and burning with defiance.

"Thank you," said Tiffany, and straightened up.

Death is right behind us, she thought. Life ends, and there's death, waiting. So . . . it must be close. Very close.

It would be . . . a door. Yes. An old door, old wood. Dark, too.

She turned. Behind her, there was a black door in the air.

The hinges would creak, she thought.

When she pushed it open, they did.

So-oo . . . she thought, this isn't exactly *real*. I'm telling myself a story I can understand, about doors, and I'm fooling myself just enough for it all to work. I just have to keep balanced on that edge for it to go on working, too. That's as hard as not thinking about a pink rhinoceros. And if Granny Weatherwax can do that, I can too.

Beyond the door, black sand stretched away under a sky of pale stars. There were some mountains on the distant horizon.

You must help us through, said the voices of the hiver.

"If you'll tak' my advice, you'll no' do that," said Rob Anybody from Tiffany's ankle. "I dinna trust the scunner one wee bitty!"

"There's part of me in there. I trust that," she said. "I did say you don't have to come, Rob."

"Oh, aye? An' I'm tae see ye go through there alone, am I? Ye'll not find me leavin' ye now!"

"You've got a clan and a wife, Rob!"

"Aye, an' so I willna dishonor them by lettin' yer step across Death's threshold alone," said Rob Anybody firmly.

So, thought Tiffany as she stared through the doorway, *this* is what we do. We live on the edges. We help those who can't find the way. . . .

She took a deep breath and stepped across.

Nothing much changed. The sand felt gritty underfoot and crunched when she walked over it, as she expected, but when it was kicked up, it fell back as slowly as thistledown, and she hadn't expected that. The air wasn't cold, but it was thin and prickly to breathe.

The door shut softly behind her.

Thank you, said the voices of the hiver. *What do we do now?*

Tiffany looked around her, and up at the stars. They weren't ones that she recognized.

"You die, I think," she said.

But there is no "me" to die, said the voices of the hiver. *There is only us.*

Tiffany took a deep breath. This was about words, and she knew about words. "Here is a story to believe," she said. "Once we were blobs in the sea, and then fishes, and then lizards and rats, and then monkeys, and hundreds of things in between. This hand was once a fin, this hand once had claws! In my human mouth I have the pointy teeth of a wolf and the chisel teeth of a rabbit and the grinding teeth of a cow! Our blood is as salty as the sea we used to live in! When we're frightened, the hair on our skin stands up, just like it did when we had fur. We *are* history! Everything we've ever been on the way to becoming us, we still are. Would you like the rest of the story?"

Tell us, said the hiver.

"I'm made up of the memories of my parents and grandparents, all my ancestors. They're in the way I look, in the color of my hair. And I'm made up of everyone I've ever met who's changed the way I think. So who is 'me'?"

The piece that just told us that story, said the hiver. *The piece that's truly you.*

"Well . . . yes. But you must have that too. You know you say you're 'us'—who is it saying it? Who is saying you're not you? You're not different from us. We're just much, much better at forgetting. And we know when not to listen to the monkey."

You've just puzzled us, said the hiver.

"The old bit of our brains that wants to be head monkey, and attacks when it's surprised," said Tiffany. "It reacts. It doesn't think. Being human is knowing when not to be the monkey or the lizard or any of the other old echoes. But when *you* take people over, you silence the human part. You listen to the monkey. The monkey doesn't know what it needs, only what it wants. No, you are not an 'us.' You are an 'I.'"

I, me, said the hiver. *I. Who am I?*

"Do you want a name? That helps."

Yes. A name. . . .

"I've always liked Arthur as a name."

Arthur, said the hiver. *I like Arthur too. And if I am, I can stop. What happens next?*

"The creatures you . . . took over, didn't they die?"

Yes, said the Arthur. *But we—but I didn't see what happened. They just stopped being here.*

Tiffany looked around at the endless sand. She couldn't see anybody, but there was something out there that suggested movement. It was the occasional change in the light, perhaps, as if she was catching glimpses of something she was not supposed to see.

"I think," she said, "that you have to cross the desert."

What's on the other side? asked Arthur.

Tiffany hesitated.

"Some people think you go to a better world," she said. "Some people think you come back to this one in a different body. And some think there's just nothing. They think you just stop."

And what do you think? Arthur asked.

"I think that there are no words to describe it," said Tiffany.

Is that true? said Arthur.

"I think that's why you have to cross the desert," said Tiffany. "To find out."

I will look forward to it. Thank you.

"Good-bye . . . Arthur."

She felt the hiver fall away. There wasn't much sign of it—a movement of a few sand grains, a sizzle in the air—but it slid away slowly across the black sand.

"An' bad cess an' good riddance tae ye!" Rob Anybody shouted after it.

"No," said Tiffany. "Don't say that."

"Aye, but it killed folk to stay alive."

"It didn't want to. It didn't know how people work."

"That was a fine load of o' blethers ye gave it, at any rate," said Rob admiringly. "Not even a gonnagle could make up a load o' blethers like that."

Tiffany wondered if it had been. Once, when the wandering teachers had come to the village, she had paid half a dozen eggs for a morning's education on "***WONDERS OF THE UNIVERS!!***" That was expensive, for education, but it had been thoroughly worth it. The teacher had been a little bit crazy, even for a teacher, but what he'd said had seemed to make absolute sense. One of the most amazing things about the universe, he had said, was that, sooner or later, everything is made of everything else, although it'll probably take millions and millions of years for this to happen. The other children had giggled or argued, but Tiffany knew that what had once been tiny living creatures was now the chalk of the hills. Everything went around, even stars.

That had been a very good morning, especially since she'd been refunded half an egg for pointing out that *universe* had been spelled wrong.

Was it true? Maybe that didn't matter. Maybe it just had to be true enough for Arthur.

Her eyes, the inner eyes that opened twice, were beginning to close. She could feel the power draining away. You couldn't stay in that state for long. You became so aware of the universe that you stopped being aware of you. How clever of humans to have learned how to close their minds. Was there anything so amazing in the universe as boredom?

She sat down, just for a moment, and picked up a handful of the sand. It rose above her hand, twisting like smoke, reflecting the starlight, then settled back as if it had all the time in the world.

She had never felt this tired.

She still heard the inner voices. The hiver had left memories behind, just a few. She could remember when there had been no stars and when there had been no such thing as "yesterday." She knew what was beyond the sky and beneath the grass. But she couldn't remember when she had last slept, properly *slept*, in a *bed*. Being unconscious didn't count. She closed her eyes, and closed her eyes again—

Someone kicked her hard on the foot.

"Dinna gae to sleep!" Rob Anybody shouted. "Not here! Ye canna gae to sleep *here*! Rise an' shine!"

Still feeling muzzy, Tiffany pushed herself back onto her feet, through gentle swirls of rising dust, and turned to the dark door.

It wasn't there.

There were her footprints in the sand, but they went only a few feet and, anyway, were slowly disappearing. There was nothing around her but dead desert, forever.

She turned back to look toward the distant mountains, but her view was blocked by a tall figure, all in black, holding a scythe. It hadn't been there before.

GOOD AFTERNOON, said Death.

CHAPTER 12

The Egress

Tiffany stared up into a black hood. There was a skull in it, but the eye sockets glowed blue.

At least bones had never frightened Tiffany. They were only chalk that had walked around.

"Are you——?" she began, but Rob Anybody gave a yell and leaped straight for the hood.

There was a thud. Death took a step backward and raised a skeletal hand to his cowl. He pulled Rob Anybody out by his hair and held him at arm's length while the Nac Mac Feegle cursed and kicked.

IS THIS YOURS? Death asked Tiffany. The voice was heavy and all around her, like thunder.

"No. Er . . . he's his."

I WAS NOT EXPECTING A NAC MAC FEEGLE TODAY, said Death. OTHERWISE I WOULD HAVE WORN PROTECTIVE CLOTHING, HA HA.

"They do fight a lot," Tiffany admitted. "You *are* Death, aren't you? I know this might sound like a silly question."

YOU ARE NOT AFRAID?

"Not yet. But, er . . . which way to the egress, please?"

There was a pause. Then Death said, in a puzzled voice: ISN'T THAT A FEMALE EAGLE?

"No," said Tiffany. "Everyone thinks that. Actually, it's the way out. The exit."

Death pointed, with the hand that still held the incandescently angry Rob Anybody.

THAT WAY. YOU HAVE TO WALK THE DESERT.

"All the way to the mountains?"

YES. BUT ONLY THE DEAD CAN TAKE THAT WAY.

"Ye've got tae let me go sooner or later, ye big 'natomy!" yelled Rob Anybody. "And then ye're gonna get sich a kickin'!"

"There was a door here!" said Tiffany.

AH, YES, said Death. BUT THERE ARE RULES. THAT WAS A WAY *IN*, YOU SEE.

"What's the difference?

A FAIRLY IMPORTANT ONE, I'M SORRY TO SAY. YOU WILL HAVE TO SEE YOURSELVES OUT. DO NOT FALL ASLEEP HERE. SLEEP HERE NEVER ENDS.

Death vanished. Rob Anybody dropped to the sand and came up ready to fight, but they were alone.

"Ye'll have to make a door oout," he said.

"I don't know how! Rob, I told you not to come with me. Can't *you* get out?"

"Aye. Probably. But I've got to see ye safe. The kelda put a geas on me. I must save the hag o' the hills."

"*Jeannie* told you that?"

"Aye. She was verra *definite*," said Rob Anybody.

Tiffany slumped down onto the sand again. It fountained up around her.

"I'll never get out," she said. How to get in, yes, *that* wasn't hard. . . .

She looked around. They weren't obvious, but there were occasional changes in the light, and little puffs of dust.

People she couldn't see were walking past her. People were crossing the desert. Dead people, going to find out what was beyond the mountains . . .

I'm eleven, she thought. People will be upset. She thought about the farm, and how her mother and father would react. But there wouldn't be a body, would there? So people would hope and hope that she'd come back and was just . . . missing, like old Mrs. Happens in the village, who lit a candle in the window every night for her son who'd been lost at sea thirty years ago.

She wondered if Rob could send a message—but what could she say? "I'm not dead, I'm just stuck"?

"I should have thought of other people," she said aloud.

"Aye, weel, ye did," said Rob, sitting down by her foot. "Yon Arthur went off happy, and ye saved other folk fra' being killed. Ye did what ye had to do."

Yes, thought Tiffany. That's what we have to do. And there's no one to protect you, because *you're* the one who's supposed to do that sort of thing.

But her Second Thoughts said: I'm *glad* I did it. I'd do it again. I stopped the hiver killing anyone else, even though we led it right into the Trials. And that thought was followed by a space. There should have been another thought, but she was too tired to have it. It had been important.

"Thank you for coming, Rob," she said. "But when . . . you can leave, you must go straight back to Jeannie, understand? And tell her I'm grateful she sent you. Say I wish we'd had a chance to get to know each other better."

"Oh, aye. I've sent the lads back anyway. Hamish is waitin' for me."

At which point the door appeared, and opened.

Granny Weatherwax stepped through and beckoned urgently.

"Some people don't have the sense they were born with! Come on, right now!" she commanded. Behind her the door started to swing shut, but she swung around savagely and rammed her boot against the jamb, shouting, "Oh, no you don't, you sly devil!"

"But . . . I thought there were rules!" said Tiffany, getting up and hurrying forward, all tiredness sudden gone. Even a tired body wants to survive.

"Oh? Really?" said Granny. "Did you sign anything? Did you take any kind of oath? No? Then they weren't *your* rules! Quickly, now! And you, Mr. Anyone!"

Rob Anybody jumped onto her boot just before she pulled it away. The door shut with another click, disappeared, and left them in . . . dead light, it seemed, a space of gray air.

"Won't take long," said Granny Weatherwax. "It doesn't usually. It's the world getting back into line. Oh, don't look like that. You showed it the Way, right? Out of pity. Well, I know this path already. You'll tread it again, no doubt, for some other poor soul, open the door for them as can't find it. But we don't talk about it, understand?"

"Miss Level never—"

"We don't talk about it, I said," said Granny Weatherwax. "Do you know what a part of being a witch is? It's making the choices that have to be made. The hard choices. But you did . . . quite well. There's no shame in pity."

She brushed some grass seed off her dress.

"I hope Mrs. Ogg has arrived," she said. "I need her recipe for apple chutney. Oh . . . when we arrive you might feel a bit dizzy. I'd better warn you."

"Granny?" said Tiffany, as the light began to grow brighter. It brought tiredness back with it, too.

"Yes?"

"What *exactly* happened just then?"

"What do you think happened?"

Light burst in upon them.

◆　◆　◆

Someone was wiping Tiffany's forehead with a damp cloth.

She lay, feeling the beautiful coolness. There were voices around her, and she recognized the chronic-complainer tones of Annagramma:

". . . And she was really making a fuss in Zakzak's. Honestly, I don't think she's quite right in the head! I think she's literally gone cuckoo! She was shouting things and using some kind of, oh, I don't know, some peasant trick to make us think she'd turned that fool Brian into a frog. Well, of course, she didn't fool *me* for one minute—"

Tiffany opened her eyes and saw the round pink face of Petulia, screwed up with concern.

"Um, she's awake!" said the girl.

The space between Tiffany and the ceiling filled up with pointy hats. They drew back, reluctantly, as she sat up. From above, it must have looked like a dark daisy, closing and opening.

"Where is this?" she said.

"Um, the First Aid and Lost Children's Tent," said Petulia. "Um . . . you fainted when Mistress Weatherwax brought you back from . . . from wherever you'd gone. *Everyone's* been in to see you!"

"She said you'd, like, *dragged* the monster into, like, the Next World!" said Lucy Warbeck, her eyes gleaming. "Mistress Weatherwax told everyone all about it!"

"Well, it wasn't quite—" Tiffany began. She felt something prod her in the back. She reached behind her, and her hand came out holding a pointy hat. It was almost gray with age and quite battered. Zakzak wouldn't have dared try to sell something like this, but the other girls stared at it like starving dogs watching a butcher's hand.

"Um, Mistress Weatherwax gave you her *hat*," breathed Petulia. "Her actual *hat*."

"She said you were a born witch and no witch should be without a hat!" said Dimity Hubbub, watching.

"That's nice," said Tiffany. She was used to secondhand clothes.

"It's only an old hat," said Annagramma.

Tiffany looked up at the tall girl and let herself smile slowly.

"Annagramma?" she said, raising a hand with the fingers open.

Annagramma backed away. "Oh no," she said. "Don't you do that! *Don't* you do that! Someone stop her doing that!"

"Do you want a *balloon*, Annagramma?" said Tiffany, sliding off the table.

"No! Please!" Annagramma took another step back, holding her arms in front of her face, and fell over a bench. Tiffany picked her up and patted her cheerfully on a cheek.

"Then I shan't buy you one," she said. "But *please* learn what *literally* really means, will you?"

Annagramma smiled in a frozen kind of way. "Er, yes," she managed.

"Good. And then we will be friends."

She left the girl standing there and went back to pick up the hat.

"Um, you're probably still a bit woozy," said Petulia. "You probably don't understand."

"Ha, I wasn't *actually* frightened, you know," said Annagramma. "It was all for fun, of course." No one paid any attention.

"Understand what?" said Tiffany.

"It's her actual *hat*!" the girls chorused.

"It's like, if that hat could talk, what stories it would have to, you know, tell," said Lucy Warbeck.

"It was just a joke," said Annagramma to anyone who was listening.

Tiffany looked at the hat. It was very battered, and not extremely clean. If that hat could talk, it would probably mutter.

"Where's Granny Weatherwax now?" she said.

There was a gasp from the girls. This was nearly as impressive as the hat.

"Um . . . she doesn't mind you calling her that?" said Petulia.

"She invited me to," said Tiffany.

"Only we heard you had to have known her for, like, a hundred years before she let you call her that . . ." said Lucy Warbeck.

Tiffany shrugged. "Well, anyway," she said, "do you know where she is?"

"Oh, having tea with the other old witches and yacking on about chutney and how witches today aren't what they were when she was a girl," said Lulu Darling.

"What?" said Tiffany. "Just having *tea*?"

The young witches looked at one another in puzzlement.

"Um, there's buns too," said Petulia. "If that's important."

"But she opened the door for me. The door into—out of the . . . the desert! You can't just sit down after that and have *buns*!"

"Um, the ones I saw had icing on them," Petulia ventured nervously. "They weren't just homemade—"

"Look," said Lucy Warbeck, "we didn't really, you know, *see* anything? You were just standing there with this like *glow* around you and we couldn't get in and then Gran—Mistress Weatherwax walked up and stepped right in and you both, you know, *stood* there? And then the glow went *zip* and vanished and you, like, fell over."

"What Lucy's failing to say very accurately," said Annagramma, "is that we didn't actually see you go anywhere. I'm telling you this as a friend, of course. There was just this glow, which could have been *anything*."

Annagramma was going to be a good witch, Tiffany considered. She could tell herself stories that she literally believed. And she could bounce back like a ball.

"Don't forget, I saw the horse," said Harrieta Bilk.

Annagramma rolled her eyes. "Oh yes, Harrieta thinks she saw some kind of horse in the sky. Except it didn't look like a horse, she says. She says it looked like a horse would look if you took the actual horse away and just left the horsiness, right, Harrieta?"

"I didn't say that!" snapped Harrieta.

"Well, pardon *me*. That's what it sounded like."

"Um, and some people said they saw a white horse grazing in the next field, too," said Petulia. "And a lot of the older witches said they felt a tremendous amount of—"

"Yes, some people thought they saw a horse in a field, but it isn't there anymore," said Annagramma in the singsong voice she used when she thought it was all stupid. "That must be very rare in the country, seeing horses in fields. Anyway, if there really *was* a white horse, it was gray."

Tiffany sat on the edge of the table, staring at her knees. Anger at Annagramma had jolted her to life, but now the tiredness was creeping back again.

"I suppose none of you saw a little blue man, about six inches high, with red hair?" she said quietly.

"Anyone?" said Annagramma with malicious cheerfulness. There was a general mumbling of "no."

"Sorry, Tiffany," said Lucy.

"Don't worry," said Annagramma. "He probably just rode away on his white horse!"

This is going to be like Fairyland all over again, thought Tiffany. Even I can't remember if it was real. Why should anyone believe me? But she had to try.

"There was a dark doorway," she said slowly, "and beyond it was a desert of black sand, and it was light although there were stars in the sky, and Death was there. I spoke to him. . . ."

"You spoke to him, did you?" said Annagramma. "And what did he say, pray?"

"He didn't say pray," said Tiffany. "We didn't talk about much. But he didn't know what an egress was."

"It's a small type of heron, isn't it?" said Harrieta.

There was silence, except for the noise of the Trials outside.

"It's not your fault," said Annagramma in what was, for her, almost a friendly voice. "It's like I said: Mistress Weatherwax messes with people's heads."

"What about the glow?" said Lucy.

"That was probably ball lightning," said Annagramma. "That's very strange stuff."

"But people were, like, hammering on it! It was as hard as ice!"

"Ah, well, it probably *felt* like that," said Annagramma, "but it was . . . probably affecting people's muscles, maybe. I'm only trying to be helpful here," she added. "You've got to be sensible. She just stood there. You saw her. There weren't any doors or deserts. There was just her."

Tiffany sighed. She felt tired. She wanted to crawl off somewhere. She wanted to go home. She'd walk there now if her boots weren't suddenly so uncomfortable.

While the girls argued, she undid the laces and tugged one off.

Silver-black dust poured out. When it hit it the ground, it bounced slowly, curving up into the air again like mist.

The girls turned, watching in silence. Then Petulia reached down and caught some of the dust. When she lifted her hand, the fine stuff flowed between her fingers. It fell as slowly as feathers.

"Sometimes things go wrong," she said, in a faraway voice. "Mistress Blackcap told me. Haven't any of you been there when old folk are dying?" There were one or two nods, but everyone was watching the dust.

"Sometimes things go wrong," said Petulia again. "Sometimes they're dying but they can't leave because they don't know the Way. She said that's when they need you to be there, close to them, to help them find the door so they don't get lost in the dark."

"Petulia, we're not supposed to talk about this," said Harrieta gently.

"No!" said Petulia, her face red. "It is time to talk about it, just here, just us! Because she said it's the last thing you can do for someone. She said there's a dark desert they have to cross, where the sand—"

"Hah! Mrs. Earwig says that sort of thing is black magic," said Annagramma, her voice as sharp and sudden as a knife.

"Does she?" said Petulia dreamily as the sand poured down. "Well, Mistress Blackcap said that sometimes the moon is light and sometimes it's in shadow, but you should always remember it's the same moon. And . . . Annagramma?"

"Yes?"

Petulia took a deep breath.

"Don't you *ever* dare interrupt me again as long as you live. Don't you dare. Don't you *dare*! I mean it."

CHAPTER 13

The Witch Trials

And then . . . there were the Trials themselves. That was the point of the day, wasn't it? But Tiffany, stepping out with the girls around her, sensed the buzz in the air. It said: Was there any point *now*? After what had happened?

Still, people had put up the rope square again, and a lot of the older witches dragged their chairs to the edge of it, and it seemed that it was going to happen after all. Tiffany wandered up to the rope, found a space, and sat down on the grass with Granny Weatherwax's hat in front of her.

She was aware of the other girls behind her, and also of a buzz or susurration of whispering spreading out into the crowd.

"*. . . She really did do it, too. . . . No, really . . . all the way to the desert. . . . Saw the dust . . . her boots were full, they say. . . .*"

Gossip spreads faster among witches than a bad cold. Witches gossip like starlings.

There were no judges and no prizes. The Trials weren't like that, as Petulia had said. The point was to show what you could do, to show what you'd become, so that people would go away thinking things like "That Caramella Bottlethwaite, she's coming along nicely." It wasn't a competition, honestly. No one *won*.

And if you believed *that*, you'd believe that the moon is pushed around the sky by a goblin called Wilberforce.

What *was* true was that one of the older witches generally opened the thing with some competent but not surprising trick that everyone had seen before but still appreciated. That broke the ice. This year it was old Goodie Trample and her collection of singing mice.

But Tiffany wasn't paying attention. On the other side of the roped-off square, sitting on a chair and surrounded by older witches like a queen on her throne, was Granny Weatherwax.

The whispering went on. Maybe opening her eyes had opened her ears, too, because Tiffany felt she could hear the whispers all around the square.

"... *Din't have no trainin', just did it. ... Did you see that horse? ... I never saw no horse! ... Din't just open the door, she stepped right in! ... Yeah, but who was it fetched her back? Esme Weatherwax, that's who! ... Yes, that's what I'm sayin', any little fool could've opened the door by luck, but it takes a real witch to bring her back, that's a winner, that is. ... Fought the thing, left it there! ... I didn't see you doing anything, Violet Pulsimone! That child ... Was there a horse or not? ... Was going to do my dancing broom trick, but that'd be wasted now, of course. ... Why did Mistress Weatherwax give the girl her hat, eh? What's she want us to think? She never takes off her hat to no one!*"

You could feel the tension, crackling from pointy hat to pointy hat like summer lighting.

The mice did their best with "I'm Forever Blowing Bubbles," but it was easy to see that their minds weren't on it. Mice are high-strung and very temperamental.

Now people were leaning down beside Granny Weatherwax. Tiffany could see some animated conversations going on.

"You know, Tiffany," said Lucy Warbeck, behind her, "all you've got to do is, like, stand up and admit it. Everyone knows you did it. I mean no one's ever, like, done something like *that* at the Trials!"

"And it's about time the old bully lost," said Annagramma.

But she's not a bully, Tiffany thought. She's tough, and she expects other witches to be tough, because the edge is no place for people who break. Everything with her is a kind of test. And her Third Thoughts handed over the thought that had not quite made it back in the tent: Granny Weatherwax, you *knew* the hiver would only come for me, didn't you? You talked to Dr. Bustle, you *told* me. Did you just turn me into your trick for today? How much did you guess? Or know?

"You'd win," said Dimity Hubbub. "Even some of the older ones would like to see her taken down a peg. They know big magic happened. There's not a whole shamble for *miles*."

So I'd win because some people don't like somebody else? Tiffany thought. Oh, *yes*, that's *really* be something to be proud of. . . .

"You can bet *she'll* stand up," said Annagramma. "You watch. She'll explain how the poor child got dragged into the Next World by a monster, and she brought her back. That's what I'd do, if I was her."

I expect you would, Tiffany thought. But you're not, and you're not me, either.

She stared at Granny Weatherwax, who was waving away a couple of elderly witches.

I wonder, she thought, if they've been saying things like "This girl needs taking down a peg, Mistress Weatherwax." And as she thought that, Granny turned back and caught her eye—

The mice stopped singing, mostly in embarrassment. There was a pause, and then people started to clap, because it was the sort of thing you had to do.

A witch, someone Tiffany didn't know, stepped out into the square, still clapping in that fluttery, hands-held-close-together-at-shoulder-height way that people use when they want to encourage the audience to go on applauding just that little bit longer.

"Very well done, Doris, excellent work, as ever," she trilled. "They've come along marvelously since last year, thank you very much, wonderful, well done . . . ahem . . ."

The woman hesitated, while behind her Doris Trample crawled around on hands and knees trying to urge her mice back into their box. One of them was having hysterics.

"And now, perhaps . . . some lady would like to, er . . . take the, er . . . stage?" said the mistress of ceremonies, as brightly as a glass ball about to shatter. "Anyone?"

There was stillness, and silence.

"Don't be shy, ladies!" The voice of the mistress of ceremonies was getting more strained by the second. It's no fun trying to organize a field full of born organizers. "Modesty does not become us! Anyone?"

Tiffany *felt* the pointy hats turning, some toward her, some toward Granny Weatherwax. Away across the few yards of grass, Granny reached up and brushed someone's hand from her shoulder, sharply, without breaking eye contact with Tiffany. And we're not wearing hats, thought Tiffany. You gave me a virtual hat once, Granny Weatherwax, and I thank you for it. But I don't need it today. Today, I know I'm a witch.

"Oh, come now, ladies!" said the mistress of ceremonies, now almost frantic. "This is the Trials! A place for friendly and instructive contestation in an atmosphere of fraternity and goodwill!

Surely some lady . . . or young lady, perhaps . . . ?"

Tiffany smiled. It should be *sorority*, not *fraternity*. We're sisters, mistress, not brothers.

"Come *on*, Tiffany!" Dimity urged. "They *know* you're good!"

Tiffany shook her head.

"Oh, well, that's it," said Annagramma, rolling her eyes. "The old baggage has messed with the girl's head, *as usual*—"

"I don't know who's messed with whose head," snapped Petulia, rolling up her sleeves. "But *I'm* going to do the pig trick." She got to her feet, and there was a general stir in the crowd.

"Oh, I see it's going to be—oh, it's you, Petulia," said the mistress of ceremonies, slightly disappointed.

"Yes, Miss Casement, and I intend to perform the pig trick," said Petulia loudly.

"But, er, you don't seem to have brought a pig with you," said Miss Casement, taken aback.

"Yes, Miss Casement. I shall perform the pig trick . . . *without a pig!*"

This caused a sensation, and cries of "Impossible!" and "There are children here, you know!"

Miss Casement looked around for assistance and found none.

"Oh well," she said helplessly. "If you are sure, dear . . ."

"Yes. I am. I shall use . . . a sausage!" said Petulia, producing one from a pocket and holding it up. There was another sensation.

Tiffany didn't see the trick. Nor did Granny Weatherwax. Their gaze was like an iron bar, and even Miss Casement instinctively didn't step into it.

But Tiffany heard the squeal, and the gasp of amazement, and then the thunder of applause. People would have applauded anything at that point, in the same way that pent-up water would take any route out of a dam.

And *then* witches got up. Miss Level juggled balls that stopped and reversed direction in midair. A middle-aged witch demonstrated a new way to stop people from choking, which doesn't even sound magical until you understand that a way of turning nearly dead people into fully alive people is worth a dozen spells that just go *twing!* And other women and girls came up one at a time, with big tricks and handy tips and things that went *wheee!* or stopped toothache or, in one case, exploded—

—and then there were no more entries.

Miss Casement walked back into the center of the field, almost drunk with relief that there *had* been a Trials, and made one final invitation to any ladies *"or, indeed, young ladies"* who might like to come forward.

There was a silence so thick you could have stuck pins in it.

And then she said: "Oh, well . . . in that case, I declare the Trials well and truly closed. Tea will be in the big tent!"

Tiffany and Granny stood up at the same time, to the second, and bowed to each other. Then Granny turned away and joined the stampede toward the teas. It was interesting to see how the crowd parted, all unaware, to let her through, like the sea in front of a particularly good prophet.

Petulia was surrounded by other young witches. The pig trick had gone down very well. Tiffany lined up to give her a hug.

"But *you* could have won!" said Petulia, red in the face with happiness and worry.

"That doesn't matter. It really doesn't," said Tiffany.

"You gave it away," said a sharp voice behind her. "You had it in your hand, and you gave it all away. How do you feel about that, Tiffany? Do you have a taste for humble pie?"

"Now you listen to me, Annagramma," Petulia began, pointing a furious finger.

Tiffany reached out and lowered the girl's arm. Then she turned and smiled so happily at Annagramma that it was disturbing.

What she wanted to say was: "Where I come from, Annagramma, they have the Sheepdog Trials. Shepherds travel there from all over to show off their dogs. And there're silver crooks and belts with silver buckles and prizes of all kinds, Annagramma, but do you know what the big prize is? No, you wouldn't. Oh, there are judges, but they don't count, not for the *big* prize. There is—there *was* a little old lady who was always at the front of the crowd, leaning on the hurdles with her pipe in her mouth with the two finest sheepdogs ever pupped sitting at her feet. Their names were Thunder and Lightning, and they moved so fast, they set the air on fire and their coats outshone the sun, but she never, ever put them in the Trials. She knew more about sheep than even sheep know. And what every young shepherd wanted, really *wanted*, wasn't some silly cup or belt but to see her take her pipe out of her mouth as he left the arena and quietly say, 'That'll do,' because that meant he was a *real* shepherd and all the other shepherds would know it, too. And if you'd told him he had to challenge her, he'd cuss at you and stamp his foot and tell you he'd sooner spit the sun dark. How could he ever win? She *was* shepherding. It was the whole of her life. What you took away from her you'd take away from yourself. You don't understand that, do you? But it's the heart and soul and center of it! The soul . . . and . . . center!"

But it would be wasted, so what she said was: "Oh, just shut up, Annagramma. Let's see if there's any buns left, shall we?"

Overhead, a buzzard screamed. She looked up.

The bird turned on the wind and, racing through the air as it began the long glide, headed back toward home.

They were always there.

◆　◆　◆

Beside her cauldron, Jeannie opened her eyes.

"He's comin' hame!" she said, scrambling to her feet. She waved a hand urgently at the watching Feegles. "Don't ye just stand there gawping!" she commanded. "Catch some rabbits to roast! Build up the fire! Boil up a load o' water, 'cuz I'm takin' a bath! Look at this place, 'tis like a midden! Get it cleaned up! I want it sparkling for the Big Man! Go an' steal some Special Sheep Liniment! Cut some green boughs, holly or yew, mebbe! Shine up the golden plates! The place must sparkle! What're ye all standin' there for?"

"Er, what did ye want us to do first, Kelda?" asked a Feegle nervously.

"All of it!"

In her chamber they filled the kelda's soup-bowl bath and she scrubbed, using one of Tiffany's old toothbrushes, while outside there were the sounds of Feegles working hard at cross-purposes. The smell of roasting rabbit began to fill the mound.

Jeannie dressed herself in her best dress, did her hair, picked up her shawl, and climbed out of the hole. She stood there watching the mountains until, after about an hour, a dot in the sky got bigger and bigger.

As a kelda, she would welcome home a warrior. As a wife, she would kiss her husband and scold him for being so long away. As a woman, she thought she would melt with relief, thankfulness, and joy.

CHAPTER 14

Queen of the Bees

⌁

And one afternoon about a week later, Tiffany went to see Granny Weatherwax.

It was only fifteen miles as the broomstick flies, and as Tiffany still didn't like flying a broomstick, Miss Level took her.

It was the invisible part of Miss Level. Tiffany just lay flat on the stick, holding on with arms and legs and knees and ears if possible, and took along a paper bag to be sick into, because no one likes anonymous sick dropping out of the sky. She was also holding a large burlap sack, which she handled with care.

She didn't open her eyes until the rushing noises had stopped and the sounds around her told her she was probably very close to the ground. In fact Miss Level had been very kind. When she fell off, because of the cramp in her legs, the broomstick was just above some quite thick moss.

"Thank you," said Tiffany as she got up, because it always pays to mind your manners around invisible people.

She had a new dress. It was green, like the last one. The complex world of favors and obligations and gifts that Miss Level lived and moved in had thrown up four yards of nice material (for the trouble-free birth of Miss Quickly's baby boy) and a few hours' dressmaking (Mrs. Hunter's bad leg feeling a lot better, thank you). She'd given the black one away. When I'm old, I shall wear midnight, she'd decided. But for now she'd had enough of darkness.

She looked around at this clearing on the side of a hill, surrounded by oak and sycamore on three sides but open on the downhill side with a wide view of the countryside below. The sycamores were shedding their spinning seeds, which whirled down lazily across a patch of garden. It was unfenced, even though some goats were grazing nearby. If you wondered why the goats weren't eating the garden, it was because you'd forgotten who lived here. There was a well. And, of course, a cottage.

Mrs. Earwig would definitely have objected to the cottage. It was out of a storybook. The walls leaned against one another for support, the thatched roof was slipping off like a bad wig, and the chimneys were corkscrewed. If you thought a gingerbread cottage would be too fattening, this was the next worst thing.

In a cottage deep in the forest lived the Wicked Old Witch. . . .

It was a cottage out of the nastier kind of fairy tale.

Granny Weatherwax's beehives were tucked away down one side of the cottage. Some were the old straw kind, most were patched-up wooden ones. They thundered with activity, even this late in the year.

Tiffany turned aside to look at them, and the bees poured out in a dark stream. They swarmed toward Tiffany, formed a column, and—

She laughed. They'd made a witch of bees in front of her, thousands of them all holding station in the air. She raised her right hand. With a rise in the level of buzzing, the bee-witch raised its right hand. She turned around. It turned around, the bees carefully copying every swirl and flutter of her dress, the ones on the very edge buzzing desperately because they had farthest to fly.

She carefully put down the big sack and reached out toward the figure. With another roar of wings it went shapeless for a moment, then re-formed a little way away, but with a hand outstretched toward her. The bee that was the tip of its forefinger hovered just in front of Tiffany's fingernail.

"Shall we dance?" said Tiffany.

In the clearing full of spinning seeds, she circled the swarm. It kept up pretty well, moving fingertip to buzzing tip, turning when she turned, although there were always a few bees racing to catch up.

Then it raised both its arms and twirled in the opposite direction, the bees in the "skirt" spreading out again as it spun. It was learning.

Tiffany laughed and did the same thing. Swarm and girl whirled across the clearing.

She felt happy and wondered if she'd ever felt this happy before. The gold light, the falling seeds, the dancing bees . . . it was all one thing. This was the opposite of the dark desert. Here, light was everywhere and filled her up inside. She could feel herself here but see herself from above, twirling with a buzzing shadow that sparkled golden as the light struck the bees. Moments like this paid for it all.

Then the witch made of bees leaned closer to Tiffany, as if staring at her with its thousands of little jeweled eyes. There was a faint piping noise from inside the figure and the bee-witch exploded into a spreading, buzzing cloud of insects that raced away across the clearing and disappeared. The only movement now was the whirring fall of the sycamore seeds.

Tiffany breathed out.

"Now, some people would have found that scary," said a voice behind her.

Tiffany didn't turn around immediately. First she said, "Good afternoon, Granny Weatherwax." *Then* she turned around. "Have *you* ever done this?" she demanded, still half drunk with delight.

"It's rude to start with questions. You'd better come in and have a cup of tea," said Granny Weatherwax.

You'd barely know that anyone *lived* in the cottage. There were two chairs by the fire, one of them a rocking chair, and by the table were two chairs that didn't rock but did wobble because of the uneven stone floor. There was a dresser, and a rag rug in front of the huge hearth. A broomstick leaned against the wall in one corner, next to something mysterious and pointy, under a cloth. There was a very narrow and dark flight of stairs. And that was it. There was nothing shiny, nothing new, and nothing unnecessary.

"To what do I owe the pleasure of this visit?" said Granny Weatherwax, taking a sooty black kettle off the fire and filling an equally black teapot.

Tiffany opened the sack she had brought with her.

"I've come to bring you your hat back," she said.

"Ah," said Granny Weatherwax. "Have you? And why?"

"Because it's *your* hat," said Tiffany, putting it on the table. "Thank you for the loan of it, though."

"I daresay there's plenty of young witches who'd give their high teeth for an ol' hat of mine," said Granny, lifting up the battered hat.

"There are," said Tiffany, and did *not* add, "and it's *eye*teeth, actually." What she did add was: "But I think everyone has to find their own hat. The right hat for them, I mean."

"I see you're now wearing a shop-bought one, then," said

Granny Weatherwax. "One of them Sky Scrapers. With *stars*," she added, and there was so much acid in the word "stars" that it would've melted copper and then dropped through the table and the floor and melted more copper in the cellar below. "Think that makes it more magical, do you? *Stars?*"

"I . . . did when I bought it. And it'll do for now."

"Until you find the right hat," said Granny Weatherwax.

"Yes."

"Which ain't mine?"

"No."

"Good."

The old witch walked across the room and tugged the cloth off the thing in the corner. It turned out to be a big wooden spike, just about the size of a pointy hat on a tall stand. A hat was being . . . *constructed* on it, with thin strips of willow and pins and stiff black cloth.

"I make my own," she said. "Every year. There's no hat like the hat you make yourself. Take my advice. I stiffens the calico and makes it waterproof with special jollop. It's amazing what you can put into a hat you make yourself. But you didn't come to talk about hats."

Tiffany let the question out at last.

"Was it real?"

Granny Weatherwax poured the tea, picked up her cup and saucer, then carefully poured some of the tea out of the cup and into the saucer. She held this up and, with care, like someone dealing with an important and delicate task, blew gently on it. She did this slowly and calmly, while Tiffany tried hard to conceal her impatience.

"The hiver's not around anymore?" said Granny.

"No. But—"

"And how did it all feel? When it was happening? Did it *feel* real?"

"No," said Tiffany. "It felt more than real."

"Well, there you are, then," said Granny Weatherwax, taking a sip from the saucer. "And the answer is: If it wasn't real, it wasn't *false*."

"It was like a dream where you've nearly woken up and can control it, you know?" said Tiffany. "If I was careful, it worked. It was like making myself rise up in the air by pulling hard on my bootlaces. It was like telling myself a story—"

Granny nodded.

"There's always a story," she said. "It's all stories, really. The sun coming up every day is a story. Everything's got a story in it. Change the story, change the world."

"And what was your plan to beat the hiver?" asked Tiffany. "Please? I've got to know!"

"My plan?" said Granny Weatherwax innocently. "My plan was to let you deal with it."

"Really? So what would you have done if I'd lost?"

"The best I can," said Granny calmly. "I always do."

"Would you have killed me if I'd become the hiver again?"

The saucer was steady in the old witch's hand. She looked reflectively at the tea.

"I would have spared you if I could," she said. "But I didn't have to, right? The Trials was the best place to be. Believe me, witches can act together if they must. It's harder'n herding cats, but it can be done."

"It's just that I think we . . . turned it all into a little show," said Tiffany.

"Hah, no. We made it into a *big* show!" said Granny Weatherwax with great satisfaction. "Thunder and lightning and white horses and wonderful rescues! Good value, eh, for a penny? And you'll learn, my girl, that a bit of a show every now and again does no harm to your reputation. I daresay Miss Level's findin' that out already, now she can juggle balls and raise her hat at the same time! Depend upon what I say!"

She delicately drank her tea out of the saucer, then nodded at the old hat on the table.

"Your grandmother," she said, "did *she* wear a hat?"

"What? Oh . . . not usually," said Tiffany, still thinking about the big show. "She used to wear an old sack as a kind of bonnet when the weather was really bad. She said hats only blow away up on the hill."

"She made the sky her hat, then," said Granny Weatherwax. "And did she wear a coat?"

"Hah, all the shepherds used to say that if you saw Granny Aching in a coat, it'd mean it was blowing rocks!" said Tiffany proudly.

"Then she made the wind her coat, too," said Granny Weatherwax. "It's a skill. Rain don't fall on a witch if she doesn't want it to, although personally I prefer to get wet and be thankful."

"Thankful for what?" said Tiffany.

"That I'll get dry later." Granny Weatherwax put down the cup and saucer. "Child, you've come here to learn what's true and what's not, but there's little I can teach you that you don't already know. You just don't know you know it, and you'll spend the rest of your life learning what's already in your bones. And that's the truth."

She stared at Tiffany's hopeful face and sighed.

"Come outside then," she said. "I'll give you lesson one. It's the only lesson there is. It don't need writing down in no book with eyes on it."

She led the way to the well in her back garden, looked around on the ground, and picked up a stick.

"Magic wand," she said. "See?" A green flame leaped out of it, making Tiffany jump. "Now you try."

It didn't work for Tiffany, no matter how much she shook it.

"Of course not," said Granny. "It's a stick. Now, maybe I made a flame come out of it, or maybe I made you *think* one did. That don't matter. It was *me* is what I'm sayin', not the stick. Get your mind right and you can make a stick your wand and the sky your hat and a puddle your magic . . . your magic . . . er, what're them fancy cups called?"

"Er . . . goblet," said Tiffany.

"Right. Magic goblet. Things aren't important. People are." Granny Weatherwax looked sidelong at Tiffany. "And I could teach you how to run across those hills of yours with the hare, I could teach you how to fly above them with the buzzard. I could tell you the secrets of the bees. I could teach you all this and much more besides, if you'd do just one thing, right here and now. One simple thing, easy to do."

Tiffany nodded, eyes wide.

"You understand, then, that all the glittery stuff is just toys, and toys can lead you astray?"

"Yes!"

"Then take off that shiny horse you wear around your neck, girl, and drop it in the well."

Obediently, half hypnotized by the voice, Tiffany reached behind her neck and undid the clasp.

The pieces of the silver Horse shone as she held it over the water.

She stared at it as if she was seeing it for the first time. And then . . .

She tests people, she thought. All the time.

"Well?" said the old witch.

"No," said Tiffany. "I can't."

"Can't or won't?" said Granny sharply.

"Can't," said Tiffany and stuck out her chin. "*And* won't!"

She drew her hand back and refastened the necklace, glaring defiantly at Granny Weatherwax.

The witch smiled.

"Well done," she said quietly. "If you don't know when to be a human being, you don't know when to be a witch. And if you're too afraid of goin' astray, you won't go anywhere. May I see it, please?"

Tiffany looked into those blue eyes. Then she undid the clasp again and handed over the necklace. Granny held it up.

"Funny, ain't it, that it seems to gallop when the light hits it," said the witch, watching it twist this way and that. "Well-made thing. O' course, it's not what a horse looks like, but it's certainly what a horse *is*."

Tiffany stared at her with her mouth open. For a moment Granny Aching stood there grinning, and then Granny Weatherwax was back. Did she do that, she wondered, or did I do it myself? And do I dare find out?

"I didn't just come to bring the hat back," she managed to say. "I brought you a present, too."

"I'm sure there's no call for anyone to bring *me* a present," said Granny Weatherwax, sniffing.

Tiffany ignored this, because her mind was still spinning. She fetched her sack again and handed over a small, soft parcel, which moved as it changed shape in her hands.

"I took most of the stuff back to Mr. Stronginthearm," she said. "But I thought you might have a . . . a *use* for this."

The old woman slowly unwrapped the white paper. The Zephyr Billow cloak unrolled itself under her fingers and filled the air like smoke.

"It's lovely, but I couldn't wear it," said Tiffany as the cloak shaped itself over the gentle currents of the clearing. "You need gravitas to carry off a cloak like that."

"What's gravitarse?" said Granny Weatherwax sharply.

"Oh . . . dignity. Seniority. Wisdom. Those sorts of things," said Tiffany.

"Ah," said Granny, relaxing a little. She stared at the gently rippling cloak and sniffed. It really was a wonderful creation. The wizards had got at least one thing right when they had made it. It was one of those things that fill a hole in your life that you didn't know was there until you'd seen it.

"Well, I suppose there's those as can wear a cloak like this, and those as can't," she conceded. She let it curl around her neck and fastened it there with a crescent-shaped brooch.

"It's a bit too grand for the likes of me," she said. "A bit too fancy. I could look like a flibbertigibbet wearing something like this." It was spoken like a statement but it had a curl like a question.

"No, it suits you, it really does," said Tiffany cheerfully. "If you don't know when to be a human being, you don't know when to be a witch."

Birds stopped singing. Up in the trees, squirrels ran and hid. Even the sky seemed to darken for a moment.

"Er . . . that's what I heard," said Tiffany, and added, "from someone who knows these things."

The blue eyes stared into hers. There were no secrets from Granny Weatherwax. Whatever you said, she watched what you meant.

"Perhaps you'll call again sometimes," she said, turning slowly and watching the cloak curve in the air. "It's always very quiet here."

"I should like that," said Tiffany. "Shall I tell the bees before I come, so you can get the tea ready?"

For a moment Granny Weatherwax glared, and then the lines faded into a wry grin.

"Clever," she said.

What's inside you? Tiffany thought. Who are you really, in there? Did you *want* me to take your hat? You pretend to be the big bad wicked witch, and you're not. You test people all the time, test, test, test, but you really want them to be clever enough to beat you. Because it must be hard, being the best. You're not allowed to stop. You can only be beaten, and you're too proud ever to lose. Pride! You've turned it into terrible strength, but it eats away at you. Are you afraid to laugh in case you hear an early cackle?

We'll meet again, one day. We both know it. We'll meet again, at the Witch Trials.

"I'm clever enough to know how you manage *not* to think of a pink rhinoceros if someone says 'pink rhinoceros,'" she managed to say aloud.

"Ah, that's deep magic, that is," said Granny Weatherwax.

"No. It's not. You don't know what a rhinoceros looks like, do you?"

Sunlight filled the clearing as the old witch laughed, as clear as a downland stream.

"That's right!" she said.

CHAPTER 15

A Hat Full of Sky

It was one of those strange days in late February when it's a little warmer than it should be and, although there's wind, it seems to be all around the horizons and never quite where you are.

Tiffany climbed up onto the downs where, in the sheltered valleys, the early lambs had already found their legs and were running around in a gang in that strange jerky run that lambs have, which makes them look like wooly rocking horses.

Perhaps there was something about that day, because the old ewes joined in, too, and skipped with their lambs. They jumped and spun, half happy, half embarrassed, big winter fleeces bouncing up and down like a clown's trousers.

It had been an interesting winter. She'd learned a lot of things. One of them was that you could be a bridesmaid to two people who between them were over 170 years old. This time Mr. Weavall, with his wig spinning on his head and his big spectacles gleaming, had *insisted* on giving one of the gold pieces to "our little helper," which more than made up for the wages that she hadn't asked for and Miss Level couldn't afford. She'd used some of it to buy a really good brown cloak. It didn't billow, it didn't fly out behind her, but it was warm and thick and kept her dry.

She'd learned lots of other things too. As she walked past the sheep and their lambs, she gently touched their minds, so softly that they didn't notice. . . .

Tiffany had stayed up in the mountains for Hogswatch, which officially marked the changing of the year. There'd been a lot to do there, and anyway it wasn't much celebrated on the Chalk. Miss Level had been happy to give her leave now, though, for the lambing festival, which the old people called Sheepbellies. It was when the shepherds' year began. The hag of the hills couldn't miss that. That was when, in warm nests of straw shielded from the wind by hurdles and barriers of cut furze, the future happened. She'd helped it happen, working with the shepherds by lantern light, dealing with the difficult births. She'd worked with the pointy hat on her head and had felt the shepherds watching her as, with knife and needle and thread and hands and soothing words, she'd saved ewes from the black doorway and helped new lambs into the light. You had to give them a show. You had to give them a story. And she'd walked back home proudly in the morning, bloody to the elbows, but it had been the blood of life.

Later she had gone up to the Feegles' mound and slid down the hole. She'd thought about this for some time and had gone prepared—with clean torn-up handkerchiefs and some soapwort shampoo made from a recipe Miss Level had given her. She had a feeling that Jeannie would have a use for these. Miss Level always visited new mothers. It was what you did.

Jeannie had been pleased to see her. Lying on her stomach so that she could get part of her body into the kelda's chamber, Tiffany had been allowed to hold all eight of what she kept thinking of as the Roblets, born at the same time as the lambs. Seven of them were bawling and fighting one another. The eighth lay quietly, biding her time. The future happened.

It wasn't only Jeannie who thought of her differently. News had got around. The people of the Chalk didn't like witches. They had always come from outside. They had always come as strangers. But there was *our* Tiffany, birthing the lambs like her granny did, and they say she's been learning witchery in the mountains! Ah, but that's still our Tiffany, that is. Okay, I'll grant you that she's wearing a hat with big stars on it, but she makes good cheese and she knows about lambing and she's Granny Aching's granddaughter, right? And they'd tap their noses knowingly. *Granny Aching's granddaughter.* Remember what the old woman could do? So if witch she be, then she's *our* witch. She knows about sheep, she does. Hah, and I heard they had a big sort of trial for witches up in them mountains and our Tiffany showed 'em what a girl from the Chalk can do. It's modern times, right? We got a witch now, and she's better'n anyone else's! No one's throwing Granny Aching's granddaughter in a pond!

Tomorrow she'd go back to the mountains again. It had been a busy three weeks, quite apart from the lambing. Roland had invited her to tea at the castle. It had been a bit awkward, as these things are, but it was funny how, in a couple of years, he'd gone from a lumbering oaf to a nervous young man who forgot what he was talking about when she smiled at him. And they had *books* in the castle!

He'd shyly presented her with a *Dictionary of Amazingly Uncommon Words*, and she had been prepared enough to bring him a hunting knife made by Zakzak Stronginthearm, who was excellent at blades even if he was rubbish at magic. The hat wasn't mentioned, very carefully. And when she'd got home, she'd found a bookmark in the P section and a faint pencil underline under the word *plongeon*: "a small curtsy, about one third as deep as the traditional one. No longer used." Alone in her bedroom, she'd blushed. It's always surprising to be reminded that while you're watching and thinking about people, all knowing and superior, they're watching and thinking about you, right back at you.

She'd written it down in her diary, which was a lot thicker now, what with all the pressed herbs and extra notes and bookmarks. It had been trodden on by cows, struck by lightning, and dropped in tea. And it didn't have an eye on it. An eye would have got knocked off on day one. It was a *real* witch's diary.

Tiffany had stopped wearing the hat, except in public, because it kept getting bent by low doorways and completely crushed by her bedroom ceiling. She was wearing it today, though, clutching it occasionally whenever a gust tried to snatch it off her head.

She reached the place where four rusty iron wheels were half buried in the turf and a potbellied stove stood up from the grass. It made a useful seat.

Silence spread out around Tiffany, a living silence, while the sheep danced with their lambs and the world turned.

Why do you go away? So that you can come back. So that you can see the place you came from with new eyes and extra colors. And the people there see you differently, too. Coming back to where you started is not the same as never leaving.

The words ran through Tiffany's mind as she watched the sheep, and she found herself filling up with joy—at the new lambs, at life, at everything. Joy is to fun what the deep sea is to a puddle. It's a feeling inside that can hardly be contained.

"I've come back!" she announced to the hills. "Better than I went!"

She snatched off the hat with stars on it. It wasn't a bad hat, for show, although the stars made it look like a toy. But it was never *her* hat. It couldn't be. The only hat worth wearing was the one you made for yourself, not one you bought, not one you were given. Your own hat, for your own head. Your own future, not someone else's.

She hurled the starry hat up as high as she could. The wind there caught it neatly. It tumbled for a moment and then was lifted by a gust and, swooping and spinning, sailed away across the downs and vanished forever.

Then Tiffany made a hat out of the sky and sat on the old potbellied stove, listening to the wind around the horizons while the sun went down.

As the shadows lengthened, many small shapes crept out of the nearby mound and joined her in the sacred place, to watch.

The sun set, which is everyday magic, and warm night came.

The hat filled up with stars. . . .

AUTHOR'S NOTE

The Doctrine of Signatures mentioned on page 67 really exists in this world, although now it's better known by historians than doctors. For hundreds of years, perhaps thousands, people believed that God, who of course had made everything, had "signed" each thing in a way that showed humanity what it could be used for. For example, goldenrod is yellow and so "must" be good for jaundice, which turns the skin yellow. (A certain amount of guesswork was involved, but sometimes patients survived.)

By an amazing coincidence, the Horse carved on the Chalk is remarkably similar to the Uffington White Horse, which in this world is carved on the downlands near the village of Uffington in southwest Oxfordshire. It's 374 feet long, several thousand years old, and carved on the hill in such a way that you can only see all of it in one go from the air. This suggests that a) it was carved for the gods to see or b) flying was invented a lot earlier that we thought or c) people used to be much, much taller.

Oh, and this world had Witch Trials, too. They were not fun.

The adventures of Tiffany Aching
and the Wee Free Men continue in

Wintersmith.

Here's a sneak peek!

CHAPTER ONE

The Big Snow

When the storm came, it hit the hills like a hammer. No sky should hold as much snow as this, and because no sky could, the snow fell, fell in a wall of white.

There was a small hill of snow where there had been, a few hours ago, a little cluster of thorn trees on an ancient mound. This time last year there had been a few early primroses; now there was just snow.

Part of the snow moved. A piece about the size of an apple rose up, with smoke pouring out around it. A hand no larger than a rabbit's paw waved the smoke away.

A very small but very angry blue face, with the lump of snow still balanced on top of it, looked out at the sudden white wilderness.

"Ach, crivens!" it grumbled. "Will ye no' look at this? 'Tis the work o' the Wintersmith! Noo there's a scunner that willna tak' 'no' fra' an answer!"

Other lumps of snow were pushed up. More heads peered out.

"Oh waily, waily, waily!" said one of them. "He's found the big wee hag again!"

The first head turned toward this head, and said, "Daft Wullie?"

"Yes, Rob?"

"Did I no' tell ye to lay off that waily business?"

"Aye, Rob, ye did that," said the head addressed as Daft Wullie.

"So why did ye just do it?"

"Sorry, Rob. It kinda bursted oot."

"It's so dispiritin'."

"Sorry, Rob."

Rob Anybody sighed. "But I fear ye're right, Wullie. He's come for the big wee hag, right enough. Who's watchin' over her doon at the farm?"

"Wee Dangerous Spike, Rob."

Rob looked up at clouds so full of snow that they sagged in the middle.

"Okay," he said, and sighed again. "It's time fra' the Hero."

He ducked out of sight, the plug of snow dropping neatly back into place, and slid down into the heart of the Feegle mound.

It was quite big inside. A human could just about stand up in the middle, but would then bend double with coughing because the middle was where there was a hole to let smoke out.

All around the inner wall were tiers of galleries, and every one of them was packed with Feegles. Usually the place was awash with noise, but now it was frighteningly quiet.

Rob Anybody walked across the floor to the fire, where his wife, Jeannie, was waiting. She stood straight and proud, like a kelda should, but close up it seemed to him that she had been crying. He put his arm around her.

"All right, ye probably ken what's happenin'," he told the blue-and-red audience looking down on him. "This is nae common storm. The Wintersmith has found the big wee hag—noo then, settle doon!"

He waited until the shouting and sword rattling had died down, then went on: "We canna fight the Wintersmith for her! That's her road! We canna walk it for her! But the hag o' hags has set us on another path! It's a dark one, and dangerous!"

A cheer went up. Feegles liked the idea of this, at least.

"Right!" said Rob, satisfied. "Ah'm awa' tae fetch the Hero!"

There was a lot of laughter at this, and Big Yan, the tallest of the Feegles, shouted, "It's tae soon. We've only had time tae gie him a couple o' heroing lessons! He's still nae more than a big streak o' nothin'!"

"He'll be a Hero for the big wee hag and that's an end o' it," said Rob sharply. "Noo, off ye go, the whole boilin' o' ye! Tae the chalk pit! Dig me a path tae the Underworld!"

*   *   *

It had to be the Wintersmith, Tiffany Aching told herself, standing in front of her father in the freezing farmhouse. She could feel it out there. This wasn't normal weather even for midwinter, and this was springtime. It was a challenge. Or perhaps it was just a game. It was hard to tell, with the Wintersmith.

Only it can't be a game because the lambs are dying. I'm only just thirteen, and my father, and a lot of other people older than me, want me to do something. And I can't. The Wintersmith has found me again. He is here now, and I'm too weak.

It would be easier if they were bullying me, but no, they're begging. My father's face is gray with worry and he's begging. *My father is begging me.*

Oh no, he's taking his hat off. He's *taking off his hat* to speak to me!

They think magic comes free when I snap my fingers. But if I can't do this for them, now, what good am I? I can't let them see I'm afraid. Witches aren't allowed to be afraid.

And this is my fault. I: I started all this. I must finish it.

Mr. Aching cleared his throat.

"...And, er, if you could ... er, magic it away, uh, or something? For us ...?"

Everything in the room was gray, because the light from the windows was coming through snow. No one had wasted time digging the horrible stuff away from the houses. Every person who could hold a shovel was needed elsewhere, and still there were not enough of them. As it was, most people had been up all night, walking the flocks of yearlings, trying to keep the new lambs safe ... in the dark, in the snow. . . .

Her snow. It was a message to her. A challenge. A summons.

"All right," she said. "I'll see what I can do."

"Good girl," said her father, grinning with relief. No, not a good girl, thought Tiffany. I brought this on us.

"You'll have to make a big fire, up by the sheds," she said aloud. "I mean a big fire, do you understand? Make it out of anything that will burn, and you must keep it going. It'll keep trying to go out, but you must keep it going. Keep piling on the fuel, whatever happens. *The fire must not go out!*"

She made sure that the "not!" was loud and frightening. She didn't want people's minds to wander. She put on the heavy brown woollen cloak that Miss Treason had made for her and grabbed the black pointy hat that hung on the back of the farmhouse door. There was a sort of communal grunt from the people who'd crowded into the kitchen, and some of them backed away.

We want a witch now, we need a witch now, but—we'll back away now, too.

That was the magic of the pointy hat. It was what Miss Treason called "Boffo."

Tiffany Aching stepped out into the narrow corridor that had been cut through the snow-filled farmyard where the drifts were more than twice the height of a man. At least the deep snow kept off the worst of the wind, which was made of knives.

A track had been cleared all the way to the paddock, but it had been heavy going. When there are fifteen feet of snow everywhere, how can you clear it? Where can you clear it to?

She waited by the cart sheds while the men hacked and scraped at the snowbanks. They were tired to the bone by now; they'd been digging for hours.

The important thing was—

But there were lots of important things. It was important to look calm and confident, it was important to keep your mind clear, it was important not to show how pants-wettingly scared you were. . . .

She held out a hand, caught a snowflake, and took a good look at it. It wasn't one of the normal ones, oh no. It was one of his special snowflakes. That was nasty. He was taunting her. Now she could hate him. She'd never hated him before. But he was killing the lambs.

She shivered and pulled the cloak around her.

"This I choose to do," she croaked, her breath leaving little clouds in the air. She cleared her throat and started again. "This I choose to do. If there is a price, this I choose to pay. If it is my death, then I choose to die. Where this takes me, there I choose to go. I choose. This I choose to do."

It wasn't a spell, except in her own head, but if you couldn't make spells work in your own head, you couldn't make them work at all.

Tiffany wrapped her cloak around her against the clawing wind and watched dully as the men brought straw and wood. The fire started slowly, as if frightened to show enthusiasm.

She'd done this before, hadn't she? Dozens of times. The trick was not that hard when you got the feel of it, but she'd done it with time to get her mind right, and anyway, she'd never done it with anything more than a kitchen fire to warm her freezing feet. In theory it should be just as easy with a big fire and a field of snow, right?

Right?

The fire began to roar up. Her father put his hand on her shoulder. Tiffany jumped. She'd forgotten how quietly he could move.

"What was that about choosing?" he said. She'd forgotten what good hearing he had, too.

"It's a . . . witch thing," she answered, trying not to look at his face. "So that if this . . . doesn't work, it's no one's fault but mine." And this is my fault, she added to herself. It's unfair, but no one said it wasn't going to be.

Her father's hand caught her chin and gently turned her head around. How soft his hands are, Tiffany thought. Big man's hands but soft as a baby's, because of the grease on the sheep's fleeces.

"We shouldn't have asked you, should we . . ." he said.

Yes, you should have asked me, Tiffany thought. The lambs are dying under the dreadful snow. And I should have said no, I should have said I'm not that good yet. But the lambs are dying under the dreadful snow!

There will be other lambs, said her Second Thoughts.

But these aren't those lambs, are they? These are the lambs that are dying, here and now. And they're dying because I listened to my feet and dared to dance with the Wintersmith.

"I can do it," she said.

Her father held her chin and stared into her eyes.

"Are you sure, jiggit?" he asked. It was the nickname her grand-mother had had for her—Granny Aching, who never lost a lamb to the dreadful snow. He'd never used it before. Why had it risen up in his mind now?

"Yes!" She pushed his hand away, and broke his gaze before she could burst into tears.

"I . . . haven't told your mother this yet," said her father very slowly, as if the words required enormous care, "but I can't find your brother. I think he was trying to help. Abe Swindell said he saw him with his little shovel. Er . . . I'm sure he's all right, but . . . keep an eye open for him, will you? He's got his red coat on."

His face, with no expression at all, was heartbreaking to see. Little Wentworth, nearly seven years old, always running after the men, always wanting to be one of them, always trying to help . . . how easily a small body could get overlooked. . . . The snow was still coming fast. The horribly wrong snowflakes were white on her father's shoulders. It's these little things you remember when the bottom falls out of the world, and you're falling—

That wasn't just unfair; that was . . . cruel.

Remember the hat you wear! Remember the job that is in front of you! Balance! Balance is the thing. Hold balance in the center, hold the balance. . . .

Tiffany extended her numb hands to the fire, to draw out the warmth.

"Remember, don't let the fire go out," she said.

"I've got men bringing up wood from all over," said her father. "I told 'em to bring all the coal from the forge, too. It won't run out of feeding, I promise you!"

The flame danced and curved toward Tiffany's hands. The trick was, the trick, the trick . . . was to fold the heat somewhere close, draw it with you and . . . balance. Forget everything else!

"I'll come with—" her father began.

"No! Watch the fire!" Tiffany shouted, too loud, frantic with fear. "You will do what I say!"

I am not your daughter today! her mind screamed. I am your witch! *I* will protect *you*!

She turned before he could see her face and ran through the flakes, along the track that had been cut toward the lower paddocks. The snow had been trodden down into a lumpy, hummocky path, made slippery with fresh snow. Exhausted men with shovels pressed themselves into the snowbanks on either side rather than get in her way.

She reached the wider area where other shepherds were digging into the wall of snow. It tumbled in lumps around them.

"Stop! Get back!" her voice shouted, while her mind wept.

The men obeyed quickly. The mouth that had given that order had a pointy hat above it. You didn't argue with that.

Remember the heat, the heat, remember the heat, balance, balance . . .

This was witching cut to the bone. No toys, no wands, no Boffo, no headology, no tricks. All that mattered was how good you were.

But sometimes you had to trick yourself. She wasn't the Summer Lady and she wasn't Granny Weatherwax. She needed to give herself all the help she could.

She pulled the little silver horse out of her pocket. It was greasy and stained, and she'd meant to clean it, but there had been no time, no time. . . .

Like a knight putting on his helmet, she fastened the silver chain around her neck.

She should have practiced more. She should have listened to people. She should have listened to herself.

She took a deep breath and held out her hands on either side of her, palms up. On her right hand a white scar glowed.

"Thunder on my right hand," she said. "Lightning in my left hand. Fire behind me. Frost in front of me."

She stepped forward until she was only a few inches away from the snowbank. She could feel its coldness already pulling the heat out of her. Well, so be it. She took a few deep breaths. This I choose to do. . . .

"Frost to fire," she whispered.

In the yard, the fire went white and roared like a furnace.

The snow wall spluttered and then exploded into steam, sending chunks of snow into the air. Tiffany walked forward slowly. Snow pulled back from her hands like mist at sunrise. It melted in the heat of her, becoming a tunnel in the deep drift, fleeing from her, writhing around her in clouds of cold fog.

Yes! She smiled desperately. It was true. If you had the perfect center, if you got your mind right, you could balance. In the middle of the seesaw is a place that never moves. . . .

Her boots squelched over warm water. There was fresh green grass under the snow, because the awful storm had been so late in the year. She walked on, heading to where the lambing pens were buried.

Her father stared at the fire. It was burning white-hot, like a furnace, eating through the wood as if driven by a gale. It was collapsing into ashes in front of his eyes. . . .

Water was pouring around Tiffany's boots now.

Yes! But don't think about it! Hold the balance! More heat! Frost to fire!

There was a bleat.

Sheep could live under the snow, at least for a while. But as Granny Aching used to say, when the gods made sheep, they must've left their brains in their other coat. In a panic, and sheep were always just an inch from panicking, they'd trample their own lambs.

Now ewes and lambs appeared, steaming and bewildered as the snow melted around them, as if they were sculptures left behind.

Tiffany moved on, staring straight ahead of her, only just aware of the excited cries of the men behind her. They were following her, pulling the ewes free, cradling the lambs. . . .

Her father yelled at the other men. Some of them were hacking at a farm cart, throwing the wood down into the white-hot flames. Others were dragging furniture up from the house. Wheels, tables, straw bales, chairs—the fire took everything, gulped it down, and roared for more. And there wasn't any more.

No red coat. No red coat! Balance, balance. Tiffany waded on, water and sheep pouring past her. The tunnel ceiling fell in a splashing and slithering of slush. She ignored it. Fresh snowflakes fell down through the hole and boiled in the air above her head. She ignored that, too. And then, ahead of her . . . a glimpse of red.

Frost to fire! The snow fled, and there he was. She picked him up, held him close, sent some of her heat into him, felt him stir, whispered: "It weighed at least forty pounds! At least forty pounds!"

Wentworth coughed and opened his eyes. Tears falling like melting snow, she ran over to a shepherd and thrust the boy into his arms.

"Take him to his mother! *Do it now!*" The man grabbed the boy and ran, frightened of her fierceness. Today she was their witch!

Tiffany turned back. There were more lambs to be saved.

Her father's coat landed on the starving flames, glowed for a moment, then fell into gray ashes. The other men were ready; they grabbed the man as he went to jump after it and pulled him back, kicking and shouting.

The flint cobbles had melted like butter. They spluttered for a moment, then froze.

The fire went out.

Tiffany Aching looked up, into the eyes of the Wintersmith.

And up on the roof of the cart shed, the small voice belonging to Wee Dangerous Spike said, "Ach, crivens!"

*   *   *

All this hasn't happened yet. It might not happen at all. The future is always a bit wobbly. Any little thing, like the fall of a snowflake or the dropping of the wrong kind of spoon, can send it spinning off along a new path. Or perhaps not.

Where it all *began* was last autumn, on the day with a cat in it. . . .

*Also look for the astonishing
final adventure of Tiffany Aching:*

I Shall Wear Midnight